Thankful's Inheritance

Joseph C. Lincoln

Contents

THANKFUL'S INHERITANCE

by

Joseph C. Lincoln

CHAPTER I

THE road from Wellmouth Centre to East Wellmouth is not a good one; even in dry weather and daylight it is not that. For the first two miles it winds and twists its sandy way over bare hills, with cranberry swamps and marshy ponds in the hollows between. Then it enters upon a three-mile stretch bordered with scrubby pines and bayberry thickets, climbing at last a final hill to emerge upon the bluff with the ocean at its foot. And, fringing that bluff and clustering thickest in the lowlands just beyond, is the village of East Wellmouth, which must on no account be confused with South Wellmouth, or North Wellmouth, or West Wellmouth, or even Wellmouth Port.

On a bright sunny summer day the East Wellmouth road is a hard one to travel. At nine o'clock of an evening in March, with a howling gale blowing and rain pouring in torrents, traveling it is an experience. Winnie S., who drives the East Wellmouth depot-wagon, had undergone the experience several times in the course of his professional career, but each time he vowed vehemently that he would not repeat it; he would "heave up" his job first.

He was vowing it now. Perched on the edge of the depot wagon's front seat, the reins leading from his clenched fists through the slit in the "boot" to the rings on the collar of General Jackson, the aged horse, he expressed his opinion of the road, the night, and the job.

"By Judas priest!" declared Winnie S.—his name was Winfield Scott Hancock Holt, but no resident of East Wellmouth called him anything but Winnie S.—"by Judas priest! If this ain't enough to make a feller give up tryin' to earn a livin', then I don't know! Tell him he can't ship aboard a schooner 'cause goin' to sea's a dog's life, and then put him on a job like this! Dog's life! Judas priest! What kind of a life's THIS, I want to know?"

From the curtain depths of the depot-wagon behind him a voice answered, a woman's voice:

"Judgin' by the amount of dampness in it I should think you might call it a duck's life," it suggested.

Winnie S. accepted this pleasantry with a grunt. "I 'most wish I was a duck," he declared, savagely. "Then I could set in three inches of ice-water and like it, maybe. Now what's the matter with you?" This last a roar to the horse, whose splashy progress along the gullied road had suddenly ceased. "What's the matter with you now?" repeated Winnie. "What have you done; come to anchor? Git dap!"

But General Jackson refused to "git dap." Jerks at the reins only caused him to stamp and evince an inclination to turn around. Go ahead he would not.

"Judas priest!" exclaimed the driver. "I do believe the critter's drowndin'! Somethin's wrong. I've got to get out and see, I s'pose. Set right where you be, ladies. I'll be back in a minute," adding, as he took a lighted lantern from beneath the seat and pulled aside the heavy boot preparatory to alighting, "unless I get in over my head, which ain't so dummed unlikely as it sounds."

Lantern in hand he clambered clumsily from beneath the boot and disappeared. Inside the vehicle was blackness, dense, damp and profound.

"Auntie," said a second feminine voice, "Auntie, what DO you suppose has happened?"

"I don't know, Emily. I'm prepared for 'most anything by this time. Maybe we've landed on Mount Ararat. I feel as if I'd been afloat for forty days and nights. Land sakes alive!" as another gust shot and beat its accompanying cloudburst through and between the carriage curtains; "right in my face and eyes! I don't wonder that boy wished he was a duck. I'd like to be a fish—or a mermaid. I couldn't be much wetter if I was either one, and I'd have gills so I could breathe under water. I SUPPOSE mermaids have gills, I don't know."

Emily laughed. "Aunt Thankful," she declared, "I believe you would find something funny in a case of smallpox."

"Maybe I should; I never tried. 'Twouldn't be much harder than to be funny with—with rain-water on the brain. I'm so disgusted with myself I don't know what to do. The idea of me, daughter and granddaughter of seafarin' folks that studied the weather all their lives, not knowin' enough to stay to home when it looked as much like a storm as it did this mornin'. And draggin' you into it, too. We could have come tomorrow or next day just as well, but no, nothin' to do but I must start today 'cause I'd planned to. This comes of figgerin' to profit by what folks leave to you in wills. Talk about dead men's shoes! Live men's rubber boots would be worth more to you and me this minute. SUCH a cruise as this has been!"

It had been a hard trip, certainly, and the amount of water through which they had traveled the latter part of it almost justified its being called a "cruise." Old Captain Abner Barnes, skipper, for the twenty years before his death, of the coasting schooner T. I. Smalley, had, during his life-long seafaring, never made a much rougher voyage, all things considered, than that upon which his last will and testament had sent his niece and her young companion.

Captain Abner, a widower, had, when he died, left his house and land at East Wellmouth to his niece by marriage, Mrs. Thankful Barnes. Thankful, whose husband, Eben Barnes, was lost at sea the year after their marriage, had been living with and acting as housekeeper for an elderly woman named Pearson at South Middleboro. She, Thankful, had never visited her East Wellmouth inheritance. For four years after she inherited it she received the small rent paid her by the tenant, one Laban Eldredge. His name was all she knew concerning him. Then he died and for the next eight months the house stood empty. And then came one more death, that of old Mrs. Pearson, the lady for whom Thankful had "kept house."

Left alone and without present employment, the Widow Barnes considered what she should do next. And, thus considering, the desire to visit and inspect her East Wellmouth property grew and strengthened. She thought more and more concerning it. It was hers, she could do what she pleased with it, and she began to formulate vague ideas as to what she might like to do. She kept these ideas to herself, but she spoke to Emily Howes concerning the possibilities of a journey to East Wellmouth.

Emily was Mrs. Barnes' favorite cousin, although only a second cousin. Her mother, Sarah Cahoon, Thankful's own cousin, had married a man named Howes. Emily was the only child by this marriage. But later there was another marriage, this time to a person named Hobbs, and there were five little Hobbses. Papa Hobbs worked occasionally, but not often. His wife and Emily worked all the time. The latter had been teaching school in Middleboro, but now it was spring vacation. So when Aunt Thankful suggested the Cape Cod tour of inspection Emily gladly agreed to go. The Hobbs house was not a haven of joy, especially to Mr. Hobbs' stepdaughter, and almost any change was likely to be an agreeable one.

They had left South Middleboro that afternoon. The rain began when the train reached West Ostable. At Bayport it had become a storm. At Wellmouth Centre it was a gale and a miniature flood. And now, shut up in the back part of the depot-wagon, with the roaring wind and splashing, beating rain outside, Thankful's references to fish and ducks and mermaids, even to Mount Ararat, seemed to Emily quite appropriate. They had planned to spend the night at the East Wellmouth hotel and visit the Barnes' property in the morning. But it was five long miles to that hotel from the Wellmouth Centre station. Their progress so far had been slow enough. Now they had stopped altogether.

A flash of light showed above the top of the carriage boot.

"Mercy on us!" cried Aunt Thankful. "Is that lightnin'? All we need to make this complete is to be struck by lightnin'. No, 'tain't lightnin', it's just the lantern. Our pilot's comin' back, I guess likely. Well, he ain't been washed away, that's one comfort."

Winnie S., holding the lantern in his hand, reappeared beneath the boot. Raindrops sparkled on his eyebrows, his nose and the point of his chin.

"Judas priest!" he gasped. "If this ain't—"

"You needn't say it. We'll agree with you," interrupted Mrs. Barnes, hastily. "Is anything the matter?"

The driver's reply was in the form of elaborate sarcasm.

"Oh, no!" he drawled, "there wasn't nothin' the matter. Just a few million pines blowed across the road and the breechin' busted and the for'ard wheel about ready to come off, that's all. Maybe there's a few other things I didn't notice, but that's all I see."

"Humph! Well, they'll do for a spell. How's the weather, any worse?"

"Worse? No! they ain't no worse made. Looks as if 'twas breakin' a little over to west'ard, fur's that goes. But how in the nation we'll ever fetch East Wellmouth, I don't know. Git dap! GIT DAP! Have you growed fast?"

General Jackson pulled one foot after the other from the mud and the wagon rocked and floundered as its pilot steered it past the fallen trees. For the next twenty minutes no one spoke. Then Winnie S. breathed a sigh of thankfulness.

"Well, we're out of that stretch of woods, anyhow," he declared. "And it 'tain't rainin' so hard, nuther. Cal'late we can get to civilization if that breechin' holds and the pesky wheel don't come off. How are you, in aft there; tolerable snug?"

Emily said nothing. Aunt Thankful chuckled at the word.

"Snug!" she repeated. "My, yes! If this water was salt we'd be as snug as a couple of pickled mackerel. How far off is this civilization you're talkin' about?"

"Well, our hotel where you're bound is a good two mile, but there's—Judas priest! there goes that breechin' again!"

There was another halt while the breeching underwent temporary repairs. The wind blew as hard as ever, but the rain had almost stopped. A few minutes later it stopped altogether.

"There!" declared Winnie S. "The fust mile's gone. I don't know's I hadn't ought to stop—"

Aunt Thankful interrupted. "Stop!" she cried. "For mercy sakes, don't stop anywheres unless you have to. We've done nothin' but stop ever since we started. Go on as far as you can while this—this machine of yours is wound up."

But that was not destined to be far. From beneath the forward end of the depot-wagon sounded a most alarming creak, a long-drawn, threatening groan. Winnie S. uttered his favorite exclamation.

"Judas priest!" he shouted. "There goes that wheel! I've, been expectin' it."

He tugged at the right hand rein. General Jackson, who, having been brought up in a seafaring community, had learned to answer his helm, swerved sharply from the road. Emily screamed faintly.

"Where are you goin'?" demanded Mrs. Barnes.

The driver did not answer. The groan from beneath the carriage was more ominously threatening than ever. And suddenly the threat was fulfilled. The depot-wagon jerked on for a few feet and then, with a crack, settled down to port in a most alarming fashion. Winnie S. settled down with it, still holding tight to the reins and roaring commands to General Jackson at the top of his lungs.

"Whoa!" he hollered. "Whoa! Stand still! Stand still where you be! Whoa!"

General Jackson stood still. Generally speaking he needed but one hint to do that. His commander climbed out, or fell out, from beneath the boot. The ground upon which he fell was damp but firm.

"Whoa!" he roared again. Then scrambling to his feet he sprang toward the wagon, which, the forward wheel detached and flat beneath it, was resting on the remaining three in a fashion which promised total capsizing at any moment.

"Be you hurt? Be you hurt?" demanded Winnie S.

From inside, the tightly drawn curtains there came a variety of sounds, screams, exclamations, and grunts as of someone gasping for breath.

"Be you hurt?" yelled the frantic Mr. Holt.

It was the voice of the younger passenger which first made coherent reply.

"No," it panted. "No, I—I think I'm not hurt. But Aunt Thankful—Oh, Auntie, are you—"

Aunt Thankful herself interrupted. Her voice was vigorous enough, but it sounded as if smothered beneath a heavy weight.

"No, no," she gasped. "I—I'm all right. I'm all right. Or I guess I shall be when you get—off of me."

"Judas priest!" cried Winnie S., and sprang to the scene. It was the younger woman, Emily, whom he rescued first. She, being on the upper side of the tilted wagon, had slid pell-mell along the seat down upon the body of her companion. Mrs. Barnes was beneath and getting her out was a harder task. However, it was accomplished at last.

"Mercy on us!" exclaimed the lady, as her companions assisted her to rise. "Mercy on us! I feel like a pancake. I never knew you weighed so much, Emily Howes. Well, that's all right and no bones broke. Where are we now? Why—why, that's a house, I do believe! We're in somebody's yard."

They were, that was plain even on a night as dark as this. Behind them, bordering the stretch of mud and puddles which they had just left, was the silhouette of a dilapidated picket fence; and in front loomed the shadowy shapes of buildings.

"We're in somebody's yard," repeated Thankful. "And there's a house, as sure as I live! Well, I never thought I'd be so grateful just at the bare sight of one. I'd begun to think I never would see a house again. If we'd run afoul of a ship I shouldn't have been so surprised. Come on, Emily!"

She seized her companion by the hand and led the way toward the nearest and largest building. Winnie S., having retrieved and relighted the overturned lantern, was inspecting the wreck of the depot-wagon. It was some minutes before he noticed that his passengers had disappeared. Then he set up a shout.

"Hi! Where you be?" he shouted.

"Here," was the answer. "Here, by the front door."

"Hey? Oh, all right. Stay where you be. I'll be there pretty soon."

The "pretty soon" was not very soon. Mrs. Barnes began to lose patience.

"I ain't goin' to roost on this step till mornin'," she declared. "I'm goin' inside. Ain't that a bell handle on your side of the door, Emily? Give it a pull, for mercy sakes!"

"But, Auntie—"

"Give it a pull, I tell you! I don't know who lives here and I don't care. If 'twas the President of the United States he'd have to turn out and let us in this night. Here, let me do it!"

She gave the glass knob a sharp jerk. From within sounded the jingle of an old-fashioned spring bell.

"There!" she exclaimed, "I guess they'll hear that. Anyway, I'll give 'em one more for good measure."

She jerked the bell again. The peal died away in a series of lessening tinkles, but there was no other sound from within.

"They must be sound sleepers," whispered Emily, after a moment.

"They must be dead," declared Thankful. "There's been smashin' and crackin' and hollerin' enough to wake up anybody that wa'n't buried. How that wind does blow! I—Hello! here comes that man at last. About time, I should say!"

Winnie S. appeared, bearing the lantern.

"What you doin'?" he asked. "There ain't no use ringin' that bell. Nobody'll hear it."

Thankful, who had just given the bell a third pull, took her hand from the knob.

"Why not?" she demanded. "It makes noise enough. I should think a graven image would hear it. What is this, a home for deaf people?"

Winnie S. grinned. "'Tain't nobody's home, not now," he said. "This house is empty. Ain't nobody lived in it for 'most a year."

The two women looked at each other. Mrs. Barnes drew along breath.

"Well," she observed, "if this ain't the last straw. Such a cruise as we've had; and finally be shipwrecked right in front of a house and find it's an empty one! Don't talk to ME! Well," sharply, "what shall we do next?"

The driver shook his head.

"Dummed if I know!" he answered. "The old wagon can't go another yard. I—I cal'late you folks'll have to stay here for a spell."

"Stay? Where'll we stay; out here in the middle of this howlin' wilderness?"

"I guess so. Unless you want to walk the rest of the way, same's I'm cal'latin' to. I'm goin' to unharness the horse and put him under the shed here and then hoof it over to the village and get somebody to come and help. You can come along if you want to, but it'll be a tougher v'yage than the one we've come through."

"How far off is this—this village of yours?"

"Oh, about a mile and a half!"

"A mile and a half! And it's beginnin' to rain again! Emily, I don't know how you feel, but if the horse can wait under the shed until somebody comes I guess we can. I say let's do it."

Emily nodded. "Of course, Auntie," she said, emphatically. "We couldn't walk a mile and a half in a storm like this. Of course we must wait. Where is the shed?"

Winnie S. led the way to the shed. It was a ramshackle affair, open on one side. General Jackson, tethered to a rusty ring at the back, whinnied a welcome.

The driver, holding the lantern aloft, looked about him. His two passengers looked also.

"Well," observed Thankful, "this may have been a shed once, but it's more like a sieve now. There's more leaks to the roof than there is boards, enough sight. However, any port in a storm, and we've got the storm, sartin. All right, Mister What's-your-name, we'll wait."

Winnie S. turned away. Then he turned back again.

"Maybe I'd better leave you the lantern," he said, doubtfully. "I guess likely I could get along without it and—and 'twould make it more sociable for you."

He put the lantern down on the earth floor beside them and strode off into the dark. Mrs. Barnes called after him.

"Ain't there any way of gettin' into that house?" she asked. "It acts as if 'twas goin' to storm hard as ever and this shed ain't the most—what did you call it?—sociable place in creation, in spite of the lantern. If we could only get inside that house—"

Winnie S. interrupted. They could not see him, but there was a queer note in his voice.

"Get inside!" he repeated. "Get into THAT house this time of night! Well—well, maybe you could, but I wouldn't do it, not for nothin'. You better wait in the shed. I'll be back soon as ever I can."

They heard him splashing along the road. Then a gust of wind and a torrent of rain beating upon the leaky roof drowned all other sounds. Emily turned to her companion.

"Auntie," she said, "if you and I were superstitious we might think all this, all that we've been through, was what people call a sign, a warning. That is what ever so many South Middleboro people would say."

"Humph! if I believed in signs I'd have noticed the weather signs afore we started. Those are all the 'signs' I believe in and I ought to have known better than to risk comin' when it looked so threatenin'. I can't forgive myself for that. However, we did come, and here we are—wherever 'here' is. Now what in the world did that man mean by sayin' we better not try to get into that house? I don't care what he meant. Give me that lantern."

"Auntie, where are you going?"

"I'm goin' to take an observation of those windows. Nine chances to one they ain't all locked, and if there's one open you and I can crawl into it. I wish we could boost the horse in, too, poor thing, but self-preservation is the first law of nature and if he's liable to perish it's no reason we should. I'm goin' to get into that house if such a thing's possible."

"But, Auntie—"

"Don't say another word. I'm responsible for your bein' here this night, Emily Howes. You wouldn't have come if I hadn't coaxed you into it. And you shan't die of pneumonia or—or drownin' if I can help it. I'm goin' to have a look at those doors and windows. Don't be scared. I'll be back in a jiffy. Goodness me, what a puddle! Well, if you hear me holler you'll know I'm goin' under for the third time, so come quick. Here goes!"

Lantern in hand, she splashed out into the wet, windy darkness.

CHAPTER II

MISS HOWES, left to share with General Jackson the "sociability" of the shed, watched that lantern with faint hope and strong anxiety. She saw it bobbing like a gigantic firefly about the walls of the house, stopping here and there and then hurrying on. Soon it passed around the further corner and disappeared altogether. The wind howled, the rain poured, General Jackson stamped and splashed, and Emily shivered.

At last, just as the watcher had begun to think some serious accident had happened to her courageous relative and was considering starting on a relief expedition, the lantern reappeared.

"Emily!" screamed Mrs. Barnes. "Emily! Come here!"

Emily came, fighting her way against the wind. She found her cousin standing by the corner of the house.

"I've got it," cried Aunt Thankful, panting but triumphant. "I've got it. One of the windows on the other side is unfastened, just as I suspicioned it might be. I think one of us can get in if t'other helps."

She seized the arm of her fellow castaway and together they turned the corner, struggled on for a short distance and then stopped.

"This is the window," gasped the widow. "Here, right abreast of us. See!"

She held up the lantern. The window was "abreast" of them, but also it was a trifle high.

"It ain't fastened," shouted Thankful; she was obliged to shout in order to be heard. "I could push it open a little mite from the bottom, but I couldn't reach to get it up all the way. You can if I steady you, I guess. Here! Put your foot on that box.

I lugged it around from the back yard on purpose."

Standing on an empty and shaky cranberry crate and held there by the strong arm of Mrs. Barnes, Emily managed to push up the lower half of the window. The moment she let go of it, however, it fell with a tremendous bang.

"One of the old-fashioned kind, you might know," declared Thankful. "No weights nor nothin'. We'll have to prop it up with a stick. You wait where you are and I'll go get one. There's what's left of a woodpile out back here; that's where that crate came from."

She hastened away and was back in a moment with a stout stick. Emily raised the window once more and placed the stick beneath it.

"There!" panted her companion. "We've got a gangway anyhow. Next thing is to get aboard. You come down and give me a boost."

But Emily declined.

"Of course I shan't do any such thing," she declared, indignantly. "I can climb through that window a great deal easier than you can, Auntie. I'm ever so much younger. Just give me a push, that's all."

Her cousin demurred. "I hate to have you do it," she said. "For anybody that ain't any too strong or well you've been through enough tonight. Well, if you're so set on it. I presume likely you could make a better job of climbin' than I could. It ain't my age that bothers me though, it's my weight. All ready? Up you go! Humph! It's a mercy there ain't anybody lookin' on. . . . There! all right, are you?"

Emily's head appeared framed by the window sash. "Yes," she panted. "I—I think I'm all right. At least I'm through that window. Now what shall I do?"

"Take this lantern and go to one of the doors and see if you can unfasten it. Try the back door; that's the most liable to be only bolted and hooked. The front one's probably locked with a key."

The lantern and its bearer disappeared. Mrs. Barnes plodded around to the back door. As she reached it it opened.

"It was only hooked," said Emily. "Come in, Auntie. Come in quick!"

Thankful had not waited for the invitation; she was in already. She took the lantern from her relative's hand. Then she shut the door behind her.

"Whew!" she exclaimed. "If it don't seem good to get under cover, real cover! What sort of a place is this, anyhow, Emily?"

"I don't know. I—I've been too frightened to look. I—I feel like a—O, Aunt Thankful, don't you feel like a burglar?"

"Me? A burglar? I feel like a wet dishcloth. I never was so soaked, with my clothes on, in my life. Hello! I thought this was an empty house. There's a stove and a chair, such as it is. Whoever lived here last didn't take away all their furniture. Let's go into the front rooms."

The first room they entered was evidently the dining-room. It was quite bare of furniture. The next, however, that which Emily had entered by the window, contained another stove, a ramshackle what-not, and a broken-down, ragged sofa.

"Oh!" gasped Miss Howes, pointing to the sofa, "see! see! This ISN'T an empty house. Suppose—Oh, SUPPOSE there were people living here! What would they say to us?"

For a moment Thankful was staggered. Then her common-sense came to her rescue.

"Nonsense!" she said, firmly. "A house with folks livin' in it has somethin' in the dinin'-room besides dust. Anyhow, it's easy enough to settle that question. Where's that door lead to?"

She marched across the floor and threw open the door to which she had pointed.

"Humph!" she sniffed. "Best front parlor. The whole shebang smells shut up and musty enough, but there's somethin' about a best parlor smell that would give it away any time. Phew! I can almost smell wax wreaths and hair-cloth, even though they have been took away. No, this is an empty house all right, but I'll make good and sure for your sake, Emily. Ain't there any stairs to this old rattle-trap? Oh, yes, here's the front hall. Hello! Hello, up there! Hi-i!"

She was shouting up the old-fashioned staircase. Her voice echoed above with the unmistakable echo of empty rooms. Only that echo and the howl of the wind and roar of rain answered her.

She came back to the apartment where she had left her cousin.

"It's all right, Emily," she said. "We're the only passengers aboard the derelict. Now let's see if we can't be more comf'table. You set down on that sofa and rest. I've got an idea in my head."

The idea evidently involved an examination of the stove, for she opened its rusty door and peered inside. Then, without waiting to answer her companion's questions, she hurried out into the kitchen, returning with an armful of shavings and a few sticks of split pine.

"I noticed that woodbox in the kitchen when I fust come in," she said. "And 'twa'n't quite empty neither, though that's more or less of a miracle. Matches? Oh, yes, indeed! I never travel without 'em. I've been so used to lookin' out for myself and other folks that I'm a reg'lar man in some ways. There! now let's see if the draft is rusted up as much as the stove."

It was not, apparently, for, with the dampers wide open, the fire crackled and snapped. Also it smoked a little.

"'Twill get over that pretty soon," prophesied Mrs. Barnes. "I can stand 'most any amount of smoke so long's there's heat with it. Now, Emily, we'll haul that sofa up alongside and you lay down on it and get rested and warm. I'd say get dry, too, but 'twould take a reg'lar blast furnace to dry a couple of water rats like you and me this night. Perhaps we can dry the upper layer, though; that'll be some help. Now, mind me! Lay right down on that sofa."

Emily protested. She was no wetter and no more tired than her cousin, she said. Why should she lie down while Aunt Thankful sat up?

"'Cause I tell you to, for one thing," said the widow, with decision. "And because I'm well and strong and you ain't. When I think of how I got you, a half invalid, as you might say, to come on this crazy trip I'm so provoked I feel like not speakin' to myself for a week. There! now you LOOK more comf'table, anyhow. If I only had somethin' to put over you, I'd feel better. I wonder if there's an old bed quilt or anything upstairs. I've a good mind to go and see."

Emily's protest was determined this time.

"Indeed you shan't!" she cried. "You shan't stir. I wouldn't have you go prowling about this poky old place for anything. Do you suppose I could stay down here alone knowing that you might be—might be meeting or—or finding almost anything up there. Sit right down in that chair beside me. Don't you think it is almost time for that driver to be back?"

"Land sakes—no! He's hardly started yet. It's goin' to take a good long spell afore he can wade a mile and a half in such a storm as this and get another horse and wagon and come back again. He'll come by and by. All we've got to do is to stay by this fire and be thankful we've got it."

Emily shivered. "I suppose so," she said. "And I know I am nervous and a trial instead of a help. If you had only been alone—"

"Alone! Heavens to Betey! Do you think I'd like this—this camp-meetin' any better if I was the only one to it. My! Just hear that wind! Hope these old chimneys are solid."

"Auntie, what do you suppose that man meant by saying he wouldn't enter this house at night for anything?"

"Don't know. Perhaps he meant he'd be afraid of bein' arrested."

"But you don't think we'll be arrested?"

"No, no, of course not. I'd be almost willin' to be arrested if they'd do it quick. A nice, dry lock-up and somethin' to eat wouldn't be so bad, would it? But no constable but a web-footed one would be out this night. Now do as I say—you lay still and give your nerves a rest."

For a few moments the order was obeyed. Then Miss Rowes said, with another shiver: "I do believe this is the worst storm I have ever experienced."

"'Tis pretty bad, that's a fact. Do you know, Emily, if I was a believer in signs such as mentioned a little while ago, I might almost be tempted to believe this storm was one of 'em. About every big change in my life has had a storm mixed up with it, comin' at the time it happened or just afore or just after. I was born, so my mother used to tell me, on a stormy night about like this one. And it poured great guns the day I was married. And Eben, my husband, went down with his vessel in a hurricane off Hatteras. And when poor Jedediah run off to go gold-diggin' there was such a snowstorm the next day that I expected to see him plowin' his way home again. Poor old Jed! I wonder where he is tonight? Let's see; six years ago, that was. I wonder if he's been frozen to death or eat up by polar bears, or what. One thing's sartin, he ain't made his fortune or he'd have come home to tell me of it. Last words he said to me was, 'I'm a-goin', no matter what you say. And when I come back, loaded down with money, you'll be glad to see me.'"

Jedediah Cahoon was Mrs. Barnes' only near relative, a brother. Always a visionary, easy-going, impractical little man, he had never been willing to stick at steady employment, but was always chasing rainbows and depending upon his sister for a home and means of existence. When the Klondike gold fever struck the country he was one of the first to succumb to the disease. And, after an argument—violent on his part and determined on Thankful's—he had left South Middleboro and gone—somewhere. From that somewhere he had never returned.

"Yes," mused Mrs. Barnes, "those were the last words he said to me."

"What did you say to him?" asked Emily, drowsily. She had heard the story often enough, but she asked the question as an aid to keeping awake.

"Hey? What did I say? Oh, I said my part, I guess. 'When you come back,' says I, 'it'll be when I send money to you to pay your fare home, and I shan't do it. I've sewed and washed and cooked for you ever since Eben died, to say nothin' of goin' out nursin' and housekeepin' to earn money to buy somethin' TO cook. Now I'm through. This is my house—or, at any rate, I pay the rent for it. If you leave it to go gold-diggin' you needn't come back to it. If you do you won't be let in.' Of course I never thought he'd go, but he did. Ah hum! I'm afraid I didn't do right. I ought to have realized that he wa'n't really accountable, poor, weak-headed critter!"

Emily's eyes were fast shutting, but she made one more remark.

"Your life has been a hard one, hasn't it, Auntie," she said.

Thankful protested. "Oh, no, no!" she declared. "No harder'n anybody else's, I guess likely. This world has more hards than softs for the average mortal and I never flattered myself on bein' above the average. But there! How in the nation did I get onto this subject? You and me settin' here on other folks's furniture—or what was furniture once—soppin' wet through and half froze, and me talkin' about troubles that's all dead and done with! What DID get me started? Oh, yes, the storm. I was just thinkin' how most of the important things in my life had had bad weather mixed up with 'em. Come to think of it, it rained the day Mrs. Pearson was buried. And her dyin' was what set me to thinkin' of cruisin' down here to East Wellmouth and lookin' at the property Uncle Abner left me. I've never laid eyes on that property and I don't even know what the house looks like. I might have asked that depot-wagon driver, but I thought 'twas no use tellin' him my private affairs, so I said we was bound to the hotel, and let it go at that. If I had asked he might at least have told me where. . . . Hey? Why—why—my land! I never thought of it, but it might be! It might! Emily!"

But Miss Howes' eyes were closed now. In spite of her wet garments and her nervousness concerning their burglarious entry of the empty house she had fallen asleep. Thankful did not attempt to wake her. Instead she tiptoed to the kitchen and the woodbox, took from the latter the last few slabs of pine wood and, returning, filled the stove to the top. Then she sat down in the chair once more.

For some time she sat there, her hands folded in her lap. Occasionally she glanced about the room and her lips moved as if she were talking to herself. Then she rose and peered out of the window. Rain and blackness and storm were without, but nothing else. She returned to the sofa and stood looking down at the sleeper. Emily stirred a little and shivered.

That shiver helped to strengthen the fears in Mrs. Barnes' mind. The girl was not strong. She had come home from her school duties almost worn out. A trip such as this had been was enough to upset even the most robust constitution. She was wet and cold. Sleeping in wet clothes was almost sure to bring on the dreaded pneumonia. If only there might be something in that house, something dry and warm with which to cover her.

"Emily," said Thankful, in a low tone. "Emily."

The sleeper did not stir. Mrs. Barnes took up the lantern. Its flame was much less bright than it had been and the wick sputtered. She held the lantern to her ear and shook it gently. The feeble "swash" that answered the shake was not reassuring. The oil was almost gone.

Plainly if exploring of those upper rooms was to be done it must be done at once. With one more glance at the occupant of the sofa Mrs. Barnes, lantern in hand, tiptoed from the room, through the barren front hall and up the stairs. The stairs creaked abominably. Each creak echoed like the crack of doom.

At the top of the stairs was another hall, long and narrow, extending apparently the whole length of the house. At intervals along this hall were doors. One after the other Thankful opened them. The first gave entrance to a closet, with a battered and ancient silk hat and a pasteboard box on the shelf. The next opened into a large room, evidently the spare bedroom. It was empty. So was the next and the next and the next. No furniture of any kind. Thankful's hope of finding a quilt or a wornout blanket, anything which would do to cover her sleeping and shivering relative, grew fainter with the opening of each door.

There were an astonishing number of rooms and closets. Evidently this had been a big, commodious and comfortable house in its day. But that day was long past its sunset. Now the bigness only emphasized the dreariness and desolation. Dampness and spider webs everywhere, cracks in the ceiling, paper peeling from the walls. And around the gables and against the dormer-windows of these upper rooms the gale shrieked and howled and wailed like a drove of banshees.

The room at the very end of the long hall was a large one. It was at the back of the house and there were windows on two sides of it. It was empty like the others, and Mrs. Barnes, reluctantly deciding that her exploration in quest of coverings had been a failure, was about to turn and retrace her steps to the stairs when she noticed another door.

It was in the corner of the room furthest from the windows and was shut tight. A closet, probably, and all the closets she had inspected so far had contained nothing but rubbish. However, Thankful was not in the habit of doing things by halves, so, the feebly sputtering lantern held in her left hand, she opened the door with the other and looked in. Then she uttered an exclamation of joy.

It was not a closet behind that door, but another room. A small room with but one little window, low down below the slope of the ceiling. But this room was to some extent furnished. There was a bed in it, and a rocking chair, and one or two pictures hanging crookedly upon the wall. Also, and this was the really important thing, upon that bed was a patchwork comforter.

Thankful made a dash for that comforter. She set the lantern down upon the floor and snatched the gayly colored thing from the bed. And, as she did so, she heard a groan.

There are always noises in an empty house, especially an old house. Creaks and cracks and rustlings mysterious and unexplainable. When the wind blows these noises are reenforced by a hundred others. In this particular house on this particular night there were noises enough, goodness knows. Howls and rattles and moans and shrieks. Every shutter and every shingle seemed to be loose and complaining of the fact. As for groans—old hinges groan when the wind blows and so do rickety gutters and water pipes. But this groan, or so it seemed to Mrs. Barnes, had a different and distinct quality of its own. It sounded—yes, it sounded human.

Thankful dropped the patchwork comforter.

"Who's that?" she asked, sharply.

There was no answer. No sounds except those of the storm. Thankful picked up the comforter.

"Humph!" she said aloud—talking to herself was a habit developed during the years of housekeeping for deaf old Mrs. Pearson. "Humph! I must be gettin' nerves, I guess."

She began folding the old quilt in order to make it easier to carry downstairs. And then she heard another groan, or sigh, or combination of both. It sounded, not outside the window or outside the house, but in that very room.

Again Mrs. Barnes dropped the comforter. Also she went out of the room. But she did not go far. Halfway across the floor of the adjoining room she stopped and put her foot down, physically and mentally.

"Fool!" she said, disgustedly. Then, turning on her heel, she marched back to the little bedroom and picked up the lantern; its flame had dwindled to the feeblest of feeble sparks.

"Now then," said Thankful, with determination, "whoever—or—or whatever thing you are that's makin' that noise you might just as well show yourself. If you're hidin' you'd better come out, for I'll find you."

But no one or no "thing" came out. Thankful waited a moment and then proceeded to give that room a very thorough looking-over. It was such a small apartment that the process took but little time. There was no closet. Except for the one window and the door by which she had entered, the four walls, covered with old-fashioned ugly paper, had no openings of any kind. There could be no attic or empty space above the ceiling because she could hear the rain upon the sloping roof. She looked under the bed and found nothing but dust. She looked in the bed, even under the rocking-chair.

"Well, there!" she muttered. "I said it and I was right. I AM gettin' to be a nervous old fool. I'm glad Emily ain't here to see me. And yet I did—I swear I did hear somethin'."

The pictures on the wall by the window caught her eye. She walked over and looked at them. The lantern gave so little light that she could scarcely see anything, but she managed to make out that one was a dingy chromo with a Scriptural subject. The other was a battered "crayon enlargement," a portrait of a man, a middle-aged man with a chin beard. There was something familiar about the face in the portrait. Something—

Thankful gasped. "Uncle Abner!" she cried. "Why—why—"

Then the lantern flame gave a last feeble sputter and went out. She heard the groan again. And in that room, the room she had examined so carefully, so close as to seem almost at her very ear, a faint voice wailed agonizingly, "Oh, Lord!"

Thankful went away. She left the comforter and the lantern upon the floor and she did not stop to close the door of the little bedroom. Through the black darkness of the long hall she rushed and down the creaky stairs. Her entrance to the sitting-room was more noisy than her exit had been and Miss Howes stirred upon the sofa and opened her eyes.

"Auntie!" she cried, sharply. "Aunt Thankful, where are you?"

"I'm—I'm here, Emily. That is, I guess—yes, I'm here."

"But why is it so dark? Where is the lantern?"

"The lantern?" Mrs. Barnes was trying to speak calmly but, between agitation and loss of breath, she found it hard work. "The lantern? Why—it's—it's gone," she said.

"Gone? What do you mean? Where has it gone?"

"It's gone—gone out. There wa'n't enough oil in it to last any longer, I suppose."

"Oh!" Emily sat up. "And you've been sitting here alone in the dark while I have been asleep. How dreadful for you! Why didn't you speak to me? Has anything happened? Hasn't that man come back yet?"

It was the last question which Thankful answered. "No. No, he ain't come back yet," she said. "But he will pretty soon, I'm sure. He—he will, Emily, don't you fret."

"Oh, I'm not worried, Auntie. I am too sleepy to worry, I guess."

"Sleepy! You're not goin' to sleep AGAIN, are you?"

Mrs. Barnes didn't mean to ask this question; certainly she did not mean to ask it with such evident anxiety. Emily noticed the tone and wondered.

"Why, no," she said. "I think not. Of course I'm not. But what made you speak in that way? You're not frightened, are you?"

Thankful made a brave effort.

"Frightened!" she repeated, stoutly. "What on earth should I be frightened of, I'd like to know?"

"Why, nothing, I hope."

"I should say not. I—Good heavens above! What's that?"

She started and clutched her companion by the arm. They both listened.

"I don't hear anything but the storm," said Emily. "Why, Auntie, you ARE frightened; you're trembling. I do believe there is something."

Thankful snatched her hand away.

"There isn't," she declared. "Of course there isn't."

"Then why are you so nervous?"

"Me? Nervous! Emily Howes, don't you ever say that to me again. I ain't nervous and I ain't goin' to be nervous. There's no—no sane reason why I should be and I shan't. I shan't!"

"But, Auntie, you are. Oh, what is it?"

"Nothin'. Nothin' at all, I tell you. The idea!" with an attempt at a laugh. "The idea of you thinkin' I'm nervous. Young folks like you or rich old women are the only ones who can afford nerves. I ain't either young nor rich."

Emily laughed, too. This speech was natural and characteristic.

"If you were a nervous wreck," she said, "it would be no wonder, all alone in the dark as you have been in a deserted house like this. I can't forgive myself for falling asleep. Whose house do you suppose it is?"

Aunt Thankful did not answer. Emily went on. Her short nap had revived her courage and spirit.

"Perhaps it is a haunted house," she said, jokingly. "Every village has a haunted house, you know. Perhaps that's why the stage-driver warned us not to go into it."

To her surprise Mrs. Barnes seemed to take offense at this attempt at humor.

"Don't talk silly," she snapped. "If I've lived all these years and been as down on spooks and long-haired mediums as I've been, and then to—there—there! Don't let's be idiots altogether. Talk about somethin' else. Talk about that depot-wagon driver and his pesky go-cart that got us into this mess. There's plenty of things I'd like to say about THEM."

They talked, in low tones. Conversation there in the dark and under such circumstances, was rather difficult. Emily, although she was determined not to admit it, was growing alarmed for the return of Winnie S. and his promised rescue expedition. Aunt Thankful was thinking of the little back bedroom upstairs. An utter lack of superstition was something upon which she had prided herself. But now, as she thought of that room, of the portrait on the wall, and what she had heard—

"Listen!" whispered Emily, suddenly. "Listen! I—I thought I heard something."

Mrs. Barnes leaned forward.

"What? Where? Upstairs?" she asked, breathlessly.

"No. Out—out there somewhere." She pointed in the direction of the front hall. "It sounded as if someone had tried the front door. Hark! There it is again."

Aunt Thankful rose to her feet. "I heard it, too," she said. "It's probably that driver man come back. I'll go and see."

"No—no, Auntie, you mustn't. I—I shan't let you."

"I shall! I shall, I tell you! If I've got any common-sense at all, I ain't goin' to be scared of—Of course it's that driver man. He's wonderin' where we are and he's lookin' for us. I'll go let him in."

She broke away from Miss Howes' grasp and started for the front hall. The action was a braver one than her cousin realized. If there was one thing on earth that Thankful Barnes did not wish to do at that moment, it was to go nearer the stairs landing to the rooms above.

But she went, and Emily went with her. Cautiously they peered through the little windows at the sides of the front door. There was no one in sight, and, listening, they heard nothing.

"I—I guess we was mistaken, Emily," whispered Thankful. "Let's go back to the fire."

"But Auntie, I DID hear something. Didn't you?"

"Well, I thought I did, but I guess—Oh, DON'T stay here another minute! I—I shall be hearin' 'most anything if we do."

They returned to the room they had left. But they had scarcely entered it when they stopped short and, clinging to each other, listened.

It was the latch of the kitchen door they heard click now. And the door was opening. In the kitchen they heard the sounds of cautious footsteps, footsteps which entered the dining-room, which came on toward the sitting-room. And a voice, a man's voice, whispered:

"I told you so! I—I told you so! I said I see a light. And—and that door was undone and—and—By time! Obed Bangs, you can go on if you want to, but I tell you you're riskin' your life. I—I ain't goin' to stay no longer. I'm goin' to fetch the constable—or—or the minister or somebody. I—"

Another voice interrupted.

"Shut up! Belay!" it ordered. "If there's anybody or anything in this house we'll have a look at it, that's all. You can go to the minister afterwards, if you want to. Just now you'll come along with me if I have to haul you by the neck. Let's see what's in here."

There was a flash of light in the crack of the door leading from the dining-room. That door was thrown open and the light became a blaze from a big lantern held aloft.

"Hey! What!" exclaimed the second voice. "Who—women, by the everlastin'!"

Mrs. Barnes and Emily clinging to each other, blinked in the lantern light.

"Women! Two women!" said the voice again.

Thankful answered. The voice was real and it came from a human throat. Anything human—and visible—she did not fear.

"Yes," she said, crisply, "we're women. What of it? Who are you?"

The man with the lantern entered the room. He was big and broad-shouldered and bearded. His companion was short and stout and smooth-faced; also he appeared very much frightened. Both men wore oilskin coats and sou'westers.

"Who are you?" repeated Aunt Thankful.

The big man answered. His sunburned, good-humored face was wrinkled and puckered with amazement.

"Well," he stammered, "I—we—Humph! well, we're neighbors and—but—but, I don't know as I know you, ma'am, do I?"

"I don't know why you should. I don't know you, fur's that goes. What are you doin' here? Did that depot-wagon man send you?"

"Depot-wagon man? No, ma'am; nobody sent us. Kenelm—er—Mr. Parker here, saw a light a spell ago and, bein' as this house is supposed to be empty, he—"

"Wait a minute!" Miss Howes interrupted. "Whose house is this?"

"Why—why, it ain't anybody's house, ma'am. That is, nobody lives here."

"But somebody used to live here, it's likely. What was his name?"

"His name? Well, old Laban Eldredge used to live here. The house belongs to Captain Abner Cahoon's heirs, I believe, and—"

Again Thankful interrupted.

"I knew it!" she cried, excitedly. "I wondered if it mightn't be so and when I see that picture of Uncle Abner I was sure. All right, Mr. Whoever-you-are, then I'm here because I own the house. My name's Barnes, Thankful Barnes of South Middleboro, and I'm Abner Cahoon's heir. Emily, this—this rattle-trap you and I broke into is the 'property' we've talked so much about."

CHAPTER III

EMILY said—well, the first thing she said was, "Oh, Aunt Thankful!" Then she added that she couldn't believe it.

"It's so," declared Mrs. Barnes, "whether we believe it or not. When you come to think it over there's nothin' so wonderful about it, after all. I had a sneakin' suspicion when I was sittin' here by you, after you'd gone to sleep. What I saw afterwards made me almost sure. I—Hum! I guess likely that'll keep till we get to the hotel, if we ever do get there. Perhaps Mr.—Mr.—"

"Bangs is my name, ma'am," said the big man with the lantern. "Obed Bangs."

"Thank you, Mr. Bangs. Or it's 'Cap'n Bangs,' ain't it?"

"They generally call me Cap'n, ma'am, though I ain't been doin' any active seafarin' for some time."

"I thought as much. Down here on Cape Cod, and givin' orders the way I heard you afore you come into this room, 'twas nine chances to one you was a cap'n, or you had been one. Bangs—Bangs—Obed Bangs? Why, that name sounds kind of familiar. Seems as if—Cap'n Bangs, you didn't use to know Eben Barnes of Provincetown, did you?"

"Eben Barnes? Cap'n Eben of the White Foam, lost off Cape Hatteras in a gale?"

"Yes, that's the one. I thought I heard him speak of you. He was my husband."

Captain Obed Bangs uttered an exclamation. Then he stepped forward and seized Mrs. Barnes' hand. The lady's hand was not a very small one but the Captain's was so large that, as Thankful remarked afterward, it might have shaken hers twice at the same time.

"Eben Barnes' wife!" exclaimed Captain Obed. "Why, Eben and I was mess-mates on I don't know how many v'yages! Well, well, well, ma'am, I'm real glad to see you."

"You ain't so glad as we are to see you—and your friend," observed Thankful, drily. "Is he a captain, too?"

He didn't look like one, certainly. He had removed his sou'wester, uncovering a round head, with reddish-gray hair surrounding a bald spot at the crown. He had a double chin and a smile which was apologetic but ingratiating. He seemed less frightened than when he first entered the room, but still glanced about him with evident apprehension.

"No—no, ma'am," he stammered, in answer to the question. "No, ma'am, I—I—my name's Parker. I—I ain't a cap'n; no, ma'am."

"Kenelm ain't been promoted yet," observed Captain Obed gravely. "He's wait-in' until he get's old enough to go to sea. Ain't that it, Kenelm?"

Kenelm smiled and shifted his sou'wester from his right hand to his left.

"I—I cal'late so," he answered.

"Well, it don't make any difference," declared Thankful. "My cousin and I are just as glad to see him as if he was an admiral. We've been waitin' so long to see any human bein' that we'd begun to think they was all drowned. But you haven't met my cousin yet. Her name's Howes."

Emily, who had stood by, patient but chilly, during the introductions and rem-iniscences, shook hands with Captain Bangs and Mr. Parker. Both gentlemen said they were pleased to meet her; no, Captain Obed said that—Kenelm said that he was "glad to be acquaintanced."

"I don't know as we hadn't ought to beg your pardon for creepin' in on you this way," said the captain. "We thought the house was empty. We didn't know you was visitin' your—your property."

"Well, so far as that goes, neither did we. I don't wonder you expected to find burglars or tramps or whatever you did expect. We've had an awful time this night, ain't we, Emily?"

"We certainly have," declared Miss Howes, with emphasis.

"Yes, you see—"

She gave a brief history of the cruise and wreck of the depot-wagon. Also of their burglarious entry of the house.

"And now, Cap'n," she said, in conclusion, "if you could think up any way of our gettin' to that hotel, we'd be ever so much obliged. . . . Hello! There's that driver, I do believe! And about time, I should say!"

From without came the sound of wheels and the voice of Winnie S., hailing his missing passengers.

"Hi! Hi-i! Where be ye?"

"He'll wear his lungs out, screamin' that way," snapped Thankful. "Can't he see the light, for goodness sakes?"

Captain Obed answered. "He couldn't see nothin' unless 'twas hung on the end of his nose," he said. "That boy's eyes and brains ain't connected. Here, Kenelm," turning to Mr. Parker, "you go out and tell Win to shut down on his fog whistle; he's wastin' steam. Tell him the women-folks are in here. Look alive, now!"

Kenelm looked alive, but not much more than that.

"All right, Cap'n," he stammered. "A—a—all right. What—what—shall I say— what shall I—had I better—"

"Thunderation! Do you need a chart and compass? Stay where you are. I'll say it myself."

He strode to the window, threw it open, and shouted in a voice which had been trained to carry above worse gales than the present one:

"Ahoy! Ahoy! Win! Fetch her around aft here. Lay alongside the kitchen door! D'you hear? Ahoy! Win! d'you hear?"

Silence. Then, after a moment, came the reply. "Yup, I hear ye. Be right there."

The captain turned from the window.

"Took some time for him to let us know he heard, didn't it," he observed. "Cal'late he had to say 'Judas priest' four or five times afore he answered. If you cut all the 'Judas priests' out of that boy's talk he'd be next door to tongue-tied."

Thankful turned to her relative.

"There, Emily," she said, with a sigh of relief. "I guess likely we'll make the hotel this tack. I begun to think we never would."

Captain Bangs shook his head.

"You won't go to no hotel this night," he said, decidedly. "It's a long ways off and pretty poor harbor after you make it. You'll come right along with me and Kenelm to his sister's house. It's only a little ways and Hannah's got a spare room and she'll be glad to have you. I'm boardin' there myself just now. Yes, you will," he added. "Of course you will. Suppose I'm goin' to let relations of Eben Barnes put up at the East Wellmouth tavern? By the everlastin', I guess not! I wouldn't send a—a Democrat there. Come right along! Don't say another word."

Both of the ladies said other words, a good many of them, but they might as well have been orders to the wind to stop blowing. Captain Obed Bangs was, evidently, a person accustomed to having his own way. Even as they were still protesting their new acquaintance led them to the kitchen door, where Winnie S. and a companion, a long-legged person who answered to the name of "Jabez," were waiting on the front seat of a vehicle attached to a dripping and dejected horse. To the rear of this vehicle "General Jackson" was tethered by a halter. Winnie S. was loaded to the guards with exclamatory explanations.

"Judas priest!" he exclaimed, as the captain assisted Mrs. Barnes and Emily into the carriage. "If I ain't glad to see you folks! When I got back here and there wa'n't a sign of you nowheres, I was took some off my pins, I tell ye. Didn't know what to do. I says to Jabez, I says—"

Captain Obed interrupted. "Never mind what you said to Jabez, Win," he said. "Why didn't you get back sooner? That's what we want to know."

Winnie S. was righteously indignant. "Sooner!" he repeated. "Judas priest! I tell ye right now I'm lucky to get back at all. Took me pretty nigh an hour to get to the village. Such travelin' I never see. Tried to save time by takin' the short cut acrost the meadow, and there ain't no meadow no more. It's three foot under water. You never see such a tide. So back I had to frog it and when I got far as Jabe's house all hands had turned in. I had to pretty nigh bust the door down 'fore I could wake anybody up. Then Jabe he had to get dressed and we had to harness up and—hey? Did you say anything, ma'am?"

The question was addressed to Mrs. Barnes, who had been vainly trying to ask one on her own account.

"I say have you got our valises?" asked Thankful. "Last I saw of them they was in that other wagon, the one that broke down."

The driver slapped his knee. "Judas priest!" he cried. "I forgot all about them satchels. Here, Jabe," handing the reins to his companion. "You take the hellum while I run back and fetch 'em."

He was back in a few moments with the missing satchels. Then Jabez, who was evidently not given to wasting words, drawled: "Did you get the mail? That's in there, too, ain't it?"

"Judas priest! So 'tis. Why didn't you remind me of it afore? Set there like—like a wooden figurehead and let me run my legs off—"

His complaints died away in the distance. At last, with the mail bag under the seat, the caravan moved on. It was still raining, but not so hard, and the wind blew less fiercely. They jogged and rocked and splashed onward. Suddenly Winnie S. uttered another shout.

"The lantern!" he cried. "Where's that lantern I lent ye?"

"It's there in the house," said Thankful. "It burned itself out and I forgot it. Mercy on us! You're not goin' back after that, I hope."

"Well, I dunno. That lantern belongs to the old man—dad, I mean—and he sets a lot of store by it. If I've lost that lantern on him, let alone leavin' his depot-wagon all stove up, he'll give me—"

"Never mind what he'll give you," broke in Captain Bangs. "You keep on your course or I'LL give you somethin'. Don't you say another word till we get abreast of Hannah Parker's."

"Humph! We're there now. I thought these folks was goin' to our hotel."

"Take my advice and don't think so much. You'll open a seam in your head and founder, first thing you know. Here we are! And here's Hannah! Hannah, Kenelm and I've brought you a couple of lodgers. Now, ma'am, if you'll stand by. Kenelm, open that hatch."

Mr. Parker opened the hatch—the door of the carriage—and the captain assisted the passengers to alight. Emily caught a glimpse of the white front of a little house and of a tall, angular woman standing in the doorway holding a lamp. Then she and Mrs. Barnes were propelled by the strong arms of their pilot through that doorway and into a little sitting-room, bright and warm and cheery.

"There!" declared Captain Obed. "That cruise is over. Kenelm! Where is Kenelm? Oh, there you are! You tell that Winnie S. to trot along. We'll settle for passage tomorrow mornin'. Now, ma'am," turning to Thankful, "you and your relation want to make yourselves as comf'table as you can. This is Miss Parker, Kenelm's sister. Hannah, this is Mrs. Barnes, Eben Barnes' widow. You've heard me speak of him. And this is Miss Howes. I cal'late they're hungry and I know they're wet. Seems's if dry clothes and supper might be the next items on the manifest."

Miss Parker rose to the occasion. She flew about preparing the "items." Thankful and Emily were shown to the spare room, hot water and towels were provided, the valise was brought in. When the ladies again made their appearance in the sitting-room, they were arrayed in dry, warm garments, partly their own and partly supplied from the wardrobe of their hostess. As to the fit of these latter, Mrs. Barnes expressed her opinion when she said:

"Don't look at me, Emily. I feel like a barrel squeezed into an umbrella cover. This dress is long enough, land knows, but that's about all you can say of it. However, I suppose we hadn't ought to—to look a gift dress in the waistband."

Supper was ready in the dining-room and thither they were piloted by Kenelm, whose hair, what there was of it, was elaborately "slicked down," and whose celluloid collar had evidently received a scrubbing. In the dining-room they found Captain Bangs awaiting them. Miss Parker made her appearance bearing a steaming teapot. Hannah, now that they had an opportunity to inspect her, was seen to be as tall and sharp-featured as her brother was short and round. She was at least fifteen years older than he, but she moved much more briskly. Also she treated Kenelm as she might have treated a child, an only child who needed constant suppression.

"Please to be seated, everybody," she said. "Cap'n Obed, you take your reg'lar place. Mrs. Barnes, if you'll be so kind as to set here, and Miss Howes next to you. Kenelm, you set side of me. Set down, don't stand there fidgetin'. WHAT did you put on that necktie for? I told you to put on the red one."

Kenelm fingered his tie. "I—I cal'late I must have forgot, Hannah," he stammered. "I never noticed. This one's all right, ain't it?"

"All right! It'll have to be. You can't change it now. But, for goodness sakes, look out it stays on. The elastic's all worn loose and it's li'ble to drop into your tea or anywheres else. Now," with a sudden change from a family to a "company" manner, "may I assist you to a piece of the cold ham, Miss Howes? I trust you are feelin' quite restored to yourself again?"

Emily's answer being in the affirmative, their hostess continued:

"I'm so sorry to be obliged to set nothin' but cold ham and toast and tea before you," she said. "If I had known you was comin' I should have prepared somethin' more fittin'. After such an experience as you must have been through this night to set down to ham and toast! I—I declare I feel real debilitated and ashamed to offer 'em to you."

Thankful answered.

"Don't say a word, Miss Parker," she said, heartily. "We're the ones that ought to be ashamed. Landin' on you this way in the middle of the night. You're awfully good to take us in at all. My cousin and I were on our way to the hotel, but Cap'n Bangs wouldn't hear of it. He's responsible for our comin' here."

Miss Parker nodded.

"Cap'n Obed is the most hospital soul livin'," she said, grandly. "He done just right. If he'd done anything else Kenelm and I would have felt hurt. I—Look out!" with a sudden snatch at her brother's shirt front. "There goes that tie. Another second and 'twould have been right in your plate."

Kenelm snapped the loop of the "made" tie over his collar button. "Don't grab at me that way, Hannah," he protested mildly. "I'm kind of nervous tonight, after what I've been through. 'Twouldn't have done no great harm if I had dropped it. I could pick it up again, couldn't I?"

"You could, but I doubt if you would. You might have ate it, you're so absent-minded. Nervous! YOU nervous! What do you think of me? Mrs. Barnes," turning to Thankful and once more resuming the "company" manner, "you'll excuse our bein' a little upset. You see, when my brother came home and said he'd seen lights movin' around in the old Barnes' house, he frightened us all pretty near to death. All Cap'n Obed could think of was tramps, or thieves or somethin'. Nothin' would do but he must drag Kenelm right back to see who or what was in there. And I was left alone to imagine all sorts of dreadful things. Tramps I might stand. They belong to this world, anyhow. But in THAT house, at eleven o'clock at night, I—Mrs. Barnes, do you believe in aberrations?"

Thankful was nonplused. "In—in which?" she asked.

"In aberrations, spirits of dead folks comin' alive again?"

For just a moment Mrs. Barnes hesitated. Then she glanced at Emily, who was trying hard not to smile, and answered, with decision: "No, I don't."

"Well, I don't either, so far as that goes. I never see one myself, and I've never seen anybody that has. But when Kenelm came tearin' in to say he'd seen a light in a house shut up as long as that one has been, and a house that folks—"

Captain Bangs interrupted. He had been regarding Thankful closely and now he changed the subject.

"How did it happen you saw that light, Kenelm?" he asked. "What was you doin' over in that direction a night like this?"

Kenelm hesitated. He seemed to find it difficult to answer.

"Why—why—" he stammered, "I'd been up to the office after the mail. And—and—it was so late comin' that I give it up. I says to Lemuel Ryder, 'Lem,' I says—"

His sister broke in.

"Lem Ryder!" she repeated. "Was he at the post-office?"

"Well—well—" Kenelm's confusion was more marked than ever. "Well—well—" he stammered, "I see him, and I says—"

"You see him! Where did you see him? Kenelm Parker, I don't believe you was at the postoffice at all. You was at the clubroom, that's where you was. At that clubroom, smokin' and playin' cards with that deprivated crowd of loafers and gamblers. Tell me the truth, now, wasn't you?"

Mr. Parker's tie fell off then, but neither he nor his sister noticed it.

"Gamblers!" he snorted. "There ain't no gamblers there. Playin' a hand or two of California Jack just for fun ain't gamblin'. I wouldn't gamble, not for a million dollars."

Captain Obed laughed. "Neither would I," he observed. "Nor for two cents, with that clubroom gang; 'twould be too much nerve strain collectin' my winnin's. I see now why you come by the Barnes' house, Kenelm. It's the nighest way home from that clubhouse. Well, I'm glad you did. Mrs. Barnes and Miss Howes would have had a long session in the dark if you hadn't. Yes, and a night at Darius Holt's hotel, which would have been a heap worse. So you've been livin' at South Middleboro, Mrs. Barnes, have you? Does Miss Howes live there, too?"

Thankful, very grateful for the change of topic, told of her life since her husband's death, of her long stay with Mrs. Pearson, of Emily's teaching school, and their trip aboard the depot-wagon.

"Well," exclaimed Miss Parker, when she had finished, "you have been through enough, I should say! A reg'lar story-book adventure, ain't it? Lost in a storm and shut up in an empty house, the one you come purpose to see. It's a mercy you wa'n't either of you hurt, climbin' in that window the way you did. You might have broke your arms or your necks or somethin'. Mr. Alpheus Bassett, down to the Point—a great, strong, fleshy man, weighs close to two hundred and fifty and never sick a day in his life—he was up in the second story of his buildin' walkin' around spry as anybody—all alone, which he shouldn't have been at his age—and he stepped on a fish and away he went. And the next thing we hear he's in bed with his collar-bone. Did you ever hear anything like that in your life, Miss Howes?"

It was plain that Emily never had. "I—I'm afraid I don't understand," she faltered. "You say he was in the second story of a building and he stepped on—on a FISH?"

"Yes, just a mackerel 'twas, and not a very big one, they tell me. At first they was afraid 'twas the spine he'd broke, but it turned out to be only the collar-bone, though that's bad enough."

Captain Obed burst into a laugh. "'Twa'n't the mackerel's collar-bone, Miss Howes," he explained, "though I presume likely that was broke, too, if Alpheus stepped on it. He was up in the loft of his fish shanty icin' and barrelin' fish to send to Boston, and he fell downstairs. Wonder it didn't kill him."

Miss Parker nodded. "That's what I say," she declared. "And Sarah—that's his wife—tells me the doctors are real worried because the fraction ain't ignited yet."

Thankful coughed and then observed that she should think they would be.

"If you don't mind," she added, "I think it's high time all hands went to bed. It must be way along into the small hours and if we set here any longer it'll be time for breakfast. You folks must be tired, settin' up this way and I'm sure Emily and I am. If we turn in now we may have a chance to look over that precious property of mine afore we go back to South Middleboro. I don't know, though, as we haven't seen enough of it already. It don't look very promisin' to me."

The captain rose from the table and, walking to the window, pushed aside the shade.

"It'll look better tomorrow—today, I should say," he observed. "The storm's about over, and the wind's hauled to the west'ard. We'll have a spell of fair weather now, I guess. That property of yours, Mrs. Barnes, 'll look a lot more promisin' in the sunshine. There's no better view along shore than from the front windows of that house. 'Tain't half bad, that old house ain't. All it needs is fixin' up."

Good nights—good mornings, for it was after two o'clock—were said and the guests withdrew to their bedroom. Once inside, with the door shut, Thankful and Emily looked at each other and both burst out laughing.

"Oh, dear me!" gasped the former, wiping her eyes. "Maybe it's mean to laugh at folks that's been as kind to us as these Parkers have been, but I never had such a job keepin' a straight face in my life. When she said she was 'debilitated' at havin' to give us ham and toast that was funny enough, but what come afterwards was funnier. The 'fraction' ain't 'ignited' yet and the doctors are worried. I should think they'd be more worried if it had."

Emily shook her head. "I am glad I didn't have to answer that remark, Auntie," she said. "I never could have done it without disgracing myself. She is a genuine Mrs. Malaprop, isn't she?"

This was a trifle too deep for Mrs. Barnes, who replied that she didn't know, she having never met the Mrs. What's-her-name to whom her cousin referred. "She's a genuine curiosity, this Parker woman, if that's what you mean, Emily," she said. "And so's her brother, though a different kind of one. We must get Cap'n Bangs to tell us more about 'em in the mornin'. He thinks that—that heirloom house of mine will look better in the daylight. Well, I hope he's right; it looked hopeless enough tonight, what I could see of it."

"I like that Captain Bangs," observed Emily.

"So do I. It seems as if we'd known him for ever so long. And how his salt-water talk does take me back. Seems as if I was hearin' my father and Uncle Abner—yes, and Eben, too—speakin'. And it is so sort of good and natural to be callin' somebody 'Cap'n.' I was brought up amongst cap'ns and I guess I've missed 'em more'n I realized. Now you must go to sleep; you'll need all the sleep you can get, and that won't be much. Good night."

"Good night," said Emily, sleepily. A few minutes later she said: "Auntie, what did become of that lantern our driver was so anxious about? The last I saw of it it was on the floor by the sofa where I was lying. But I didn't seem to remember it after the captain and Mr. Parker came."

Mrs. Barnes' reply was, if not prompt, at least conclusive.

"It's over there somewhere," she said. "The light went out, but it ain't likely the lantern went with it. Now you go to sleep."

Miss Howes obeyed. She was asleep very soon thereafter. But Thankful lay awake, thinking and wondering—yes, and dreading. What sort of a place was this she had inherited? She distinctly did not believe in what Hannah Parker had called "aberrations," but she had heard something—something strange and inexplicable in that little back bedroom. The groans might have been caused by the gale, but no gale spoke English, or spoke at all, for that matter. Who, or what, was it that had said "Oh Lord!" in the darkness and solitude of that bedroom?

CHAPTER IV

THANKFUL opened her eyes. The sunlight was streaming in at the window. Beneath that window hens were clucking noisily. Also in the room adjoining someone was talking, protesting.

"I don't know, Hannah," said Mr. Parker's voice. "I tell you I don't know where it is. If I knew I'd tell you, wouldn't I? I don't seem to remember what I done with it."

"Well, then, you've got to set down and not stir till you do remember, that's all. When you went out of this house last evenin' to go to the postoffice—Oh, yes! To the postoffice—that's where you said you was goin'—you had the lantern and that umbrella. When you came back, hollerin' about the light you see in the Cap'n Abner house, you had the lantern. But the umbrella you didn't have. Now where is it?"

"I don't know, Hannah. I—I—do seem to remember havin' had it, but—"

"Well, I'm glad you remember that much. You lost one of your mittens, too, but 'twas an old one, so I don't mind that so much. But that umbrella was your Christmas present and 'twas good gloria silk with a real gilt-plated handle. I paid two dollars and a quarter for that umbrella, and I told you never to take it out in a storm because you were likely to turn it inside out and spile it. If I'd seen you take it last night I'd have stopped you, but you was gone afore I missed it."

"But—but, consarn it all, Hannah—"

"Don't swear, Kenelm. Profanity won't help you none."

"I wa'n't swearin'. All I say is what's the use of an umbrella if you can't hist it in a storm? I wouldn't give a darn for a schooner load of 'em when 'twas fair weather.

I—I cal'late I—I left it somewheres."

"I cal'late you did. I'm goin' over to the village this mornin' and I'll stop in at that clubhouse, myself."

"I—I don't believe it's at the clubhouse, Hannah."

"You don't? Why don't you?"

"I—I don't know. I just guess it ain't, that's all. Somethin' seems to tell me 'tain't."

"Oh, it does, hey? I want to know! Hum! Was you anywheres else last night? Answer me the truth now, Kenelm Parker. Was you anywheres else last night?"

"Anywheres else. What do you mean by that?"

"I mean what I say. You know what I mean well enough. Was you—well, was you callin' on anybody?"

"Callin' on anybody? CALLIN' on 'em?"

"Yes, callin' on 'em. Oh, you needn't look so innocent and buttery! You ain't above it. Ain't I had experience? Haven't I been through it? Didn't you use to say that I, your sister that's been a mother to you, was the only woman in this world for you, and then, the minute I was out of sight and hardly out of hearin', you—"

"My soul! You've got Abbie Larkin in your head again, ain't you? It—it—I swear it's a reg'lar disease with you, seems so. Ain't I told you I ain't seen Abbie Larkin, nor her me, for the land knows how long? And I don't want to see her. My time! Do you suppose I waded and paddled a mile and a quarter down to call on Abbie Larkin a night like last night? What do you think I am—a bull frog? I wouldn't do it to see the—the Queen of Rooshy."

This vehement outburst seemed to have some effect. Miss Parker's tone was more conciliatory.

"Well, all right," she said. "I s'pose likely you didn't call on her, if you say so, Kenelm. I suppose I am a foolish, lone woman. But, O Kenelm, I do think such a sight of you. And you know you've got money and that Abbie Larkin is so worldly she'd marry you for it in a minute. I didn't know but you might have met her."

"Met her! Tut—tut—tut! If that ain't—and in a typhoon like last night! Oh, sartin, I met her! I was up here on top of Meetin'-house Hill, larnin' her to swim in the mud puddles. You do talk so silly sometimes, Hannah."

"Maybe I do," with a sniff. "Maybe I do, Kenelm, but you mean so much to me.

I just can't let you go."

"Go! I ain't goin' nowheres, am I? What kind of talk's that?"

"And to think you'd heave away that umbrella—the umbrella I gave you! That's what makes me feel so bad. A nice, new, gilt-plated umbrella—"

"I never hove it away. I—I—well, I left it somewhere, I—I cal'late. I'll go look for it after breakfast. Say, when are we goin' to have breakfast, anyhow? It's almost eight o'clock now. Ain't them women-folks EVER goin' to turn out?"

Thankful had heard enough. She was out of bed the next instant.

"Emily! Emily!" she cried. "It's late. We must get up now."

The voices in the sitting-room died to whispers.

"I—I can't help it," pleaded Kenelm. "I never meant nothin'. I thought they was asleep. And 'TIS most eight. By time, Hannah, you do pick on me—"

A vigorous "Sshh!" interrupted him. The door between the sitting-room and dining-room closed with a slam. Mrs. Barnes and Emily dressed hurriedly.

They gathered about the breakfast table, the Parkers, Captain Obed and the guests. Miss Parker's "company manner" was again much in evidence and she seemed to feel it her duty to lead the conversation. She professed to have discovered a striking resemblance between Miss Howes and a deceased relative of her own named Melinda Ellis.

"The more I see of you, Miss Howes," she declared, "the more I can't help thinkin' of poor Melindy. She was pretty and had dark eyes and hair same's you've got, and that same sort of—of consumptic look to her. Not that you've got consumption, I don't mean that. Only you look the way she done, that's all. She did have consumption, poor thing. Everybody thought she'd die of it, but she didn't. She got up in the night to take some medicine and she took the wrong kind—toothache lotion it was and awful powerful—and it ate right through to her diagram. She didn't live long afterwards, poor soul."

No one said anything for a moment after this tragic recital. Then Captain Bangs observed cheerfully:

"Well, I guess Miss Howes ain't likely to drink any toothache lotion."

Hannah nodded sedately. "I trust not," she said. "But accidents do happen. And Melindy and Miss Howes look awful like each other. You're real well, I hope, Miss Howes. After bein' exposed the way you was last night I HOPE you haven't caught cold. You never can tell what'll follow a cold—with some people."

Thankful was glad when the meal was over. She, too, was fearful that her cousin might have taken cold during the wet chill of the previous night. But Emily declared she was very well indeed; that the very sight of the sunlit sea through the dining-room windows had acted like a tonic.

"Good enough!" exclaimed Captain Obed, heartily. "Then we ought to be gettin' a bigger dose of that tonic. Mrs. Barnes, if you and Miss Howes would like to walk over and have a look at that property of yours, now's as good a time as any to be doin' it. I'll go along with you if I won't be in the way."

Thankful looked down rather doubtfully at the borrowed gown she was wearing, but Miss Parker came to the rescue by announcing that her guests' own garments must be dry by this time, they had been hanging by the stove all night. So, after the change had been made, the two left the Parker residence and took the foot-path at the top of the bluff. Captain Obed seemed at first rather uneasy.

"Hope I ain't hurryin' you too much," he said. "I thought maybe it would be just as well to get out of sight of Hannah as quick as possible. She might take a notion to come with us. I thought sure Kenelm would, but he's gone on a cruise of his own somewheres. He hustled outdoor soon as breakfast was over."

Emily burst out laughing. "Excuse me, please," she said, "but I've been dying to do this for so long. That—that Miss Parker is the oddest person!"

The captain grinned. "Thinkin' about that 'diagram' yarn?" he asked. "'Tis funny when you hear it the first four or five times. Hannah Parker can get more wrong words in the right places than anybody I ever run across. She must have swallowed a dictionary some time or 'nother, but it ain't digested well, I'm afraid."

Thankful laughed, too. "You must find her pretty amusin', Cap'n Bangs," she said.

The captain shook his head. "She's a reg'lar dime show," he observed. Then he added: "Only trouble with that kind of a show is it gets kind of tiresome when you have to set through it all winter. There! now you can see your property, Mrs. Barnes, and ten mile either side of it. Look's some more lifelike and cheerful than it did last night, don't it?"

It most assuredly did. They had reached the summit of a little hill and before and behind and beneath them was a view of shore and sea that caused Emily to utter an exclamation of delight.

"Oh!" she cried. "WHAT a view! What a wonderful view!"

Behind them, beyond the knoll upon which stood the little Parker house which they had just left, at the further side of the stretch of salt meadow with the creek and bridge, was East Wellmouth village. Along the white sand of the beach, now garlanded with lines of fresh seaweed torn up and washed ashore by the gale, were scattered a half dozen fishhouses, with dories and lobster pots before them, and at the rear of these began the gray and white huddle of houses and stores, with two white church spires and the belfry of the schoolhouse rising above their roofs.

At their right, only a few yards from the foot-path where they stood, the high sand bluff broke sharply down to the beach and the sea. The great waves, tossing their white plumes on high, came marching majestically in, to trip, topple and fall, one after the other, in roaring, hissing Niagaras upon the shore. Over their raveled crests the gulls dipped and soared. The air was clear, the breeze keen and refreshing and the salty smell of the torn seaweed rose to the nostrils of the watchers.

To the left were barren hills, dotted with scrub, and farther on the pine groves, with the road from Wellmouth Centre winding out from their midst.

All these things Thankful and Emily noticed, but it was on the prospect directly ahead that their interest centered. For there, upon the slope of the next knoll stood the "property" they had come to see and to which they had been introduced in such an odd fashion.

Seen by daylight and in the glorious sunshine the old Barnes house did look, as their guide said, more "lifelike and cheerful." A big, rambling, gray-gabled affair, of colonial pattern, a large yard before it and a larger one behind, the tumble-down shed in which General Jackson had been tethered, a large barn, also rather tumble-down, with henhouses and corncribs beside it and attached to it in haphazard fashion. In the front yard were overgrown clusters of lilac and rose bushes and, behind the barn, was the stubble of a departed garden. Thankful looked at all these.

"So that's it," she said.

"That's it," said Captain Obed. "What do you think of it?"

"Humph! Well, there's enough of it, anyhow, as the little boy said about the spring medicine. What do you think, Emily?"

Emily's answer was prompt and emphatic.

"I like it," she declared. "It looks so different this morning. Last night it seemed lonesome and pokey and horrid, but now it is almost inviting. Think what it must be in the spring and summer. Think of opening those upper windows on a summer morning and looking out and away for miles and miles. It would be splendid!"

"Um—yes. But spring and summer don't last all the time. There's December and January and February to think of. Even March ain't all joy; we've got last night to prove it by. However, it doesn't look quite so desperate as I thought it might; I'll give in to that. Last night I was about ready to sell it for the price of a return ticket to South Middleboro. Now I guess likely I ought to get a few tradin' stamps along with the ticket. Humph! This sartin isn't ALL Poverty Lane, is it? THAT place wa'n't built with tradin' stamps. Who lives there?"

She was pointing to the estate adjoining the Barnes house and fronting the sea further on. "Estate" is a much abused term and is sometimes applied to rather insignificant holdings, but this one deserved the name. Great stretches of lawns and shrubbery, ornamental windmill, greenhouses, stables, drives and a towered and turreted mansion dominating all.

"I seem to have aristocratic neighbors, anyhow," observed Mrs. Barnes. "Whose tintype belongs in THAT gilt frame?"

Captain Obed chuckled at the question.

"Why, nobody's just now," he said. "There was one up to last fall, though I shouldn't have called him a tintype. More of a panorama, if you asked me—or him, either. That place belonged to our leadin' summer resident, Mr. Hamilton Colfax, of New York. There's a good view from there, too, but not as fine as this one of yours, Mrs. Barnes. When your uncle, Cap'n Abner, bought this old house it used to set over on a part of that land there. The cap'n didn't like the outlook so well as the one from here, so he bought this strip and moved the house down. Quite a job movin' a house as old as this one.

"Mr. Colfax died last October," he added, "and the place is for sale. Good deal of a shock, his death was, to East Wellmouth. Kind of like takin' away the doughnut and leavin' nothin' but the hole. The Wellmouth Weekly Advocate pretty nigh gave up the ghost when Mr. Colfax did. It always cal'lated on fillin' at least three columns with the doin's of the Colfaxes and their 'house parties' and such. All summer it told what they did do and all winter it guessed what they was goin' to do.

It ain't been much more than a patent medicine advertisin' circular since the blow struck. Well, have you looked enough? Shall we heave ahead and go aboard your craft, Mrs. Barnes?"

They walked on, down the little hill and up the next, and entered the front yard of the Barnes house. There were the marks in the mud and sand where the depot-wagon had overturned, but the wagon itself was gone. "Cal'late Winnie S. and his dad come around early and towed it home," surmised Captain Obed. "Seemed to me I smelled sulphur when I opened my bedroom window this mornin'. Guess 'twas a sort of floatin' memory of old man Holt's remarks when he went by. That depot-wagon was an antique and antiques are valuable these days. Want to go inside, do you?"

Thankful hesitated. "I haven't got the key," she said. "I suppose it's at that Badger man's in the village. You know who I mean, Cap'n Bangs."

The captain nodded.

"Christopher S. H. Badger, tinware, groceries, real estate, boots and shoes, and insurance," he said. "Likewise justice of the peace and first mate of all creation. Yes, I know Chris."

"Well, he's been in charge of this property of mine. He collected the rent from that Mr. Eldredge who used to live here. I had a good many letters from him, mainly about paintin' and repairs."

"Um—hum; I ain't surprised. Chris sells paint as well as tea and tinware. He's got the key, has he?"

"I suppose he has. I ought to have gone up and got it from him."

"Well, I wouldn't fret about it. Of course we can't go in the front door like the minister and weddin' company, but the kitchen door was unfastened last night and I presume likely it's that way now. You haven't any objection to the kitchen door, have you? When old Laban lived here it's a safe bet he never used any other. Cur'ous old critter, he was."

They entered by the kitchen door. The inside of the house, like the outside, was transformed by day and sunshine. The rooms downstairs were large and well lighted, and, in spite of their emptiness, they seemed almost cheerful.

"Whose furniture is this?" asked Thankful, referring to the stove and chair and sofa in the dining-room.

"Laban's; that is, it used to be. When he died he didn't have chick nor child nor relation, so fur's anybody knew, and his stuff stayed right here. There wa'n't very much of it. That is—" He hesitated.

"But, there must have been more than this," said Thankful. "What, became of it?"

Captain Obed shook his head. "You might ask Chris Badger," he suggested. "Chris sells antiques on the side—the high side."

"Did old Mr. Eldredge live here ALL alone?" asked Emily.

"Yup. And died all alone, too. Course I don't mean he was alone all the time he was sick. Most of that time he was out of his head and folks could stay with him, but he came to himself occasional and when he did he'd fire 'em out because feedin' 'em cost money. He wa'n't what you'd call generous, Laban wa'n't."

"Where did he die?" asked Thankful, who was looking out of the window.

"Upstairs in the little back bedroom. Smallest room in the house 'tis, and folks used to say he slept there 'cause he could heat it by his cussin' instead of a stove. 'Most always cussin', he was—cussin' and groanin'.'"

Thankful was silent. Emily said: "Groaning? You mean he groaned when he was ill?"

"Yes, and when he was well, too. A habit of his, groanin' was. I don't know why he done it—see himself in the lookin'-glass, maybe; that was enough to make anybody groan. He'd groan in his sleep—or snore—or both. He was the noisiest sleeper ever I set up with. Shall we go upstairs?"

The narrow front stairs creaked as loudly in the daytime as they had on the previous night, but the long hall on the upper floor was neither dark nor terrifying. Nevertheless it was with just a suspicion of dread that Mrs. Barnes approached the large room at the end of the hall and the small one adjoining it. Her common-sense had returned and she was naturally brave, but an experience such as hers had been is not forgotten in a few hours. However, she was determined that no one should know her feelings; therefore she was the first to enter the little room.

"Here's where Laban bunked," said the captain. "You'd think with all the big comf'table bedrooms to choose from he wouldn't pick out this two-by-four, would you? But he did, probably because nobody else would. He was a contrary old rooster, and odd as Dick's hat-band."

Thankful was listening, although not to their guide's remarks. She was listening for sounds such as she had heard—or thought she had heard—on the occasion of her previous visit to that room. But there were no such sounds. There was the bed, the patchwork comforter, the chair and the pictures on the walls, but when she approached that bed there came no disturbing groans. And, by day, the memory of her fright seemed absolutely ridiculous. For at least the tenth time she solemnly resolved that no one should ever know how foolish she had been.

Emily uttered an exclamation and pointed.

"Why, Auntie!" she cried. "Isn't that—where did that lantern come from?"

Captain Obed looked where she was pointing. He stepped forward and picked up the overturned lantern.

"That's Darius Holt's lantern, I do believe," he declared. "The one Winnie S. was makin' such a fuss about last night. How in the nation did it get up here?"

Thankful laughed. "I brought it up," she said. "I come on a little explorin' cruise when Emily dropped asleep on that sittin'-room lounge, but I hadn't much more'n got in here when the pesky thing went out. You ought to have seen me hurryin' along that hall to get down before you woke up, Emily. No, come to think of it, you couldn't have seen me—'twas too dark to see anything. . . . Well," she added, quickly, in order to head off troublesome questioning, "we've looked around here pretty well. What else is there to see?"

They visited the garret and the cellar; both were spacious and not too clean.

"If I ever come here to live," declared Thankful, with decision, "there'll be some dustin' and sweepin' done, I know that."

Emily looked at her in surprise.

"Come here to live!" she repeated. "Why, Auntie, are you thinking of coming here to live?"

Her cousin's answer was not very satisfactory. "I've been thinkin' a good many things lately," she said. "Some of 'em was even more crazy than that sounds."

The inside of the house having been thus thoroughly inspected they explored the yard and the outbuildings. The barn was a large one, with stalls for two horses and a cow and a carriage-room with the remnants of an old-fashioned carryall in it.

"This is about the way it used to be in Cap'n Abner's day," said Captain Obed.

"That carryall belonged to your uncle, the cap'n, Mrs. Barnes. The boys have had it out for two or three Fourth of July Antiques and Horribles' parades; 'twon't last for many more by the looks of it."

"And what," asked Thankful, "is that? It looks like a pigsty."

They were standing at the rear of the house, which was built upon a slope. Under the washshed, which adjoined the kitchen, was a rickety door. Beside that door was a boarded enclosure which extended both into the yard and beneath the washshed.

Captain Bangs laughed. "You've guessed it, first crack," he said. "It is a pigpen. Some of Laban's doin's, that is. He used to keep a pig and 'twas too much trouble to travel way out back of the barn to feed it, so Labe rigged up this contraption. That door leads into the potato cellar. Labe fenced off half the cellar to make a stateroom for the pig. He thought as much of that hog as if 'twas his own brother, and there WAS a sort of family likeness."

Thankful snorted. "A pigsty under the house!" she said. "Well, that's all I want to know about THAT man!"

As they were returning along the foot-path by the bluff Captain Obed, who had been looking over his shoulder, suddenly stopped.

"That's kind of funny," he said.

"What?" asked Emily.

"Oh, nothin', I guess. I thought I caught a sight of somebody peekin' around the back of that henhouse. If 'twas somebody he dodged back so quick I couldn't be sure. Humph! I guess I was mistaken, or 'twas just one of Solon Taylor's young ones. Solon's a sort of—sort of stevedore at the Colfax place. Lives there and takes care of it while the owners are away. No-o; no, I don't see nobody now."

Thankful was silent during the homeward walk. When she and Miss Howes were alone in their room, she said:

"Emily, are you real set on gettin' back to South Middleboro tonight?"

"No, Auntie. Why?"

"Well, if you ain't I think I'd like to stay over another day. I've got an idea in my head and, such a thing bein' kind of unusual, I'd like to keep company with it for a spell. I'll tell you about it by and by; probably 'twon't come to anything, anyway."

"But do you think we ought to stay here, as Miss Parker's guests? Wouldn't it be—"

"Of course it would. We'll go over to that hotel, the one we started for in the first place. Judgin' from what I hear of that tavern it'll be wuth experiencin'; and—and somethin' may come of that, too."

She would not explain further, and Emily, knowing her well, did not press the point.

Hannah Parker protested volubly when her "company" declared its intention of going to the East Wellmouth Hotel.

"Of course you shan't do no such thing," she declared. "The idea! It's no trouble at all to have you, and that hotel really ain't fit for such folks as you to stay at. Mrs. Bacon, from Boston, stayed there one night in November and she pretty nigh famished with the cold, to say nothin' of havin' to eat huckleberry preserves for supper two nights runnin'. Course they had plenty of other things in the closet, but they'd opened a jar of huckleberries, so they had to be et up afore they spiled. That's the way they run THAT hotel. And Mrs. Bacon is eastern Massachusetts delegate from the State Grange. She's Grand Excited Matron. Just think of treatin' her that way! Well, where've you been all the forenoon?"

The question was addressed to her brother, who entered the house by the side door at that moment. Kenelm seemed a trifle confused.

"I—I been lookin' for that umbrella, Hannah," he explained. "I knew I must have left it somewheres 'cause—'cause, you see I—I took it out with me last night and—and—"

"And come home without it. It wouldn't take a King Solomon to know that. Did you find it?"

Kenelm's embarrassment appeared to increase.

"Well," he stammered, "I ain't exactly found it—but—"

"But what?"

"I—I'm cal'latin' to find it, Hannah."

"Yes, I know. You're cal'latin' to get to Heaven some time or other, I s'pose, but if the path is as narrow and crooked as they say 'tis I should be scared if I was you. You'll find a way to lose it, if there is one. Oh, dear me!" with a sudden change to a tone almost pleading. "Be you goin' to smoke again?"

Kenelm's reply was strange for him. He scratched a match and lit his pipe with calm deliberation.

"I'm cal'latin' to," he said, cheerfully. And his sister, to the surprise of Mrs. Barnes and Emily, did not utter another word of protest.

Captain Obed volunteered to accompany them to the hotel and to the store of Mr. Badger. On the way Thankful mentioned Mr. Parker's amazing independence in the matter of the pipe.

The captain chuckled. "Yes," he said, "Kenelm smokes when he wants to, and sometimes when he don't, I guess, just to keep his self-respect. Smokin' is one p'int where he beat out Hannah. It's quite a yarn, the way he done it is. Some time I'll tell it to you, maybe."

The hotel—it was kept by Darius Holt, father of Winnie S.—was no more inviting than Miss Parker's and Captain Bangs' hints had led them to expect. But Thankful insisted on engaging a room for the night and on returning there for dinner, supper and breakfast the following day.

"After that, we'll see," she said. "Now let's go and make a call on that rent collector of mine."

Mr. Badger was surprised to meet the owner of the Barnes house, surprised and a bit taken aback, so it seemed to Mrs. Barnes and her cousin. He was very polite, almost obsequiously so, and his explanations concerning the repairs which he had found it necessary to make and the painting which he had had done were lengthy if not convincing.

As they left him, smiling and bowing in the doorway of his store, Thankful shook her head. When they were out of earshot she said:

"Hum! The paint he says he put on that precious property of mine don't show as much as you'd expect, but he used enough butter and whitewash this morning to make up. He's a slick party, that Mr. Badger is, or I miss my guess. His business arithmetic don't go much further than addition. Everything in creation added to one makes one and he's the one. Mr. Chris Badger's got jobs enough, accordin' to his sign. He won't starve if he don't collect rents for me any more."

The hotel dinner was neither bountiful nor particularly well cooked. The Holts joined them at table and Winnie S. talked a good deal. He expressed much joy at the recovery of his lantern.

"But when I see you folks in that house last night," he said, "I thought to myself, 'Judas priest!' thinks I. 'Them women has got more spunk than I've got.' Gettin' into a house like that all alone in the dark—Whew! Judas priest! I wouldn't do it!"

"Why not?" asked Emily.

"Oh, just 'cause I wouldn't, I suppose. Now I don't believe in such things, of course, but old Laban he did die there. I never heard nothin', but they tell me—"

"Rubbish!" broke in Mr. Holt, Senior. "'Tain't nothin' but fool yarns, the whole of it. Take an old house, a hundred year old same as that is, and shut her up and 'tain't long afore folks do get to pretendin' they hear things. I never heard nothin'. Have some more pie, Miss Howes? Huh! There AIN'T no more, is there!"

After dinner Emily retired to her room for a nap. She did so under protest, declaring that she was not tired, but Thankful insisted.

"If you ain't tired now you will be when the excitement's over," she said. "My conscience is plaguin' me enough about fetchin' you on this cruise, as it is. Just take it as easy as you can, Emily. Lie down and rest, and please me."

So Emily obeyed orders and Mrs. Barnes, after drawing the curtains and asking over and over again if her cousin was sure she was comfortable, went out. It was late in the afternoon when she returned.

"I've been talkin' until my face aches," she declared. "And my mind is about made up to do—to do what may turn out to be the craziest thing I ever DID do. I'll tell you the whole thing after supper, Emily. Let's let my tongue have a vacation till then."

And, after supper, which, by the way, was no better than the dinner, she fulfilled her promise. They retired to the bedroom and Thankful, having carefully closed the windows and door and hung a towel over the keyhole, told of her half-formed plan.

"Emily," she began, "I presume likely you'll feel that you'd ought to go back home tomorrow? Yes, I knew you'd feel that way. Well, I ain't goin' with you. I've made up my mind to stay here for a few days longer. Now I'll tell you why.

"You see, Emily," she went on, "my comin' down here to East Wellmouth wa'n't altogether for the fun of lookin' at the heirloom Uncle Abner left me. The first thing I wanted to do was see it, but when I had seen it, and if it turned out to be what I hoped it might be, there was somethin' else. Emily, Mrs. Pearson's dyin' leaves me without a job. Oh, of course I know I could 'most likely get another chance at nursin' or keepin' house for somebody, but, to tell you the truth, I'm gettin' kind of tired of that sort of thing. Other folks' houses are like other folks' ailments; they don't interest you as much as your own do. I'm sick of askin' somebody else what they want for dinner; I'd like to get my own dinner, or, at least, if somebody else is to eat with me, I want to decide myself what they'll have to eat. I want to run my own house once more afore I die. And it seems—yes, it seems to me as if here was the chance; nothin' but a chance, and a risky one, but a chance just the same. Emily, I'm thinkin' of fixin' up Uncle Abner's old rattletrap and openin' a boardin'-house for summer folks in it.

"Yes, yes; I know," she continued, noticing the expression on her companion's face. "There's as much objection to the plan as there is slack managin' in this hotel, and that's some consider'ble. Fust off, it'll cost money. Well; I've saved a little money and those cranberry bog shares Mrs. Pearson left me will sell for two thousand at least. That would be enough, maybe, if I wanted to risk it all, but I don't. I've got another scheme. This property of mine down here is free and clear, but, on account of its location and the view, Cap'n Bangs tells me it's worth consider'ble more than I thought it was. I believe—yes, I do believe I could put a mortgage on it for enough to pay for the fixin' over, maybe more."

Emily interrupted.

"But, Auntie," she said, "a mortgage is a debt, isn't it? A debt that must be paid. And if you borrow from a stranger—"

"Just a minute, Emily. Course a mortgage is a debt, but it's a debt on the house and land and, if worse comes to worst, the house and land can go to pay for it. And I don't mean to borrow from a stranger, if I can help it. I've got a relation down here on the Cape, although he's a pretty fur-off, round-the-corner relation, third cousin, or somethin' like that. His name's Solomon Cobb and he lives over to Trumet, about nine mile from here, so Cap'n Bangs says. And he and Uncle Abner used to sail together for years. He was mate aboard the schooner when Uncle Abner died on a v'yage from Charleston home. This Cobb man is a tight-fisted old bachelor, they say, but his milk of human kindness may not be all skimmed. And, anyhow, he does take mortgages; that's the heft of his business—I got that from the cap'n without tellin' him what I wanted to know for."

Miss Howes smiled.

"You and Captain Bangs have been putting your heads together, I see," she said.

"Um—hm. And his head ain't all mush and seeds like a pumpkin, if I'm any judge. The cap'n tells me that east Wellmouth needs a good summer boardin'-house. This—this contraption we're in now is the nighest thing there is to it, and that's as far off as dirt is from soap; you can see that yourself. 'Cordin' to Cap'n Bangs, lots and lots of city people would come here summers if there was a respectable, decent place to go to. Now, Emily, why can't I give 'em such a place? Seems to me I can. Anyhow, if I can mortgage the place to Cousin Sol Cobb I think—yes, I'm pretty sure I shall try. Now what do you think? Is your Aunt Thankful Barnes losin' her sense—always providin' she's ever had any to lose—or is she gettin' to be a real business woman at last?"

Emily's reply was at first rather doubtful. She raised one objection after the other, but Mrs. Barnes was always ready with an answer. It was plain that she had looked at her plan from every angle. And, at last, Miss Howes, too, became almost enthusiastic.

"I do believe," she said, "it may turn out to be a splendid thing for you, Auntie. At least, I'm sure you will succeed if anyone can. Oh dear!" wistfully. "I only wish it were possible for me to stay here and help with it all. But I can't—I can't. Mother and the children need the money and I must go back to my school."

Thankful nodded. "Yes," she admitted, "I suppose likely you must, for the present. But—but if it SHOULD be a go and I SHOULD see plainer sailin' ahead, then I'd need somebody to help manage, somebody younger and more up-to-date than I am. And I know mighty well who I shall send for."

They talked for a long time, but at last, after they were in bed and the lamp was extinguished, Emily said:

"I hate to go back and leave you here, Auntie; indeed I do. I shall be so interested and excited I shall scarcely be able to wait for your letters. You will write just as soon as you have seen this Mr. Cobb, won't you?"

"Yes, sartin sure I will. I know it's goin' to be hard for you to go and leave me, Emily, but I shan't be havin' a Sunday-school picnic, exactly, myself. From what I used to hear about Cousin Solomon, unless he's changed a whole lot since, gettin' a dollar from him won't be as easy as pullin' a spoon out of a kittle of soft-soap. I'll have to do some persuadin', I guess. Wish my tongue was as soothin'-syrupy as that Mr. Badger's is. But I'm goin' to do my best. And if talkin' won't do it I'll—I swear I don't know as I shan't give him ether. Maybe he'd take THAT if he could get it for nothin'. Good night."

CHAPTER V

"WELL," said Thankful, with a sigh, "she's gone, anyhow. I feel almost as if I'd cut my anchor rope and was driftin' out of sight of land. It's queer, ain't it, how you can make up your mind to do a thing, and then, when you've really started to do it, almost wish you hadn't. Last night—yes, and this mornin'—I was as set on carryin' through this plan of mine as a body could be, but just now, when I saw Emily get aboard those cars, it was all I could do to keep from goin' along with her."

Captain Obed nodded. "Sartin," he agreed. "That's natural enough. When I was a youngster I was forever teasin' to go to sea. I thought my dad was meaner than a spiled herrin' to keep on sayin' no when I said yes. But when he did say yes and I climbed aboard the stagecoach to start for Boston, where my ship was, I never was more homesick in my life. I was later on, though—homesick and other kinds."

They were standing on the station platform at Wellmouth Centre, and the train which was taking Emily back to South Middleboro was a rapidly moving, smoking blur in the distance. The captain, who seemed to have taken a decided fancy to his prospective neighbor and her young relative, had come with them to the station. Thankful had hired a horse and "open wagon" at the livery stable in East Wellmouth and had intended engaging a driver as well, but Captain Bangs had volunteered to act in that capacity.

"I haven't got much to do this mornin'," he said. "Fact is, I generally do have more time on my hands than anything else this season of the year. Later on, when I put out my fish weirs, I'm pretty busy, but now I'm a sort of 'longshore loafer. You're figurin' to go to Trumet after you've seen Miss Emily leave the dock, you said, didn't you? Well, I've got an errand of my own in Trumet that might as well be done now as any time. I'll drive you over and back if you're willin' to trust the vessel in my hands. I don't set up to be head of the Pilots' Association when it comes to steerin' a horse, but I cal'late I can handle any four-legged craft you're liable to charter in East Wellmouth."

His offer was accepted and so far he had proved a competent and able helmsman. Now, Miss Howes having been started on her homeward way, the next port of call was to be the office of Mr. Solomon Cobb at Trumet.

During the first part of the drive Thankful was silent and answered only when spoken to. The parting with Emily and the sense of heavy responsibility entailed by the project she had in mind made her rather solemn and downcast. Captain Obed, noticing this, and suspecting the cause, chatted and laughed, and after a time his passenger seemed to forget her troubles and to enjoy the trip.

They jogged up the main street of Trumet until they reached the little three-cornered "square" which is the business center of the village. Next beyond the barbershop, which is two doors beyond the general store and postoffice, was a little one-story building, weather-beaten and badly in need of paint. The captain steered his "craft" up to the sidewalk before this building and pulled up.

"Whoa!" he ordered, addressing the horse. Then, turning to Thankful, he said:

"Here you are, ma'am. This is Sol Cobb's place."

Mrs. Barnes looked at the little building. Its exterior certainly was not inviting. The windows looked as if they had not been washed for weeks, the window shades were yellow and crooked, and one of the panes of glass in the front door was cracked across. Thankful had not seen her "Cousin Solomon" for years, not since she was a young woman, but she had heard stories of his numerous investments and business prosperity, and she could scarcely believe this dingy establishment was his.

"Are you sure, Cap'n Bangs?" she faltered. "This can't be the Solomon Cobb I mean. He's well off and it don't seem as if he would be in an office like this—if 'tis an office," she added. "It looks more like a henhouse to me. And there's no signs anywhere."

The captain laughed. "Signs cost money," he said. "It takes paint to make a sign, same as it does to keep a henhouse lookin' respectable. This is the only Sol Cobb in Trumet, fur's I ever heard, and he's well off, sartin. He ought to be; I never heard of him lettin' go of anything he got hold of. Maybe you think I'm talkin' pretty free about your relation, Mrs. Barnes," he added, apologetically. "I hadn't ought to, I suppose, but I've had one or two little dealin's with Sol, one time or 'nother, and I—well, maybe I'm prejudiced. Excuse me, won't you? He may be altogether different with his own folks."

Thankful was still staring at the dubious and forbidding front door.

"It doesn't seem as if it could be," she said. "But if you say so of course 'tis."

"Yes, ma'am, I guess 'tis. That's Sol Cobb's henhouse and the old rooster is in, judgin' by the signs. Those are his rubbers on the step. Wearin' rubbers winter or summer is a habit of his. Humph! I'm talkin' too much again. You're goin' in, I suppose, ma'am?"

Thankful threw aside the carriage robe and prepared to clamber from the wagon.

"I surely am," she declared. "That's what I came way over here for."

The captain sprang to the ground and helped her to alight.

"I'll be right across the road at the store there," he said. "I'll be on the watch when you came out. I—I—"

He hesitated. Evidently there was something else he wished to say, but he found the saying difficult. Thankful noticed the hesitation.

"Yes, what was it, Cap'n Bangs?" she asked.

Captain Obed fidgeted with the reins.

"Why, nothin', I guess," he faltered. "Only—only—well, I tell you, Mrs. Barnes, if—if you was figgerin' on doin' any business with Mr. Cobb, any money business, I mean, and—and you'd rather go anywheres else I—I—well, I'm pretty well acquainted round here on the Cape amongst the bank folks and such and I'd be real glad to—"

Thankful interrupted. She had, after much misgiving and reluctance, made up her mind to approach her distant relative with the mortgage proposition, but to discuss that proposition with strangers was, to her mind, very different. She had mentioned the proposed mortgage to Emily, but she had told no one else, not even the captain himself. And she did not mean to tell. The boarding house plan must stand or fall according to Mr. Cobb's reception of it.

"No, no," she said, hastily. "It ain't anything important—that is, very important."

"Well, all right. You see—I only meant—excuse me, Mrs. Barnes. I hope you don't think I meant to be nosey or interferin' in your affairs."

"Of course I don't. You've gone to a lot of trouble on my account as 'tis, and you've been real kind."

The captain hurriedly muttered that he hadn't been kind at all and watched her as she walked up the short path to Mr. Cobb's front door. Then, with a solemn shake of the head, he clinched again at the wagon seat and drove across the road to the hitching-posts before the store. Thankful opened the door of the "henhouse" and entered.

The interior of the little building was no mare inviting than its outside. One room, dark, with a bare floor, and with cracked plastered walls upon which a few calendars and an ancient map were hanging. There was a worn wooden settee and two wooden armchairs at the front, near the stove, and at the rear an old-fashioned walnut desk.

At this desk in a shabby, leather-cushioned armchair, sat a little old man with scant gray hair and a fringe of gray throat whiskers. He wore steel-rimmed spectacles and over these he peered at his visitor.

"Good mornin'," said Thankful. It seemed to her high time that someone said something, and the little man had not opened his lips. He did not open them even now.

"Um," he grunted, and that was all.

"Are you Mr. Solomon Cobb?" she asked. She knew now that he was; he had changed a great deal since she had last seen him, but his eyes had not changed, and he still had the habit she remembered, that of pulling at his whiskers in little, short tugs as if trying to pull them out. "Like a man hauling wild carrots out of a turnip patch," she wrote Emily when describing the interview.

He did not answer the question. Instead, after another long look, he said:

"If you're sellin' books, I don't want none. Don't use 'em."

This was so entirely unexpected that Mrs. Barnes was, for the moment, confused and taken aback.

"Books!" she repeated, wonderingly. "I didn't say anything about books. I asked you if you was Mr. Cobb."

Another look. "If you're sellin' or peddlin' or agentin' or anything I don't want none," said the little man. "I'm tellin' you now so's you can save your breath and mine. I've got all I want."

Thankful looked at him and his surroundings. This ungracious and unlooked for reception began to have its effect upon her temper; as she wrote Emily in the letter, her "back fin began to rise." It was on the tip of her tongue to say that, judging by appearances, he should want a good many things, politeness among others. But she did not say it.

"I ain't a peddler or a book agent," she declared, crisply. "When I ask you to buy, seems to me 'twould be time enough to say no. If you're Solomon Cobb, and I know you are, I've come to see you on business."

The word "business" had an effect. Mr. Cobb swung about in his chair and regarded her fixedly. There was a slight change in his tone.

"Business, hey?" he repeated. "Well, I'm a business man, ma'am. What sort of business is it you've got?"

Thankful did not answer the question immediately. Instead she walked nearer to the desk.

"Yes," she said, slowly, "you're Solomon Cobb. I should know you anywhere now. And I ain't seen you for twenty year. I presume likely you don't know me."

The man of business stared harder than ever. He took off his spectacles, rubbed them with his handkerchief, put them on and stared again.

"No, ma'am, I don't," he said. "You don't live in Trumet, I know that. You ain't seen me for twenty year, eh? Twenty year is quite a spell. And yet there's somethin' sort of—sort of familiar about you, now that I look closer. Who be you?"

"My name is Thankful Barnes—now. It didn't used to be. When you knew me 'twas Thankful Cahoon. My grandmother, on my father's side, was your mother's own cousin. Her name was Matilda Myrick. That makes you and me sort of distant relations, Mr. Cobb."

If she expected this statement to have the effect of making the little man more cordial she was disappointed. In fact, if it had any effect at all, it was the opposite, judging by his manner and expression. His only comments on the disclosure of kinship were a "Humph!" and a brief "Want to know!" He stared at Thankful and she at him. Then he said:

"Well?"

Mrs. Barnes was astonished.

"Well?" she repeated. "What's well? What do you mean by that?"

"Nothin's I know of. You said you came to see me about some business or other. What sort of business?"

"I came to see you about gettin' some money. I need some money just now and—"

Solomon interrupted her.

"Humph!" he grunted. "I cal'lated as much."

"You cal'lated it! For the land sakes—why?"

"Because you begun by sayin' you was a relation of mine. I've got a good many relations floatin' around loose and there ain't nary one of 'em ever come to see me unless 'twas to get money. If I give money to all my relations that asked for it I'd be a dum sight poorer'n I be now."

Thankful was by this time thoroughly angry.

"Look here," she snapped. "If I'd come to you expectin' you to GIVE me any money I'd be an idiot as well as a relation. Far's that last part goes I ain't any prouder of it than you are."

This pointed remark had no more effect than the statement of relationship. Mr. Cobb was quite unruffled.

"You came to see me," he said, "and you ain't come afore for twenty year—you said so. Now, when you do come, you want money, you said that, too."

"Well, what of it?"

"Nothin' of it, 'special. Only when a party comes to me and commences by sayin' he or she's a relation I know what's comin' next. Relations! Humph! My relations never done much for me."

Thankful's fingers twitched. "'Cordin' to all accounts you never done much for them, either," she declared. "You don't even ask 'em to sit down. Well, you needn't worry so far's I'm concerned. Good-by."

She was on her way out of the office, but he called her back.

"Hi, hold on!" he called. "You ain't told me what that business was yet. Come back! You—you can set down, if you want to."

Thankful hesitated. She was strongly tempted to go and never return. And yet, if she did, she must go elsewhere to obtain the mortgage she wished. And to whom should she go? Reluctantly she retraced her steps.

"Set down," said Mr. Cobb, pulling forward a chair. "Now what is it you want?"

Mrs. Barnes sat down. "I'll tell you what I don't want," she said with emphasis. "I don't want you to give me any money or to lend me any, either—without it's bein' a plain business deal. I ain't askin' charity of you or anybody else, Solomon Cobb. And you'd better understand that if you and I are goin' to talk any more."

Mr. Cobb tugged at his whiskers.

"You've got a temper, ain't you," he declared. "Temper's a good thing to play with, maybe, if you can afford it. I ain't rich enough, myself. I've saved a good many dollars by keepin' mine. If you don't want me to give you nor lend you money, what do you want?"

"I want you to take a mortgage on some property I own. You do take mortgages, don't you?"

More whisker pulling. Solomon nodded.

"I do sometimes," he admitted; "when I cal'late they're safe to take. Where is this property of yours?"

"Over in East Wellmouth. It's the old Abner Barnes place. Cap'n Abner willed it to me. He was my uncle."

And at last Mr. Cobb showed marked interest. Slowly he leaned back in his chair. His spectacles fell from his nose into his lap and lay there unheeded.

"What? What's that you say?" he asked, sharply. "Abner Barnes was your uncle? I—I thought you said your name was Cahoon."

"I said it used to be afore I was married, when I knew you. Afterwards I married Eben Barnes, Cap'n Abner's nephew. That made the captain my uncle by marriage."

Solomon's fingers groped for his spectacles. He picked them up and took his handkerchief from his pocket. But it was his forehead he rubbed with his handkerchief, not the glasses.

"You're—you're Abner Barnes' niece!" he said slowly.

"Yes—niece by marriage."

"The   one   he   used   to   talk   so   much   about?   What   was   her name—Patience—Temp'rance—"

"Thankful—that's my name. I presume likely Uncle Abner did use to talk about me. He always declared he thought as much of me as if I was his own child."

There was an interval of silence. Mr. Cobb replaced his spectacles and stared through them at his visitor. His manner was peculiar—markedly so.

"I went mate for Cap'n Abner a good many v'yages," he said, after a moment.

"Yes, I know you did."

"He—he told you so, I suppose."

"Yes."

"What else did he tell you; about—about me, I mean?"

"Why, nothin' 'special that I know of. Why? What was there to tell?"

"Nothin'. Nothin' much, I guess. Abner and me was sort of—sort of chums and I didn't know but he might have said—might have told you considerable about me. He didn't, hey?"

"No. He told me you was his mate, that's all."

It may have been Thankful's imagination, but it did seem as if her relative was a trifle relieved. But even yet he did not seem quite satisfied. He pulled at his whiskers and asked another question.

"What made you come here to me?" he asked.

"Mercy on us! I've told you that, haven't I? I came to see about gettin' a mortgage on his old place over to East Wellmouth. I knew you took mortgages—at least folks said you did—and bein' as you was a relation I thought—"

A wave of the hand interrupted her.

"Yes, yes," broke in Solomon, hastily. "I know that. Was that the only reason?"

"I presume likely 'twas. I did think it was a natural one and reason enough, but I guess THAT was a mistake. It looks as if 'twas."

She made a move to rise, but he leaned forward and detained her.

"There! there!" he said. "Set still, set still. So you're Abner Barnes' niece?"

"My soul! I've told you so three times."

"Abner's niece! I want to know!"

"Well, I should think you might know by this time. Now about that mortgage."

"Hey? Oh, yes—yes! You want a mortgage on Abner's place over to East Wellmouth. Um! Well, I know the property and about what it's wuth—which ain't much. What are you cal'latin' to do—live there?"

"Yes, if I can carry out the plan I've got in my head. I'm thinkin' of fixin' up that old place and livin' in it. I'm figgerin' to run it as a boardin'-house. It'll cost money to put it in shape and a mortgage is the simplest way of raisin' that money, I suppose. That's the long and short of it."

The dealer in mortgages appeared to hear and there was no reason why he should not have understood. But he seemed still unsatisfied, even suspicious. The whiskers received another series of pulls and he regarded Thankful with the same questioning stare.

"And you say," he drawled, "that you come to me just because—"

"Mercy on us! If you don't know why I come by this time, then—"

"All right, all right. I—I'm talkin' to myself, I guess. Course you told me why you come. So you're cal'latin' to start a boardin'-house, eh? Risky things, boardin'-houses are. There's a couple of hundred launched every year and not more'n ten ever make a payin' v'yage. Let's hear what your plan is, the whole of it."

Fighting down her impatience Thankful went into details concerning her plan. She explained why she had thought of it and her growing belief that it might be successful. Mr. Cobb listened.

"Humph!" he grunted, when she had finished. "So Obed Bangs advised you to try it, hey? That don't make me think no better of it, as I know of. I know Bangs pretty well."

"Yes," dryly; "I supposed likely you did. Anyhow, he said he knew you."

"He did, hey? Told you some things about me, hey?"

"No, he didn't tell me anything except that you and he had had some dealin's. Now, Mr. Cobb, we've talked a whole lot and it don't seem to me we got anywheres. If you don't want to take a mortgage on that place—"

"Sshh! Who said I didn't want to take it? How do I know what I want to do yet? Lord! How you women do go on! Suppose I should take a mortgage on that place— mind, I don't say I will, but suppose I should—how would I know that the mortgage would be paid, or the interest, or anything?"

"If it ain't paid you can foreclose when the time comes, I presume likely. As for the interest—well, I'm fairly honest, or I try to be, and that'll be paid reg'lar if I live."

"Ya'as. Well, fur's honesty goes, I could run a seine through Ostable County any day in the week and load a schooner with honest folks; and there wouldn't nary one of 'em have cash enough to pay for the wear and tear on the net. Honesty's good policy, maybe, but it takes hard money to pay bills."

Thankful stood up.

"All right," she said, decidedly, "then I'll go where they play the honest game. And you needn't set there and weed your face any more on my account."

Mr. Cobb rose also. "There! there!" he protested. "Don't get het up. I don't say I won't take your mortgage, do I?"

"You've said a good deal. If you say any more of the same kind you can say it to yourself. I tell you, honest, I don't like the way you say it."

The owner of the "hen-house" looked as if he wished very much to retort in kind. The glare he gave his visitor prophesied direful things. But he did not retort; nor, to her surprise, did he raise his voice or order her off the premises. Instead his tone, when he spoke again, was quiet, even conciliatory.

"I—I'm sorry if I've said anything I shouldn't," he stammered. "I'm gettin' old and—and sort of short in my talk, maybe. I—I—there's a good many folks round here that don't like me, 'count of my doin' business in a business way, 'stead of doin' it like the average poor fool. I suppose they've been talkin' to you and you've got sort of prejudiced. Well, I don't know's I blame you for that. I shan't hold no grudge. How much of a mortgage do you cal'late to want on Abner's place?"

"Two thousand dollars."

"Two thousand! . . . There, there! Hold on, hold on! Two thousand dollars is a whole lot of money. It don't grow on every bush."

"I know that as well as you do. If I did I'd have picked it afore this."

"Um—hm. How long a time do you want?"

"I don't know. Three years, perhaps."

Solomon shook his head.

"Too long," he said. "I couldn't give as long a mortgage as that to anybody. No, I couldn't do it. . . . Tell you what I will do," he added. "I—I don't want to act mean to a relation. I think as much of relations as anybody does. I'd like to favor you and

I will if I can. You give me a week to think this over in and then I'll let you know what I'll do. That's fair, ain't it?"

Mrs. Barnes declined the offer.

"It may be fair to you," she said, "but I can't wait so long. I want to settle this afore I go back to South Middleboro. And I shall go back tomorrow, or the day after at the latest."

Another session of "weeding." Then said Mr. Cobb: "Well, all right, all right. I'll think it over and then I'll drive across to East Wellmouth, have another look at the property, and let you know. I'll see you day after tomorrow forenoon. Where you stoppin' over there?"

Thankful told him. He walked as far as the door with her.

"Hope you ain't put out with me, ma'am," he said. "I have to be kind of sharp and straight up and down in my dealin's; they'd get the weather gauge on me a dozen times a day if I wa'n't. But I'm real kind inside—to them I take a notion to. I'll—I'll treat you right—er—er—Cousin Thankful; you see if I don't. I'm real glad you come to me. Good day."

Thankful went down the path. As she reached the sidewalk she turned and looked back. The gentleman with the kind interior was standing peering at her through the cracked glass of the door. He was still tugging at his whiskers and if, as he had intimated, he had "taken a notion" to her, his expression concealed the fact wonderfully.

Captain Obed, who had evidently been on the lookout for his passenger, appeared on the platform of the store on the other side of the road. After asking if she had any other "port of call" in that neighborhood, he assisted her into the carriage and they started on their homeward trip. The captain must have filled with curiosity concerning the widow's interview with Mr. Cobb, but beyond asking if she had seen the latter, he did not question. Thankful appreciated his reticence; the average dweller in Wellmouth—Winnie S., for instance—would have started in on a vigorous cross-examination. Her conviction that Captain Bangs was much above the average was strengthened.

"Yes," she said, "he was there. I saw him. He's a—a kind of queer person, I should say. Do you know him real well, Cap'n Bangs?"

The captain nodded. "Yes," he said, "I know him about as well as anybody outside of Trumet does. I ain't sure that anybody really knows him all the way through. Queer!" he chuckled. "Well, yes—you might say Sol Cobb was queer and you wouldn't be strainin' the truth enough to start a plank. He's all that and then consider'ble."

"What sort of a man is he?"

"Sol? Hum! Well, he's smart; anybody that beats Sol Cobb in a trade has got to get up a long ways ahead of breakfast time. Might stay up all night and then not have more leeway than he'd be liable to need."

"Yes, Yes, I'm sure he's smart in business. But is he—is he a GOOD man?"

The captain hesitated before replying.

"Git dap!" he ordered, addressing the horse. "Good? Is Sol good? Well, I cal'late that depends some on what dictionary you hunt up the word in. He's pious, sartin. There ain't many that report on deck at the meetin'-house more reg'lar than he does. He don't cal'late to miss a prayer-meetin' and when there's a revival goin' on he's right up front with the mourners. Folks do say that his favorite hymn is 'I'm Glad Salvation's Free' and they heave out consider'ble many hints that if 'twa'n't free he wouldn't have got it; but then, that's an old joke and I've heard 'em say the same thing about other people."

"But do you think he's honest?"

"I never heard of his doin' anything against the law. He'll skin honesty as close as he can, there ain't much hide left when he gets through; but I cal'late he thinks he's honest. And maybe he is—maybe he is. It all depends on the definition, same as I said. Sol's pious all right. I cal'late he'd sue anybody that had a doubt as to how many days Josiah went cabin passenger aboard the whale. His notion of Heaven may be a little mite hazy, although he'd probably lay consider'ble stress on the golden streets, but he's sot and definite about t'other place. Yes, siree!" he added, reflectively, "Sol is sartin there's a mighty uncomf'table Tophet, and that folks who don't believe just as he does are bound there. And he don't mean to go himself, if 'tendin' up to meetin' 'll keep him clear.

"It's kind of queer to me," he went on, slowly, "to see the number of folks that make up their minds to be good—or what they call good—because they're scared to be bad. Doin' right because right IS right, and lettin' the Almighty credit 'em with that, because He's generally supposed to know it's right full well as they do—that ain't enough for their kind. They have to keep hollerin' out loud how good they are so He'll hear and won't make any mistake in bookin' their own particular passage. Sort of takin' out a religious insurance policy, you might say 'twas. . . . Humph!" he added, coming out of his reverie and looking doubtfully at his companion, "I—I hope I ain't shocked you, ma'am. I don't mean to be irreverent, you understand. I've thought consider'ble about such things and I have funny ideas maybe."

Thankful declared that she was not shocked. She had heard but little of her driver's long dissertation. She was thinking of her interview with Mr. Cobb and the probability of his accepting her proposal and taking a mortgage on her East Wellmouth property. If he refused, what should she do then? And if he accepted and she went on to carry her plan into execution, what would be the outcome? The responsibility was heavy. She would be risking all she had in the world. If she succeeded, well and good. If she failed she would be obliged to begin all over again, to try for another position as housekeeper, perhaps to "go out nursing" once more. She was growing older; soon she would be beyond middle life and entering upon the first stages of old age. And what a lonely old age hers was likely to be! Her husband was dead; her only near relative, brother Jedediah, was—well, he might be dead also, poor helpless, dreamy incompetent. He might have died in the Klondike, providing he ever reached that far-off country, which was unlikely. He would have been but an additional burden upon her had he lived and remained at home, but he would have been company for her at least. Emily was a comfort, but she had little hope of Emily's being able to leave her school or the family which her salary as teacher helped to support. No, she must carry her project through alone, all alone.

She spoke but seldom and Captain Obed, noticing the change in her manner and possibly suspecting the cause, did his best to divert her thoughts and cheer her. He chatted continuously, like, as he declared afterwards, "a poll parrot with its bill greased." He changed the topic from Mr. Cobb and his piety to the prospects of good fishing in the spring, from that to the failure of the previous fall's cranberry crop, and from that again to Kenelm Parker and his sister Hannah. And, after a time, Thankful realized that he was telling a story.

CHAPTER VI

T AKIN' other folks' advice about your own affairs," began Cap'n Obed, "is like a feller readin' patent medicine circulars to find somethin' to cure a cold. Afore he gets through his symptoms have developed into bronchitis and pneumony, with gallopin' consumption dead ahead. You never can tell what'll happen.

"You noticed how Hannah Parker sort of riz up when Kenelm started smokin' yesterday? Yes, I know you did, 'cause you spoke of it. And you notice, too, how meek and lowly she laid down and give in when he kept right on doin' it. That ain't her usual way with Kenelm by a consider'ble sight. I told you there was quite a yarn hitched to that smokin' business. So there is.

"Kenelm's an old bach, you know. One time he used to work, or pretend to, because he needed the money; but his Aunt Phoebe up to Brockton died and left him four or five thousand dollars and he ain't worked of any account since. He's a gentleman now, livin' on his income—and his sister.

"Hannah ain't got but precious little money of her own, but she knows how to take care of it, which her brother don't. She was housekeepin' for some folks at Wapatomac, but when the inheritances landed she headed straight for East Wellmouth, rented that little house they're in now, and took charge of Kenelm. He wa'n't overanxious to have her do it, but that didn't make any difference. One of her pet bugaboos was that, now her brother was well-off—'cordin' to her idea of well-offness—some designin' woman or other would marry him for his money. Down she come, first train, and she's been all hands and the cook, yes, and paymaster—with Kenelm a sort of steerage passenger, ever since. She keeps watch over him same as the sewin' circle does over the minister's wife, and it's 'No Anchorage for Females' around that house, I can tell you.

"Another of her special despisin's—next to old maids and young widows—used to be tobacco smoke. We had a revival preacher in East Wellmouth that first winter and he stirred up things like a stick in a mudhole. He was young and kind of good-lookin', with a voice like the Skakit foghorn, and he took the sins of the world in his mouth, one after the other, as you might say, and shook 'em same's a pup would a Sunday bunnit. He laid into rum and rum sellin', and folks fairly got in line to sign the pledge. 'Twas 'Come early and avoid the rush.' Got so that Chris Badger hardly dast to use alcohol in his cigar-lighter.

"Then, havin' dried us up, that revival feller begun to smoke us out. He preached six sermons on the evils of tobacco, and every one was hotter'n the last. Accordin' to him, if you smoked now you'd burn later on. Lots of the men folks threw their pipes away, and took to chewin' slipp'ry ellum.

"Now, Kenelm smoked like a peat fire. He lit up after breakfast and puffed steadily until bedtime, only puttin' his pipe down to eat, or to rummage in his pocket for more tobacco. Hannah got him to go to one of the anti-tobacco meetin's. He set through the whole of it, interested as could be. Then, when 'twas over, he stopped in the church entry to load up his pipe, and walked home with his sister, blowin' rings and scratchin' matches and talkin' loud about how fine the sermon was. He talked all next day about that sermon; said he'd go every night if they'd let you smoke in there.

"So Hannah was set back a couple of rows, but she wa'n't discouraged—not by a forty fathom. She got after her brother mornin', noon and night about the smokin' habit. The most provokin' part of it, so she said, was that he always agreed with her.

"'It's ruinin' your health,' she'd say.

"'Yes,' says Kenelm, lookin' solemn, 'I cal'late that's so. I've been feelin' poorly for over a year now. Worries me consider'ble. Pass me that plug on the top of the clock, won't you, Hannah?'

"Now what can you do with a feller like that?

"She couldn't start him with fussin' about HIS health, so she swung over on a new tack and tried her own. She said so much smoke in the house was drivin' her into consumption, and she worked up a cough that was a reg'lar graveyard quickstep. I heard her practicin' it once, and, I swan, there was harps and halos all through it!

"That cough made Kenelm set up and take notice; and no wonder. He listened to a hundred or so of Hannah's earthquakes, and then he got up and pranced out of the house. When he came back the doctor was with him.

"Now, this wa'n't exactly what his sister was lookin' for. She didn't want to see the doctor. But Kenelm said she'd got to have her lungs sounded right off, and he guessed they'd have to use a deep-sea lead, 'cause that cough seemed to come from the foundations. He waylaid the doctor after the examination was over and asked all kinds of questions. The doctor tried to keep a straight face, but I guess Kenelm smelt a rat.

"Anyway, Hannah coughed for a day or two more, and then her brother come totin' in a big bottle of med'cine.

"'There!' he says. 'That'll fix you!'

"'Where'd you get it?' says she.

"'Down to Henry Tubman's,' he says.

"'Henry Tubman! What on earth! Why, Henry Tubman's a horse doctor!'

"'I know he is,' says Kenelm, solemn as a roostin' pullet, 'but we've been fishin' with the wrong bait. 'Tain't consumption that's ailin' you, Hannah; you've got the heaves.'

"So Hannah didn't cough much more, 'cause, when she did, Kenelm would trot out the bottle of horse med'cine, and chuck overboard a couple of barrels of sarcasm. She tried openin' all the windows, sayin' she needed fresh air, but he locked himself up in the kitchen and filled that so full of smoke that you had to navigate it by dead reckonin'—couldn't see to steer. So she was about ready to give up; somethin' that anybody but a stubborn critter like her would have done long afore.

"But one afternoon she was down to the sewin' circle, and the women folks there, havin' finished pickin' to pieces the characters of the members not on hand, started in to go on about the revivals and how much good they was doin'. 'Most everybody had some relation, if 'twa'n't nothin' more'n a husband, that had stopped smokin' and chewin'. Everybody had some brand from the burnin' to brag about—everybody but Hannah; she could only set there and say she'd done her best, but that Kenelm still herded with the goats.

"They was all sorry for her, but the only one that had any advice to give was Abbie Larkin, she that was Abbie Dillin'ham 'fore she married old man Larkin. Larkin had one foot in the grave when she married him, and she managed to crowd the other one in inside of a couple of years afterward. Abbie is a widow, of course, and she is middlin' good-lookin' and dresses pretty gay. Larkin left her a little money, but I guess she's run through most of it by this time. The circle folks was dyin' to talk about her, but she was always on hand so early that they hardly ever got a chance.

"Well, after supper was over, Abbie gets Hannah over in a corner, and says she:

"'Miss Parker,' says she, 'here's an advertisement I cut out of the paper and saved a-purpose for you. I want you to look at it, but you mustn't tell anybody I gave it to you.'

"So Hannah unfurls the piece of newspaper, and 'twas an advertisement of 'Kill-Smudge,' the sure cure for the tobacco habit. You could give it to the suff'rer unbeknownst to him, in his tea or soup or somethin', and in a couple of shakes he'd no more smoke than he'd lend money to his brother-in-law, or do any other ridic'lous thing. There was testimonials from half a dozen women that had tried it, and everyone showed a clean bill.

"Hannah read the advertisement through twice. 'Well, I never!' says she.

"'Yes,' says Abbie, and smiles.

"'Of course,' says Hannah, lookin' scornful, 'I wouldn't think of tryin' the stuff, but I'll just take this home and read it over. It's so curious,' she says.

"'Ain't it?' says Abbie, and smiles some more.

"So that night, when Kenelm sat by the stove, turnin' the air blue, his sister set at the other side of the table with that advertisement hid behind the Wellmouth Advocate readin' and thinkin'. She wrote a letter afore she went to bed and bought a dollar's worth of stamps at the postoffice next day. And for a week she watched the mails the way one of these city girls does when the summer's 'most over and eight or nine of her fellers have finished their vacations and gone back to work.

"About ten days after that Kenelm begins to feel kind of off his feed, so's to speak. Somethin' seemed to ail him and he couldn't make out what 'twas. They'd had a good many cranberries on their bog that year and Hannah'd been cookin' 'em up fast so's they wouldn't spile. But one night she brings on a cranberry pie, and Kenelm turned up his nose at it.

"'More of that everlastin' sour stuff!' he snorts. 'I've et cranb'ries till my stomach's puckered up as if it worked with a gath'rin' string. Take it away! I don't want it!'

"'But, Kenelm, you're always so fond of cranb'ry pie.'

"'Me? It makes me shrivel just to look at it. Pass that sugar bowl, so's I can sweeten ship.'

"Next day 'twas salt fish and potatoes that wa'n't good. He'd been teasin' for a salt-fish dinner for ever so long, so Hannah'd fixed up this one just to please him, but he swallered two or three knifefuls and then looked at her kind of sad and mournful.

"'To think,' says he, 'that I've lived all these years to be p'isoned fin'lly! And by my own sister, too! Well, that's what comes of bein' wuth money. Give me my pipe and let me forget my troubles.'

"'Course this kind of talk made Hannah mad, but she argued that 'twas the Kill-Smudge gettin' in its work, so she put a double dose into his teacup that night, and trusted in Providence.

"And the next day she noticed that he swallered hard between every pull at his pipe, and when, at last, he jumped out of his chair, let out a swear word and hove his pipe at the cat, she felt consider'ble encouraged. She thought 'twas her duty, however, to warn him against profane language, but the answer she got was so much more prayerful than his first remarks, that she come about and headed for the sittin'-room quick.

"Well, to make a long yarn short, the Kill-Smudge done the bus'ness. Kenelm stuck to smokin' till he couldn't read a cigar sign without his ballast shiftin', and then he give it up. And—as you might expect from that kind of a man—he was more down on tobacco than the Come-Outer parson himself. He even got up in revival meetin' and laid into it hammer and tongs. He was the best 'horrible example' they had, and Hannah was so proud of him that she couldn't sleep nights. She still stuck to the Kill-Smudge, though—layin' in a fresh stock every once in a while—and she dosed the tea about every other day, so's her brother wouldn't run no danger of relapse. I'm 'fraid Kenelm didn't get any too much joy out of his meals.

"And so everything was all right—'cordin' to Hannah's reckonin'—and it might have stayed all right if she hadn't took that trip to Washington. Etta Ellis was goin' on a three weeks' cut-rate excursion, and she talked so much about it, that Hannah got reckless and fin'lly said she'd go, too.

"The only thing that worried her was leavin' Kenelm. She hated to do it dreadful, but he seemed tame enough and promised to change his flannels if it got cold, and to feed the cat reg'lar, and to stay to home, and one thing and another, so she thought 'twas safe to chance it. She cooked up a lot of pie and frosted cake, and wrote out a kind of time-table for him to eat and sleep by, and then cried and kissed him good-by.

"The first three days after she was gone Kenelm stayed 'round the house and turned in early. He was feelin' fine, but 'twas awful lonesome. The fourth day, after breakfast, he had a cravin' to smoke. Told me afterward it seemed to him as if he MUST smoke or die of the fidgets. At last he couldn't stand it no longer, but turned Hannah's time-table to the wall and went out for a walk. He walked and walked and walked. It got 'most dinner time and he had an appetite that he hadn't had afore for months.

"Just as he was turnin' into the road by the schoolhouse who should come out on the piazza of the house on the corner but Abbie Larkin. She'd left the door open, and the smell of dinner that blew through it was tantalizin'. Abbie was dressed in her Sunday togs and her hair was frizzed till she couldn't wrinkle her forehead. If the truth was known, I cal'late she'd seen Kenelm go past her house on the way downtown and was layin' for him when he come back, but she acted dreadful surprised.

"'Why, Mr. Parker!' says she, 'how DO you do? Seems's if I hadn't seen you for an age! Ain't it dreadful lonesome at your house now your sister's away?'

"Kenelm colored up some—he always h'isted danger signals when women heave in sight—and agreed that 'twas kind of poky bein' all alone. Then they talked about the weather, and about the price of coal, and about the new plush coat Cap'n Jabez Bailey's wife had just got, and how folks didn't see how she could afford it with Jabez out of work, and so on. And all the time the smell of things cookin' drifted through the doorway. Fin'lly Abbie says, says she:

"'Was you goin' home, Mr. Parker?'

"'Yes, ma'am,' says Kenelm. 'I was cal'latin' to go home and cook somethin' for dinner.'

"'Well, there, now!' says Abbie. 'I wonder why I didn't think of it afore! Why don't you come right in and have dinner with me? It's ALL ready and there's plenty for two. DO come, Mr. Parker, to please ME!'

"'Course Kenelm said he couldn't, and, likewise, of course, he did. 'Twas a smashin' dinner—chicken and mashed potatoes and mince pie, and the land knows what. He ate till he was full clear to the hatches, and it seemed to him that nothin' ever tasted quite so good. The widow smiled and purred and colored up and said it seemed SO good to have a man at the table; seemed like the old days when Dan'l—meanin' the late lamented—was on deck, and so forth.

"Then, when the eatin' was over, she says, 'I was expectin' my cousin Benjamin down for a week or so, but he can't come. He's a great smoker, and I bought these cigars for him. You might as well use them afore they dry up.'

"'Afore Kenelm could stop her she rummaged a handful of cigars out of the table drawer in the settin'-room.

"'There!' she says. 'Light right up and be comfortable. It'll seem just like old times. Dan'l was such a 'smoker! Oh, my!' and she gave a little squeal; 'I forgot you've stopped smokin'.'

"Well, there was the cigars, lookin' as temptin' as a squid to a codfish; and there was Kenelm hankerin' for 'em so his fingers twitched; and there was Abbie lookin' dreadful disapp'inted, but tryin' to make believe she wasn't. You don't need a spyglass to see what happened.

"'I'd like to,' says Kenelm, pickin' up one of the cigars. 'I'd like to mighty well, but'—here he bites off the end—''twouldn't hardly do, now would it? You see—'

"'I see,' says Abbie, scratchin' a match; 'but WE'LL never tell. We'll have it for our secret; won't we, Mr. Parker?'

"So that's how Kenelm took his first tumble from grace. He told me all about it one day a good while afterward. He smoked three of the cigars afore he went home, and promised to come to supper the next afternoon.

"'You DO look so comfortable, Mr. Parker,' purrs Abbie, as sweet and syrupy as a molasses stopper. 'It must be SUCH a comfort to a man to smoke. I don't care

WHAT the minister says, you can smoke here just as much as you want to! It must be pretty hard to live in a house where you can't enjoy yourself. I shouldn't think it would seem like home. A man like you NEEDS a good home. Why, how I do run on!'

"Oh, there ain't really nothin' the matter with the Widow Larkin—so fur's smartness is concerned, there ain't.

"And for five days more Kenelm ate his meals at Abbie's and smoked and was happy, happier'n he'd been for months.

"Meantime, Hannah and Etta was visitin' the President—that is to say, they was lookin' over the White House fence and sayin' 'My stars!' and 'Ain't it elegant!' Nights, when the sightseein' was over, what they did mostly was to gloat over how mean and jealous they'd make the untraveled common tribe at sewin' circle feel when they got back home. They could just see themselves workin' on the log-cabin quilt for the next sale, and slingin' out little reminders like, 'Land sakes! What we're talkin' about reminds me of what Etta and me saw when we was in the Congressional Libr'ry. YOU remember that, Etta?' And that would be Etta's hint to look cute and giggle and say, 'Well! I should say I DID!' And all the rest of the circlers would smile kind of unhealthy smiles and try to look as if trips to Washington wa'n't nothin'; THEY wouldn't go if you hired 'em to. You know the game if you've ever been to sewin' circle.

"But all this plannin' was knocked in the head by a letter that Hannah got on an afternoon about a week after she left home. It was short but there was meat in it. It said: 'If you want to keep your brother from marryin' Abbie Larkin you had better come home quick!' 'Twas signed 'A Friend.'

"Did Hannah come home? Well, didn't she! She landed at Orham the next night. And she done some thinkin' on the way, too. She kept out of the way of everybody and went straight up to the house. 'Twas dark and shut up, but the back door key was under the mat, as usual, so she got in all right. The plants hadn't been watered for two days, at least; the clock had stopped; the cat's saucer was licked dry as a contribution box, and the critter itself was underfoot every second, whoopin' for somethin' to eat. The whole thing pretty nigh broke Hannah's heart, but she wa'n't the kind to give up while there was a shot in the locker.

"She went to the closet and found that Kenelm's Sunday hat and coat was gone.

Then she locked the back door again and cut acrost the lots down to Abbie's. She crept round the back way and peeked under the curtain at the settin'-room window. There set Abbie, lookin' sweet and sugary. Likewise, there was Kenelm, lookin' mighty comfortable, with a big cigar in his mouth and more on the table side of him. Hannah gritted her teeth, but she kept quiet.

"About ten minutes after that Chris Badger was consider'ble surprised to hear a knock at the back door of his store and to find that 'twas Hannah that had knocked.

"'Mr. Badger,' says Hannah, polite and smilin', 'I want to buy a box of the best cigars you've got.'

"'Ma'am!' says Chris, thinkin' 'twas about time to send for the constable or the doctor—one or t'other.

"'Yes,' says Hannah; 'if you please. Oh! and, Mr. Badger, please don't tell anyone I bought 'em. PLEASE don't, to oblige me.'

"So Chris trotted out the cigars—ten cents straight, they was—and said nothin' to nobody, which is a faculty he has when it pays to have it.

"When Kenelm came home that night he was knocked pretty nigh off his pins to find his sister waitin' for him. He commenced a long rigmarole about where he'd been, but Hannah didn't ask no questions. She said that Washington was mighty fine, but home and Kenelm was good enough for her. Said the thoughts of him alone had been with her every minute, and she just HAD to cut the trip short. Kenelm wa'n't any too enthusiastic to hear it.

"Breakfast next mornin' was a dream. Hannah had been up since five o'clock gettin' it ready. There was everything on that table that Kenelm liked 'special. And it all tasted fine, and he ate enough for four. When 'twas over Hannah went to the closet and brought out a bundle.

"'Kenelm,' she says, 'here's somethin' I brought you that'll surprise you. I've noticed since I've been away that about everybody smokes—senators and judges, and even Smithsonian Institute folks. And when I see how much comfort they get out of it, my conscience hurt me to think that I'd deprived my brother of what he got such a sight of pleasure from. Kenelm, you can begin smokin' again right off. Here's a box of cigars I bought on purpose for you; they're the kind the President smokes.'

"Which wa'n't a bad yarn for a church member that hadn't had any more prac- tice than Hannah had.

"Well, Kenelm was paralyzed, but he lit up one of the cigars and found 'twas better than Abbie's brand. He asked Hannah what she thought the church folks would say, but she said she didn't care what they said; her travels had broadened her mind and she couldn't cramp herself to the ideas of a little narrow place like East Wellmouth.

"Dinner that day was a bigger meal than breakfast, and two of the cigars went fine after it. Kenelm hemmed and hawed and fin'lly said that he wouldn't be home to supper; said he'd got to go downtown and would get a bite at the Trav'lers' Rest or somewheres. It surprised him to find that Hannah didn't raise objections, but she didn't, not a one. Just smiled and said, 'All right,' and told him to have a good time. And Abbie's supper didn't seem so good to him that night, and her cigars—bein' five centers—wa'n't in it with that Washington box.

"Hannah didn't have dinner the next day until two o'clock, but 'twas worth waitin' for. Turkey was twenty-three cents a pound, but she had one, and plum puddin', too. She kept pressin' Kenelm to have a little more, so 'twas after three when they got up from the table.

"'Twas a rainy, drizzly afternoon and the stove felt mighty homey and cozy. So did the big rocker that Hannah transplanted from the parlor to the settin'-room. That chair had been a kind of sacred throne afore, and to set in it had been sort of sacrilegious, but there 'twas, and Kenelm didn't object. And those President cigars certainly filled the bill.

"About half-past five Kenelm got up and looked out of the window. The rain come spattin' against the pane and the wind whined and sounded mean. Kenelm went back to the chair again. Then he got up and took another observation. At last he goes back to the chair, stretches himself out, puts his feet against the stove, pulls at the cigar, and says he:

"'I was cal'latin' to go downtown on a bus'ness trip, same's I did last night. But I guess,' he says—'I guess I won't. It's too comfort'ble here,' says he.

"And I cal'late," said Captain Obed, in conclusion, "that afore Hannah turned in that night she gave herself three cheers. She'd gained a tack on Abbie Larkin that had put Abbie out of the race, for that time, anyhow."

"But who sent the 'friend' letter?" asked Thankful, whose thoughts had been diverted from her own troubles by hearing those of Miss Parker.

The captain laughed.

"That's a mystery, even yet," he said. "I'm pretty sure Hannah thinks 'twas Elvira Paine. Elvira lives acrost the road from Abbie Larkin and, bein' a single woman with mighty little hopes of recovery, naturally might be expected to enjoy upsettin' anybody else's chance. But, at any rate, Mrs. Barnes, the whole thing bears out what I said at the beginnin': takin' other folks' advice about your own affairs is mighty risky. I hope, if you do go ahead with your boardin'-house plan, it won't be because I called it a good one."

Thankful smiled and then sighed. "No," she said, "if I go ahead with it it'll be because I've made up my mind to, not on account of anybody else's advice. I've steered my own course for quite a long spell and I sha'n't signal for a pilot now. Well, here we are home again—or at East Wellmouth anyhow."

"So we be. Better come right to Hannah's along with me, hadn't you? You must have had enough of the Holt Waldorf-Astory by this time."

But Thankful insisted upon going to the hotel and there her new friend—for she had begun to think of him as that—left her. She informed him of her intention to remain in East Wellmouth for another day and a half and he announced his intention of seeing her again before she left.

"Just want to keep an eye on you," he said. "With all of Mrs. Holt's temptin' meals set afore you you may get gout or somethin' from overeatin'. Either that or Winnie S.'ll talk you deef. I feel a kind of responsibility, bein' as I'm liable to be your next-door neighbor if that boardin'-house does start up, and I want you to set sail with a clean bill of health. If you sight a suspicious-lookin' craft, kind of antique in build, broad in the beam and makin' heavy weather up the hills—if you sight that kind of craft beatin' down in this direction tomorrow you'll know it's me. Good day."

Thankful lay awake for hours that night, thinking, planning and replanning. More than once she decided that she had been too hasty, that her scheme involved too great a risk and that, after all, she had better abandon it. But each time she changed her mind and at last fell asleep determining not to think any more about it, but to wait until Mr. Cobb came to accept or decline the mortgage. Then she would make a final decision.

The next day passed somehow, though it seemed to her as if it never would, and early the following forenoon came Solomon himself. The man of business was driving an elderly horse which bore a faint resemblance to its owner, being small and thin and badly in need of a hairdresser's services. If the animal had possessed whiskers and could have tugged at them Thankful was sure it would have done it.

Solomon tugged at his own whiskers almost constantly during that forenoon. He and Mrs. Barnes visited the "Captain Abner place" and Solomon inspected every inch of its exterior. For some reason or other he absolutely refused to go inside. His conversation during the inspection was, for the most part, sniffs and grunts, and it was not until it was ended and they stood together at the gate, that he spoke to the point, and then only because his companion insisted.

"Well!" said Thankful.

Mr. Cobb "weeded."

"Eh?" he said.

"That's what I say—eh? What are you goin' to do about that mortgage, Mr. Cobb?"

More weeding. Then: "Waal, I—I don't cal'late to want to be unreasonable nor nothin', but I ain't real keen about takin' no mortgage on that property; not myself, I ain't."

"Well, it is yourself I'm askin' to take it. So you won't, hey? All right; that's all I wanted to know."

"Now—now—now, hold on! Hold on! I ain't sayin' I WON'T take it. I—I'd like to be accommodatin', 'specially to a relation. But—"

"Never mind the relation business. I found out what you think of relations afore you found out I was one. And I ain't askin' accommodation. This is just plain business, seems to me. Will you let me have two thousand dollars on a mortgage on this place?"

Mr. Cobb fidgeted. "I couldn't let you have that much," he said. "I couldn't. I—I—" he wrenched the next sentence loose after what seemed a violent effort, "I might let you have half of it—a thousand, say."

But Thankful refused to say a thousand. That was ridiculous, she declared. By degrees, and a hundred at a time, Solomon raised his offer to fifteen hundred. This being the sum Mrs. Barnes had considered in the first place—and having asked for the two thousand merely because of her judgment of human nature—she announced that she would think over the offer. Then came the question of time. Here Mr. Cobb was firm. Three years—two years—he would not consider. At last he announced that he would take a one-year mortgage on the Barnes property for fifteen hundred dollars; and that was all he would do.

"And I wouldn't do that for nobody else," he declared. "You bein' my relation I don't know's it ain't my duty as a perfessin' Christian to—to help you out. I hadn't ought to afford it, but I'm willin' to go so far."

Thankful shook her head. "I'm glad you said, 'PROFESSIN' Christian.'" she observed. "Well," drawing a long breath, "then I suppose I've got to say yes or no. . . . And I'll say yes," she added firmly. "And we'll call it settled."

They parted before the hotel. She was to return to South Middleboro that afternoon. Mr. Cobb was to prepare the papers and forward them for her signature, after which, upon receipt of them duly signed, he would send her the fifteen hundred dollar check.

Solomon climbed into the buggy. "Well, good-by," he said. "I hope you'll do fust-rate. The interest'll be paid regular, of course. I'm real pleased to meet you— er—Cousin Thankful. Be sure you sign them papers in the right place. Good-by. Oh—er—er—sometimes I'll be droppin' in to see you after you get your boardin'-house goin'. I come to East Wellmouth once in a while. Yes—yes—I'll come and see you. You can tell me more about Captain Abner, you know. I'd—I'd like to hear what he said to you about me. Good-by."

That afternoon, once more in the depot-wagon, which had been refitted with its fourth wheel, Thankful, on her way to the Wellmouth railway station, passed her "property." The old house, its weather-beaten shingles a cold gray in the half-light of the mist-shrouded, sinking sun, looked lonely and deserted. A chill wind came from the sea and the surf at the foot of the bluff moaned and splashed and sighed.

Thankful sighed also.

"What's the matter?" asked Winnie S.

"Oh, nothin' much. I wish I was a prophet, that's all. I'd like to be able to look ahead a year."

Winnie S. whistled. "Judas priest!" he said. "So'd I. But if I'd see myself drivin' this everlastin' rig-out I'd wished I hadn't looked. I don't know's I'd want to see ahead as fur's that, after all."

Thankful sighed again. "I don't know as I do, either," she admitted.

CHAPTER VII

MARCH, so to speak, blew itself out; April came and went; May was here. And on the seventeenth of May the repairs on the "Cap'n Abner place" were completed. The last carpenter had gone, leaving his shavings and chips behind him. The last painter had spilled his last splash of paint on the sprouting grass beneath the spotless white window sills. The last paper-hanger had departed. Winnie S. was loading into what he called a "truck wagon" the excelsior and bagging in which the final consignment of new furniture had been wrapped during its journey from Boston. About the front yard Kenelm Parker was moving, rake in hand. In the kitchen Imogene, the girl from the Orphans' Home in Boston, who had been engaged to act as "hired help," was arranging the new pots and pans on the closet shelf and singing "Showers of Blessings" cheerfully if not tunefully.

Yes, the old "Cap'n Abner place" was rejuvenated and transformed and on the following Monday it would be the "Cap'n Abner place" no longer: it would then become the "High Cliff House" and open its doors to hoped-for boarders, either of the "summer" or "all-the-year" variety.

The name had been Emily Howes' choice. She and Mrs. Barnes had carried on a lengthy and voluminous correspondence and the selection of a name had been left to Emily. To her also had been intrusted the selection of wallpapers, furniture and the few pictures which Thankful had felt able to afford. These were but few, for the cost of repairing and refitting had been much larger than the original estimate. The fifteen hundred dollars raised on the mortgage had gone and of the money obtained by the sale of the cranberry bog shares—Mrs. Pearson's legacy—nearly half had gone also. Estimates are one thing and actual expenditures are another, a fact known to everyone who has either built a house or rebuilt one, and more than once during the repairing and furnishing process Thankful had repented of her venture and wished she had not risked the plunge. But, having risked it, backing out was impossible. Neither was it possible to stop half-way. As she said to Captain Obed, "There's enough half-way decent boardin'-houses and hotels in this neighborhood now. There's about as much need of another of that kind as there is of an icehouse at the North Pole. Either this boardin'-house of mine must be the very best there can be, price considered, or it mustn't be at all. That's the way I look at it."

The captain had, of course, agreed with her. His advice had been invaluable. He had helped in choosing carpenters and painters and it was owing to his suggestion that Mrs. Barnes had refrained from engaging an East Wellmouth young woman to help in the kitchen.

"You could find one, of course," said the captain. "There's two or three I could think of right off now who would probably take the job, but two out of the three wouldn't be much account anyhow, and the only one that would is Sarah Mullet and she's engaged to a Trumet feller. Now let alone the prospect of Sarah's gettin' married and leavin' you 'most any time, there's another reason for not hirin' her. She's the everlastin'est gossip in Ostable County, and that's sayin' somethin'. What Sarah don't know about everybody's private affairs she guesses and she always guesses out loud. Inside of a fortnight she'd have all you ever done and a whole lot you never thought of doin' advertised from Race P'int to Sagamore. She's a reg'lar talkin' foghorn, if there was such a thing—only a foghorn shuts down in clear weather and SHE don't shut down, day or night. Talks in her sleep, I shouldn't wonder. If I was you, Mrs. Barnes, I wouldn't bother with any help from 'round here. I'd hire a girl from Boston, or somewheres; then you could be skipper of your own ship."

Thankful, after thinking the matter over, decided that the advice was good. The difficulty, of course, was in determining the "somewhere" from which the right sort of servant, one willing to work for a small wage, might be obtained. At length she wrote to a Miss Coffin, once a nurse in Middleboro but now matron of an orphans' home in Boston. Miss Coffin's reply was to the effect that she had, in her institution, a girl who might in time prove to be just the sort which her friend desired.

Of course [she wrote], she isn't at all a competent servant now, but she is bright and anxious to learn. And she is a good girl, although something of a character. Her Christian name is Marguerite, at least she says it is. What her other name is goodness only knows. She has been with us now for nearly seven years. Before that she lived with and took care of a drunken old woman who said she was the girl's aunt, though I doubt if she was. Suppose I send her to you on trial; you can send her back to us if she doesn't suit. It would be a real act of charity to give her a chance, and I think you will like her in spite of her funny ways.

This doubtful recommendation caused Thankful to shake her head. She had great confidence in Miss Coffin's judgment, but she was far from certain that "Marguerite" would suit. However, guarded inquiries in Wellmouth and Trumet strengthened her conviction that Captain Obed knew what he was talking about, and, the time approaching when she must have some sort of servant, she, at last, in desperation wrote her friend to send "the Marguerite one" along for a month's trial.

The new girl arrived two days later. Winnie S. brought her down in the depot-wagon, in company with her baggage, a battered old valise and an ancient umbrella. She clung to each of these articles with a death grip, evidently fearful that someone might try to steal them. She appeared to be of an age ranging from late sixteen to early twenty, and had a turned-up nose and reddish hair drawn smoothly back from her forehead and fastened with a round comb. Her smile was of the "won't come off" variety.

Thankful met her at the back door and ushered her into the kitchen, the room most free from workmen at the moment.

"How do you do?" said the lady. "I'm real glad to see you. Hope you had a nice trip down in the cars."

"Lordy, yes'm!" was the emphatic answer, accompanied by a brilliant smile. "I never had such a long ride in my life. 'Twas just like bein' rich. I made believe I WAS rich most all the way, except when a man set down in the seat alongside of me and wanted to talk. Then I didn't make believe none, I bet you!"

"A man?" grinned Thankful. "What sort of a man?"

"I don't know. One of the railroad men I guess 'twas; anyhow he was a fresh young guy, with some sort of uniform hat on. He asked me if I didn't want him to put my bag up in the rack. He said you couldn't be too careful of a bag like that. I told him never mind my bag; it was where it belonged and it stayed shut up, which was more'n you could say of some folks in this world. I guess he understood; anyhow he beat it. Lordy!" with another smile. "I knew how to treat HIS kind. Miss Coffin's told me enough times to look out for strange men. Is this where I'm goin' to live, ma'am?"

"Why—why, yes; if you're a good girl and try hard to please and to learn. Now—er—Marguerite—that's your name, isn't it?"

"No, ma'am, my name's Imogene."

"Imo—which? Why! I thought you was Marguerite. Miss Coffin hasn't sent another girl, has she?"

"No, ma'am. I'm the one. My name used to be Marguerite, but it's goin' to be Imogene now. I've wanted to change for a long while, but up there to the Home they'd got kind of used to Marguerite, so 'twas easier to let it go at that. I like Imogene lots better; I got it out of a book."

"But—but you can't change your name like that. Isn't Marguerite your real name?"

"No'm. Anyhow I guess 'tain't. I got that out of a book, too. Lordy," with a burst of enthusiasm, "I've had more names in my time! My Aunt Bridget she called me 'Mag' when she didn't make it somethin' worse. And when I first came to the Home the kids called me 'Fire Alarm,' 'cause my hair was red. And the cook they had then called me 'Lonesome,' 'cause I guess I looked that way. And the matron— not Miss Coffin, but the other one—called me 'Maggie.' I didn't like that, so when Miss Coffin showed up I told her I was Marguerite. But I'd rather be Imogene now, if you ain't particular, ma'am."

"Why—um—well, I don't know's I am; only seems to me I'd settle on one or t'other and stay put. What's your last name?"

"I ain't decided. Montgomery's a kind of nice name and so's St. John, or Wolcott—there used to be a Governor Wolcott, you know. I s'pose, now I'm out workin' for myself, I ought to have a last name. Maybe you can pick one out for me, ma'am."

"Humph! Maybe I can. I've helped pick out first names for babies in my time, but pickin' out a last name for anybody would be somethin' new, I will give in. But I'll try, if you want me to. And you must try to do what I want and to please me.

Will you promise me that?"

"Lordy, yes'm!"

"Um! Well, you might begin by tryin' not to say 'Lordy' quite so many times. That would please me, for a start."

"All right'm. I got in the habit of sayin' it, I guess. When I first come to the Home I used to say, 'God sakes,' but the matron didn't like that."

"Mercy on us! I don't wonder. Well—er—Imogene, now I'll show you the house and your room and all. I hope you like 'em."

There was no doubt of the liking. Imogene was delighted with everything. When she was shown the sunny attic bedroom which was to be hers she clapped her hands.

"It's elegant, ma'am," she cried. "Just grand! OH! it's too splendid to believe and yet there ain't any make-believe in it. Lordy! Excuse me, ma'am, I forgot. I won't say it again. I'll wait and see what you say and then I'll say that. And now," briskly, "I guess you think it's time I was gettin' to work. All right, I can work if I ain't got no other accomplishments. I'm all ready to begin."

As a worker she was a distinct success. There was not a lazy bone in her energetic body. She was up and stirring each morning at five o'clock and she evinced an eager willingness to learn that pleased Mrs. Barnes greatly. Her knowledge of cookery was limited, and deadly, but as Thankful had planned to do most of the cooking herself, for the first season at least, this made little difference. Altogether the proprietress of the High Cliff House was growing more and more sure that her female "hired help" was destined to prove a treasure.

"I am real glad you like it here so well, Imogene," she said, at the end of a fortnight. "I was afraid you might be lonesome, down here so far from the city."

Imogene laughed. "Who? Me?" she exclaimed. "I guess not, ma'am. Don't catch me bein' lonesome while there's folks around I care about. I was lonesome enough when I first came to the Home and the kids used to make fun of me. But I ain't lonesome now, with you so kind and nice. No indeedy! I ain't lonesome and I ain't goin' to be. You watch!"

Captain Obed heartily approved of Imogene. Of Kenelm Parker as man-of-all-work his approval was much less enthusiastic. He had been away attending to his fish weirs, when Kenelm was hired, and the bargain was made before he returned.

It was Hannah Parker who had recommended her brother for the position. She had coaxed and pleaded and, at last, Thankful had consented to Kenelm's taking the place on trial.

"You'll need a nice, trustworthy man to do chores," said Hannah. "Now Kenelm's honest; there ain't a more honest, conscientious man in East Wellmouth than my brother, if I do say it. Take him in the matter of that umbrella he lost the night you first came, Mrs. Barnes. Take that, for instance. He'd left it or lost it somewheres, he knew that, and the ordinary person would have been satisfied; but not Kenelm. No sir-ee! He hunted and hunted till he found that umbrella and come fetchin' of it home. 'Twas a week afore he did that, but when he did I says, 'Well,' I says, 'you have got more stick-to-it than I thought you had. You—'"

"Where did he find it?" interrupted Thankful.

"Land knows! He didn't seem to know himself—just found it, he said. He acts so sort of upsot and shameful about that umbrella that he and I don't talk about it any more. But it did show that he had a sense of responsibleness, and a good one. Anybody that'll stick to and persecute a hunt for a lost thing the way he done will stick to a job the same way. Don't you think so yourself, Mrs. Barnes?"

Thankful was not convinced, but she yielded. When she told Captain Bangs he laughed and observed: "Yup, well, maybe so. Judgin' by other jobs Kenelm's had he'll stick to this one same as he does to his bed of a Sunday mornin'—lay down on it and go to sleep. However, I presume likely he ought to have the chance. Of course Hannah's idea is plain enough. Long's he's at work over here, she can keep an eye on him. And it's a nice, satisfactory distance from the widow Larkin, too."

So Kenelm came daily to work and did work—some. When he did not he always had a plausible excuse. As a self-excuser he was a shining light.

Thankful had, during the repairs on the house, waited more or less anxiously for developments concerning the mystery of the little back bedroom. Painters and paperhangers had worked in that room as in others, but no reports of strange sounds, or groans, or voices, had come from there. During the week preceding the day of formal opening Thankful herself had spent her nights in that room, but had not heard nor seen anything unusual. She was now pretty thoroughly convinced that the storm had been responsible for the groans and that the rest had been due to her imagination. However, she determined to let that room and the larger one adjoining last of all; she would take no chances with the lodgers, she couldn't afford it.

Among the equipment of the High Cliff House or its outbuildings were a horse, a pig, and a dozen hens and two roosters. Captain Obed bought the horse at Mrs. Barnes' request, a docile animal of a sedate age. A second-hand buggy and a second-hand "open wagon" he also bought. The pig and hens Thankful bought herself in Trumet. She positively would not consent to the pig's occupying the sty beneath the woodshed and adjoining the potato cellar, so a new pen was built in the hollow at the rear of the house. Imogene was tremendously interested in the live-stock. She begged the privilege of naming each animal and fowl. Mrs. Barnes had been encouraging the girl to read literature more substantial than the "Fireside Companion" tales in which she had hitherto delighted, and had, as a beginning, lent her a volume of United States history, one of several discarded schoolbooks which Emily Howes sent at her cousin's request. Imogene was immensely interested in the history. She had just finished the Revolution and the effect of her reading was evident when she announced the names she had selected.

The horse, being the most important of all the livestock, she christened George Washington. The pig was named Patrick Henry. The largest hen was Martha Washington. "As to them two roosters," she explained, "I did think I'd name the big handsome one John Hancock and the littlest one George Three. They didn't like each other, ma'am, that was plain at the start, so I thought they'd ought to be on different sides. But the very first fight they had George pretty near licked the stuffin' out of John, so I've decided to change the names around. That ought to fix it; don't you think so, ma'am?"

On the seventeenth the High Cliff House was formally opened. It was much too early to expect "summer" boarders, but there were three of the permanent variety who had already engaged rooms. Of these the first was Caleb Hammond, an elderly widower, and retired cranberry grower, whose wife had died fifteen years before and who had been "boarding around" in Wellmouth Centre and Trumet ever since. Caleb was fairly well-to-do and although he had the reputation of being somewhat "close" in many matters and "sot" in his ways, he was a respected member of society. He selected a room on the second floor—not a front room, but one on the side looking toward the Colfax estate. The room on the other side, across the hall, was taken by Miss Rebecca Timpson, who had taught the "upstairs" classes in the Wellmouth school ever since she was nineteen, a considerable period of time.

The large front rooms, those overlooking the bluff and the sea, Thankful had intended reserving for guests from the city, but when Mr. Heman Daniels expressed a wish to engage and occupy one of them, that on the left of the hall, she reconsidered and Mr. Daniels obtained his desire. It was hard to refuse a personage like Mr. Daniels anything. He was not an elderly man; neither was he, strictly speaking, a young one. His age was, perhaps, somewhere in the late thirties or early forties and he was East Wellmouth's leading lawyer, in fact its only one.

Heman was a bachelor and rather good-looking. That his bachelorhood was a matter of choice and not necessity was a point upon which all of East Wellmouth agreed. He was a favorite with the ladies, most of them, and, according to common report, there was a rich widow in Bayport who would marry him at a minute's notice if he gave the notice. So far, apparently, he had not given it. He was a "smart" lawyer, everyone said that, and it is probable that he himself would have been the last to deny the accusation. He was dignified and suave and gracious, also persuasive when he chose to be.

He had been boarding with the Holts, but, like the majority of the hotel lodgers and "mealers," was very willing to change. The location of the High Cliff House was, so he informed Thankful, the sole drawback to its availability as a home for him.

"If a bachelor may be said to have a home, Mrs. Barnes," he added, graciously. "However, I am sure even an unfortunate single person like myself may find a real home under your roof. You see, your reputation had preceded you, ma'am. Ha, ha! yes. As I say, the location is the only point which has caused me to hesitate. My—er—offices are on the Main Road near the postoffice and that is nearly a mile from here. But, we'll waive that point, ma'am. Six dollars a week for the room and seven for meals, you say. Thirteen dollars—an unlucky number: Ha, ha! Suppose we call it twelve and dodge the bad luck, eh? That would seem reasonable, don't you think?"

Thankful shook her head. "Altogether too reasonable, Mr. Daniels, I'm afraid," she replied. "I've cut my rates so close now that I'm afraid they'll catch cold in bad weather. Thirteen dollars a week may be unlucky, but twelve would be a sight more unlucky—for me. I can let you have a side room, of course, and that would be cheaper."

But Mr. Daniels did not wish a side room; he desired a front room and, at last, consented to pay the regular rate for it. But when the arrangement was concluded Thankful could not help feeling that she had taken advantage of an unworldly innocence.

Captain Obed Bangs, when she told him, reassured her.

"Don't worry, ma'am," he said. "I wouldn't lay awake nights fearin' I'd got ahead of Heman Daniels much. If you have got ahead of him you're the only person I ever see that did, and you ought to be proud instead of ashamed. And I'd get him to make his offer in writin' and you lock up the writin'."

"Why! Why, Captain Obed! How you do talk! You don't mean that Mr. Daniels is a cheat, do you? You don't mean such a thing as THAT?"

The captain waved a protesting hand.

"No, no," he declared. "I wouldn't call any lawyer a cheat. That's too one-sided a deal to be good business. The expense of hirin' counsel is all on one side if it ever comes to a libel suit. And besides, I don't think Daniels is a cheat. I never heard of him doin' anything that wa'n't legally honest. He's sharp and he's smart, but he's straight enough. I was only jokin', Mrs. Barnes. Sometimes I think I ought to hang a lantern on my jokes; then folks would see 'em quicker."

So Mr. Daniels came, and Mr. Hammond came, and so also did Miss Timpson. The first dinner was served in the big dining-room and it was a success, everyone said so. Beside the boarders there were invited guests, Captain Bangs and Hannah Parker, and Kenelm also. It was a disappointment to Thankful, although she kept the disappointment to herself, the fact that the captain had not shifted what he called his "moorings" to her establishment. She had hoped he might; she liked him and she believed him to be just the sort of boarder she most desired. It may be that he, too, was disappointed. What he said was:

"You see, ma'am, I've been anchorin' along with Hannah and Kenelm now for quite a spell. They took me in when 'twas a choice between messin' at the Holt place or eatin' grass in the back yard like King Nebuchadnezzar. Hannah don't keep a reg'lar boardin'-house but she does sort of count on me as one of the family, and I don't feel 'twould be right to shift—not yet, anyhow. But maybe I can pilot other craft into High Cliff Harbor, even if I don't call it my own home port."

That first dinner was a bountiful meal. Miss Parker expressed the general opin-ion, although it was expressed in her own way, when she said:

"My sakes alive, Mrs. Barnes! If THIS is the way you're goin' to feed your board-ers right along then I say it's remarkable. I've been up to Boston a good many times in my life, and I've been to Washington once, but in all MY experience at high-toned hotels I never set down to a better meal. It's a regular Beelzebub's feast, like the one in Scriptur'—leavin' out the writin' on the wall of course."

Kenelm ate enough for two and then, announcing that he couldn't heave away no more time, having work to do, retired to the rear of the barn where, the rake beside him, he slumbered peacefully for an hour.

"There!" said Thankful to Imogene that night. "We've started anyhow. And 'twas a good start if I do say it."

"Good!" exclaimed Imogene. "I should say 'twas good! But if them boarders eat as much every day as they have this one 'twon't be a start, 'twill be a finish. Lor—I mean mercy on us, ma'am—if this is a boardin'-house I'd like to know what a pal-ace is. Why a king never had better grub served to him. Huh! I guess he didn't. Old George Three used to eat gruel, like a—like a sick orphan at the Home. Oh, he did, ma'am, honest! I read about it in one of them history books you lent me. He was a tight-wad old gink, he was. Are you goin' to give these guys as much every meal, ma'am?"

"I mean to, of course," declared Mrs. Barnes. "Nobody shall starve at my table. And please, Imogene, don't call people ginks and guys. That ain't nice talk for a young woman."

Imogene apologized and promised to be more careful. But she thought a great deal and, at the end of the first week, she imparted her thoughts to Captain Obed.

"Say, Captain Bangs," she said, "do you know what is the matter with the name of this place? I tell you what I think is the matter. It hadn't ought to be the HIGH Cliff House. The CHEAP Cliff House would be a sight better. Givin' guys—folks, I mean—fifteen-dollar-a-week board for seven dollars may be mighty nice for them, but it's plaguy poor business for Mrs. Thankful."

The captain shook his head; he had been thinking, too, and his conclusions were much the same.

"You mustn't find fault with Mrs. Barnes, Imogene," he said. "She's a mighty fine woman."

"Fine woman! You bet she is! She's too plaguy fine, that's the trouble with her. She's so afraid her boarders'll starve that she forgets all about makin' money. She's the best woman there is in the world, but she needs a mean partner. Then the two of them might average up all right, I guess."

Captain Obed rubbed his chin. "Think she needs a business manager, eh?" he observed.

Imogene nodded emphatically. "She needs two of them," she declared. "One to manage the place and another to keep that Parker man workin'. He can eat more and talk more and work less than any guy ever I see. Why, he'd spend half his time in this kitchen gassin' with me, if I'd let him. But you bet I don't let him."

The captain thought more and more during the days that followed. At length he wrote a letter to Emily Howes at South Middleboro. In it he expressed his fear that Mrs. Barnes, although in all other respects perfect, was a too generous "provider" to be a success as a boarding-house keeper in East Wellmouth.

She'll have boarders enough, you needn't worry about that, [he wrote] but she'll lose money on every one. I've tried to hint, but she don't take the hint, and it ain't any of my affair, rightly speaking, so I can't speak out plain. Can't you write her a sort of warning afore it's too late? Or better still, can't you come down here and talk to her? I wish you would. Excuse my nosing in and writing you this way, please. I'm doing it just because I want to see her win out in the race, that's all. I wish you'd answer this pretty prompt, if you don't mind.

But the reply he hoped for did not come and he began to fear that he had made a bad matter worse by writing. Doubtless Miss Howes resented his "nosing in."

Thankful now began advertising in the Boston papers. And the answers to the ads began to arrive. Sometimes men and women from the city came down to inspect the High Cliff House, preparatory to opening negotiations for summer quarters. They inspected the house itself, interviewed Thankful, strolled along the bluff admiring the view, and sampled a meal. Then, almost without exception, they agreed upon terms and selected rooms. That the house would be full from top to bottom by the first of July was now certain. But, as Imogene said to Captain Bangs, "If we lose five dollars a week on everyone of 'em that ain't nothin' to hurrah about, seems to me."

The captain had not piloted any new boarders to the High Cliff. Perhaps he thought, under the circumstances, this would be a doubtful kindness. But the time came when he did bring one there. And the happenings leading to that result were these:

It was a day in the first week in June and Captain Obed, having business in Wellmouth Centre, had hired George Washington, Mrs. Barnes' horse, and the buggy and driven there. The business done he left the placid George moored to a hitching-post by the postoffice and strolled over to the railway station to watch the noon train come in.

The train was, of course, late, but not very late in this instance, and the few passengers alighted on the station platform. The captain, seated on the baggage-truck, noticed one of these passengers in particular. He was a young fellow, smooth-faced and tall, and as, suitcase in hand, he swung from the last car and strode up the platform it seemed to Captain Obed as if there was something oddly familiar in that stride and the set of his square shoulders. His face, too, seemed familiar. The captain felt as if he should recognize him—but he did not.

He came swinging on until he was opposite the baggage-truck. Then he stopped and looked searchingly at the bulky form of the man seated upon it. He stepped closer and looked again. Then, with a twinkle in his quiet gray eye, he did a most amazing thing—he began to sing. To sing—not loudly, of course, but rather under his breath. And this is what he sang:

> "Said all the little fishes that swim there below:
> 'It's the Liverpool packet! Good Lord, let her go!'"

To the average person this would have sounded like the wildest insanity. But not to Captain Obed Bangs of East Wellmouth. The captain sprang from the truck and held out his hand.

"Johnnie Kendrick!" he shouted. "It's Johnnie Kendrick, I do believe! Well, I swan to man!"

The young man laughed, and, seizing the captain's hand, shook it heartily.

"I am glad you do," he said. "If you hadn't swanned to man I should have been afraid there was more change in Captain Obed Bangs than I cared to see. Captain Obed, how are you?"

Captain Obed shook his head. "I—I—" he stammered. "Well, I cal'late my timbers are fairly strong if they can stand a shock like this. Johnnie Kendrick, of all folks in the world!"

"The very same, Captain."

"And you knew me right off! Well done for you, John! Why, it's all of twenty odd year since you used to set on a nail keg in my boathouse and tease me into singing the Dreadnought chanty. I remember that. Good land! I ought to remember the only critter on earth that ever ASKED me to sing. Ho! ho! but you was a little towheaded shaver then; and now look at you! What are you doin' away down here?"

John Kendrick shook his head. "I don't know that I'm quite sure myself, Captain," he said. "I have some suspicions, of course, but they may not be confirmed. First of all I'm going over to East Wellmouth; so just excuse me a minute while I speak to the driver of the bus."

He was hurrying away, but his companion caught his arm.

"Heave to, John!" he ordered. "I've got a horse and a buggy here myself, such as they are, and unless you're dead sot on bookin' passage in Winnie S.'s—what did you call it?—bust—I'd be mighty glad to have you make the trip along with me. No, no. 'Twon't be any trouble. Come on!"

Five minutes later they were seated in the buggy and George Washington was jogging with dignified deliberation along the road toward East Wellmouth.

"And why," demanded Captain Obed, "have you come to Wellmouth again, after all these years?"

Mr. Kendrick smiled.

"Well, Captain Bangs," he said, "it is barely possible that I've come here to stay."

"To stay! You don't mean to stay for good?"

"Well, that, too, is possible. Being more or less optimistic, we'll hope that if I do stay it will be for good. I'm thinking of living here."

His companion turned around on the seat to stare at him.

"Livin' here!" he repeated. "You? What on earth—? What are you goin' to do?"

The passenger's eyes twinkled, but his tone was solemn enough.

"Nothing, very likely," he replied. "That's what I've been doing for some time."

"But—but, the last I heard of you, you was practicin' law over to New York."

"So I was. That, for a young lawyer without funds or influence, is as near doing nothing as anything I can think of."

"But—but, John—"

"Just a minute, Captain. The 'buts' are there, plenty of them. Before we reach them, however, perhaps I'd better tell you the story of my life. It isn't exciting enough to make you nervous, but it may explain a few things."

He told his story. It was not the story of his life, his whole life, by any means. The captain already knew the first part of that life. He had known the Kendricks ever since he had known anyone. Every person in East Wellmouth of middle age or older remembered when the two brothers, Samuel Kendrick and Bailey Kendrick— Bailey was John's father—lived in the village and were the "big" men of the community. Bailey was the more important and respected at that time, for Samuel speculated in stocks a good deal and there were seasons when he was so near bankruptcy that gossip declared he could not pass the poorhouse without shivering. If it had not been for his brother Bailey, so that same gossip affirmed, he would most assuredly have gone under, but Bailey lent him money and helped him in many ways. Both brothers were widowers and each had a son; but Samuel's boy Erastus was fifteen years older than John.

The families moved from Wellmouth when John was six years old. They went West and there, so it was said, the positions of the brothers changed. Samuel's luck turned; he made some fortunate stock deals and became wealthy. Bailey, however, lost all he had in bad mining ventures and sank almost to poverty. Both had been dead for years now, but Samuel's son, Erastus—he much preferred to be called E. Holliday Kendrick—was a man of consequence in New York, a financier, with offices on Broad Street and a home on Fifth Avenue. John, the East Wellmouth people had last heard of as having worked his way through college and law school and as practicing his profession in the big city.

So much Captain Bangs knew. And John Kendrick told him the rest. The road to success for a young attorney in New York he had found hard and discouraging. For two years he had trodden it and scarcely earned enough to keep himself alive. Now he had decided, or practically decided, to give up the attempt, select some small town or village and try his luck there. East Wellmouth was the one village he knew and remembered with liking. So to East Wellmouth he had come, to, as Captain Obed described it, "take soundin's and size up the fishin' grounds."

"So there you are, Captain," he said, in conclusion. "That is why I am here."

The captain nodded reflectively.

"Um—yes," he said. "I see; I see. Well, well; and you're figgerin' on bein' a lawyer here—in East Wellmouth?"

Mr. Kendrick nodded also. "It may, and probably will be, pretty close figuring at first," he admitted, "but at least there will be no more ciphers in the sum than there were in my Manhattan calculations. Honestly now, Captain Bangs, tell me—what do you think of the idea?"

The captain seemed rather dubious.

"Humph!" he grunted. "Well, I don't know, John. East Wellmouth ain't a very big place."

"I know that. Of course I shouldn't hope to do much in East Wellmouth alone. But it seemed to me I might do as other country lawyers have done, have an office—or a desk—in several other towns and be in those towns on certain days in the week. I think I should like to live in East Wellmouth, though. It is—not to be sentimental but just truthful—the one place I remember where I was really happy. And, as I remember too, there used to be no lawyer there."

Captain Obed's forehead puckered.

"That's just it, John," he said. "There is a lawyer here now. Good deal of a lawyer, too—if you ask HIM. Name's Heman Daniels. You used to know him as a boy, didn't you?"

Kendrick nodded assent.

"I think I did," he said. "Yes, I remember him. He was one of the big boys when I was a little one, and he used to bully us small chaps."

"That's the feller. He ain't changed his habits so much, neither. But he's our lawyer and I cal'late he's doin' well."

"Is he? Well, that's encouraging, at any rate. And he's the only lawyer you have? Only one lawyer in a whole town. Why in New York I couldn't throw a cigar stump from my office window without running the risk of hitting at least two and starting two damage suits."

The captain chuckled.

"I presume likely you didn't throw many," he observed. "That would be expensive fun."

"It would," was the prompt reply. "Cigars cost money."

They jogged on for a few minutes in silence. Then said Captain Obed:

"Well, John, what are you plannin' to do first? After we get into port, I mean."

"I scarcely know. Look about, perhaps. Possibly try out a boarding-house and hunt for a prospective office. By the way, Captain, you don't happen to know of a good, commodious two by four office that I could hire at a two by four figure, do you? One not so far from the main street that I should wear out an extravagant amount of shoe leather walking to and from it?"

More reflection on the captain's part. Then he said:

"Well, I don't know as I don't. John, I'll tell you: I've got a buildin' of my own. Right abreast the post-office; Henry Cahoon has been usin' it for a barber-shop. But Henry's quit, and it's empty. The location's pretty good and the rent—well, you and me wouldn't pull hair over the rent question, I guess."

"Probably not, but I should insist on paying as much as your barber friend did. This isn't a charity proposition I'm making you, Captain Bangs. Oh, let me ask this: Has this—er—office of yours got a good front window?"

"Front window! What in time—? Yes, I guess likely the front window's all right. But what does a lawyer want of a front window?"

"To look out of. About all a young lawyer does is look out of the window. Now about a boarding-place?"

Captain Obed had been waiting for this question.

"I've got a boardin'-place for you, John," he declared. "The office I may not be so sartin about, but the boardin'-place I am. There ain't a better one this side of Boston and I know it. And the woman who keeps it is—well, you take my word for it she's all RIGHT."

His passenger regarded him curiously.

"You seem very enthusiastic, Captain," he observed, with a smile.

Captain Bangs' next remark was addressed to the horse. He gruffly bade the animal "gid-dap" and appeared a trifle confused.

"I am," he admitted, after a moment. "You'll be, too, when you see her."

He described the High Cliff House and its owner. Mr. Kendrick asked the terms for board and an "average" room. When told he whistled.

"That isn't high," he said. "For such a place as you say this is it is very low. But I am afraid it is too high for me. Isn't there any other establishment where they care for men—and poor lawyers?"

"Yes, there is, but you shan't go to it, not if I can stop you. You come right along with me now to the High Cliff and have dinner. Yes, you will. I ain't had a chance to treat you for twenty year and I'm goin' to buy you one square meal if I have to feed you by main strength. Don't you say another word. There! There's east Wellmouth dead ahead of us. And there's the High Cliff House, too. Git dap, Father of your Country! See! He's hungry, too, and he knows what he'll get, same as I do."

They drove into the yard of Mrs. Barnes' "property" and Thankful herself met them at the door. Captain Obed introduced his passenger and announced that the latter gentleman and he would dine there. The lady seemed glad to hear this, but she seemed troubled, too. When she and the captain were alone together she disclosed the cause of her trouble.

"I'm afraid I'm goin' to lose my best boarder," she said. "Mr. Daniels says he's afraid he must take his meals nearer his place of business. And, if he does that, he'll get a room somewheres uptown. I'm awful sorry. He's about the highest payin' roomer I have and I did think he was permanent. Oh, dear!" she added. "It does seem as if there was just one thing after the other to worry me. I—I don't seem to be makin' both ends meet the way I hoped. And—and lookin' out for everything myself, the way I have to do, keeps me stirred up all the time. I feel almost sort of discouraged. I know I shouldn't, so soon, of course. It's—it's because I'm tired today, I guess likely."

"Yes, I guess likely 'tis. Tired! I shouldn't wonder? It ain't any of my affairs at all, Mrs. Barnes, and I beg your pardon for sayin' it, but if you don't have some good capable person to take some of the care and managin' of this place off your shoulders you'll be down sick afore the summer's through."

Thankful sighed, and then smiled. "I know I need help, the right kind of help, just as well as you do, Cap'n Bangs," she said. "But I know, too, that I can't afford to pay for it, so I must get along best I can without it. As for gettin' sick—well, I can't afford that, either."

At dinner John Kendrick met Mr. Heman Daniels and Miss Timpson and Caleb Hammond. All three were evidently very curious concerning the business which had brought the young man to East Wellmouth, but their curiosity was not satisfied. Kendrick himself refused to notice hints and insinuations and, though he talked freely on most subjects, would not talk of his own affairs. Captain Obed, of course, disclosed nothing of the knowledge he had gained. So the table talk dealt mainly with the changes in the village since John was a boy there, and of old times and old residents long gone.

Mr. Daniels was very gracious and very affable. He spoke largely of cases intrusted to his care, of responsibilities and trusts, and if the guest gained the idea that Mr. Daniels was a very capable and prosperous lawyer indeed—if he gained such an idea and did not express it, how could Heman be expected to contradict?

After dinner—Kendrick informed his friend it was one of the best he had ever eaten—he and the captain walked over to the village, where they spent the afternoon wandering about, inspecting the ex-barber-shop and discussing chances and possibilities. The young man was still doubtful of East Wellmouth's promise of professional opportunities. He should like to live there, he said, and he might decide to do so, but as yet he had not so decided. He seemed more pessimistic than during the drive down from the station. Captain Obed, however, and oddly enough, was much more optimistic than he had been at first.

"I don't know, John," he said, "but I ain't sure you couldn't make good, and pretty good, too, by settlin' here. This section needs a good lawyer."

"Another good lawyer you mean. Daniels is here, remember. Judging by his remarks this noon he is very much here."

"Um—yes, I know. If you take his remarks at the value he marks 'em with he's the whole bank and a safe-deposit vault hove in. But I wouldn't wonder if those remarks was subject to a discount. Anyhow I know mighty well there's a lot of folks in this town—good substantial folks, too—who don't like him. They hire him once in a while because there ain't another lawyer short of Trumet and that's quite a ways. But maybe they'd be mighty glad to shift if there was a chance right at hand. Don't you strike the colors yet awhile. Think it over first."

He insisted upon Kendrick's returning to the High Cliff House that night. "I want Mrs. Barnes to show you the room she's got vacant," he said. "Ain't no harm lookin' at a brindle calf, as the feller said; you don't have to buy the critter unless you want to."

So Mr. Kendrick inspected the rooms and expressed himself as delighted with them.

"They're all right in every respect, Captain," he declared. "And the food is more than that. But the price—although it's surprisingly low considering the value offered—is too steep for me. I'm afraid, if I should locate here, for a trial trip, I couldn't afford to be comfortable and I shouldn't expect to."

Captain Bangs remained to take supper with his friend. The meal over, they and the rest of the boarders were seated in the big living-room—once Captain Abner's "best parlor"—when there came from outside the rattle of wheels and the voice of Winnie S. shouting "Whoa!" to General Jackson.

Thankful, who had been in the kitchen superintending Imogene, who was learning rapidly, came hurrying to the front door. The group in the parlor heard her utter an exclamation, an exclamation of surprise and delight. There were other exclamations, also in a feminine voice, and the sounds of affectionate greetings. Then Mrs. Barnes, her face beaming, ushered into the living-room a young woman. And this young woman was her cousin, Emily Howes.

Captain Obed rose to greet her.

"Well, I swan to man, Miss Howes!" he cried. "This IS a surprise! I didn't know you was due for a v'yage in this latitude."

Thankful laughed. "Neither did I," she declared. "It's as big a surprise to me as it is to you, Cap'n. She didn't write me a word."

Emily laughed.

"Of course I didn't, Auntie," she said. "I wanted to surprise you. But you're glad to see me, aren't you?"

"GLAD! I don't believe I was ever so glad to see anybody in MY life."

"We're all glad to see you, Miss Howes," announced the captain. "Come down to make us a little visit, hey?"

"Oh, more than a little one. You can't escape so easily. I am going to stay all summer at least, perhaps longer. There, Aunt Thankful, what do you think of that?"

CHAPTER VIII

WHAT Thankful thought of it was evidenced by the manner in which she received the news. She did not say much, then, but the expression of relief and delight upon her face was indication sufficient. She did ask a number of questions: Why had Emily come then, so long before her school closed? How was it that she could leave her teaching? Why hadn't she written? And many others.

Miss Howes answered the questions one after the other. She had come in May because she found that she could come.

"I meant to come the very first moment it was possible for me to do so," she said. "I have been more interested in this new project of yours, Auntie, than anything else in the world. You knew that; I told you so before I left and I have written it many times since. I came now because—well, because—you mustn't be alarmed, Auntie; there is nothing to be frightened about—but the school committee seemed to feel that I needed a change and rest. They seemed to think that I was not as well as I should be, that I was tired, was wearing myself out; that is the way they expressed it. It was absurd, of course, I am perfectly well. But when they came to me and told me that they had decided to give me a vacation, with pay, until next fall, and even longer if I felt that I needed it, you may be sure I didn't refuse their kind offer. I thanked them and said yes before they could have changed their minds, even if they had wished to. They said I should go into the country. That was just where I wanted to go, and so here I am, IN the country. Aren't you glad?"

"Glad! Don't talk! But, Emily, if you ain't well, don't you think—"

"I am well. Don't say another word about that. And, Oh, the things I mean to do to help you, Aunt Thankful!"

"Help me! Indeed you won't! You'll rest and get strong again, that's what you'll do. I don't need any help."

"Oh, yes, you do. I know it."

"How do you know?"

For just an instant Emily glanced at Captain Bangs. The captain's face expressed alarm and embarrassment. He was standing where Mrs. Barnes could not see him and he shook his head warningly. Miss Howes' eyes twinkled, but she did not smile.

"Oh, I knew!" she repeated.

"But HOW did you know? I never wrote you such a thing, sartin."

"Of course you didn't. But I knew because—well, just because. Everyone who takes boarders needs help. It's a—it's a chronic condition. Now, Auntie, don't you think you could find some supper for me? Not much, but just a little. For an invalid ordered to the country I am awfully hungry."

That was enough for Thankful. She seized her cousin by the arm and hurried her into the dining-room. A few moments later she reappeared to order Miss Howes' trunk carried upstairs to the "blue room."

"You'll have to excuse me, folks," she said, addressing her guests. "I know I didn't introduce you to Emily. I was so flustered and—and tickled to see her that I forgot everything, manners and all. Soon's she's had a bite to eat I'll try to make up. You'll forgive me, won't you?"

When she had gone Captain Obed was bombarded with questions. Who was the young lady? Where did she come from? If she was only a cousin, why did she call Mrs. Barnes "Auntie"? And many others.

Captain Obed answered as best he could.

"She's real pretty, isn't she," affirmed Miss Timpson. "I don't know when I've seen a prettier woman. Such eyes! And such hair! Ah hum! When I was her age folks used to tell me I had real wonderful hair. You remember that, don't you, Mr. Hammond?"

Mr. Hammond chuckled. "I remember lots of things," he observed diplomatically.

"You think she's pretty, don't you, Mr. Daniels?" persisted Miss Timpson.

East Wellmouth's legal light bowed assent. "A—ahem—a very striking young lady," he said with dignity. He had scarcely taken his eyes from the newcomer while she was in the room. John Kendrick said nothing.

When Emily and Thankful returned to the living-room there were introductions and handshakings. And, following these, a general conversation lasting until ten o'clock. Then Miss Howes excused herself, saying that she was a bit tired, bade them all good night and went to her room.

Captain Obed left soon afterward.

"Well, John," he said to his friend, as they stood together on the front step, "what do you think of this for a boardin'-house? All I prophesied, ain't it?"

Kendrick nodded. "All that, and more," he answered, emphatically.

"Like Mrs. Barnes, don't you?"

"Very much. No one could help liking her."

"Um-hm. Well, I told you that, too. And her niece—cousin, I mean—is just as nice as she is. You'll like her, too, when you know her. . . . Eh?"

"I didn't speak, Captain."

"Oh, didn't you? Well, it's high time for me to be headin' for home. Hannah'll be soundin' the foghorn for me pretty soon. She'll think I'VE been tagged by Abbie Larkin if I don't hurry up and report. See you in the mornin', John. Good night."

The next forenoon he was on hand, bright and early, and he and Kendrick went over to the village on another tour of inspection. Captain Obed was extremely curious to know whether or not his friend had made up his mind to remain in East Wellmouth, but, as the young man himself did not volunteer the information, the captain asked no questions. They walked up and down the main road until dinner time. John said very little, and was evidently thinking hard. Just before twelve Captain Bangs did ask a question, his first one.

"Well, John," he said, looking up at the clock in the steeple of the Methodist Church, "it's about time for us to be thinkin' about takin' in cargo. Where shall we eat this noon? At the High Cliff again, or do you want to tackle Darius Holt's? Course you understand I'm game for 'most anything if you say so, and 'most anything's what we're liable to get at that Holt shebang. I don't want you to think I've got any personal grudge. When it comes to that I'm—ho! ho!—well, I'm a good deal in the frame of mind Kenelm Parker was at the revival meetin' some year ago. Kenelm just happened in and took one of the back seats. The minister—he was a stranger in town—was walkin' up and down the aisles tryin' to influence the mourners to come forward. He crept up on Kenelm from behind, when he wa'n't expected, and says he, 'Brother,' he says, 'do you love the Lord?' Kenelm was some took by surprise and his wits was in the next county, I cal'late. 'Why—why—' he stammers. 'I ain't got nothin' AG'IN' Him.' Ho! ho! That's the way I feel about Darius Holt. I don't love his hotel, but I ain't got nothin' ag'in' him. What do you say?"

Kendrick hesitated.

"The Holt board is cheaper, isn't it?" he asked.

"Yup. It costs less and it's wuth it."

"Humph! Well—well, I guess we may as well go back to the High Cliff House."

Captain Obed was much surprised, but he said nothing.

At dinner there was a sprightly air of cheerfulness and desire to please among the boarders. Everyone talked a good deal and most of the remarks were addressed to Miss Howes, who sat at the foot of the table, opposite her cousin. Thankful noticed the change and marveled at it. Dinners had hitherto been rather hurried and silent affairs. Miss Timpson usually rushed through the meal in order to get back to her school. Mr. Daniels' habit was to fidget when Imogene delayed serving a course, to look at his watch and hint concerning important legal business which needed prompt attention. Caleb Hammond's conversation too often was confined to a range bordered by rheumatism on the one hand and bronchitis on the other.

Now all this was changed. No one seemed in a hurry, no one appeared to care what the time might be, and no one grumbled. Mr. Daniels was particularly affable and gracious; he even condescended to joke. He was wearing his best and newest suit and his tie was carefully arranged. Emily was in high spirits, laughed at the jokes, whether they were new or old, and seemed to be very happy. She had been for a walk along the bluff, and the sea breeze had crimsoned her cheeks and blown her hair about. She apologized for the disarrangement of the hair, but even Miss Timpson—her own tresses as smooth as the back of a haircloth sofa—declared the effect to be "real becomin'." Heman Daniels, who, being a bachelor, was reported to be very particular in such matters, heartily concurred in this statement. Mr. Hammond said it reminded him some of Laviny Marthy's hair. "Laviny Marthy was my wife that was," he added, by way of explanation. John Kendrick said very little; in fact, he was noticeably silent during dinner. Miss Timpson said afterward: "That Mr. Kendrick isn't much of a talker, is he? I guess he's what they call a good listener, for he seemed to be real interested, especially when Miss Howes was talkin'. He'd look at her and look at her, and time and time again I thought he was goin' to say somethin', but he didn't."

He was not talkative when alone with Captain Obed that afternoon. They paid one more visit to the building "opposite the postoffice" and while there he asked a few questions concerning the rent. The figure named by the captain was a low one and John seemed to think it too low. "I'm not asking charity," he declared. "At least you might charge me enough to pay for the paint I may rub off when I open the door."

But Captain Obed obstinately refused to raise his figure. "I've charged enough to risk what paint there is," he announced. "If I charged more I'd feel as if I had to paint fresh, and I don't want to do that. What's the matter with you, John? Want to heave your money away, do you? Better keep the odd change to buy cigars. You can heave them away, if you want to—and you won't be liable to hit many lawyers neither."

At supper time as they stood by the gate of the High Cliff House the captain, who was to eat at his regular boarding-place, the Parkers', that evening, ventured to ask the question he had been so anxious to ask.

"Well, John?" he began.

"Well, Captain?"

"Have you—have you made up your mind yet?"

Kendrick turned over, with his foot, a stone in the path.

"I—" he paused and turned the stone back again. Then he drew a long breath. "I must make it up," he said, "and I can do it as well now as a week later, I suppose. Wherever I go there will be a risk, a big risk. Captain Bangs, I'll take that risk here. If you are willing to let me have that office of yours for six months at the figure you have named—and I think you are crazy to do it—I will send for my trunk and my furniture and begin to—look out of the window."

Captain Obed was delighted. "Shake, John," he exclaimed. "I'm tickled to death. And I'll tell you this: If you can't get a client no other way I'll—I'll break into the meetin'-house and steal a pew or somethin'. Then you can defend me. Eh . . . And now what about a place for you to eat and sleep?" he added, after a moment.

The young man seemed to find the question as hard to answer as the other.

"I like it here," he admitted. "I like it very much indeed. But I must economize and the few hundred dollars I have scraped together won't—"

He was interrupted. Emily Howes appeared at the corner of the house behind them.

"Supper is ready," she called cheerfully.

Both men turned to look at her. She was bareheaded and the western sun made her profile a dainty silhouette, a silhouette framed in the spun gold of her hair.

"John's comin', Miss Emily," answered the captain. "He'll be right there."

Emily waved her hand and hurried back to the dining-room door. Mr. Kendrick kicked the stone into the grass.

"I think I may as well remain here, for the present at least," he said. "After all, there is such a thing as being too economical. A chap can't always make a martyr of himself, even if he knows he should."

The next morning Mrs. Barnes, over at the village on a marketing expedition, met Captain Bangs on his way to the postoffice.

"Oh, Cap'n," she said, "I've got somethin' to tell you. 'Tain't bad news this time; it's good. Mr. Heman Daniels has changed his mind. He's goin' to keep his room and board with me just as he's been doin'. Isn't that splendid!"

The sewing circles and the club and the noon and evening groups at the post-office had two new subjects for verbal dissection during the next fortnight. This was, in its way, a sort of special Providence, for this was the dull season, when there were no more wrecks alongshore or schooners aground on the bars, and the boarders and cottagers from the cities had not yet come to East Wellmouth. Also the opening of the High Cliff House was getting to be a worn-out topic. So Emily Howes, her appearance and behavior, and John Kendrick, HIS behavior and his astonishing recklessness in attempting to wrest a portion of the county law practice from Heman Daniels, were welcomed as dispensations and discussed with gusto.

Emily came through the gossip mill ground fine, but with surprisingly little chaff. She was "pretty as a picture," all the males agreed upon that point. And even the females admitted that she was "kind of good-lookin'," although Hannah Parker's diagnosis that she was "declined to be consumptic" and Mrs. Larkin's that she was older than she "made out to be," had some adherents. All agreed, however, that she knew how to run a boarding-house and that she was destined to be the "salvation" of Thankful Barnes' venture at the Cap'n Abner place.

Certainly she did prove herself to possess marked ability as a business manager. Quietly, and without undue assertion, she reorganized the affairs of the High Cliff House. No one detected any difference in the quality of the meals served there, in their variety or ample sufficiency. But, little by little, she took upon herself the buying of supplies, the regulation of accounts, the prompt payment of bills and the equally prompt collection of board and room rent. Thankful found the cares upon her shoulders less and less heavy, and she was more free to do what she was so capable of doing, that is, superintend the cooking and the housekeeping.

But Thankful herself was puzzled.

"I don't understand it," she said. "I've always had to look out for myself, and others, too. There ain't been a minute since I can remember that I ain't had somebody dependent upon me. I cal'lated I could run a boardin'-house if I couldn't do anything else. But I'm just as sure as I am that I'm alive that if you hadn't come when you did I'd have run this one into the ground and myself into the poorhouse. I don't understand it."

Emily smiled and put her arm about her cousin's waist. "Oh, no, you wouldn't, Auntie," she said. "It wasn't as bad as that. You needed help, that was all. And you are too generous and kind-hearted. You were always fearful that your boarders might not be satisfied. I have been teaching bookkeeping and accounting, you see, and, besides, I have lived in a family where the principal struggle was to satisfy the butcher and the baker and the candlestick maker. This is real fun compared to that."

Thankful shook her head.

"I know," she said; "you always talk that way, Emily. But I'm afraid you'll make yourself sick. You come down here purpose for your health, you know."

Emily laughed and patted Mrs. Barnes' plump shoulder.

"Health!" she repeated. "Why, I have never been as well since I can remember. I couldn't be sick here, in this wonderful place, if I tried. Do you think I look ill? . . . Oh, Mr. Daniels!" addressing the lawyer, who had just entered the dining-room,

"I want your opinion, as a—a specialist. Auntie is afraid I am ill. Don't you think I look about as well as anyone could look?"

Heman bowed. "If my poor opinion is worth anything," he observed, "I should say that to find fault with your appearance, Miss Howes, would be like venturing to—er—-paint the lily, as the saying is. I might say more, but—ahem—perhaps I had better not."

Judging by the young lady's expression he had said quite enough already.

"Idiot!" she exclaimed, after he had left the room. "I ask him a sensible question and he thinks it necessary to answer with a silly compliment. Thought I was fishing for one, probably. Why will men be such fools—some men?"

Mr. Daniels' opinion concerning his professional rival was asked a good many times during that first fortnight. He treated the subject as he did the rival, with condescending toleration. It was quite plain that he considered his own position too secure to be shaken. In fact, his feeling toward John Kendrick seemed to be a sort of kindly pity.

"He appears to be a very well-meaning young man," he said, in reply to one of the questions. "Rash, of course; very young men are likely to be rash—and perhaps more hopeful than some of us older and—ahem—wiser persons might be under the same circumstances. But he is well-meaning and persevering. I have no doubt he will manage to pick up a few crumbs, here and there. I may be able to throw a few in his way. There are always cases—ah—which I can't—or don't wish to—accept."

When this remark was repeated to Captain Obed the latter sniffed.

"Humph!" he observed, "I don't know what they are. I never see a case Heman wouldn't accept, if there was as much as seventy-five cents in it. If bananas was a nickel a bunch the only part he'd throw in anybody else's way would be the skins."

John, himself, did not seem to mind or care what Mr. Daniels or anyone else said. He wrote a letter to New York and, in the course of time, a second-hand desk, a few chairs, and half a dozen cases of law books arrived by freight and were installed in the ex-barber-shop. The local sign-painter perpetrated a sign with "John Kendrick, Attorney-at-law" upon it in gilt letters, and the "looking out of the window" really began.

And that was about all that did begin for days and days. Each morning or afternoon, Sundays excepted, Captain Bangs would drop in at the office and find no one there, no one but the tenant, that is. The latter, seated behind the desk, with a big sheepskin-bound volume spread open upon it, was always glad to see his visitor. Their conversations were characteristic.

"Hello, John!" the captain would begin. "How are the clients comin'?"

"Don't know, Captain. None of them has as yet got near enough so that I could see how he comes."

"Humph! I want to know. Mr. John D. Jacob Vanderbilt ain't cruised in from Newport to put his affairs in your hands? Sho'! He's pretty short-sighted, ain't he?"

"Very. He's losing valuable time."

"Well, I expected better things of him, I must say. Ain't gettin' discouraged, are you, John?"

"No, indeed. If there was much discouragement in my make-up I should have stopped before I began. How is the fish business, Captain?"

"Well, 'tain't what it ought to be this season of the year. Say, John, couldn't you subpoena a school of mackerel for me? Serve an order of the court on them to come into my weirs and answer for their sins, or somethin' like that? I'd be willin' to pay you a fairly good fee."

On one occasion the visitor asked his friend what he found to do all the long days. "Don't study law ALL the time, do you, John?" he queried.

Kendrick shook his head. "No," he answered, gravely. "Between studies I enjoy the view. Magnificent view from this window, don't you think?"

Captain Obed inspected the "view." The principal feature in the landscape was Dr. Jameson's cow, pastured in the vacant lot between the doctor's home and the postoffice.

"Very fine cow, that," commented the lawyer. "An inspiring creature. I spend hours looking at that cow. She is a comfort to my philosophic soul."

The captain observed that he wanted to know.

"Yes," continued Kendrick. "She is happy; you can see that she is happy. Now why?"

"'Cause she's eatin' grass," declared Captain Obed, promptly.

"That's it. Good for you! You have a philosophic soul yourself, Captain. She is happy because she has nothing to do but eat, and there is plenty to eat. That's my case exactly. I have nothing to do except eat, and at Mrs. Barnes' boarding-house there is always enough, and more than enough, to eat. The cow is happy and I ought to be, I suppose. If MY food was furnished free of cost I should be, I presume."

Kenelm Parker heard a conversation like the foregoing on one occasion and left the office rubbing his forehead.

"There's two lunatics in that place," he told the postmaster. "And if I'd stayed there much longer and listened to their ravin's there'd have been another one."

Kenelm seemed unusually contented and happy in his capacity as man-of-all-work at the High Cliff House. Possibly the fact that there was so very little real work to do may have helped to keep him in this frame of mind. He had always the appearance of being very busy; a rake or a hoe or the kindling hatchet were seldom out of reach of his hand. He talked a great deal about being "beat out," and of the care and responsibility which were his. Most of these remarks were addressed to Imogene, to whom he had apparently taken a great fancy.

Imogene was divided in her feelings toward Mr. Parker.

"He's an awful interestin' talker," she confided to Emily. "Every time he comes into this kitchen I have to watch out or he'll stay and talk till noontime. And yet if I want to get him to do somethin' or other he is always chock full of business that can't wait a minute. I like to hear him talk—he's got ideas on 'most every kind of thing—but I have to work, myself."

"Do you mean that he doesn't work?" asked Emily.

"I don't know whether he does or not. I can't make out. If he don't he's an awful good make-believe, that's all I've got to say. One time I caught him back of the woodpile sound asleep, but he was hanging onto the axe just the same. Said he set up half the night before worryin' for fear he mightn't be able to get through his next day's work, and the want of rest had been too much for him. Then he started in to tell me about his home life and I listened for ten minutes before I come to enough to get back to the house."

"Do you think he is lazy, Imogene?"

"I don't know. He says he never had no chance and it might be that's so. He says the ambition's been pretty well drove out of him, and I guess it has. I should think 'twould be. The way that sister of his nags at him all the time is enough to drive out the—the measles."

Imogene and Hannah Parker, as Captain Obed said, "rubbed each other the wrong way." Hannah was continually calling to see her brother, probably to make sure that he was there and not in the dangerous Larkin neighborhood. Imogene resented these visits—"usin' up Mrs. Thankful's time," she said they were—and she and Hannah had some amusing clashes. Miss Parker was inclined to patronize the girl from the Orphan's Home, and Imogene objected.

"Well," observed Hannah, on one occasion, "I presume likely you find it nice to be down here, where folks are folks and not just 'inmates.' It must be dreadful to be an 'inmate.'"

Imogene sniffed. "There's all kinds of inmates," she said, "same as there's all kinds of folks. Far's that goes, there's some folks couldn't be an inmate, if they wanted to. They wouldn't be let in."

"Oh, is that so? Judgin' by what I've seen I shouldn't have thought them that run such places was very particular. Where's Kenelm?"

"I don't know. He's to work, I suppose. That's what he's hired for, they tell me."

"Oh, indeed! Well," with emphasis, "he doesn't have to work, unless he wants to. My brother has money of his own, enough to subside on comf'tably, if he wanted to do it. His comin' here is just to accommodate Mrs. Barnes, that's all. Where is he?"

"Last I saw of him he was accommodatin' the horse stall. He may be uptown by this time, for all I know."

"Uptown?" in alarm. "What would he be uptown for? He ain't got any business there, has he?"

"Search ME. Good many guys—folks, I mean—seem to be always hangin' 'round where they haven't business. Well, I've got some of my own and I guess I'd better attend to it. Good mornin', ma'am."

Miss Howes cautioned Imogene against arousing the Parkers' enmity.

"Lordy! I mean mercy sakes, ma'am," exclaimed Imogene, "you needn't be afraid so far as Kenelm's concerned. I do boss him around some, when I think it's needful, but it ain't my bossin' that worries him, it's that Hannah woman's. He says she's at him all the time. Don't give him the peace of his life, he says. He's a misunderstood man, he tells me. Maybe he is; there are such, you know. I've read about 'em in stories."

Emily smiled. "Well," she said, "I wouldn't drive him too hard, if I were you, Imogene. He isn't the hardest worker in the world, but he does do some work, and men who can be hired to work about a place in summer are scarce here in East Wellmouth. You must be patient with him."

"Lor—land sakes! I am. But he does make me cross. He'd be settin' in my kitchen every evenin' if I'd let him. Don't seem to want to go home. I don't know's I blame him for that. You think I ought to let him set, I suppose, Miss Howes?"

"Why, yes, if he doesn't annoy you too much. We must keep him contented. You must sacrifice your own feelings to help Aunt Thankful. You would be willing to make some sacrifice for her, wouldn't you?"

"You bet your life I would! She's the best woman on earth, Mrs. Barnes is. I'd do anything for her, sacrifice my head, if that was worth five cents to anybody. All right, he can set if he wants to. I—I suppose I might improve his mind, hey, ma'am? By readin' to him, I mean. Mrs. Thankful, she's been givin' me books to improve my mind; perhaps they'd improve his if I read 'em out loud to him. His sister prob'ly won't like it, but I don't care. You couldn't improve HER mind; she ain't got any. It all run off the end of her tongue long ago."

By the Fourth of July the High Cliff House was filled with boarders. Every room was taken, even the little back bedroom and the big room adjoining it. These were taken by a young couple from Worcester and, if they heard any unusual noises in their apartment, they did not mention them. Thankful's dread of that little room had entirely disappeared. She was now thoroughly convinced that her imagination and the storm were responsible for the "spooks."

John Kendrick continued to sleep and eat at the new boarding-house. He was a general favorite there, although rather silent and disinclined to take an active part in the conversation at table. He talked more with Emily Howes than with anyone and she and he were becoming very friendly. Emily, Thankful and Captain Obed Bangs were the only real friends the young man had; he might have had more, but he did not seem to care for them. With these three, however, and particularly with Emily, he was even confidential, speaking of his professional affairs and prospects, subjects which he never mentioned to others.

These—the prospects—were brighter than at first. He had accepted one case and refused another. The refusal came as a surprise to East Wellmouth and caused much comment. Mr. Chris Badger was a passenger on the train from Boston and that train ran off the track at Buzzard's Bay. No one was seriously hurt except Mr. Badger. The latter gentleman purchased a pair of crutches and limped about on them, proclaiming himself a cripple for life. He and Heman Daniels had had a disagreement over a business matter so Chris took his damage suit against the railroad to John Kendrick. And John refused it.

Captain Obed, much disturbed, questioned his friend.

"Land of love, John!" he said. "Here you've been roostin' here, lookin' out of this window and prayin' for a job to come along. Now one does come along and you turn it down. Why?"

Kendrick laughed. "I'm cursed with a strong sense of contrast, Captain," he replied. "Those crutches are too straight for me."

The captain stared. "Straight!" he repeated. "All crutches are straight, ain't they?"

"Possibly; but some cripples are crooked."

So it was to Mr. Daniels, after all, that the damage suit came, and Heman brought about a three-hundred-dollar settlement. Most of East Wellmouth pronounced Kendrick "too pesky particular," but in some quarters, and these not by any means the least influential, his attitude gained approval and respect. This feeling was strengthened by his taking Edgar Wingate's suit against that same railroad. Edgar's woodlot was set on fire by sparks from the locomotive and John forced payment, and liberal payment, for the damage. Other cases, small ones, began to come his way. Lawyer Daniels had enemies in the community who had been waiting to take their legal affairs elsewhere.

Heman still professed entire indifference, but he no longer patronized his rival. John had a quiet way of squelching such patronage and of turning the laugh, which was annoying to a person lacking a sense of humor. And then, too, it was quite evident that Emily Howes' liking for the younger man displeased Daniels greatly. Heman liked Emily, seemed to like her very much indeed. On one or two occasions he had taken her to ride behind his fast horse, and he often brought bouquets and fruit, "given me by my clients and friends," he explained. "One can't refuse little gifts like that, but it is a comfort, to a bachelor like me, to be able to hand them on—hand them on—yes."

The first of August brought a new sensation and a new resident to East
Wellmouth. The big Colfax estate was sold and the buyer was no less a personage than E. Holliday Kendrick, John Kendrick's aristocratic Fifth Avenue cousin.
His coming was as great a surprise to John as to the rest of the community, but he
seemed much less excited over it. The purchase was quietly completed and, one
pleasant morning, the great E. Holliday himself appeared in East Wellmouth accompanied by a wife and child, two motor cars and six servants.

Captain Obed Bangs, who had been spending a week in Orham on business
connected with his fish weirs, returned to find the village chanting the praises of
the new arrival. Somehow or other E. Holliday had managed already to convey
the impression that he was the most important person in creation. The captain
happening in at the High Cliff House after supper, found the group in the living-
room discussing the all-important topic. Most of the city boarders were out enjoying a "marshmallow toast" about a bonfire on the beach, but the "regulars" were
present.

"Where's Mrs. Thankful?" was Captain Obed's first question.

"She's in the kitchen, I think," replied John. "Shall I call her?"

"Oh, no, no! It ain't particular. I just—just wondered where she was, that's all.
I wouldn't trouble her on no account."

John smiled. He seemed quietly amused about something. He regarded his
friend, who, after a glance in his direction, was staring at the lamp on the table, and
said:

"I'm sure it would be no trouble, Captain. Better let me tell her you are here."

Captain Obed was saved the embarrassment of further protestations by the entrance of Thankful herself; Emily accompanied her. The captain shook hands with
Mrs. Barnes and her cousin and hastened to announce that he heard "big news"
down street and had run over to find out how much truth there was in it.

"Couldn't scurcely believe it, myself," he declared. "John here, never said a
word about his high-toned relation comin' to East Wellmouth. Had you any idea
he was comin', John?"

John shook his head.

"No," he said. "The last time I saw him in New York, which was two years or more ago, he did say something about being on the lookout for a summer residence. But he did not mention East Wellmouth; nor did I. I remember hearing that he and the late Mr. Colfax were quite friendly, associated in business affairs, I believe. Probably that accounts for his being here."

"Set down, everybody," urged Thankful. "I'm willin' to set down, myself, I can tell you. Been on my feet 'most of the day. What sort of a person is this relation of yours, Mr. Kendrick? He ought to be all right, if there's anything in family connections."

Heman Daniels answered the question. He spoke with authority.

"Mr. Holliday is a fine gentleman," he announced, emphatically. "I've seen him two or three times since he came. He's a millionaire, but it doesn't make him pompous or stand-offish. He and I spoke—er—conversed together as friendly and easy as if we had known each other all our lives. He is very much interested in East Wellmouth. He tells me that, if the place keeps on suiting him as it has so far, he intends making it his permanent home. Of course he won't stay here ALL the year—the family have a house in Florida and one in New York, I believe—but he will call East Wellmouth his real home and his interests will center here."

There was a general expression of satisfaction. Miss Timpson declared that it was "real lovely" of Mr. Holliday Kendrick. Caleb Hammond announced that he always cal'lated there was a boom coming for the town. Had said so more times than he could count. "Folks'll tell you I said it, too," he proclaimed stoutly. "They'll bear me out in it, if you ask 'em."

"I'm glad we're goin' to have such nice neighbors," said Thankful. "It's always worried me a little wonderin' who that Colfax place might be sold to. I didn't know but somebody might get it with the notion of startin' another hotel."

"Hannah Parker ain't opened her mouth to talk of anything else since I got back," said Captain Bangs. "And it's been open most of the time, too. She says John's rich relation's locatin' here is a dissipation of Providence, if you know what that is."

John smiled but he said nothing. Emily was silent, also; she was regarding the young man intently.

"Yes, sir," continued Mr. Daniels, evidently pleased at the approval with which his statement had been met. "Yes, sir, Mr. E. Holliday Kendrick is destined to be a great acquisition to this town; mark my words. He tells me he shall hire no one to do his work except East Wellmouth people. And there will be a lot of work to be done, if he carries out his plans. He intends building an addition to his house, and enlarging his estate—"

Thankful interrupted.

"Enlargin' it!" she repeated. "Mercy sakes! What for? I should think 'twas large enough now!"

Heman smiled tolerantly. "To us—the ordinary—er—citizens, it might appear so," he observed. "But the—er—New York ideas is broader than the average Cape Codder's, if you'll excuse me, Mrs. Barnes. Mr. Kendrick has begun to spend money here already, and he will doubtless spend more. He contemplates public improvements as well as private. He asked me what sort of spirit there was in our community. Ahem!"

He paused, apparently to let the importance of the announcement sink in. It sank, or seemed to. Mr. Hammond, however, was somewhat puzzled.

"Now what do you cal'late he meant by that?" he queried.

John Kendrick answered. He and Emily had exchanged smiles. Neither of them seemed as deeply impressed with the Daniels proclamation as the others of the group.

"Perhaps he wanted to buy a drink," suggested John, gravely.

Miss Timpson was shocked; her expression showed it. Caleb Hammond did not seem to know whether to be shocked or not; the Hammond appreciation of a joke generally arrived on a later train. Mrs. Barnes and Captain Obed laughed, but not too heartily.

Mr. Daniels did not laugh. The frivolous interruption evidently jarred him.

"I scarcely imagine that to be the reason," he said, drily. "If Mr. E. Holliday Kendrick does indulge I guess likely—that is, I presume he would not find it necessary to buy his—er—beverages here. He meant public spirit, of course. He asked me who our leading men were."

"Who were they—the others, I mean?" asked John.

Emily rubbed away a smile with her handkerchief. Heman noticed her action, and his color brightened.

"They WERE public," he said, rather sharply. "They were men of standing—

long standing in the community. Prominent and prosperous citizens, who have lived here long enough for East Wellmouth to know them—and respect them."

This was a shot in the bull's eye. Miss Timpson evidently thought so, for she nodded approval. Daniels continued.

"They were men of known worth," he went on. "Practical citizens whose past as well as present is known. Your cousin—I believe he is your cousin, Kendrick, although he did not mention the relationship—was grateful to me for giving him their names. He is a practical man, himself."

John nodded. "He must be," he admitted. "No one but a practical man could get all that advice, free, from a lawyer."

Captain Obed laughed aloud.

"That's a good one," he declared. "Lawyers ain't in the habit of GIVIN' much, 'cordin' to all accounts. How about it, Heman?"

Mr. Daniels ignored the question and the questioner. He rose to his feet.

"There are SOME lawyers," he observed, crisply, "whose advice is not asked—to any great extent. I—I think I will join the group on the beach. It's a beautiful evening. Won't you accompany me, Miss Howes?"

Emily declined the invitation. "No, thank you, Mr. Daniels," she said. "I am rather tired and I think I won't go out tonight. By the way, Mr. Kendrick," she added, "was the great man asking your advice also? I happened to see him go into your office yesterday."

Everyone was surprised—everyone except the speaker and the person addressed, that is—but Heman's surprise was most manifest. His hand was on the knob of the door, but now he turned.

"In HIS office?" he repeated. "Kendrick, was he in to see YOU?"

John bowed assent. "Yes," he said. "He seems to be contemplating retaining a sort of—of resident attorney to look after his local affairs. I mentioned your name, Daniels."

Mr. Daniels went out. The door banged behind him.

A half hour later, after Mr. Hammond also had gone to join the marshmallow toasters and Miss Timpson had retired to her room, John told the others the story. Mr. E. Holliday Kendrick HAD called upon him at his office and he did contemplate engaging a resident lawyer. There were likely to be many of what he termed "minor details" connected with the transfer of the Colfax estate to him and the purchases which he meant to make later on, and an attorney at his beck and call would be a great convenience. Not this only; he had actually offered his young cousin the position, had offered to engage him and to pay him several hundred dollars as a retaining fee.

He told his hearers so much, and then he stopped. Emily, who had seemed much interested, waited a moment and then begged him to continue.

"Well?" she said. "Why don't you tell us the rest? We are all waiting to congratulate you. You accepted, of course."

John shook his head. "Why, no," he replied, "I didn't accept, exactly. I did say I would think it over; but I—well, I'm not sure that I shall accept."

Here was the unexpected. His hearers looked at each other in amazement.

"You won't accept!" cried Thankful. "Why, Mr. Kendrick."

"Won't accept!" shouted Captain Obed. "What on earth! Why, John Kendrick, what's the matter with you? Ain't you been settin' in that office of yours waitin' and waitin' for somethin' worth while to come along? And now a really big chance does come, and you say you don't know as you'll take it! What kind of talk's that, I'd like to know!"

John smiled. Miss Howes, who seemed as much surprised as the others, did not smile.

"Why won't you take it?" demanded the captain.

"Oh, I don't know. The proposition doesn't appeal to me as strongly as it should, perhaps. Cousin Holliday and I ARE cousins, but we—well, we differ in other ways besides the size of our incomes. When I was in New York I went to him at one time. I was—I needed—well, I went to him. He consented to see me and he listened to what I had to say, but he was not too cordial. He didn't ask me to call again. Now he seems changed, I admit. Remembers perfectly well that I am his father's brother's only child and all that, and out of the kindness of his heart offers me employment. But—but I don't know."

No one spoke for a moment. Then Emily broke the silence.

"You don't know?" she repeated, rather sharply. "Why not, may I ask?"

"Oh, I don't, that's all. For one thing, there is just a little too much condescension in my dear cousin's manner. I may be a yellow dog, but I don't like to sit up and beg when my master threatens to throw me a bone. Perhaps I'm particular as to who that master may be."

Again it was Emily who spoke.

"Perhaps you are—TOO particular," she said. "Can you afford to be so particular?"

"Probably not. But, you see, there is another thing. There is a question of professional ethics involved. If I take that retainer I am bound in honor to undertake any case Cousin Holliday may give me. And—and, I'm not sure I should care to do that. You know how I feel about a lawyer's duty to his client and his duty to himself. There are certain questions—"

She interrupted.

"I think there are, too many questions," she said. "I lose patience with you sometimes. Often and often I have known of your refusing cases which other lawyers have taken and won."

"Meaning Brother Daniels?" He asked it with a smile, but with some sarcasm in his tone. Both he and Miss Rowes seemed to have forgotten that the captain and Thankful were present.

"Why, yes. Mr. Daniels has accepted cases which you have refused. No one thinks the less of him for it. He will accept your cousin's retainer if you don't."

"I presume he will. That would be the practical thing to do, and he prides himself on his practicality."

"Practicality is not altogether bad. It is often necessary in this practical world. What case is Mr. Kendrick likely to put in your hands which you would hesitate to undertake?"

"None that I know of. But if he did, I—"

"You could refuse to take it."

"Why, not easily. I should have accepted his retainer and that, according to legal etiquette, would make me honor bound to—"

She interrupted again. Her patience was almost gone, that was plain. For the matter of that, so was Captain Obed's.

"Don't you think that you are a trifle too sensitive concerning honor?" she asked. "And too suspicious besides? I do. Oh, I am tired of your scruples. I don't like to see you letting success and—and all the rest of it pass you by, when other men, not so overscrupulous, do succeed. Don't you care for success? Or for money?"

John interrupted her. He leaned forward and spoke, deliberately but firmly. And he looked her straight in the face.

"I do," he said. "I care for both—now—more than I ever thought I could care."

And, all at once, the young lady seemed to remember that her cousin and the captain were in the room. She colored, and when she spoke it was in a different tone.

"Then," she said, "it seems to me, if I were you, I should accept the opportunities that came in my way. Of course, it's not my affair. I shouldn't have presumed to advise." She rose and moved toward the door. "Good night, Mr. Kendrick," she said. "Good night, Captain Bangs. Auntie, you will excuse me, won't you? I am rather tired tonight, and—"

But once more Kendrick interrupted.

"One moment, please, Miss Howes," he said, earnestly. "Do I understand—do you mean that you wish me to accept Cousin Holliday's retainer?"

Emily paused.

"Why," she answered, after an instant's hesitation, "I—I really don't see why my wish one way or the other should be very strong. But—but as a friend of yours—of course we are all your friends, Mr. Kendrick—as one of your friends I—we, naturally, like to see you rise in your profession."

"Then you advise me to accept?"

"If my advice is worth anything—yes. Good night."

Next day, when Captain Obed made his customary call at the ex-barber-shop, he ventured to ask the question uppermost in his mind.

"Have you decided yet, John?" he asked.

His friend looked at him.

"Meaning—what?" he queried.

"Meanin'—you know what I mean well enough. Have you decided to take your cousin's offer?"

"I've done more than that, Captain. I have accepted the offer and the retaining fee, too."

Captain Obed sprang forward and held out his hand.

"Bully for you, John!" he shouted. "That's the best thing you ever done in your life. NOW you've really started."

Kendrick smiled. "Yes," he admitted, "I have started. Where I may finish is another matter."

"Oh, you'll finish all right. Don't be a Jeremiah, John. Well, well! This is fine. Won't all hands be pleased!"

"Yes, won't they! Especially Brother Daniels. Daniels will be overcome with joy. Captain, have a cigar. Have two cigars. I have begun to spend my retainer already, you see."

CHAPTER IX

THE August days were busy ones at the High Cliff House. Every room was filled and the tables in the dining-room well crowded. Thankful told Captain Bangs that she could not spare time even to look out of the window. "And yet Emily and I are about the only ones who don't look out," she added. "There's enough goin' on to look at, that's sartin."

There was indeed. Mr. E. Holliday Kendrick having taken possession of his new estate, immediately set about the improving and enlarging which Mr. Daniels had quoted him as contemplating. Carpenters, painters and gardeners were at work daily. The Kendrick motor cars and the Kendrick servants were much in evidence along East Wellmouth's main road. What had been done by the great man and his employees and what would be done in the near future kept the gossips busy. He was planning a new rose garden—"the finest from Buzzard's Bay down"; he had torn out the "whole broadside" of the music-room and was "cal'latin'" to make it twice as large as formerly; he was to build a large conservatory on the knoll by the stables. Hannah Parker declared she could not see the need of this. "There's a tower onto the main buildin' already," she said, "pretty nigh as high as a lighthouse. I should think a body could see fur enough from that tower, without riggin' up a conservatory. Well, Mrs. Kendrick needn't ask ME to go up in it. I went to the top of the conservatory on Scargo Hill one time and I was so dizzy in the head I thought sure I'd fall right over the railin'."

The High Cliff boarders—Miss Timpson and Caleb Hammond especially—spent a great deal of time peering from the living-room windows and watching what they called the "goin's on" at the Kendrick estate. Occasionally they caught a glimpse of E. Holliday himself. The great man was inclined to greatness even in the physical meaning of the word, for he was tall and stout, and dignified, not to say pompous. Arrayed in white flannels he issued orders to his hirelings and the hirelings obeyed him. When one is monarch of the larger portion of all he surveys it must be gratifying to feel that one looks the part. E. Holliday looked it and apparently felt it.

Thankful, during this, her most prosperous season, was active from morning until night. When that night came she was ready for sleep, ready for more than she could afford to take. Emily was invaluable as manager and assistant, and Captain Obed Bangs assisted and advised in every way that he could. The captain had come to be what Mrs. Barnes called the "sheet anchor" of the High Cliff House. Whenever the advice of a man, or a man's help was needed, it was to Captain Bangs that she turned. And Captain Obed was always only too glad to help. Hannah Parker declared he spent more time at the boarding house than he did at her home.

If Emily Howes noticed how frequently the captain called—and it is probable that she did—she said nothing about it. John Kendrick must have noticed it, for occasionally, when he and Captain Obed were alone, he made an irrelevant remark like the following:

"Captain," he said, on one occasion, "I think you're growing younger every day."

"Who? Me? Go on, John! How you talk! I'm so old my timbers creak every time I go up a flight of stairs. They'll be sendin' me to the junk pile pretty soon."

"I guess not. You're as young as I am, every bit. Not in years, perhaps, but in spirit and energy. And you surprise me, too. I didn't know you were such a lady's man."

"Me? A lady's man? Tut, tut! Don't talk foolish. If I've cruised alone all these years I cal'late that's proof enough of how much a lady's man I am."

"That's no proof. You haven't happened upon the right sort of consort, that's all. Look at Brother Daniels; he is a bachelor, too, but everyone knows what a lady's man he is."

"Humph! You ain't comparin' me to Heman Daniels, are you?"

"No. No, of course not. I shouldn't dare. Comparing any mortal with Daniels would be heresy, wouldn't it? But you certainly are popular with the fair sex. Why, even Imogene has fallen under the influence. She says Mrs. Barnes thinks you are the finest man in the world."

"She does, hey? Well," tartly, "she better mind her own affairs. I thought she rated Kenelm Parker about as high as anybody these days. He spends more time in that kitchen of hers—"

"There, there, Captain! Don't sidestep. The fair Imogene may be susceptible to Mr. Parker's charms, but that is probably because you haven't smiled upon her. If you—"

"Say, look here, John Kendrick! If you keep on talkin' loony in this way I'll begin to heave out a few hints myself. I may be as popular as you say, with Imogene and—and the help, but I know somebody else that is catchin' the same disease."

"Meaning Mr. Daniels, I suppose? He is popular, I admit."

"Is he? Well, you ought to know best. Seems to me I can call to mind somebody else that is fairly popular—in some latitudes. By the way, John, you don't seem to be as popular with Heman as you was at first."

"I'm sorry. My accepting my cousin's retainer may—"

"Oh, I didn't mean that. What was you and Emily doin' at Chris Badger's store yesterday afternoon?"

"Doing? Yesterday? Oh, yes! I did meet Miss Howes while I was on my way to the office and I waited while she did a little marketing. What in the world—"

"Nothin'. Fur's that goes I don't think either of you knew you was IN the world. I passed right by and you didn't see me. Heman saw you, too. What was your marketin'—vegetables?"

"I believe so. Captain, you're sidestepping again. It was of you, not me, I was speaking when—"

"Yes, I know. Well, I'm speakin' about you now. Heman saw you buyin' them vegetables. Tomatters, wa'n't they?"

"Perhaps so. Have you been drinking? What difference does it make whether we bought tomatoes or potatoes?"

"Didn't make none—to me. But I bet Heman didn't like to see you two buyin' tomatters."

"For heaven's sake, why not?"

"Oh, 'cause he probably remembered, same as I did, what folks used to call 'em in the old days."

"You HAVE been drinking! What did they use to call them?"

"Love apples," replied Captain Obed, and strode away chuckling. John watched him go. He, too, laughed at first, but his laugh broke off in the middle and when he went into the house his expression was troubled and serious.

One remark of the captain's was true enough; John Kendrick's popularity with his professional rival was growing daily less. The pair were scrupulously polite to each other, but they seldom spoke except when others were present, and Mr. Daniels made it a point apparently to be present whenever Miss Howes was in the room. He continued to bring his little offerings of fruit and flowers and his invitations for drives and picnics and entertainments at the town hall were more frequent. Sometimes Emily accepted these invitations; more often she refused them. John also occasionally invited her to drive with him or to play tennis on his cousin's courts, and these invitations she treated as she did Heman's, refusing some and accepting others. She treated the pair with impartiality and yet Thankful was growing to believe there was a difference. Imogene, outspoken, expressed her own feelings in the matter when she said,

"Miss Emily likes Mr. Kendrick pretty well, don't she, ma'am?"

Thankful regarded her maidservant with disapproval.

"What makes you say that, Imogene?" she demanded. "Of course she likes him. Why shouldn't she?"

"She should, ma'am. And she does, too. And he likes her; that's plain enough."

"Imogene, what are you hintin' at? Do you mean that my cousin is in—in love with Mr. John Kendrick?"

"No'm. I don't say that, not yet. But there's signs that—"

"Signs! If you don't get those ridiculous story-book notions out of your head I don't know what I'll do to you. What do you know about folks bein' in love? You ain't in love, I hope; are you?"

Imogene hesitated. "No, ma'am," she replied. "I ain't. But—but maybe I might be, if I wanted to."

"For mercy sakes! The girl's crazy. You MIGHT be—if you wanted to! Who with? If you're thinkin' of marryin' anybody seems to me I ought to know it. Why, you ain't met more'n a dozen young fellers in this town, and I've taken good care to know who they were. If you're thinkin' of fallin' in love—or marryin'—"

Imogene interrupted. "I ain't," she declared. "And, anyhow, ma'am, gettin' married don't necessarily mean you're in love."

"It don't! Well, this beats all I ever—"

"No, ma'am, it don't. Sometimes it's a person's duty to get married."

Thankful gasped. "Duty!" she repeated. "You HAVE been readin' more of those books, in spite of your promisin' me you wouldn't."

"No, ma'am, I ain't. Honest, I ain't."

"Then what do you mean? Imogene, what man do you care enough for to make you feel it's your—your duty to marry him?"

"No man at all," declared Imogene, promptly and decisively. And that is all she would say on the subject.

Thankful repeated this astonishing conversation, or part of it, to Emily. The latter considered it a good joke. "That girl is a strange creature," she said, "and great fun. You never can tell what she will say or think. She is very romantic and that nonsense about duty and the rest of it undoubtedly is taken from some story she has read. You needn't worry, Auntie. Imogene worships you, and she will never leave you—to be married, or for any other reason."

So Thankful did not worry about Imogene. She had other worries, those connected with a houseful of boarders, and these were quite sufficient. And now came another. Kenelm Parker was threatening to leave her employ.

The statement is not strictly true. Kenelm, himself, never threatened to do anything. But another person did the threatening for him and that person was his sister. Hannah Parker, for some unaccountable reason, seemed to be developing a marked prejudice against the High Cliff House. Her visits to the premises were not less frequent than formerly, but they were confined to the yard and stable; she no longer called at the house. Her manner toward Emily and Thankful was cordial enough perhaps, but there was constraint in it and she asked a good many questions concerning her brother's hours of labor, what he did during the day, and the like.

"She acts awful queer, seems to me," said Thankful. "Not the way she did at first at all. In the beginnin' I had to plan pretty well to keep her from runnin' in and sp'ilin' my whole mornin' with her talk. Now she seems to be keepin' out of my way. What we've done to make her act so I can't see, and neither can Emily."

Captain Bangs, to whom this remark was addressed, laughed.

"You ain't done anything, I guess," he said. "It ain't you she's down on; it's your hired girl, the Imogene one. She seems to be more down on that Imogene than a bow anchor on a mud flat. They don't hitch horses, those two. You see she tries to boss and condescend and Imogene gives her as good as she sends. It's got so that Hannah is actually scared of that girl; don't pretend to be, of course; calls her 'the inmate' and all sorts of names. But she is scared of her and don't like her."

Thankful was troubled. "I'm sorry," she said. "Imogene is independent, but she's an awful kind-hearted girl. I do hate trouble amongst neighbors."

"Oh, there won't be any trouble. Hannah's jealous, that's all the trouble—jealous about Kenelm. You see, she wanted him to come here to work so's she could have him under her thumb and run over and give him orders every few minutes. Imogene gives him orders, too, and he minds; she makes him. Hannah don't like that; 'cordin' to her notion Kenelm hadn't ought to have any skipper but her. It's all right, though, Mrs. Barnes. It's good for Kenelm and it's good for Hannah. Do 'em both good, I cal'late."

But when Kenelm announced that he wasn't sure but that he should "heave up his job" in a fortnight or so, the situation became more serious.

"He mustn't leave," declared Thankful. "August and early September are the times when I've got to have a man on the place, and you say yourself, Captain Bangs, that there isn't another man to be had just now. If he goes—"

"Oh, he won't go. This is more of Hannah's talk; she's put him up to this leavin' business. Offer him another dollar a week, if you have to, and I'll do some preachin' to Hannah, myself."

When Thankful mentioned the matter to Imogene the latter's comment was puzzling but emphatic.

"Don't you fret, ma'am," she said. "He ain't left yet."

"I know; but he says—"

"HE don't say it. It's that sister of his does all the sayin'. And SHE ain't workin' for you that I know of."

"Now, Imogene, we mustn't, any of us, interfere between Kenelm and his sister. She IS his sister, you know."

"Yes'm. But she isn't his mother and his grandmother and his aunt and all his relations. And, if she was, 'twouldn't make no difference. He's the one to say whether he's goin' to leave or not."

"But he does say it. That is, he—"

"He just says he 'cal'lates.' He never said he was GOIN' to do anything; not for years, anyhow. It's all right, Mrs. Thankful. You just wait and see. If worst comes to worst I've got a—"

She stopped short. "What have you got, Imogene?" asked Mrs. Barnes.

"Oh, nothin', ma'am. Only you just wait."

So Thankful waited and Kenelm, perfectly aware of the situation, and backed by the counsel of his sister, became daily more independent. He did only such work as he cared to do and his hours for arriving and departing were irregular, to say the least.

On the last Thursday, Friday and Saturday of August the Ostable County Cattle Show and Fair was to be held at the county seat. The annual Cattle Show is a big event on the Cape and practically all of East Wellmouth was planning to attend. Most of the High Cliff boarders were going to the Fair and, Friday being the big day, they were going on Friday. Imogene asked for a holiday on that day. The request was granted. Then Kenelm announced that he and Hannah were cal'latin' to go. Thankful was somewhat reluctant; she felt that to be deprived of the services of both her hired man and maid on the same day might be troublesome. But as the Parker announcement was more in the nature of an ultimatum than a request, she said yes under protest. But when Captain Obed appeared and invited her and John Kendrick and Emily Howes to go to the Fair with him in a hired motor car she was more troubled than ever.

"I'd like to go, Cap'n," she said. "Oh, I WOULD like to go! I haven't had a day off since this place opened and I never rode in an automobile more'n three times in my life. But I can't do it. You and Emily and John can, of course, and you must; but I've got to stay here. Some of the boarders will be here for their meals and I can't leave the house alone."

Captain Obed uttered a dismayed protest.

"Sho!" he exclaimed. "Sho! That's too bad. Why, I counted more on your goin' than—Humph! You've just got to go, that's all. Can't Imogene look after the house?"

"She could if she was goin' to be here, but she's goin' to the Fair herself. I promised her she could and I must keep my promise."

"Yes, yes; I presume likely you must. But now, Mrs. Thankful—"

"I'm afraid there can't be any 'but,' Cap'n. You and Mr. Kendrick and Emily go and I'll get my fun thinkin' what a good time you'll have."

She was firm and at last the captain yielded. But his keen disappointment was plainly evident. He said but little during his stay at the boarding-house and went home early, glum and disconsolate. At the Parker domicile he found Kenelm and his sister in a heated argument.

"I don't care, Hannah," vowed Kenelm. "I'm a-goin' to that Fair, no matter if I do have to go alone. Didn't you tell me I was goin'? Didn't you put me up to askin' for the day off? Didn't you—"

"Never mind what I did. I give in I had planned for you to go, but that was when I figgered on you and me goin' together. Now that Mr. Hammond has invited me to go along with him—"

Captain Obed interrupted. "Hello! Hello!" he exclaimed. "What's this? Has Caleb Hammond offered to go gallivantin' off to the Ostable Cattle Show along with you, Hannah? Well, well! Wonders'll never cease. Caleb's gettin' gay in his old age, ain't he? Humph! there'll be somethin' else for the postoffice gang to talk about, first thing you know. Hannah, I'm surprised!"

Miss Parker colored and seemed embarrassed. Her brother, however, voiced his disgust.

"Surprised!" he repeated. "Huh! That's nuthin' to what I am. I'm more'n surprised—I'm paralyzed. To think of that tightfisted old fool lettin' go of money enough to hire a horse and team and—"

"Kenelm!" Hannah's voice quivered with indignation. "Kenelm Parker! The idea!"

"Yes, that's what I say, the idea! Here's an old critter—yes, he is old, too. He's so nigh seventy he don't dast look at the almanac for fear he'll find it's past his birthday. And he's always been so tight with money that he'd buy second-hand postage stamps if the Gov'ment wouldn't catch him. And his wife's been dead a couple of hundred year, more or less, and yet, by thunder-mighty, all to once he starts in—"

"Kenelm Parker, you stop this minute! I'm ashamed of you. Mr. Hammond's a real, nice, respectable man. As to his money—well, that's his business anyhow, and, besides, he ain't hirin' the horse and buggy; he's goin' to borrow it off his nephew over to the Centre. His askin' me to go is a real neighborly act."

"Huh! If he's so plaguy neighborly why don't he ask me to go, too? I'm as nigh a neighbor as you be, ain't I?"

"He don't ask you because the buggy won't hold but two, and you know it. I should think you'd be glad to have me save the expense of my fare. Winnie S. would charge me fifty cents to take me to the depot, and the fare on the excursion train is—"

"Now what kind of talk's that! I ain't complainin' 'cause you save the expense. And I don't care if you go along with all the old men from here to Joppa. What I'm sayin' is that I'm goin' to that Fair tomorrow. I can go alone in the cars, I guess. There won't nobody kidnap me, as I know of."

"But, Kenelm, I don't like to have you over there all by yourself. It'll be so lonesome for you. If you'll only wait maybe I'll go again, myself. Maybe we could both go together on Saturday."

"I don't want to go Saturday; I want to go tomorrow. Tomorrow's the big day, when they have the best horse-racin'. Why, Darius Holt is cal'latin' to make money tomorrow. He's got ten dollars bet on Exie B. in the second race and—"

"Kenelm Parker! Is THAT what you want to go to that Cattle Show for? To bet on horse trots! To gamble!"

"Aw, dry up. How'd I gamble? You don't let me have money enough to put in the collection box Sundays, let alone gamblin'. I have to shove my fist clear way down to the bottom of the plate whenever they pass it for fear Heman Daniels'll see that I'm only lettin' go of a nickel. Aw, Hannah, have some sense, won't you! I'd just as soon go to that Fair alone as not. I won't be lonesome. Lots of folks I know are goin'; men and women, too."

"Women? What women?"

"Oh, I don't know. How should I know?"

"Well—well, I suppose likely they are. Imogene said she was goin' and—"

"Imogene! You mean that hired inmate over to Thankful Barnes'? Humph! So she told you she was goin', hey? Well, most likely she told a fib. I wouldn't trust her not to; sassy, impudent thing! I don't believe she's goin' at all. Is she, Cap'n

Bangs?"

The captain, who had remained silent during this family jar, could not resist the temptation.

"Oh yes, Imogene's goin'," he answered, cheerfully. "She's countin' on havin' the time of her life over there. But she isn't the only one. Why, about all the females in East Wellmouth'll be there. I heard Abbie Larkin arrangin' for her passage with Winnie S. yesterday afternoon. Win said, 'Judas priest!' He didn't know where he was goin' to put her, but he cal'lated he'd have to find stowage room somewhere. Oh, Kenelm won't be lonesome, Hannah. I shouldn't worry about that."

Kenelm looked as if he wished the speaker might choke. Hannah straightened in her chair.

"Hum!" she mused. "Hum!" and was silent for a moment. Then she asked:

"Is Mrs. Thankful goin', too? I suppose likely she is."

The captain's cheerfulness vanished.

"No," he said, shortly, "she isn't. She wanted to, but she doesn't feel she can leave the boardin'-house with nobody to look after it."

Miss Parker seemed pleased, for some reason or other.

"I don't wonder," she said, heartily. "She shouldn't be left all alone herself, either. If that ungrateful, selfish Orphan's Home minx is selfish enough to go and leave her, all the more reason my brother shouldn't. Whatever else us Parkers may be, we ain't selfish. We think about others. Kenelm, dear, you must stay at work and help Mrs. Barnes around the house tomorrow. You and I'll go to the Fair on Saturday. I don't mind; I'd just as soon go twice as not."

Kenelm sprang to his feet. He was so angry that he stuttered.

"You—you—YOU don't care!" he shouted. "'Cause you're goin' TWICE! That's a divil of a don't care, that is!"

"Kenelm! My own brother! Cursin' and swearin'!"

"I ain't, and—and I don't care if I be! What's the matter with you, Hannah Parker? One minute you're sailin' into me tellin' me to heave up my job and not demean myself doin' odd jobs in a boardin'-house barn. And the next minute you're tellin' me I ought to stay to home and—and help out that very boardin'-house. I won't! By—by thunder-mighty, I won't! I'm goin' to that Cattle Show tomorrow if it takes my last cent."

Hannah smiled. "How many last cents have you got, Kenelm?" she asked. "You was doin' your best to borrer a quarter of me this mornin'."

"I've got more'n you have. I—I—everything there is here—yes, and every cent there is here—belongs to me by rights. You ain't got nothin' of your own."

Miss Parker turned upon him. "To think," she wailed, brokenly, "to think that my own brother—all the brother I've got—can stand afore me and heave my—my poverty in my face. I may be dependent on him. I am, I suppose. But Oh, the disgrace of it! the—Oh! Oh! Oh!"

Captain Obed hurried upstairs to his room. Long after he had shut the door he heard the sounds of Hannah's sobs and Kenelm's pleadings that he "never meant nothin'." Then came silence and, at last, the sounds of footsteps on the stairs. They halted in the upper hall.

"I don't know, Kenelm," said Hannah, sadly. "I'll try to forgive you. I presume likely I must. But when I think of how I've been a mother to you—"

"Now, Hannah, there you go again. How could you be my mother when you ain't but four year older'n I be? You just give me a few dollars and let me go to that Cattle Show and—"

"No, Kenelm, that I can't do. You are goin' to leave Mrs. Barnes' place; I want you to do that, for the sake of your self-respect. But you must stay there and help her tomorrow. It's your duty."

"Darn my duty! I'll LEAVE tomorrow, that's what I'll do."

"Oh dear! There you go again. Profane language and bettin' on horses! WHAT'LL come next? My own brother a gambler and a prodigate! Has it come to this?"

The footsteps and voices died away. Captain Obed blew out the light and got into bed. The last words he heard that night were uttered by the "prodigate" himself on his way to his sleeping quarters. And they were spoken as a soliloquy.

"By time!" muttered Kenelm, as he shuffled slowly past the Captain's door. "By time! I—I'll do somethin' desperate!"

Next morning, when Captain Obed's hired motor car, with its owner, a Wellmouth Centre man, acting as chauffeur, rolled into the yard of the High Cliff House, a party of three came out to meet it. John Kendrick and Emily Howes were of the party and they were wrapped and ready for the trip. The captain had expected them; but the third, also dressed for the journey, was Mrs. Thankful Barnes.

Thankful's plump countenance was radiant.

"I'm goin' after all," she announced. "I'm goin' to the Fair with you, Cap'n Bangs. Now what do you think of that? . . . That is," she added, looking at the automobile, "if you can find a place to put me."

The captain's joy was as great as his surprise. "Place to put you!" he repeated. "If I couldn't do anything else I'd hang on behind, like a youngster to a truck wagon, afore you stayed at home. Good for you, Mrs. Thankful! But how'd you come to change your mind? Thought you couldn't leave."

Thankful smiled happily. "I didn't change my mind, Cap'n," she said. "Imogene changed hers. She's a real, good sacrificin' body, the girl is. When she found I'd been asked and wouldn't go, she put her foot down flat. Nothin' would do but she should stay at home today and I should go. I knew what a disappointment 'twas to her, but she just made me do it. She'll go tomorrow instead; that's the way we fixed it finally. I'm awful glad for myself, but I do feel mean about Imogene, just the same."

A few minutes later, the auto, with John, Emily and Thankful on the rear seat and Captain Obed in front with the driver, rolled out of the yard and along the sandy road toward Wellmouth Centre. About a mile from the latter village it passed a buggy with two people in it. The pair in the buggy were Caleb Hammond and Hannah Parker.

Captain Obed chuckled. "There go the sweethearts," he observed. "Handsome young couple, ain't they?"

The other occupants of the car joined in the laugh. Emily, in particular, was greatly amused.

"Why do you call them sweethearts, Captain?" she asked. "You don't really suppose—"

The captain burst into a laugh.

"What? Those two?" he said. "No, no, I was only jokin'. I don't know about Hannah—single women her age are kind of chancey—but I do know Caleb. He ain't takin' a wife to support, not unless she can support him. He had a chance to use a horse and buggy free for nothin', that's all; and it would be against his principles to let a chance like that go by. Cal'late he took Hannah 'cause he knew ice cream and peanuts don't agree with her dyspepsy and so he wouldn't have to buy any. Ho, ho! I wonder how Kenelm made out? Wonder if he went on his own hook, after all?"

In the kitchen of the High Cliff House Imogene was washing the breakfast dishes and trying to forget her disappointment. A step sounded in the woodshed and, turning, she beheld Mr. Parker. He saw her at the same time and the surprise was mutual.

"Why, hello!" exclaimed Imogene. "I thought you'd gone to the Fair."

"Hello!" cried Kenelm. "Thought you'd gone to the Cattle Show."

Explanations followed. "What ARE you cal'latin' to do, then?" demanded Kenelm, moodily.

"Me? Stay here on my job, of course. That's what you're goin' to do, too, ain't it?"

Mr. Parker thrust his hands into his pockets.

"No, by time, I ain't!" he declared, fiercely. "I ain't got any job no more. I've quit, I have."

"Quit! You mean you ain't goin' to work for Mrs. Thankful?"

"I ain't gain' to work for nobody. Why should I? I've got money enough to live on, ain't I? I've got an income of my own. I ain't told Mrs. Thankful yet, but I have quit, just the same."

Imogene put down the dishcloth.

"This is your sister's doin's, I guess likely," she observed.

"No, it ain't! If—if it was, by time, I wouldn't do it! Hannah treats me like a dog—yes, sir, like a dog. I'm goin' to show her. A man's got some feelin's, if he is a dog."

"How are you goin' to show her?"

"I don't know, but I be. I'll run away, if I can't do nothin' else. I'll show her I'm sick of her bossin'."

Imogene seemed to be thinking. She regarded Mr. Parker with a steady and reflective stare.

"What are you lookin' at me like that for?" demanded Kenelm, after the stare had become unbearable.

"I was thinkin'. Humph! What would you do to fix it so's your sister would stop her bossin' and you could have your own way once in a while?"

"Do? By time, I'd do anything! Anything, by thunder-mighty!"

"You would? You mean it?"

"You bet I mean it!"

"Would you promise to stay right here and work for Mrs. Thankful as long as she wanted you to?"

"Course I would. I ain't anxious to leave. It's Hannah that's got that notion. Fust she was dead sot on my workin' here and now she's just as sot on my leavin'."

"Do you know why she's so—what do you call it?—sot?"

Kenelm fidgeted and looked foolish. "Well," he admitted, "I—I wouldn't won-der if 'twas account of you, Imogene. Hannah knows I—I like you fust rate, that we're good friends, I mean. She's—well, consarn it all!—she's jealous, that's what's the matter. She's awful silly that way. I can't so much as look at a woman, but she acts like a plumb idiot. Take that Abbie Larkin, for instance. One time she—ho, ho! I did kind of get ahead of her then, though."

Imogene nodded. "Yes," she said; "I heard about that. Well, maybe you can get ahead of her again. You wait a minute."

She went into the living-room. When she came back she had an ink-bottle, a pen and a sheet of note-paper in her hands.

"What's them things for?" demanded Mr. Kenelm.

"I'll tell you pretty soon. Kenelm, you—you asked me somethin' a while ago, didn't you?"

Kenelm started. "Why—why, Imogene," he stammered, "I—I don't know's I know what you mean."

"I guess you know, all right. You did ask me—or, anyhow, you would if I hadn't said no before you had the chance. You like me pretty well, don't you, Kenelm?"

This pointed question seemed to embarrass Mr. Parker greatly. He turned red and glanced at the door.

"Why—why, yes, I like you fust rate, Imogene," he admitted. "I—I don't know's I ever see anybody I liked better. But when it comes to—You see, that time when I said—er—er what I said I was kind of—of desperate along of Hannah and—"

"Well, you're desperate now, ain't you? Here," sharply, "you sit still and let me finish. I've got a plan and you'd better listen to it. Kenelm, won't you sit still, for—for my sake?"

The "big day" of the Ostable County Cattle Show and Fair came to an end as all days, big or little, have to come. Captain Obed Bangs and his guests enjoyed every minute of it. They inspected the various exhibits, witnessed the horse races and the baseball game, saw the balloon ascension, and thrilled with the rest of the great crowd at the "parachute drop." It was six o'clock when they left the Fair grounds and Thankful began to worry about the condition of affairs at the High Cliff House.

"It'll be way past dinner time when you and I get there, Emily," she said, "and goodness knows what my boarders have had to eat. Imogene's smart and capable enough, but whether she can handle everything alone I don't know. We ought to have started sooner, but it's nobody's fault more'n mine that we didn't."

However, when the High Cliff House was reached its proprietor found that her fears were groundless. But a few of the boarders had planned to eat their evening meal there; most of the city contingent were stopping at various teahouses and restaurants in Ostable or along the road and would not be home until late.

"Everything's fine, ma'am," declared Imogene. "There was only three or four here for supper and I fixed them all right. Mr. Hammond came in late, but I fed him up and he's gone to bed. Tired out, I guess. I asked him if he had a good time and he said he had, but it cost him a sight of money."

Captain Obed laughed. "Caleb will have to do without his mornin' newspapers for quite a spell to make up for today's extravagance," he declared. "That's what 'tis to take the girls around. Better take warnin', John."

John Kendrick smiled. "Considering," he said, "that you and I have almost come to blows before I was permitted to even buy a package of popcorn with my own money, I think you need the warning more than I, Cap'n Bangs."

"Imogene," said Thankful, "you've been a real, nice girl today; you've helped me out a lot and I shan't forget it. Now you go to bed and rest, so's to feel like gettin' an early start for the Fair tomorrow."

Imogene shook her head. "I can't go right now, thank you, ma'am," she said. "I've got company."

Emily and Thankful looked at each other.

"Company!" repeated the former. "What company?"

Before Imogene could answer the dining-room door was flung open and Hannah Parker rushed in. She was still arrayed in her Sunday gown, which she had donned in honor of Fair Day, but her Sunday bonnet was, as Captain Obed said afterward, "canted down to leeward" and her general appearance indicated alarm and apprehension.

"Why, Hannah!" exclaimed Thankful. "Why, Miss Parker, what's the matter?"

Hannah's glance swept the group before her; then it fastened upon Imogene.

"Where's my brother?" she demanded. "Have you seen my brother?"

Captain Bangs broke in.

"Your brother? Kenelm?" he asked. "Why, what about Kenelm? Ain't he to home?"

"No. No, he ain't. And he ain't been home, either. I left a cold supper for him on the table, and I put the teapot on the rack of the stove ready for him to bile. But he ain't been there. It ain't been touched. I—I can't think what—"

Imogene interrupted. "Your brother's all right, Miss Parker," she said, calmly. "He's been havin' supper with me out in the kitchen. He's there now. He's the company I said I had, Mrs. Thankful."

Hannah stared at her. Imogene returned the gaze coolly, blandly and with a serene air of confident triumph.

"Perhaps you'd better come out and see him, ma'am," she went on. "He—we, that is—have got somethin' to tell you. The rest can come, too, if they want to," she added. "It's nothin' we want to keep from you."

Hannah Parker pushed by her and rushed for the kitchen. Imogene followed her and the others followed Imogene. As Thankful said, describing her own feelings, "I couldn't have stayed behind if I wanted to. My feet had curiosity enough to go by themselves."

Kenelm, who had been sitting by the kitchen table before a well-filled plate, had heard his sister's approach and had risen. When Mrs. Barnes and the others reached the kitchen he had backed into a corner.

"Kenelm Parker," demanded Hannah, "what are you doin' here, this time of night?"

"I—I been eatin' supper," stammered Kenelm, "but I—I'm through now."

"Through! Didn't you know your supper was waitin' for you at home? Didn't I tell you to come home early and have MY supper ready? Didn't—"

Imogene interrupted. "I guess you did, ma'am," she said, "but you see I asked him to stay here, so he stayed."

"YOU asked him! And he stayed! Well, I must say! Kenelm, have you been eatin' supper alone with that—with that—"

She was too greatly agitated to finish, but as Kenelm did not answer, Imogene did, without waiting.

"Yes'm," she said, soothingly. "It's all right. Kenelm and me can eat together, if we want to, I guess. We're engaged."

"ENGAGED!" Almost everyone said it—everyone except Hannah; she could not say anything.

"Yes," replied Imogene. "We're engaged to be married. We are, aren't we, Kenelm?"

Kenelm tried to back away still further, but the wall was behind him and he could only back against it. He was pale and he swallowed several times.

"Kenelm, dear," said Imogene, "didn't you hear me? Tell your sister about our bein' engaged."

Kenelm's mouth opened and shut. "Eh—eh—" he stammered. "I—I—"

"Don't be bashful," urged Imogene. "We're engaged to be married, ain't we?"

Mr. Parker gulped, choked and then nodded. "Yes," he admitted, faintly. "I—I cal'late we be."

His sister took a step forward, her arm raised. Captain Obed stepped in front of her.

"Just a minute, Hannah! Heave to! Come up into the wind a jiffy. Let's get this thing straight. Kenelm, do you mean—"

The gentleman addressed seemed to mean very little, just then. But Imogene's coolness was quite unruffled and again she answered for him.

"He means just what he said," she declared, "and what he said was plain enough, I should think. I don't know why there should be so much row about it. Mr. Parker and I have been good friends ever since I come here to work. He's asked me to marry him some time or other and I said maybe I would. That makes us engaged, same's I've been tryin' to tell you. And what all this row is about I can't see. It's our business, ain't it? I can't see as it's anybody else's."

But Hannah was by this time beyond holding back. She pushed aside the captain's arm and faced the engaged couple. Her eyes flashed and her fingers twitched.

"You—you designin' critter you!" she shouted, addressing Imogene. "You plannin', schemin', underhanded—"

"Shh! shh!" put in Captain Obed. "Easy, Hannah! easy, there!"

"I shan't be easy! You mind your own affairs, Obed Bangs! Kenelm Parker, how dare you say—how dare you tell me you're goin' to marry this—this INMATE? What do you mean by it?"

Poor Kenelm only gurgled. His lady love once more came to his rescue.

"He's told you times enough what he means," she asserted, firmly. "And I'll thank you not to call me names, either. In the first place I won't stand it; and, in the second, if you and me are goin' to be sisters-in-law, we'd better learn how to get along peaceable together. I—"

"Don't you talk to me! Don't you DARE talk to me! I might have expected it! I did expect it. So this is why you two didn't go to the Fair? You had this all planned between you. I was to be got out of the way, and—"

"That's enough of that, too. There wasn't any plannin' about it—not until to-day, anyhow. I didn't know he wasn't goin' to the Fair and he didn't know I wasn't. He would have gone only—only you deserted him to go off with your own—your own gentleman friend. Humph! I should think you would look ashamed!"

Miss Parker's "shame"—or her feelings, whatever they might be—seemed to render her speechless. Her brother saw his chance.

"You know that's just what you done, Hannah," he put in, pleadingly. "You know you did. I was so lonesome—"

"Hush! Hush, Kenelm!" ordered Imogene. "You left him alone to go with another man, Miss Parker. For all he knew you might be—be runnin' off to be married, or somethin'. So he come to where he had a friend, that's all. And what if he did? He can get married, if he wants to, can't he? I'd like to know who'd stop him. He's over twenty-one, I guess."

This speech was too much for Emily; she laughed aloud. That laugh was the final straw. Hannah made a dive for her brother.

"You come home with me," she commanded. "You come right straight home with me this minute. As for you," she added, turning to Imogene, "I shan't waste any more words on a—on a thing like you. After my brother's money, be you? Thought you'd get him and it, too, did you? Well, you shan't! He'll come right along home with me and there he'll stay. He's worked in this place as long as he's goin' to,

Miss Inmate. I'll take him out of YOUR clutches."

"Oh no, you won't! Him and me are goin' to the Fair tomorrow and on Monday he's comin' back to work here same as ever. You are, ain't you, Kenelm?"

Kenelm gulped and fidgeted. "I—I—I—" he stuttered.

"You see, Hannah," continued Imogene—"I suppose I might as well begin to call you 'Hannah,' seein' as we're goin' to be relations pretty soon—you see, he's engaged to me now and he'll do what I ask him to, of course."

"Engaged! He ain't engaged! I'll fix the 'engagement.' That'll be broke off this very minute."

And now Imogene played her best trump. She took from her waist a slip of paper and handed it to Captain Obed.

"Just read that out loud, won't you, please, Cap'n Bangs?" she asked.

The captain stared at the slip of paper. Then, in a choked voice, he read aloud the following:

I, Kenelm Issachar Parker, being in sound mind and knowing what I am doing, ask Imogene to be my wife and I agree to marry her any time she wants me to.

(Signed) KENELM ISSACHAR PARKER.

"There!" exclaimed Imogene. "I guess that settles it, don't it? I've got witnesses, anyhow, and right here, to our engagement. You all heard us both say we was engaged. But that paper settles it. Kenelm and I knew mighty well that you'd try to break off the engagement and say there wasn't any; but you can't break THAT."

"I can't? I like to know why I can't! What do you suppose I care for such a—a—"

"Well, if you don't, then the law does. If you make your brother break his engagement to me, Hannah Parker, I'll take that piece of paper right to a lawyer and make him sue Kenelm for—for breach of promises. You know what that means, I guess, if you've read the papers same as I have. I rather guess that paper would give me a good many dollars damage. If you don't believe it you try and see. And there's two lawyers livin' right in this house," she added triumphantly.

If she expected a sensation her expectations were realized. Hannah was again stricken dumb. Captain Bangs and Emily and John Kendrick looked at each other, then the captain doubled up with laughter. Mrs. Barnes and Kenelm, however, did not laugh. The latter seemed tremendously surprised.

"Why—why, Imogene," he protested, "how you talk! I never thought—"

"Kenelm, be still."

"But, Imogene," begged Thankful, "you mustn't say such things. I never—"

"Now, ma'am, please don't you butt in. I know what I'm doin'. Please don't talk to me now. There, Kenelm," turning to the trembling nominee for matrimonial offices, "that'll do for tonight. You go along with your sister and be on hand ready to take me to the Cattle Show tomorrow. Good night—er—dear."

Whether it was the "dear" that goaded Miss Parker into one more assault, or whether she was not yet ready to surrender, is uncertain. But, at all events, she fired a last broadside.

"He SHAN'T go with you tomorrow," she shrieked. "He shan't; I won't let him."

Imogene nodded. "All right," she said, firmly. "Then if he don't I'll come around tomorrow and tell him I'm ready to be married right away. And if he says no to THAT—then—well then, I'll go straight to the lawyer with that paper."

Ten minutes later, when the Parkers had gone and the sound of Hannah's tirade and Kenelm's protestations had died away on the path toward their home, Thankful, John and Captain Obed sat gazing at each other in the living room. Imogene and Emily were together in the kitchen. The "engaged" young lady had expressed a desire to speak with Miss Howes alone.

John and the captain were still chuckling, but Thankful refused to see the joke; she was almost in tears.

"It's dreadful!" she declared. "Perfectly awful! And Imogene! To act and speak so to our next-door neighbor! What WILL come of it? And how COULD she? How could she get engaged to THAT man, of all men? He's old enough to be her father and—and she CAN'T care for him."

Emily entered the room. She was apparently much agitated and her eyes were moist. She collapsed in a rocking-chair and put her handkerchief to her face.

"Land sakes!" cried Captain Obed. "Is it as bad as that? Does it make you cry?"

Emily removed the handkerchief. "I'm not crying," she gasped. "I—I—Oh dear! This is the funniest thing that girl has done yet."

"But what is it?" asked John. "What's the answer? We're dying to know."

Emily shook her head. "I can't tell you," she said. "I promised I wouldn't. It—it all came of a talk Imogene and I had a while ago. We were speaking of self-sacrifice and she—she adores you, Auntie, and—"

Thankful interrupted. "Mercy on us!" she cried. "Adores me! Self-sacrifice! She ain't doin' this crazy, loony thing for ME, I hope. She ain't marryin' that Parker man because—"

"She hasn't married anyone yet. Oh, it is all right, Auntie; she knows what she is doing, or she thinks she does. And, at any rate, I think there is no danger of Mr. Parker's giving up his situation here until you are ready to have him do it. There! I mustn't say another word. I have said too much already."

Captain Obed rose to his feet.

"Well," he said, "it's too thick off the bows for me to see more'n a foot; I give in to that. But I will say this: If that Imogene girl don't know what she's up to it's the fust time since I've been acquainted with her. And she sartin has spiked Hannah's guns. Either Hannah's got to say 'dum' when Imogene says 'dee' or she stands a chance to lose her brother or his money, one or t'other, and she'd rather lose the fust than the last, I'll bet you. Ho, ho! Yes, it does look as if Imogene had Hannah in a clove hitch. . . . Well, I'm goin' over to see what the next doin's in the circus is liable to be. I wouldn't miss any of THIS show for no money. Good night."

CHAPTER X

THE next morning Kenelm, arrayed in his best, was early on hand to escort the lady of his choice to the Fair. The lady, herself, was ready and the pair drove away in Winnie S.'s depot-wagon bound for Wellmouth Centre and the train. Before she left the house Imogene made an earnest request.

"If you don't mind, ma'am," she said, addressing Mrs. Barnes, "I wish you wouldn't say nothin' to nobody about Mr. Kenelm and me bein' engaged. And just ask the rest of 'em that heard the—the rough-house last night not to say anything, either, please."

"Why, Imogene," said Thankful, "I didn't know you wanted it to be a secret. Seems to me you said yourself that it wasn't any secret."

"Yes'm, I know I did. Well, I suppose 'tain't, in one way. But there ain't any use in advertisin' it, neither. Kenelm, he's promised to keep still."

"But, Imogene, why? Seems to me if I was willin' to be engaged to that—to Kenelm, I wouldn't be ashamed to have folks know it."

"Oh, I ain't ashamed exactly. I ain't ashamed of what I done, not a bit. Only what's the use of tellin'?"

"But you'll have to tell some time; when you're married, sartin."

"Yes'm. Well, we ain't married—yet."

"But you're goin' to be, I should presume likely."

"Maybe so; but not for a good while, anyhow. If I am it won't make any difference far's you and me are concerned, ma'am. Nor Mr. Parker, either; he'll stay here and work long's you want him, married or not. And so'll I."

"Well, I suppose that's one comfort, anyhow. I won't say anything about your engagement and I'll ask the others not to. But folks are bound to talk, Imogene. Miss Parker now—how are you goin' to stop her tellin'?"

Imogene nodded knowingly. "I shan't have to, I'll bet you, ma'am," she said. "She ain't so anxious to have it talked about—not s'long as there's a chance to break it off, she ain't. She'll keep still."

"Maybe so, but folks'll suspect, I guess. They'll think somethin's queer when you and Kenelm go to the Cattle Show together today."

"No, they won't. Why should they? Didn't Hannah Parker herself go yesterday with Mr. Hammond? And didn't Mr. Kendrick go with Miss Emily? Yes, and you with Cap'n Bangs? Lordy, ma'am, I—"

"Don't say 'Lordy,' Imogene," cautioned Thankful, and hastened away. Imogene looked after her and laughed to herself.

When Captain Obed made his morning call Mrs. Barnes told him of this conversation.

"And how is Hannah this mornin'?" asked Thankful. "I was surprised enough to see Kenelm in that depot-wagon. I never thought for a minute she'd let him go."

The captain chuckled. "Let him!" he repeated. "Why, Hannah helped him get ready; picked out his necktie for him and loaded him up with clean handkerchiefs and land knows what. She all but give him her blessin' afore he started; she did say she hoped he'd have a good time."

"She did! Mercy on us! Is the world comin' to an end? Last night she was—"

"Yes, I know. Well, we've got to give Hannah credit; she's got a head on her shoulders, even if the head does run pretty strong to mouth. Imogene's took her measure, judgin' by what you said the girl said to you. Hannah's thought it over, I cal'late, and she figgers that while there's life there's hope, as you might say. Her brother may be engaged, but he ain't married, and, s'long's he ain't, she's got a chance. You just see, Mrs. Thankful—you see if Hannah ain't sweeter to Kenelm from this on than a molasses jug stopper to a young one. She'll lay herself out to make his home the softest spot in creation, so he'll think twice before leavin' it. That's her game, as I see it, and she'll play it. Give Hannah credit; she won't abandon the ship while there's a plank above water. Just watch and see."

Thankful looked doubtful. "Well, maybe so," she said. "Maybe she will be nice to her brother, but how about the rest of us? She wouldn't speak to me last night, nor to Emily—and as for Imogene!"

"Yes, I know. But wait until she sees you, or Imogene either, next time. She'll be smooth as a smelt. I'll bet you anything she'll say that, after all, she guesses the engagement's a good thing and that Imogene's a nice girl. There's a whole lot in keepin' the feller you're fightin' off his guard until you've got him in a corner with his hands down. Last night Hannah give me my orders to mind my own business. This mornin' she cooked me the best breakfast I've had since I shipped aboard her vessel. And kept askin' me to have more. No, Imogene's right; Hannah'll play the game, and she'll play it quiet. As for tellin' anybody her brother's engaged, you needn't worry about that. She'll be the last one to tell."

This prophecy seemed likely to prove true. The next time Thankful met Hannah the latter greeted her like a long-lost friend. During a long conversation she mentioned the subject of her brother's engagement but once and then at the very end of the interview.

"Oh, by the way, Mrs. Thankful," she said, "I do beg your pardon for carryin' on the way I did at your house t'other night. The news was pitched out at me so sudden that I was blowed right off my feet, as you might say. I acted real unlikely, I know; but, you see, Kenelm does mean so much to me that I couldn't bear to think of givin' him up to anybody else. When I come to think it over I realized 'twa'n't no more'n I had ought to have expected. I mustn't be selfish and I ain't goin' to be. S'long's 'tain't that—that Jezebel of an Abbie Larkin I don't mind so much. I couldn't stand havin' her in the family—THAT I couldn't stand. Oh, and if you don't mind, Mrs. Thankful, just don't say nothin' about the engagin' yet awhile. I shouldn't mind, of course, but Kenelm, he's set on keepin' it secret for a spell. There! I must run on. I've got to go up to the store and get a can of that consecrated soup for supper. Have you tried them soups? They're awful cheap and handy. You just pour in hot water and there's more'n enough for a meal. Good-by."

Imogene, when she returned from the Fair, announced that she had had a perfectly lovely time.

"He ain't such bad company—Kenelm, I mean," she observed. "He talks a lot, but you don't have to listen unless you want to; and he enjoys himself real well, considerin' how little practice he's had."

"Did you meet anyone you knew?" asked Emily.

"No'm. We saw quite a lot of folks from East Wellmouth, but we saw 'em first, so we didn't meet 'em. One kind of funny thing happened: a man who was outside a snake tent, hollerin' for everybody to come in, saw us and he says to me: 'Girlie,' he says—he was a fresh guy like all them kind—'Girlie,' he says, 'ask your pa to take you in and see the Serpent King eat 'em alive. Only ten cents, Pop,' he says to Kenelm. 'Don't miss the chance to give your little girl a treat.' Kenelm was all frothed up at bein' took for my father, but I told him he needn't get mad—if I could stand it he could, I guessed."

Kenelm reported for work as usual on Monday morning and he worked—actually worked all day. For an accepted lover he appeared rather subdued and silent. Captain Obed, who noticed his behavior, commented upon it.

"Cal'late Kenelm's beginnin' to realize gettin' engaged don't mean all joy," he said, with a chuckle. "He's just got two bosses instead of one, that's all. He's scart to death of Hannah at home and when he's here Imogene orders him 'round the way a bucko mate used to order a roustabout. I said Hannah was in a clove hitch, didn't I? Well, she is, but Kenelm—well, Kenelm's like a young one runnin' 'tiddly' on thin ice—worse'n that, 'cause he can't stop on either side, got to keep runnin' between 'em and look out and not fall in."

Labor Day, the day upon which the Cape summer season really ends, did not, to the High Cliff House, mean the general exodus which it means to most of the Cape hotels. Some of Thankful's lodgers left, of course, but many stayed, and were planning to stay through September if the weather continued pleasant. But on the Saturday following Labor Day it rained. And the next day it rained harder, and on Monday began a series of cold, windy, gloomy days which threatened to last indefinitely. One after the other the sojourners from the cities passed from grumbling at the weather to trunk-packing and leaving. A few stayed on into the next week but when, at the end of that week, a storm set in which was more severe than those preceding it, even these optimists surrendered. Before that third week was over the High Cliff House was practically deserted. Except for Heman Daniels and John Kendrick and Miss Timpson and Caleb Hammond, Thankful and Emily and Imogene were alone in the big house.

This upsetting of her plans and hopes worried Thankful not a little. Emily, too, was troubled concerning her cousin's business outlook. The High Cliff House had been a success during its first season, but it needed the expected September and early October income to make it a success financially. The expense had been great, much greater than Thankful had expected or planned. It is true that the boarders, almost without exception, had re-engaged rooms and board for the following summer, but summer was a long way off. There was the winter to be lived through and if, as they had hoped, additions and enlargements to the establishment were to be made in the spring, more, a good deal more money, would be needed.

"As I see it, Auntie," said Emily, when they discussed the situation, "you have splendid prospects here. Your first season has been all or more than you dared hope for, and if we had had good weather—the sort of weather everyone says the Cape usually has in the fall months—you would have come out even or better. But, even then, to make this scheme a real money-maker, you would be obliged to have more sleeping-rooms made over, and a larger dining-room. Now why don't you go and see this—what is he?—cousin of yours, Mr. Cobb, and tell him just how you stand? Tell him of your prospects and your plans, and get him to advance you another thousand dollars—more, if you can get it. Why don't you do that?"

Thankful did not answer. She had few secrets from Emily, whom she loved as dearly as a daughter, but one secret she had kept. Just why she had kept this one she might not have been able to explain satisfactorily, even to herself. She had written Emily of her visit to Solomon Cobb's "henhouse" and of the loan on mortgage which had resulted therefrom. But she had neither written nor told all of the circumstances of that visit, especially of Mr. Cobb's attitude toward her and his reluctance to lend the money. She said merely that he had lent it and Emily had evidently taken it for granted that the loan was made because of the relationship and kindly feeling between the two. Thankful, even now, did not undeceive her. She felt a certain shame in doing so; a shame in admitting that a relative of hers could be so mean and disobliging.

"Why don't you go to Mr. Cobb again, Auntie?" repeated Emily. "He will lend you more, I'm sure, if you explain all the circumstances. It would be a perfectly safe investment for him, and you would pay interest, of course."

Mrs. Barnes shook her head. "I don't think I'd better, Emily," she said. "He's got one mortgage on this place already."

"What of it? That was only for fifteen hundred and you have improved the house and grounds ever so much since then. I think he'll be glad to let you have another thousand. The mortgage he has is to run for three years, you said, didn't you?"

Again Thankful did not answer. She had not said the mortgage was for a term of three years; Emily had presumed that it was and she had not undeceived her. She hesitated, and Emily noticed her hesitation.

"It is for three years, isn't it, Auntie?" she repeated.

Mrs. Barnes tried to evade the question.

"Why, not exactly, Emily," she replied. "It ain't. You see, he thought three years was a little mite too long, and so—and so we fixed up for a shorter time. It's all right, though."

"Is it? You are sure? Aunt Thankful, tell me truly: how long a term is that mortgage?"

"Well, it's—it's only for a year, but—"

"A year? Why, then it will fall due next spring. You can't pay that mortgage next spring, can you?"

"I don't know's I can, but—but it'll be all right, anyhow. He'll renew it, if I ask him to, I presume likely."

"Of course he will. He will have to. Auntie, you must go and see him at once. If you don't I shall."

If there was one point on which Thankful was determined, it was that Emily should not meet Solomon Cobb. The money-lender had visited the High Cliff premises but once during the summer and then Miss Howes was providentially absent.

"No, no!" declared Mrs. Barnes, hastily. "You shan't do any such thing. The idea! I guess I can 'tend to borrowin' money from my own relation without draggin' other folks into it. I'll drive over and see him pretty soon."

"You must go at once. I shan't permit you to wait another week. It is almost time for me to go back to my schoolwork, and I shan't go until I am certain that mortgage is to be renewed and that your financial affairs are all right. Do go, Auntie, please. Arrange to have the mortgage renewed and try to get another loan. Promise me you will go tomorrow."

So Thankful was obliged to promise, and the following morning she drove George Washington over the long road, now wet and soggy from the rain, to

Trumet.

Mr. Solomon Cobb's "henhouse" looked quite as dingy and dirty as when she visited it before. Solomon himself was just as shabby and he pulled at his whiskers with his accustomed energy.

"Hello!" he said, peering over his spectacles. "What do you want? . . . Oh, it's you, is it? What's the matter?"

Thankful came forward. "Matter?" she repeated. "What in the world—what made you think anything was the matter?"

Solomon stared at her fixedly.

"What did you come here for?" he asked.

"To see you. That's worth comin' for, isn't it?"

The joke was wasted, as all jokes seemed to be upon Mr. Cobb. He did not smile.

"What made you come to see me?" he asked, still staring.

"What made me?"

"Yes. What made you? Have you found—has anybody told you—er—anything?"

"Anybody told me! My soul and body! That's what you said when I was here before. Do you say it to everybody? What on earth do you mean by it? Who would tell me anything? And what would they tell?"

Solomon pulled his whiskers. "Nothin', I guess," he said, after a moment. "Only there's so much fool talk runnin' loose I didn't know but you might have heard I was—was dead, or somethin'. I ain't."

"I can see that, I hope. And if you was I shouldn't be traipsin' ten miles just to look at your remains. Time enough for that at the funeral. Dead! The idea!"

"Um—well, all right; I ain't dead, yet. Set down, won't ye?"

Thankful sat down. Mr. Cobb swung about in his own chair, so that his face was in the shadow.

"Hear you've been doin' pretty well with that boardin'-house of yours," he observed. "Hear it's been full up all summer."

"Who told you so?"

"Oh, I heard. I hear about all that's goin' on, one way or another. I was over there a fortni't ago."

"You were? Why didn't you stop in and see me? You haven't been there but once since the place started."

"Yes, I have. I've been by a good many times. Didn't stop, though. Too many of them city dudes around to suit me. Did you fetch your October interest money."

"No, I didn't. It ain't due till week after next. When it is I'll send it, same as I have the rest."

"All right, all right, I ain't askin' you for it. What did you come for?"

And then Thankful told him. He listened without comment until she had finished, peering over his spectacles and keeping up the eternal "weeding."

"There," concluded Mrs. Barnes, "that's what I came for. Will you do it?"

The answer was prompt enough this time.

"No, I won't," said Solomon, with decision.

Thankful was staggered.

"You won't?" she repeated. "You won't—"

"I won't lend you no more money. Why should I?"

"You shouldn't, I suppose, if you don't want to. But, the way I look at it, it would be a perfectly safe loan for you. My prospects are fine; everybody says so."

"Everybody says a whole lot of things. If I'd put up money on what everybody said I'd be puttin' up at the poorhouse, myself. But I ain't puttin' up there and I ain't puttin' up the money neither."

"All right; keep it then—keep it and sleep on it, if you want to. I can get along without it, I guess; or, if I can't, I can borrow it of somebody else."

"Humph! You're pretty sassy, seems to me, for anybody that's askin' favors."

"I'm not askin' favors. I told you that when I first come to you. What I asked was just business and nothin' else."

"Is that so? As I understand it you're askin' to have a mortgage renewed. That may be business, or it may be a favor, 'cordin' to how you look at it."

Thankful fought down her temper. The renewal of the mortgage was a vital matter to her. If it was not renewed what should she do? What could she do? All she had in the world and all her hopes for the future centered about her property in East Wellmouth. If that were taken from her—

"Well," she admitted, "perhaps it is a favor, then."

"Perhaps 'tis. Why should I renew that mortgage? I don't cal'late to renew mortgages, as a general thing. Did I say anything about renewin' it when I took it? I don't remember that I did."

"No, no—I guess you didn't. But I hope you will. If you don't—I—I—Solomon Cobb, that boardin'-house means everything to me. I've put all I've got in it. It has got the best kind of a start and in another year—I—I—Please, Oh PLEASE don't close me out."

"Humph!"

"Please don't. You told me when I was here before what a lot you thought of my Uncle Abner. You knew how much he thought of me. When you think of him and what he said—"

Mr. Cobb interrupted. "Said?" he repeated, sharply. "What do you mean he said? Eh? What do YOU know he said?"

"Why—why, he told you about me. You said yourself he did. How much he thought of me, and all."

"Is that all you meant?"

"Yes, of course. What else is there to mean? Solomon, you profess to be a Christian. You knew my uncle. He did lots of favors for you; I know he did. Now—"

"Sshh! shh!" Mr. Cobb seemed strangely perturbed. He waved his hand. "Hush!" he repeated. "What are you draggin' Cap'n Abner and Christianity and all that in for? They ain't got nothin' to do with that mortgage. Who said they had?"

"Why, no one said it. No one said anything; no one but me. I don't know what you mean—"

"Mean! I don't mean nothin'. There! There! Clear out and don't bother me no more today. I'm—I ain't feelin' well. Got a cold comin' on, I cal'late. Clear off home and let me alone."

"But I can't go until you tell me about that mortgage."

"Yes, you can, too. I can't tell you about nothin' just now. I got to think, ain't I? Maybe I'll renew that mortgage and maybe I won't. I'll tell you when I make up my mind. Time enough between now and spring. I—Ah, Ezry, how be you? Come on in. Glad to see you."

The last portion of the foregoing was addressed to a man who had entered the office. Mr. Cobb did look as if he was really glad to see him.

Thankful rose. "I'll go," she said, drearily. "I suppose I might as well. But I shan't sleep much until you make up that mind of yours. And do make it up the right way, for my sake—and Uncle Abner's."

Her relative waved both hands this time.

"Shh!" he ordered, desperately. "Don't say no more now; I don't want the whole creation to know my business and yours. Go on home. I—I'll come over and see you by and by."

So, because she saw there was no use remaining, Mrs. Barnes went. The drive home, through the dismal grayness of the cloudy afternoon, seemed longer and more trying than the trip over. The dream of raising money for the spring additions and alterations was over; the High Cliff House must do its best as it was for another year at least. As to the renewal of the mortgage, there was a faint hope. Mr. Cobb's final remarks had inspired that hope. He had been on the point of refusing to renew, Thankful was sure of that. Then something was said which caused him to hesitate. Mrs. Barnes looked out between the ears of jogging George Washington and spoke her thought aloud.

"It's somethin' to do with Uncle Abner," she soliloquized. "He don't like to have Uncle Abner mentioned. Hum! I wonder what the reason is. I only wish I knew."

To Emily, who was eagerly waiting to hear the result of her cousin's visit to Solomon Cobb, Thankful told but a portion of the truth. She did say, however, that the additional loan appeared to be out of the question and she guessed they would have to get on without the needed alterations for another year. Emily thought they should not.

"If this place is to become really profitable, Auntie," she insisted, "those changes should be made. I don't see why this Mr. Cobb won't lend you the money; but, if he won't, then I'm sure someone else will, if you ask. Don't you know anyone here in East Wellmouth whom you might ask for a loan—on your prospects?"

"No. No, I don't."

"Why, yes, you do. There is Captain Bangs, for instance. He is well to do, and I'm sure he is a good friend. Why don't you ask him?"

Thankful's answer was prompt and sharp.

"Indeed I shan't," she declared.

"Then I will. I'll be glad to."

"Emily Howes, if you say one word to Cap'n Obed about borrowin' money from him I'll—I'll never speak to you afterwards. Go to Captain Obed. The idea!"

"But why not, Auntie? He IS a friend, and—"

"Of course he is; that's the very reason. He is a friend and he'd probably lend it because he is, whether he knew he'd ever get it back or not. No, when I borrow money it'll be of somebody that lends it as a business deal, not from friendship."

"But, Auntie, you went to Mr. Cobb because he was your relative. You said that was the very reason why you went to him."

"Um, yes. Well, I may have GONE to him for that reason, but there ain't any relationship in that mortgage of his; don't you get the notion that there is."

Emily's next question, naturally, concerned the renewal of that mortgage. Mrs. Barnes said shortly that she guessed the renewal would be all right.

"He's comin' over to settle it with me pretty soon," she added. "Now don't worry your head off any more about mortgages and loans, Emily. You're goin' to leave me pretty soon; let's not spend our last days together frettin' about money. That mortgage is all right. Maybe the extra loan will be, too. Maybe—why, maybe Mr. Kendrick would lend it, if I asked him."

"Mr. Kendrick? Why, Auntie, Mr. Kendrick has no money, or only a very little. He is doing well—very well, considering how short a time he has practised his profession here, but I'm sure he has no money to lend. Why, he tells me—"

The expression of Mrs. Barnes' face must have conveyed a meaning; at any rate Emily's sentence broke off in the middle. She colored and seemed embarrassed.

Thankful smiled. "Yes," she observed, drily, "I notice he tells you a lot of things—a whole lot more than he does anybody else. Generally speakin', he is about the closest-mouthed young man about his personal affairs that I ever run across. However, I ain't jealous, not a mite. And 'twa'n't of him I was speakin'; 'twas his cousin, Mr. E. Holliday Kendrick. He's got money enough, I guess. Maybe he might make a loan on decent security. He's a possibility. I'll think him over."

Mr. E. Holliday and his doings were still East Wellmouth's favorite conversational topics. The great man was preparing to close his summer house and return to New York. His family had already gone—to Lenox, where they were to remain for a few weeks and then journey to Florida. E. Holliday remained, several of the servants remaining with him, but he, too, was to go very soon. There were rumors that he remained because of other schemes concerning his new estate. Just what those schemes were no one seemed to know. If John Kendrick knew he told no one, not even Emily Howes.

But E. Holliday himself disclosed his plan and it was to Thankful Barnes that he did so. He called at the High Cliff House one afternoon and asked to see its proprietor. Thankful was a trifle flustered. It was the first call which her wealthy neighbor had made upon her, and she could not understand why he came at this late date.

"For mercy sakes, come into the livin'-room with me, Emily," she begged. "I shan't know how to act in the face of all that money."

Emily was much amused. "I never knew you to be frightened of money before, Auntie," she said. "I thought you were considering borrowing some of this very—ahem—personage."

"Maybe I was, though I cal'late I should have took it out in consideration; I never would have gone to him and asked. But now the—what do you call it?— personage—come to me for somethin', the land knows what."

"Perhaps HE wants to borrow."

"Humph! Perhaps he does. Well, then, he's fishin' in the wrong puddle. Emily Howes, stop laughin' and makin' jokes and come into that livin'-room same as I ask you to."

But this Emily firmly declined to do. "He's not my caller, Auntie," she said. "He didn't even ask if I were in."

So Thankful went into the living-room alone to meet the personage. And she closed all doors behind her. "If you won't help you shan't listen," she declared. "And I don't know's I'll tell you a word after he's gone."

The call was a long one. It ended in an odd way. Emily, sitting by the dining-room window, heard the front door slam and, looking out, saw Mr. Kendrick stalking down the path, a frown on his face and outraged dignity in his bearing. A moment later Thankful burst into the dining-room. Her cheeks were flushed and she looked excited and angry.

"What do you think that—that walkin' money-bag came here for?" she demanded. "He came here to tell me I'd got to sell this place to him. Yes, sell it to him, 'cause he wanted it. It didn't seem to make any difference what I wanted. Well, it will make a difference, I tell you that!"

When she had calmed sufficiently she told of the interview with her neighbor. E. Holliday had lost no time in stating his position. The High Cliff House, it appeared, was a source of annoyance to him and his. A boarding-house, no matter how genteel or well-conducted a boarding-house it may be, could not longer be tolerated in that situation. The boarders irritated him by trespassing upon his premises, by knocking their tennis balls into his garden beds, by bathing and skylarking on the beach in plain sight from his verandas. And the house and barn interfered with his view. He wished to be perfectly reasonable in the matter; Mrs. Barnes, of course, understood that. He was willing to pay for the privilege of having his own way. But, boiled down and shorn of politeness and subterfuge, his proposition was that Thankful should sell her property to him, after which he would either tear down the buildings on that property, or move them to a less objectionable site.

"But, Auntie," cried Emily, "of course you told him you didn't want to sell."

"Sartin I did. I told him all I had was invested here, that my first season had been a good one considerin' 'twas the first, and that my prospects were all I had a right to hope for. I told him I was sorry if my boarders had plagued him and I'd try to see they didn't do so any more. But I couldn't think of sellin' out."

"And what did he say to that?"

"What didn't he say? What I said didn't make a bit of difference. He made proclamation that any reasonable price I might name he would consider. He wouldn't submit to what he called 'extortion' of course, but he would be perfectly fair, and all that. I kept sayin' no and he kept sayin' yes. Our talk got more and more sultry long towards the last of it. He told me that he made it a p'int to get what he wanted and he was goin' to get it now. One thing he told me I didn't know afore, and it's kind of odd, too. He said the land this house sits on used to belong to him once. His father left it to him. He sold it a long while ago, afore my Uncle Abner bought, I guess. Now he's sorry he sold."

"That was queer, what else did he say?"

"Oh, he said a whole lot about his desire to make East Wellmouth his permanent residence, about the taxes he paid, and what he meant to do for the town. I told him that was all right and fine and the town appreciated it, but that I'd got to think of myself; this boardin'-house idea was a life-long ambition of mine and I couldn't give it up."

"And how did it end?"

"Just where it begun. His last words to me was that if I wouldn't listen to reason then he'd have to try other ways. And he warned me that he should try 'em. I said go ahead and try, or words not quite so sassy but meanin' the same. And out he marched. Oh, Emily, WHAT do you suppose he'll try? He can't MAKE me sell out, can he? Oh, dear! Oh, dear! here's more trouble. And I thought there was enough already!"

Emily did her best to reassure her relative, telling the latter that of course she could not be forced into parting with what was her own and that Mr. Kendrick was talking merely for effect; but it was plain that Miss Howes herself was troubled.

"I think you should consult a lawyer, Auntie," she said. "I am sure I am right, and that that man can't make you do what you don't want to do. But I don't know, of course, and a lawyer would know because that is his business. Why don't you ask John—Mr. John Kendrick, I mean? He will advise you."

Thankful nodded. "I will," she said.

But John did not come home for dinner that night. He had business which called him to Wellmouth Centre that afternoon and it was late in the evening when he returned. Heman Daniels was late for dinner also, and when he entered the dining-room there was an air of mystery and importance about him which everyone noticed. Miss Timpson, who seldom permitted reticence to interfere with curiosity, asked him what was the matter.

"I do declare, Mr. Daniels," she said, "you look as if you had the cares of the nation on your shoulders tonight. Has anything gone wrong with one of those important cases of yours?"

Mr. Daniels shook his head. "No," he answered, gravely. "My cases are progressing satisfactorily. My worries just now are not professional. I heard some news this afternoon which—er—upset me somewhat, that is all."

"News? Upsettin' news? Land sakes, do tell us! What is it?"

But Mr. Daniels refused to tell. The news concerned other people, he said, and he was not at liberty to tell. He trusted Miss Timpson would excuse him under the circumstances.

Miss Timpson was therefore obliged to excuse him, though it was plain that she did so under protest. She made several more or less direct attempts to learn the secret and, failing, went out to attend prayer-meeting. Caleb Hammond went out also, though the club, not prayer-meeting, was his announced destination. Heman finished his dinner alone. When he had finished he sent word by Imogene that when Miss Howes was at liberty he should like to speak with her.

Emily, who was in the kitchen with Thankful and Captain Obed, the latter having, as usual, dropped in on his way to the postoffice, seemed in no hurry to speak with Mr. Daniels. It was not until half an hour later, when the message was repeated, that she bade the captain good night and started for the living-room. Captain Obed and Thankful smiled at each other.

"Heman's a heap more anxious to see her than she is to see him," observed the former. "He's pretty fur gone in that direction, judgin' by the weather signs."

Thankful nodded.

"I cal'late that's so," she agreed. "Still, he's been just as fur gone with others, if all they say's true. Mr. Daniels is a fascinator, so everybody says."

"Yup. Prides himself on it, always seemed to me. But there generally comes a time when that kind of a lady-killer gets hit himself. Lots of females have been willin' to marry Heman, but he's never given 'em the chance. About so fur he'll go and then shy off."

"How about that widow woman over to Bayport?"

"Well, I did think he was goin' to cast anchor there, but he ain't, up to now. That widow's wuth a lot of money—her husband owned any quantity of cranberry bog property—and all hands cal'lated Heman had his eye on it. Maybe he and the widow would have signed articles only for Miss Howes heavin' in sight."

"Well, I suppose he's a good man; I never heard a word against him that way. And he's a risin' lawyer—"

"Yes—or riz."

"Yes. But—but I somehow wouldn't want Emily to marry him."

Captain Obed agreed heartily. "Neither would I," he declared. Then, after a moment, he added: "Hasn't it seemed to you that John Kendrick was kind of—well, kind of headin' up towards—towards—"

"Yes. Ye-es, I have thought so. I joke Emily a little about him sometimes."

"So do I, John. How do you think she"—with a jerk of the head toward the living-room—"feels—er—that way?"

"I don't know. She likes him, I'm sure of that. But, so fur as I know, there's no understandin' between them. And, anyhow, John couldn't think of gettin' married, not for a long spell. He hasn't got any money."

"No, not yet he ain't, but he will have some day, or I miss my guess. He's gettin' more popular on the Cape all the time, and popular in the right places, too. Why, the last time I was in South Denboro Cap'n Elisha Warren spoke to me about him, and if Cap'n 'Lisha gets interested in a young feller it means a lot. 'Lisha's got a lot of influence."

"You say you joke with John about Emily. How's he take the jokes?"

"Oh, he takes 'em all right. You can't get him mad by teasin' him, 'cause he won't tease. He generally comes right back at me about—er—that is—"

"About what?"

"Oh—nothin'. Just nonsense, that's all. Well, I cal'late I'd better be goin' if I want to fetch the postoffice afore it's shut up."

But he was destined not to "fetch" the postoffice that night. He had risen to go when the dining-room door opened and Emily appeared. Her face was flushed, and she seemed excited and angry.

"Auntie," she said, sharply, "Auntie, will you come into the living-room a moment. I want you to hear what that—what Mr. Daniels says. Don't stop to talk. Come! Captain Bangs, you may come, too. You are—are his friend and you should hear it."

Surprised and puzzled, Thankful and the captain followed her through the dining-room to the living-room. There they found Heman Daniels, standing by the center table, looking embarrassed and uncomfortable.

"Now, Mr. Daniels," said Emily, "I want you to tell my cousin and Captain Bangs just what you have told me. It's not true—I know it's not true, and I want them to be able to contradict such a story. Tell them."

Heman fidgeted with the paper-cutter on the table.

"I merely told Miss Howes," he said, nervously, "what was told me. It was told me by one of the parties most interested and so I accepted it as the truth. I—I have no personal interest in the matter. As—as a friend and—and a lawyer—I offered my services, that is all. I—"

He was interrupted by the opening of the front door. John Kendrick, wearing his light overcoat, and hat in hand, entered the living-room.

"I'm awfully sorry to be so late, Mrs. Barnes," he began. "I was detained at the Centre. Hello, Captain! Good evening, Daniels! Good evening, Miss Howes!"

Captain Obed and Thankful said, "Good evening." Neither Emily nor Heman returned the greeting. John, for the first time, appeared to notice that something was wrong. He looked from Mrs. Barnes to Captain Bangs, standing together at one side of the table, and at Daniels and Emily at the other side. Heman had moved closer to the young lady, and in his manner was a hint of confidential understanding, almost of protection.

Kendrick looked from one pair to the other. When he next spoke it was to Emily Howes.

"Why, what's the matter?" he asked, with a smile. "This looks like a council of war."

Emily did not smile.

"Mr. Kendrick," she said, "I am very glad you came. Now you can deny it yourself."

John gazed at her in puzzled surprise.

"Deny it?" he repeated. "Deny what?"

Before Miss Howes could answer Heman Daniels spoke.

"Kendrick," he said, importantly, "Miss Howes has heard something concerning you which she doesn't like to believe."

"Indeed? Did she hear it from you, may I ask?"

"She did."

"And that is why she doesn't believe it? Daniels, I'm surprised. Even lawyers should occasionally—"

Emily interrupted. "Oh, stop!" she cried. "Don't joke, please. This is not a joking matter. If what I have been told IS true I should—But I know it isn't—I KNOW it!"

John bowed. "Thank you," he said. "What have you heard?"

"She has heard—" began Heman.

"Pardon me, Daniels. I asked Miss Howes."

Emily began a reply, but she did not finish it.

"I have been told—" she began. "I have been told—Oh, I can't tell you! I am ashamed to repeat such wicked nonsense. Mr. Daniels may tell you; it was he who told me."

John turned to his fellow practitioner.

"Very well," he said. "Now, Daniels, what is it?"

Heman did not hesitate.

"Miss Howes has heard," he said, deliberately, "that your client, Mr. Holliday Kendrick, is determined to force Mrs. Barnes here into selling him this house and land, to force her to sell whether she wishes it or not. Is that true?"

John nodded, gravely.

"I'm afraid it is," he said. "He seems quite determined. In fact, he said he had expressed that determination to the lady herself. He did that, didn't he, Mrs. Barnes?"

Thankful, who had been so far a perplexed and troubled listener, answered.

"Why, yes," she admitted. "He was here today and he give me to understand that he wanted this property of mine and was goin' to have it. If I wouldn't agree to sell it to him now then he'd drive me into sellin' later on. That's about what he said."

Captain Obed struck his fists together.

"The swab!" he exclaimed. "Well, if that don't beat all my goin' to sea! Humph! I'd like to know how he cal'lates to do it."

"Anything more, Daniels?" inquired John.

"Yes, there is something more. What we want to know from you, Kendrick, is whether or not you, as his legal adviser, propose to help him in this scheme of his. That is what we wish to know."

"We? What we? Has Mrs. Barnes—or Miss Howes—have they engaged you as their attorney, Daniels?"

Before Daniels could reply Emily asked a question.

"Did he—has he asked you to help him?" she demanded. "Has he?"

John smiled. "I doubt if it could be called asking," he observed. "He gave me orders to that effect shortly after he left here."

Emily gasped. Thankful and Captain Obed said, "Oh!" in concert. Heman Daniels smiled triumphantly.

"You see, Miss Howes?" he said.

"One moment, Daniels," broke in Kendrick, sharply. "You haven't answered my question yet. Just where do you come in on this?"

"I—I—" began Daniels, but once more Emily interrupted.

"Are you—" she cried. "Tell me; are you going to help that man force my cousin into giving up her home?"

Again John smiled. "Well, to be frank," he said, "since it IS her home and she doesn't wish to sell it I can't for the life of me see how she can be forced into selling, with or without my valuable aid. Miss Howes, I—"

"Stop! You persist in treating this affair as a joke. It is NOT a joke—to my cousin, or to me. Did you tell that man you would help him?"

"No."

"I knew it! I was certain of it! Of course you didn't!"

"Pardon me, Miss Howes," put in Daniels. "We have not heard all yet. Kendrick, do I understand that you told your cousin and—er—benefactor that you would NOT help him in his infamous scheme?"

John's patience was nearing its limits. He smiled no more.

"I don't know what you understand, Daniels," he said, crisply. "Your understanding in many matters is beyond me."

"But did you say you would not help him?" persisted Emily.

"Why no, not exactly. He did not wait to hear what I had to say. He seemed to take my assistance for granted."

Daniels laughed scornfully.

"You see, Miss Howes?" he said again. Then, turning to Thankful: "Mrs. Barnes, I met Mr. Holliday Kendrick on the street just after he had come from the interview with his—er—attorney. He told me that he intended to force you into giving up your property to him and he told me also that his cousin here had the case in his hands and would work to carry it through. There seemed to be no doubt in his mind that this gentleman," indicating John, "had accepted the responsibility. In fact he said he had."

Captain Obed snorted. "That's plaguy nonsense!" he declared. "I know better. John ain't that kind of feller. You wouldn't help anybody to turn a woman out of her house and home, would you, John? Course you wouldn't. The swab! Just 'cause he's got money he cal'lates he can run everything. Well, he can't."

"Goodness knows I hope he can't!" moaned Thankful.

"And in the meantime we are waiting to hear what his lawyer has to say," observed Heman.

John stepped forward. "Daniels," he said, "it strikes me that your 'we's' are a bit frequent. Why are you interfering in this affair?"

Mr. Daniels drew himself up. "I am not interfering," he replied. "My interest is purely that of a friend. AS a friend I told Miss Howes what your cousin said to me. She seemed to doubt my word. In justice to myself I propose to prove that I have spoken the truth, that is all. So far I think I may say that I have proved it. Now I demand to know what you intend doing. Are you for Mrs. Barnes or against her?"

"So you demand that, do you?"

"I do. Will you answer?"

"No."

"Ah ha! I thought not."

"I'll answer no demands from you. Why should I? If Mrs. Barnes or Miss Howes asks me I will answer, of course."

"Mr. Kendrick—" began Thankful. Emily interrupted.

"Wait, Auntie," she said. "He must answer me first. Mr. Kendrick, when that man came to you with his 'orders,' as you call them, you must have had some opportunity to speak. Why didn't you refuse at once?"

For the first time John hesitated. "Well," he said, slowly, "for one reason I was taken completely by surprise."

"So was Aunt Thankful, when he came to her. But she refused."

"And, for another, there were certain circumstances which made it hard to refuse point-blank. In a way, I suppose Mr. Kendrick was justified in assuming that I would work for his interests. I accepted his retaining fee. You remember that I hesitated before doing so, but—but I did accept, and I have acted as his attorney since. I—"

"Stop! I did not ask for excuses. I ask you, as Mr. Daniels asked, are you for my cousin or against her?"

"And I ask you what is Mr. Daniels' warrant for asking me anything?"

"Answer my question! Will you fight for my cousin's rights, or have you sold yourself to—to this benefactor of yours?"

John flushed at the repetition of the word.

"I have tried to give value received for whatever benefactions have come my way," he said, coldly. "This matter may be different; in a way it is. But not as Mr. Holliday Kendrick sees it. When a lawyer accepts a retaining fee—not for one case but for all cases which his client may give him—he is, by the ethics of his profession, honor bound to—"

"Honor!" scornfully. "Suppose we omit the 'honor'."

"That is not easy to do. I AM my cousin's attorney. But, as Mrs. Barnes' friend and yours, I—"

Emily stamped her foot. "Friend!" she cried. "I don't care for such friends. I have heard enough. I don't wish to hear any more. You were right, Mr. Daniels. I apologize for doubting your word. Aunt Thankful, you must settle this yourself. I—I am through. I—I am going. Please don't stop me."

She was on her way to the door of the dining-room. Heman Daniels called her name.

"One minute, Miss Howes," he said. "I trust you will not forget you have one friend who will be only too glad to work for Mrs. Barnes' interests and yours. I am at your service."

"Thank you, thank you, Mr. Daniels. I—I have no doubt we shall need your services. But please don't—"

John Kendrick was at her side.

"Miss Howes—Emily—" he pleaded. "Don't misunderstand me."

She burst out at him like, as Captain Obed said afterward, "an August thunder tempest."

"Misunderstand!" she repeated. "I don't misunderstand. I understand quite well. Don't speak to me again."

The door closed behind her. Thankful, after an instant's hesitation, hurried out after her.

"Excuse me, gentlemen," said Daniels, and followed Mrs. Barnes.

Captain Obed turned to his friend.

"For the Lord sakes, John!" he shouted. "What in the everlastin' do you mean? What did you let her go that way for? Why didn't you tell her you wouldn't do it?"

But Kendrick paid not the slightest attention. He was gazing at the door through which Emily and Thankful had disappeared. His face was white.

"John," repeated the captain.

"Hush!" ordered John. He strode to the door and opened it.

"Emily!" he cried. "Emily!"

There was no answer. John waited a moment and then turned and walked to the window, where he raised the shade and stood looking out.

"John," said the captain again.

"Hush! Don't say anything to me now."

So Captain Obed did not speak. A few minutes later the dining-room door opened and Mr. Daniels entered. His expression was one of complete, not to say malicious, satisfaction. John turned at the opening of the door.

"Emily," he began. Then, seeing Daniels, he remained silent, looking at him.

"Kendrick," said Heman, with dignity, "in the matter which we have just been discussing you will hereafter deal with me. That is Mrs. Barnes' wish and also Miss Howes'."

John did not reply. Once more he walked to the door and opened it.

"Miss Howes!" he called. "Emily! If you will let me explain—Emily!"

"I'll go fetch her," declared Captain Obed. John pushed him back.

"Don't interfere, Captain," he said, sharply. "Emily!"

No answer. Daniels made the next remark.

"I'm afraid you don't get the situation, Kendrick," he said. "Neither Miss Howes nor Mrs. Barnes cares to see you or speak with you. After this you are to deal with me. They have asked me, as a FRIEND," emphasizing the word, "to act as their representative in this and all matters."

John turned and looked at the speaker.

"In all matters?" he asked, slowly.

"Yes sir, in all."

"And they refuse to see me?"

"It would—er—seem so. . . . Is there anything further, Kendrick? If not then this affair between your—er—client and mine would appear to be a matter of skill for you and me to contest. We'll see who wins."

John still looked at him.

"So that's it then," he said, after a moment. "You and I are to determine which is the better lawyer?"

"So it would seem. Though, considering my record and experience, I don't know that—"

"That such a test is necessary? I don't know that it is, either. But we'll have it."

He walked from the room and they heard him ascending the stairs. Captain Obed swore aloud. Heman Daniels laughed.

CHAPTER XI

THE next morning the captain was an early caller. Breakfast at the High Cliff House was scarcely over when he knocked at the kitchen door. Imogene opened the door.

"Mr. Kendrick ain't here," she said, in answer to the caller's question. "He's gone."

"Gone? So early? Where's he gone; down to his office?"

"I don't know. He's gone, that's all I do know. He didn't stop for any breakfast either."

"Humph! That's funny. Where's Mrs. Thankful?"

"She's up in Miss Emily's room. Miss Emily didn't come down to breakfast neither. I'll tell Mrs. Barnes you're here."

When Thankful came she looked grave enough.

"I'm awful glad to see you, Cap'n," she said. "I've been wantin' to talk to some sane person; the one I've been talkin' to ain't sane, not now. Come into the dinin'-room. Imogene, you needn't finish clearin' away till I tell you to. You stay in the kitchen here."

When she and Captain Obed were in the dining-room alone, and with both doors closed, Thankful told of the morning's happenings.

"They're bad enough, too," she declared. "Almost as bad as that silly business last night—or worse, if such a thing's possible. To begin with, Mr. John Kendrick's gone."

"Yes, Imogene said he'd gone. But what made him go so early?"

"You don't understand, Cap'n. I mean he's gone—gone for good. He isn't goin' to board or room here any more."

Captain Obed whistled. "Whew!" he exclaimed. "You don't mean it?"

"I wish I didn't, but I do. I didn't see him this mornin', he went too early for that, but he took his suitcase and his trunk is all packed and locked. He left a note for me with a check for his room rent and board in it. The note said that under the circumstances he presumed I would agree 'twas best for him to go somewheres else at once. He thanked me for my kindness, and said some real nice things—but he's gone."

"Tut! tut! Dear, dear! Where's he gone to? Did he say?"

"No, I've told you all he said. I suppose likely I ought to have expected it, and perhaps, if he is goin' to work for that cousin of his and against me, it's best that he shouldn't stay here; but I'll miss him awful—a good deal more'n I miss the money he's paid me, and the land knows I need that. I can't understand why he acted the way he did last night. It don't seem like him at all."

"Humph! I should say it didn't. And it ain't like him either. There's a nigger in the woodpile somewheres; I wish I could smoke the critter out. What's Emily say about his goin'?"

"She don't say anything. She won't talk about him at all, and she won't let me mention his name. The poor girl looks as if she'd had a hard night of it, but she looks, too, as if her mind was made up so fur's he was concerned."

Captain Obed pulled at his beard.

"She didn't give him much of a chance last evenin', seemed to me," he said. "If she'd only come back when he called after her that time, I cal'late he was goin' to say somethin'; but she didn't come. Wouldn't answer him at all."

"Did he call after her? I didn't hear him and I don't think she did. When she slammed out of that livin'-room she went right up the back stairs to her bedroom and I chased after her. She was cryin', or next door to it, and I wanted to comfort her. But she wouldn't let me."

"I see. Probably she didn't hear him call at all. He did, though; and he called her by her first name. Matters between 'em must have gone further'n we thought they had."

"Yes, I guess that's so. Do you know, Cap'n, I wouldn't wonder if Mr. Daniels knew that and that was why he was so—so nasty to Mr. Kendrick last night. Well,

I'm afraid it's all off now. Emily's awful proud and she's got a will of her own."

"Um, so I should judge. And John's will ain't all mush and molasses either. That's the worst of young folks. I wonder how many good matches have been broke off just by two young idiots lettin' their pride interfere with their common-sense. I wish you and me had a dime for every one that had; you wouldn't have to keep boarders, and I wouldn't have to run sailin' parties with codfish passengers."

"That's so. But, Cap'n Bangs, DO you think Mr. Kendrick is goin' to try and force me into sellin' out just 'cause his boss says so? It don't seem as if he could. Why, he—he's seemed so grateful for what I've done for him. He said once I couldn't be kinder if I was his own mother. It don't seem as if he could treat me so, just for the money there was in it. But, Oh dear!" as the thought of Mr. Solomon Cobb crossed her mind, "seems as if some folks would do anything for money."

"John wouldn't. I've known of his turnin' down more'n one case there was money in account of its bein' more fishy than honest. No, if he does work for that— that half Holliday cousin of his on this job, it'll be because he's took the man's money and feels he can't decently say no. But I don't believe he will. No, sir-ee! I tell you there's a darky in this kindlin' pile. I'm goin' right down to see John this minute."

He went, but, instead of helping the situation, he merely made it worse. He found John seated at his office desk apparently engaged in his old occupation, that of looking out of the window. The young man's face was pale and drawn, but his manner was perfectly calm.

"Hello, Captain," he observed, as his caller entered. "I trust you've taken the necessary precautions, fumigated and all that sort of thing."

"Fumigated?"

"Why, yes. Unless I'm greatly mistaken, this office is destined to become the den of the moral leper. As soon as my respected fellow-townsmen, the majority of them, learn that I am to battle with Heman the Great, and in such a cause, I shall be shunned and, so to speak, spat upon. You're taking big chances by coming here."

The captain grunted. "Umph!" he sniffed. "They don't know it yet; neither do I."

"Ah yes, but they will shortly. Daniels will take care that they do."

"John, for thunder sakes—"

"Better escape contagion while you can, Captain. Unclean! Unclean!"

"Aw, belay, John! I don't feel like jokin'. What you've got to tell me now is that it ain't so. You ain't goin' to—to try to—to—"

His friend interrupted. "Captain Bangs," he said, sharply, "this is a practical world we live in. You and I have had that preached to us; at least I have and you were present during the sermon. I don't know how you feel, of course; but henceforth I propose to be the most practical man you ever saw."

"Consarn your practicality! Are you goin' to help that—that gold-dust twin—that cussed relation of yours, grab Thankful Barnes' house and land from her?"

"Look here, Bangs; when the—gold-dust twin isn't bad—when the twin offered me the position of his attorney and the blanket retainer along with it, who was it that hesitated concerning my acceptance? You? I don't remember that you did. Neither did—others. But I did accept because—well, because. Now the complications are here, and what then?"

"John—John Kendrick, if you dast to set there and tell me you're cal'latin' to—you can't do it! You can't be goin' to try such a—"

"Oh, yes, I can. I may not succeed, but I can try."

Captain Obed seldom lost his temper, but he lost it now.

"By the everlastin'!" he roared. "And this is the young feller that I've been holdin' up and backin' up as all that's fair and above board! John Kendrick, do you realize—"

"Easy, Captain, easy. Perhaps I realize what I'm doing better than you do."

"You don't neither. Emily Howes—"

John's interruption was sharper now.

"That'll do, Bangs," he said. "Suppose we omit names."

"No, we won't omit 'em. I tell you you don't realize. You're drivin' that girl right straight to Heman Daniels, that's what you're doin'."

Kendrick smiled. "I should say there was no driving necessary," he observed. "Daniels seems to be already the chosen guardian and adviser. I do realize what I'm doing, Captain, and," deliberately, "I shall do it."

"John, Emily—"

"Hush! I like you, Captain Obed. I don't wish to quarrel with you. Take my advice and omit that young lady's name."

Captain Obed made one last appeal.

"John," he pleaded, desperately, "don't! I know you're sort of—sort of tied up to Holliday Kendrick; I know you feel that you are. But this ain't a question of professional honor and that kind of stuff. It's right and wrong."

"Is it? I think not. I was quite willing to discuss the rights and wrongs, but I had no—however, that is past. I was informed last night, and in your hearing, that the question was to be purely a matter of legal skill—of law—between Daniels and myself. Very well; I am a lawyer. Good morning, Captain Bangs."

The captain left the office, still protesting. He was hurt and angry. It was not until later he remembered he had not told Kendrick that Heman Daniels must have spoken without authority when he declared himself the chosen representative of Mrs. Barnes and Emily in all matters between the pair and John. Heman could not have been given such authority because, according to Thankful's story, she and Miss Howes had immediately gone upstairs after leaving the living-room. Daniels could have spoken with them again that evening. But when Captain Obed remembered this it was too late. Thankful had asked Mr. Daniels to take her case, provided the attempt at ousting her from her property ever reached legal proceedings. And Emily Howes left East Wellmouth two days later.

She had not intended to leave for South Middleboro so soon; she had planned to remain another week before going back to her school duties. But there came a letter from the committee asking her to return as soon as possible and she suddenly announced her determination to go at once.

Thankful at first tried to dissuade her, but soon gave up the attempt. It was quite evident that Emily meant to go and equally certain, in her cousin's mind, that the reason for the sudden departure was the scene with John Kendrick. Emily refused to discuss the latter's conduct or to permit the mention of his name. She seemed reluctant even to speak of the Holliday Kendrick matter, although all of East Wellmouth was now talking of little else. When Mrs. Barnes, driven to desperation, begged her to say what should be done, she shook her head.

"I wish I could tell you, Auntie," she said, "but I can't. Perhaps you don't need to do anything yet. Mr. Daniels says the idea that that man can force you into selling is ridiculous."

"I know he does. But I'm a woman, Emily, and what I don't know about law would fill a bigger library than there is in this town by a consider'ble sight. It's always the woman, particularly a widow woman, that gets the worst of it in this kind of thing. I'd feel better if I knew somebody was lookin' out for me. Oh dear, if only Mr. John Kendrick hadn't—"

"Auntie, please."

"Yes, I know. But it don't seem as if he could act so to me. It don't seem—"

"Hush! It is quite evident he can. Don't say any more."

"Well, I won't. But what shall I do? Shall I put it all in Mr. Daniels' hands? He says he'll be glad to help; in fact about everybody thinks he is helpin', I guess. Hannah Parker told me—"

"Don't, Auntie, don't. Put it in Mr. Daniels' hands, if you think best. I suppose it is all you can do. Yes, let Mr. Daniels handle it for you."

"All right. I'll tell him you and I have agreed—"

"No. Tell him nothing of the sort. Don't bring my name into the matter."

"But, Emily, you don't think I ought to sell—"

"No! No! Of course I don't think so. If I were you I should fight to the last ditch. I would never give in—never! Oh, Auntie, I feel wicked and mean to leave you now, with all this new trouble; but I must—I must. I can't stay here—I—"

"There, there, Emily, dear! I understand, I guess. I know how hard it is for you. And I thought so much of him, too. I thought he was such a fine young—"

"Aunt Thankful, are you daring to hint that I—I—care in the least for that—him? How dare you insinuate such a thing to me? I—I despise him!"

"Yes, yes," hastily. "Course you do, course you do. Well, we won't worry about that, any of it. Mr. Daniels says there's nothin' to worry about anyhow, and I'll tell him he can do what he thinks ought to be done when it's necessary. Now let's finish up that packin' of yours, dearie."

Thankful did not trust herself to accompany her cousin to Wellmouth Centre. She was finding it hard enough to face the coming separation with outward cheerfulness, and the long ride to the railway station she found to be too great a strain. So she made the lameness of George Washington's off fore leg an excuse for keeping that personage in the stable, and it was in Winnie S.'s depot-wagon that Emily journeyed to the Centre.

They said good-by at the front gate. Emily, too, was trying to appear cheerful, and the parting was hurried.

"Good-by, Auntie," she said. "Take care of yourself. Write often and I will answer, I promise you. I know you'll be lonely after I've gone, but I have a plan—a secret. If I can carry it through you won't be SO lonely, I'm pretty sure. And don't worry, will you? The mortgage is all right and as for the other thing—well, that will be all right, too. You won't worry, will you?"

"No, no; I'll be too busy to worry. And you'll come down for the Christmas vacation? You will, won't you?"

"I'll try . . . I mean I will if I can arrange it. Good-by, dear."

The depot-wagon rattled out of the yard. Winnie S. pulled up at the gate to shout a bit of news.

"Say, Mrs. Barnes," he yelled, "we got one of your boarders over to our place now. John Kendrick's come there to live. Lots of folks are down on him 'count of his heavin' you over and takin' up along with Mr. Holliday; but Dad says he don't care about that so long's he pays his board reg'lar. Git dap, Old Hundred!"

A last wave of Thankful's hand, the answering wave of a handkerchief from the rear seat of the depot-wagon, and the parting was over. Thankful went into the house. Lonely! She had never been more lonely in her life, except when the news of her husband's death was brought to her. The pang of loneliness which followed her brother Jedediah's departure for the Klondike was as nothing to this. She had promised not to worry, and she must keep that promise, but there was certainly plenty to cause worry. The mortgage which Emily had so comfortably declared "all right" was far from that. Solomon Cobb had not been near her since their interview. He had not yet said that he would renew the mortgage when it fell due. Mrs. Barnes began to fear that he did not intend to renew it.

Heman Daniels, when he came in for supper, seemed disturbed to find that Miss Howes had gone. Somehow or other he had gained the impression that she was to leave the next morning.

"Did she—did Miss Howes leave no message for me?" he inquired, with a carelessness which, to Thankful, seemed more assumed than real.

"No," answered the latter, "no, unless you call it a message about takin' the responsibility of Holliday Kendrick and his schemes off my hands. That is," remembering Emily's desire not to have her name mentioned in the matter, "she didn't leave that. But I guess you can take charge of that mess, if you want to."

Mr. Daniels smiled a superior smile. "I intended doing so," he said, "as a matter of friendship, Mrs. Barnes. You may rest easy. I have taken pains to let the town-folks know that your interests are mine and I think our—er—late—er—friend is learning what our best citizens think of his attitude."

There was truth in this statement. John Kendrick had foreseen the effect upon his popularity which his espousal of his wealthy relative's cause might have and his prophecy concerning "moral leprosy" was in process of fulfillment. Opinion in the village was divided, of course. There were some who, like Darius Holt, announced that they did not blame the young yellow. E. Holliday had money and influence and, as a business man, his attorney would be a fool not to stick by the cash-box. But there were others, and these leading citizens and hitherto good friends, who openly expressed disgust both with the rich man and his lawyer. Several of these citizens called upon Thankful to tell her of their sympathy and of their wish to help her in any way.

"Not that you're liable to need help," said one caller. "This property's yours and even John D. himself couldn't get it from you unless you were willin'. But it's a dirty trick just the same and young Kendrick, that all hands thought was so straight and honest, takin' part in it is the dirtiest thing in it. Well, he's hurt himself more'n he has anybody else."

Captain Obed Bangs was a gloomy man that fall. He had always liked John and the liking had grown to an ardent admiration and affection. He made several attempts to speak with the young man on the subject, but the latter would not discuss it. He was always glad to see the captain and quite willing to talk of anything but Mrs. Barnes' property and of Emily Howes. These topics were taboo and Captain Obed soon ceased to mention them. Also he no longer made daily calls at the ex-barber-shop and, in spite of himself, could not help showing, when he did call, the resentment he felt. John noticed this and there was a growing coldness between the two.

"But," declared the captain, stoutly, when he and Thankful were together, "I still say 'tain't so. I give in that it looks as if 'twas, but I tell you there's a nigger in the woodpile somewheres. Some day he'll be dug out and then there's a heap of tattle-tales and character naggers in this town that'll find they've took the wrong channel. They'll be good and seasick, that's what they'll be."

Mr. E. Holliday Kendrick, if he knew that his own popularity had suffered a shock, did not appear to care. He went on with his plans for enlarging his estate and, when he left East Wellmouth for New York, which he did early in October, told those who asked him that he had left the purchase of the "boarding-house nuisance" in the hands of his attorney. "I shall have that property," he announced, emphatically. "I may not get it for some time, but I shall get it. I make it a point to get what I go after."

Emily, in her letters, those written soon after her arrival in South Middleboro, said nothing concerning her plan, the "secret" which was to cheer Mrs. Barnes' loneliness. Thankful could not help wondering what the secret might be, but in her own letters she asked no questions. And, one day in mid-October, that secret was divulged.

Thankful, busy in the kitchen with Imogene, preparing dinner, heard the sound of wheels and horse's hoofs in the yard. Going to the door, she was surprised to see Captain Obed Bangs climbing from a buggy. The buggy was her own and the horse to which it was attached was her own George Washington. Upon the seat of the buggy was a small boy. Thankful merely glanced at the boy; her interest just then centered upon the fact that the captain was, or apparently had been, using her horse and buggy without her knowledge or consent. She certainly had no objection to his so using it, but it was most unlike him to do so.

"Good mornin', ma'am," he hailed, cheerfully. His eyes were twinkling and he appeared to be in high good humor.

"Why, good mornin', Cap'n," said Thankful. "I—you—you're goin' somewhere, I should judge."

The captain shook his head. "No," he replied, "I've been. Had an errand up to the Centre. I knew somethin' was comin' on the mornin' train so I drove up to fetch it. Thought you wouldn't mind my usin' your horse and buggy. Imogene knew I was usin' it."

Thankful was surprised. "She did?" she repeated. "That's funny. She didn't say a word to me."

"No, I told her not to. You see, the—the somethin' I was expectin' was for you, so I thought we'd make it a little surprise. Emily—Miss Howes, she sent it."

"Emily—sent somethin' to me?"

"Yup."

"For the land sakes! Well," after a moment, "did it come? Where is it?"

"Oh, yes, it came. It's right there in the buggy. Don't you see it?"

Thankful looked at the buggy. The only thing in it, so far as she could see, was the little boy on the seat. The little boy grinned.

"Hello, Aunt Thankful," he said. "I've come to stay with you, I have."

Thankful started, stared, and then made a rush for the buggy.

"Georgie Hobbs!" she cried. "You blessed little scamp! Come here to me this minute. Well, well, well!"

Georgie came and was received with a bear hug and a shower of kisses.

"Well, well!" repeated Thankful. "And to think I didn't know you! I'm ashamed of myself. And you're the surprise, I suppose. You ARE one, sure and sartin. How did you get here?"

"I came on the cars," declared Georgie, proudly. "Ma and Emmie put me on 'em and told me to sit right still until I got to Wellmouth Centre and then get off. And I did, too; didn't I, Mr.—I mean Captain Bangs."

"You bet you did!" agreed the delighted captain. "That's some relation you've got there, Mrs. Barnes. He's little but Oh my! He and I have had a good talk on the way down. We got along fust-rate; hey, commodore? The commodore's agreed to ship second-mate along with me next v'yage I make, if I ever make one."

Thankful held her "relation"—he was Emily's half-brother and her own favorite next to Emily herself in that family—at arm's length. "You blessed little—little mite!" she exclaimed. "So you come 'way down here all alone just to see your old auntie. Did you ever in your life! And I suppose you're the 'secret' Emily said she had, the one that was to keep me from bein' lonesome."

Georgie nodded. "Yes," he said. "Emmie, she's wrote you all about me. I've got the letter pinned inside of me here," patting his small chest. "And I'm goin' to stay ever so long, I am. I want to see the pig and the hens and the—and the orphan, and everything."

"So you shall," declared Thankful. "I'm glad enough to see you to turn the house inside out if you wanted to look at it. And you knew all about this, I suppose?" turning to Captain Obed.

The captain laughed aloud.

"Sartin I did," he said. "Miss Howes and I have been writin' each other like a couple of courtin' young folks. I knew the commodore was goin' to set sail today and I was on hand up to the depot to man the yards. Forgive me for hookin' your horse and buggy, will you, Mrs. Thankful?"

Forgiveness was granted. Thankful would have forgiven almost anything just then. The "commodore" announced that he was hungry and he was hurried into the house. The cares of travel had not taken away his appetite. He was introduced to Imogene, at whom he stared fixedly for a minute or more and then asked if she was the "orphan." When told that she was he asked if her mamma and papa were truly dead. Imogene said she guessed they were. Then Georgie asked why, and, after then, what made them that way, adding the information that he had a kitty that went dead one time and wasn't any good any more.

The coming of the "commodore" brought a new touch of life to the High Cliff House, which had settled down for its winter nap. Thankful, of course, read Emily's letter at the first opportunity. Emily wrote that she felt sure Georgie would be company for her cousin and that she had conceived the idea of the boy's visit before leaving East Wellmouth, but had said nothing because she was not sure mother would consent. But that consent had been granted and Georgie might stay until Christmas, perhaps even after that if he was not too great a care.

He was something of a care, there was no doubt of that. Imogene, whom he liked and who liked him, declared that "that young one had more jump in him than a sand flea." The very afternoon of his arrival he frightened the hens into shrieking hysterics, poked the fat and somnolent Patrick Henry, the pig, with a sharp stick to see if he was alive and not "gone dead" like the kitten, and barked his shins and nose by falling out of the wheelbarrow in the barn. Kenelm, who still retained his position at the High Cliff House and was meek and lowly under the double domination of his fiancee and his sister, was inclined to grumble. "A feller can't set down to rest a minute," declared Kenelm, "without that young one's jumpin' out at him from behind somethin' or 'nother and hollerin', 'Boo!' Seems to like to scare me into a fit. Picks on me wuss than Hannah, he does."

But even Kenelm confessed to a liking for the "pesky little nuisance." Captain Obed idolized him and took him on excursions along the beach or to his own fishhouses, where Georgie sat on a heap of nets and came home smelling strongly of cod, but filled to the brim with sea yarns. And Thankful found in the boy the one comfort and solace for her increasing troubles and cares. Altogether the commodore was in a fair way to become a thoroughly spoiled officer.

With November came the rains again, and, compared with them, those of early September seemed but showers. Day after day and night after night the wind blew and the water splashed against the windows and poured from the overflowing gutters. Patrick Henry, the pig, found his quarters in the new pen, in the hollow behind the barn, the center of the flood zone, and being discovered one morning marooned on a swampy islet in the middle of a muddy lake, was transferred to the old sty, that built by the late Mr. Laban Eldredge, beneath the woodshed and adjoining the potato cellar. Thankful's orderly, neat soul rebelled against having a pig under the house, but, as she expressed it, "'twas either that or havin' the critter two foot under water."

Captain Obed, like every citizen of East Wellmouth, was disgusted with the weather. "I was cal'latin' to put in my spare time down to the shanty buildin' a new dory," he said, "but I guess now I'll build an ark instead. If this downpour keeps on I'll need one bad as Noah ever did."

Heman Daniels, Miss Timpson and Caleb Hammond were now the only boarders and roomers Mrs. Barnes had left to provide for. There was little or no profit in providing for them, for the rates paid by the two last named were not high, and their demands were at times almost unreasonable. Miss Timpson had a new idea now, that of giving up the room she had occupied since coming to the Barnes boarding-house and moving her belongings into the suite at the rear of the second floor, that comprising the large room and the little back bedroom adjoining, the latter the scene of Thankful's spooky adventure on the first night of her arrival in East Wellmouth. These rooms ordinarily rented for much more than Miss Timpson had paid for her former apartment, but she had no thought of paying more for them. "Of course I shouldn't expect to get 'em for the same if 'twas summer," she explained to Thankful, "but just now, with 'em standin' empty, I might as well move there as not. I know you'll be glad to have me, won't you, Mrs. Barnes, you and me being such good friends by this time."

And Thankful, although conscious of an injustice somewhere, did not like to refuse her "good friend." So she consented and Miss Timpson moved into the back rooms. But she no sooner had her trunks carried there than she was struck by another brilliant idea. Thankful, hearing unusual sounds from above that Saturday morning, ascended the back stairs to find the school mistress tugging at the bureau, which she was apparently trying to drag from the small room into the larger.

"It came to me all of a sudden," panted Miss Timpson, who was out of breath but enthusiastic. "That little room's awful small and stuffy to sleep in, and I do hate to sleep in a stuffy room. But when I was standing there sniffing and looking it came to me."

"What came to you?" demanded the puzzled Thankful. "What are you talkin' about—the bureau?"

"No, no! The idea! The bureau couldn't come to me by itself, could it? No, the idea came to me. That little room isn't good for much as a bedroom, but it will make the loveliest study. I can put my table and my books in there and move the bed and things in here. Then I'll have a beautiful, nice big bedroom and the cutest little study. And I've always wanted a study. Now if you and Imogene help me with the bureau and bed it'll be all fixed."

So Imogene, assisted by Kenelm, who was drafted in Thankful's place, spent a good part of the afternoon shifting furniture and arranging the bedroom and the "study." Miss Timpson superintended, and as she was seldom satisfied until each separate item of the suite's equipment had been changed about at least twice, in order to get the "effect," all three were nervous and tired when the shifting was over. Miss Timpson should have been happy over the attainment of the study, but instead she appeared gloomy and downcast.

"I declare," she said, as she and Thankful sat together in the living-room that evening, "I don't know's I've done right, after all. I don't know's I wish I had stayed right where I was."

"Mercy on us! Why?" demanded Thankful, a trifle impatiently.

"Oh, I don't know. Maybe 'cause I'm kind of tired and nervous tonight. I feel as if—as if something was going to happen to me. I wonder if I could have another cup of tea before I went to bed; it might settle my nerves, you know."

Considering that the lady had drunk three cups of tea at supper Mrs. Barnes could not help feeling doubtful concerning the soothing effect of a fourth. But she prepared it and brought it into the living-room. Miss Timpson sipped the tea and groaned.

"Do you ever have presentiments, Mrs. Barnes?" she asked.

"Have what?"

"Presentiments? Warnings, you know? I've had several in my life and they have always come to something. I feel as if I was going to have one now. Heavens! Hear that wind and rain! Don't they sound like somebody calling—calling?"

"No, they don't. They sound cold and wet, that's all. Dear me, I never saw such a spell of weather. I thought this mornin' 'twas goin' to clear, but now it's come on again, hard as ever."

"Well," with dismal resignation, "we'll all go when our time comes, I suppose. We're here today and gone tomorrow. I don't suppose there's any use setting and worrying. Be prepared, that's the main thing. Have you bought a cemetery lot, Mrs. Barnes? You ought to; everybody had. We can't tell when we're liable to need a grave."

"Goodness gracious sakes! Don't talk about cemetery lots and graves. You give me the blue creeps. Go to bed and rest up. You're tired, and no wonder; you've moved no less'n three times since mornin', and they say one movin's as bad as a fire. Here! Give me that tea-cup. There's nothin' left in it but grounds, and you don't want to drink THEM."

Miss Timpson relinquished the cup, took her lamp and climbed the stairs. Her good night was as mournful as a funeral march. Thankful, left alone, tried to read for a time, but the wailing wind and squeaking shutters made her nervous and depressed, so, after putting the key under the mat of the side door for Heman Daniels, who was out attending a meeting of the Masonic Lodge, she, too, retired.

It was not raining when she awoke, but the morning was gray and cloudy. She came downstairs early, so early—for it was Sunday morning, when all East Wellmouth lies abed—that she expected to find no one, not even Imogene, astir. But, to her great surprise, Miss Timpson was seated by the living-room stove.

"Land sakes!" exclaimed Thankful. "Are you up? What's the matter?"

Miss Timpson, who had started violently when Mrs. Barnes entered, turned toward the latter a face as white, so Thankful described it afterward, "as unbleached muslin." This was not a bad simile, for Miss Timpson's complexion was, owing to her excessive tea-drinking, a decided yellow. Just now it was a very pale yellow.

"Who is it?" she gasped. "Oh, it's you, Mrs. Barnes. It IS you, isn't it?"

"Me? Of course it's me. Have I changed so much in the night that you don't know me? What is it, Miss Timpson? Are you sick? Can I get you anything?"

"No, no. I ain't sick—in body, anyway. And nobody can get me anything this side of the grave. Mrs. Barnes, I'm going."

"You're GOIN'? What? You don't mean you're dyin'?"

Considering her lodger's remarks of the previous evening, those relating to "going when the time came," it is no wonder Thankful was alarmed. But Miss Timpson shook her head.

"No," she said, "I don't mean that, not yet, though that'll come next; I feel it coming already. No, Mrs. Barnes, I don't mean that. I mean I'm going away. I can't live here any longer."

Thankful collapsed upon a chair.

"Goin'!" she repeated. "You're goin' to leave here? Why—why you've just fixed up to stay!"

Miss Timpson groaned. "I know," she wailed; "I thought I had, but I—I've changed my mind. I'm going to leave—now."

By way of proof she pointed to her traveling-bag, which was beside her on the floor. Mrs. Barnes had not noticed the bag before, but now she saw that it was, apparently, packed.

"My trunks ain't ready yet," went on the schoolmistress. "I tried to pack 'em, but—but I couldn't. I couldn't bear to do it alone. Maybe you or Imogene will help me by and by. Oh, my soul! What was that?"

"What? I didn't hear anything."

"Didn't you? Well, perhaps I didn't, either. It's just my nerves, I guess! Mrs. Barnes, could you help me pack those trunks pretty soon? I'm going away. I must go. If I stay in this house any longer I shall DIE."

She was trembling and wringing her hands. Thankful tried to comfort her and did succeed in quieting her somewhat, but, in spite of her questionings and pleadings Miss Timpson refused to reveal the cause of her agitation or of her sudden determination to leave the High Cliff House.

"It ain't anything you've done or haven't done, Mrs. Barnes," she said. "I like it here and I like the board and I like you. But I must go. I'm going to my cousin's down in the village first and after that I don't know where I'll go. Please don't ask me any more."

She ate a few mouthfuls of the breakfast which Thankful hastily prepared for her and then she departed for her cousin's. Thankful begged her to stay until Kenelm came, when he might harness the horse and drive her to her destination, but she would not wait. She would not even remain to pack her trunks.

"I'll come back and pack 'em," she said. "Or perhaps you and Imogene will pack 'em for me. Oh, Mrs. Barnes, you've been so kind. I hate to leave you this way, I do, honest."

"But WHY are you leavin'?" asked Thankful once more. For the first time Miss Timpson seemed to hesitate. She looked about, as if to make sure that the two were alone; then she leaned forward and whispered in her companion's ear.

"Mrs. Barnes," she whispered, "I—I didn't mean to tell you. I didn't mean to tell anybody. 'Twas too personal, too sacred a thing to tell. But I don't know's I shan't tell you after all; seem's as if I must tell somebody. Mrs. Barnes, I shan't live much longer. I've had a warning."

Thankful stared at her.

"Rebecca Timpson!" she exclaimed. "Have you gone crazy? What are you talkin' about? A warnin'!"

"Yes, a warning. I was warned last night. You—you knew I was a twin, didn't you?"

"A which?"

"A twin. Probably you didn't know it, but I used to have a twin sister, Medora, that died when she was only nineteen. She and I looked alike, and were alike, in most everything. We thought the world of each other, used to be together daytimes and sleep together nights. And she used to—er—well, she was different from me in one way—she couldn't help it, poor thing—she used to snore something dreadful. I used to scold her for it, poor soul. Many's the time I've reproached myself since, but—"

"For mercy sakes, what's your sister's snorin' got to do with—"

"Hush! Mrs. Barnes," with intense solemnity. "As sure as you and I live and breathe this minute, my sister Medora came to me last night."

"CAME to you! Why—you mean you dreamed about her, don't you? There's nothin' strange in that. When you took that fourth cup of tea I said to myself—"

"HUSH! Oh, hush! DON'T talk so. I didn't dream. Mrs. Barnes, I woke up at two o'clock this morning and—and I heard Medora snoring as plain as I ever heard anything."

Thankful was strongly tempted to laugh, but the expression on Miss Timpson's face was so deadly serious that she refrained.

"Goodness!" she exclaimed. "Is that all? That's nothin'. A night like last night, with the rain and the blinds and the wind—"

"Hush! It wasn't the wind. Don't you suppose I know? I thought it was the wind or my imagination at first. But I laid there and listened and I kept hearing it. Finally I got up and lit my lamp; and still I heard it. It was snoring and it didn't come from the room I was in. It came from the little back room I'd made into a study."

Thankful's smile faded. She was conscious of a curious prickling at the roots of her black hair. The back bedroom! The room in which Laban Eldredge died! The room in which she herself had heard—

"I went into that room," continued Miss Timpson. "I don't know how I ever did it, but I did. I looked everywhere, but there was nobody there, not a sign of anybody. And still that dreadful snoring kept on and on. And then I realized—" with a shudder, "I realized what I hadn't noticed before; that room was exactly the size and shape of the one Medora and I used to sleep in. Mrs. Barnes, it was Medora's spirit that had come to me. Do you wonder I can't stay here any longer?"

Thankful fought with her feelings. She put a hand on the back of her neck and rubbed vigorously. "Nonsense!" she declared, bravely. "You imagined it. Nonsense! Whoever heard of a snorin' ghost?"

But Miss Timpson only shook her head. "Good-by, Thankful," she said. "I shan't tell anybody; as I said, I didn't mean to tell you. If—if you hear that anything's happened to me—happened sudden, you know—you'll understand. You can tell Imogene and Mr. Daniels and Mr. Hammond that I—that I've gone visiting to my cousin Sarah's. That'll be true, anyway. Good-by. You MAY see me again in this life, but I doubt it."

She hurried away along the path. Thankful reentered the house and stood in the middle of the kitchen floor, thinking. Then she walked steadily to the foot of the back stairs, ascended them, and walked straight to the apartments so recently occupied by the schoolmistress. Miss Timpson's trunks were there and the greater part of her belongings. Mrs. Barnes did not stop to look at these. She crossed the larger room and entered the little back bedroom.

The clouds were breaking and the light of the November sun shone in. The little room was almost cheerful. There were no sounds except those from without, the neigh of George Washington from his stall, the cackle of the hens, the hungry grunts of Patrick Henry, the pig, in his sty beside the kitchen.

Thankful looked and listened. Then she made a careful examination of the room, but found nothing mysterious or out of the ordinary. And yet there was a mystery there. She had long since decided that her own experience in that room had been imagination, but now that conviction was shaken. Miss Timpson must have heard something; she HAD heard something which frightened her into leaving the boarding-house she professed to like so well. Ghost or no ghost, Miss Timpson had gone; and one more source of income upon which Mrs. Barnes had depended went with her. Slowly, and with the feeling that not only this world but the next was conspiring to bring about the failure of her enterprise and the ruin of her plans and her hopes, Thankful descended the stairs to the kitchen and set about preparing breakfast.

CHAPTER XII

MR. CALEB HAMMOND rose that Sunday morning with a partially developed attack of indigestion and a thoroughly developed "grouch." The indigestion was due to an injudicious partaking of light refreshment—sandwiches, ice cream and sarsaparilla "tonic"—at the club the previous evening. Simeon Baker had paid for the refreshment, ordering the supplies sent in from Mr. Chris Badger's store. Simeon had received an unexpected high price for cranberries shipped to New York, and was in consequence "flush" and reckless. He appeared at the club at nine-thirty, after most of its married members had departed for their homes and only a few of the younger set and one or two bachelors, like Mr. Hammond, remained, and announced that he was going to "blow the crowd." The crowd was quite willing to be blown and said so.

Mr. Hammond ate three sandwiches and two plates of ice cream, also he smoked two cigars. He did not really feel the need of the second cream or the second cigar, but, as they were furnished without cost to him, he took them as a matter of principle. Hence the indigestion.

The "grouch" was due partially to the unwonted dissipation and its consequences and partly to the fact that his winter "flannels" had not been returned by Mrs. Melinda Pease, to whom they had been consigned for mending and overhauling.

It was the tenth of November and for a period of twenty-four years, ever since his recovery from a severe attack of rheumatic fever, Caleb had made it a point to lay aside his summer underwear on the morning of November tenth and don a heavy suit. Weather, cold or warm, was not supposed to have any bearing on this change. The ninth might be as frigid as a Greenland twilight and the tenth as balmy as a Florida noon—no matter; on the ninth Mr. Hammond wore light underwear and shivered; on the tenth he wore his "flannels" and perspired. It was another of his principles, and Caleb had a deserved reputation for adhering to principle and being "sot" in his ways.

So, when, on this particular tenth of November, this Sabbath morning, he rose, conscious of the sandwiches and "tonic," and found no suit of flannels ready for him to don, his grouch began to develop. He opened his chamber door a crack and shouted through the crack.

"Mrs. Barnes," he called. "Hi—i, Mrs. Barnes!"

Thankful, still busy in the kitchen, where she had been joined by Imogene, sent the latter to find out what was the matter. Imogene returned, grinning.

"He wants his flannels," she announced. "Wants to know where them winter flannels Mrs. Pease sent home yesterday are. Why, ain't they in his room, he says."

Thankful sniffed. Her experience with Miss Timpson, and the worry caused by the latter's leaving, had had their effect upon her patience.

"Mercy sakes!" she exclaimed. "Is that all? I thought the house was afire. I don't know where his flannels are. Why should I? Where'd Melindy put 'em when she brought 'em here?"

Imogene chuckled. "I don't think she brought 'em at all," she replied. "She wa'n't here yesterday. She—why, yes, seems to me Kenelm said he heard she was sick abed with a cold."

Thankful nodded. "So she is," she said. "Probably the poor thing ain't had time to finish mendin' 'em. It's a good deal of a job, I guess. She told me once that that Hammond man wore his inside clothes till they wa'n't anything BUT mendin', just hung together with patches, as you might say. His suits and overcoats are all right enough 'most always, but he can't seem to bear to spend money for anything underneath. Perhaps he figgers that patches are good as anything else, long's they don't show. Imogene, go tell him Melindy didn't fetch 'em."

Imogene went and returned with her grin broader than ever.

"He says she did bring 'em," she announced. "Says she always brings him his things on the ninth. He's pretty peppery this mornin', seems to me. Says he don't cal'late to stand there and freeze much longer."

"Freeze! Why, it's the warmest day we've had for a fortni't. The sun's come out and it's cleared up fine, like Indian summer. Oh, DO be still!" as another shout for "Mrs. Barnes" came from above. "Here, never mind, Imogene; I'll tell him."

She went into the front hall and called up the stairs.

"Your things ain't here, Mr. Hammond," she said. "Melindy didn't bring 'em. She's laid up with a cold and probably couldn't get 'em ready."

"Course she's got 'em ready! She always has 'em ready. She knows I want 'em."

"Maybe so, but she ain't always sick, 'tain't likely. They ain't here, anyway. You won't need 'em today."

"Need 'em? Course I need 'em. It's colder than Christmas."

"No, it isn't. It's almost as warm as September. Put on two suits of your others, if you're so cold. And come down to breakfast as soon as you can. We've all had ours."

When Mr. Hammond did come down to breakfast his manner was that of a martyr. The breakfast itself, baked beans and fishballs, did not appeal to him, and he ate little. He grumbled as he drank his coffee.

"Healthy note, this is!" he muttered. "Got to set around and freeze to death just 'cause that lazy critter ain't finished her job. I pay her for it, don't I?"

Thankful sniffed. "I suppose you do," she said, adding under her breath, "though how much you pay is another thing."

"Is this all the breakfast you've got?" queried Caleb.

"Why, yes; it's what we always have Sunday mornin's. Isn't it what you expected?"

"Oh, I expected it, all right. Take it away; I don't want no more. Consarn it! I wish sometimes I had a home of my own."

"Well, why don't you have one? I should think you would. You can afford it."

Mr. Hammond did not reply. He folded his napkin, seized his hat and coat and went out. When he crossed the threshold he shivered, as a matter of principle.

He stalked gloomily along the path by the edge of the bluff. Captain Obed Bangs came up the path and they met.

"Hello, Caleb!" hailed the captain. "Fine weather at last, eh? Almost like August. Injun summer at last, I cal'late. What you got your coat collar turned up for? Afraid of getting your neck sunburned?"

Mr. Hammond grunted and hurried on. Captain Obed had chosen a poor topic if he desired a lengthy conversation.

Mrs. Pease lived at the farther end of the village and when Caleb reached there he was met by the lady's niece, Emma Snow.

"Aunt Melindy's real poorly," said Emma. "She's been so for 'most three days. I'm stayin' here with her till she gets better. No, she ain't had time to do your mendin' yet. Anyhow it's so nice and warm you don't need the things, that's a comfort."

It may have been a comfort to her, but it was not to Caleb. He growled a reply and turned on his heel. The churchgoers along the main road received scanty acknowledgment of their greetings.

"Ain't you comin' to meetin'?" asked Abbie Larkin.

"Naw," snarled Caleb, "I ain't."

"Why not? And it's such a lovely day, too."

"Ugh!"

"Why ain't you comin' to meetin', Mr. Hammond?"

"'Cause I don't feel like it, that's why."

"I want to know! Well, you DON'T seem to be in a pious frame of mind, that's a fact. Better come; you may not feel like church, but I should say you needed it, if ever anybody did."

Caleb did not deign a reply. He stalked across the road and took the path to the shore.

As he came opposite the Parker cottage he saw Hannah Parker at the window. He nodded and his nod was returned. Hannah's experience was as gloomy as his own. She did not look happy and somehow the idea that she was not happy pleased him; Abbie Larkin had been altogether too happy; it grated on him. He was miserable and he wanted company of his own kind. He stopped, hesitated, and then turned in at the Parker gate.

Hannah opened the door.

"Good mornin', Caleb," she said. "Come in, won't you? It looks sort of chilly outdoor."

This WAS a kindred spirit. Mr. Hammond entered the Parker sitting-room.

Hannah motioned toward a chair and he sat down.

"Mornin', Hannah," said Caleb. "'Tis chilly. It'll be a mercy if we don't catch our deaths, dressed the way some of us be. How's things with you?"

Miss Parker shook her head. "Oh, I don't know, Caleb," she answered. "They ain't all they might be, I'm afraid."

"What's the matter? Ain't you feelin' up to the mark?"

"Oh, yes—yes; I'm feeling well enough in body. I ain't sick, if that's what you mean. I'm kind of blue and—and lonesome, that's all. I try to bear up under my burdens, but I get compressed in spirit sometimes, I can't help it. Ah, hum a day!"

She sighed and Mr. Hammond sighed also.

"You ain't the only one," he said. "I'm bluer'n a whetstone myself, this mornin'."

"What's the trouble?"

"Trouble? Trouble enough! Somethin' happened this mornin' that riled me all up. It—" he paused, remembering that the cause of the "rilin'" was somewhat personal, not to say delicate. "Well—well, never mind what it was," he added. "'Twas mighty aggravatin', that's all I've got to say."

Hannah sighed again. "Ah, hum!" she observed. "There's aggravations enough in this life. And they generally come on account of somebody else, too. There's times when I wish I didn't have any flesh and blood."

"Hey? Good land! No flesh and blood! What do you want—bones?"

"Oh, I don't mean that. I wish I didn't have any—any relations of my own flesh and blood."

"Humph! I don't know's you'd be any better off. I ain't got nobody and I ain't what you might call cheerful. I know what's the matter with you, though. That Kenelm's been frettin' you again, I suppose."

He had guessed it. Kenelm that morning had suddenly announced that he was to have a day off. He was cal'latin' to borrow Mrs. Barnes' horse and buggy and go for a ride. His sister promptly declared that would be lovely; she was just wishing for a ride. Whereupon Kenelm had hemmed and hawed and, at last, admitted that his company for the drive was already provided.

"Oh!" sneered Hannah. "I see. You're goin' to take that precious inmate of yours along. And I've got to set here alone at home. Well, I should think you'd be

ASHAMED."

"What for? Ain't nothin' in takin' a lady you're keepin' company with out drivin', is there? I don't see no shame in that."

"No, I presume likely YOU don't. You're way past shame, both of you. And when I think of all I've done for you. Slaved and cooked your meals—"

"Well, you're cookin' 'em yet, ain't you? I ain't asked you to stop."

"I will stop, though. I will."

"All right, then; heave ahead and stop. I cal'late my wife'll be willin' to cook for me, if it's needful."

"Your wife! She ain't your wife yet. And she shan't be. This ridiculous engaged business of yours is—is—"

"Well, if you don't like the engagin', why don't you stop it?"

"Why don't YOU stop it, you mean. You would if you had the feelin's of a man."

"Humph! And let some everlastin' lawyer sue me out of my last cent for damages. All right, I'll stop it if you say so. There's plenty of room in the poorhouse, they tell me. How'd you like to give us this place and move to the poorhouse, Hannah?"

"But—but, O Kenelm, I can't think of your gettin' married! I can't think of it!"

"Don't think of it. I ain't thinkin' of it no more'n I can help. Why ain't you satisfied with things as they be? Everything's goin' on all right enough now, ain't it? You and me are livin' together same as we have for ever so long. You're here and I—well, I—"

He did not finish the sentence, but his sister read his thought. She knew perfectly well that her brother was finding a measure of enjoyment in the situation, so far as his dealings with her were concerned. He was more independent than he had been since she took him in charge. But she realized, too, her own impotence. She could not drive him too hard or he might be driven into marrying Imogene. And THAT Hannah was determined should be deferred as long as possible.

So she said no more concerning the "ride" and merely showed her feelings by moping in the corner and wiping her eyes with her handkerchief whenever he looked in her direction. After he had gone she spent the half-hour previous to Mr. Hammond's arrival in alternate fits of rage and despair.

"So Kenelm's been actin' unlikely, has he?" queried Caleb. "Well, if he was my brother he'd soon come to time quick, or be put to bed in a hospital. That's what would happen to HIM."

Miss Parker looked as if the hospital picture was more appealing than dreadful.

"I wish he was your brother," she said. "Or I wish I was independent and had a house of my own."

"Huh! Gosh! So do I wish I had one. I've been wishin' it all the mornin'. If I had a home of my own I'd have what I wanted to eat—yes, and wear. And I'd have 'em when I wanted 'em, too."

"Don't they give you good things to eat over at Mrs. Barnes'?"

"Oh, they're good enough maybe, if they're what you want. But boardin's boardin'; 'tain't like your own home."

"Caleb, it's a wonder to me you don't rent a little house and live in it. You've got money enough; least so everybody says."

"Humph! What everybody says is 'most generally lies. What would be the sense of my hirin' a house? I'd have to have a housekeeper and a good one costs like thunder. A feller's wife has to get along on what he gives her, but a housekeeper—"

He stopped short, seemingly struck by a new and amazing idea. Miss Parker rambled on about the old days when "dear papa" was alive; how happy she was then, and so on, with occasional recourse to the handkerchief. Suddenly Caleb slapped his knee.

"It's all right," he said. "It's fine—and it's commonsense, too. Hannah, what's the matter with you and me gettin' married?"

Hannah stared at him.

"Married!" she repeated. "Me get married! Who to, for the land sakes? Are you out of your head?"

"Not a mite. What's the matter with you marryin' me?"

"My soul! Is this a funny-paper joke, or are you—"

"'Tain't a joke; I mean it. Is there any reason why we shouldn't marry and settle down together, you and me? I don't see none. You could keep house for me then, and 'twouldn't cost—that is, you could look out for me, and I—well, I suppose likely I could look out for you, too. Why not?"

"Why, how you talk, Caleb Hammond!"

"No, I don't talk neither. I mean it. You was wishin' for a home of your own; so was I. Let's have one together."

"Well, I swan! Get married at our—at our age! I never did hear such talk! We'd be a nice young bride and groom, wouldn't we? I guess East Wellmouth folks would have somethin' to laugh at then."

"Let 'em laugh. Laughin' don't cost nothin', and, if it does, we won't have to pay for it. See here, Hannah, this ain't any foolish front-gate courtin', this ain't. It's just common-sense business. Let's do it. I will if you will."

Miss Parker shook her head. The prospect of being Mrs. Caleb Hammond was not too alluring. Caleb's reputation as a husband was not, while his wife lived, that of a "liberal provider." And yet this was Hannah's first proposal, and it had come years after she had given up hoping for one. So she prolonged the delicious moment as long as possible.

"I suppose you're thinkin' about that brother of yours," suggested Mr. Hammond. "Well, he'll be all right. 'Cordin' to what I've heard, and seen myself, he's hangin' around that hired help girl at the High Cliff pretty reg'lar these days. Maybe he'll marry her and you'll be left without anybody. If he don't marry her he can come to live along of us—maybe. If he does he'll mind his p's and q's, I tell you that. He'll find out who's boss."

This speech had an effect. For the first time Hannah's determination wavered. Kenelm was, although Caleb did not know it, actually engaged to marry Imogene. His sister was even then writhing under the humiliation. And here was an opportunity to get even, not only with Kenelm, but with the "inmate." If she, Hannah, were to marry and leave the pair instead of being herself left! Oh, the glory of it— the triumphant glory of it! How she could crush her brother! How she could gloat over and sneer at Imogene! The things she might say—she, the wife of a rich man! Oh, wonderful!

"Well, come on, Hannah, come on," urged the impatient Caleb. "What do you say?"

But Miss Parker still shook her head. "It ain't any use, Caleb," she declared. "Even if—if I wanted to, how could I tell Kenelm? He'd raise an awful fuss. He'd tell everybody and they—"

"No, he wouldn't. I'd break his neck if he did. . . . And—eh—" as another idea came to him, "he needn't know till 'twas all over. We could get married right off now, and not tell a soul—Kenelm or anybody else—till it was done. Then they could talk or shut up, we wouldn't care. They couldn't change nothin'."

"Caleb Hammond, do you suppose I'd have the face to go to a minister in this town and have you tell him we'd come to get married? I'd be so ashamed—"

"Hold on! We don't have to go to a minister in this town. There's other towns with parsons in them, ain't they? We could drive over somewheres else."

"Everybody'd see us drivin' together."

"What of it? They see us drivin' to the Cattle Show together, didn't they?"

"Yes, and they've talked about it ever since, some of 'em. That Abbie Larkin said—Oh, I can't tell you what she said. No, I shan't do it. I shouldn't have the face. And everybody'd ask where we was bound, and I'd—I'd be so—so mortified and—and—why, I'd act like a reg'lar—er—er—domicile that had run away from the Idiots' Home. No, no, no! I couldn't."

Mr. Hammond thought it over. Then he said:

"See here, Hannah, I cal'late we can fix that. We'll start in the night, after all hands have gone to bed. I'll sneak out about quarter to twelve and borrow Thankful's horse and buggy out of her barn. I know where she keeps the key. I'll be ready here at twelve prompt—or not here, maybe, but down in the hollow back of your hen-house. You must be there and we'll drive over to Trumet—"

"Trumet! Why, Caleb Hammond, I know everybody in Trumet well's I do here. And gettin' to Trumet at three o'clock in the mornin' would be—"

"Then we won't go to Trumet. We'll go to Bayport. It's quite a trip, but that's all the better 'cause we won't make Bayport till daylight. Then we'll hunt up a parson to marry us and come back here and tell folks when we get good and ready. Thankful'll miss the horse and team, I cal'late, but I'll fix that; I'll leave a note sayin' I took the critter, bein' called away on business."

"Yes, but what will I tell Kenelm?"

"Don't tell him anything, the foolhead. Why, yes, you can leave a note sayin' you've gone up to the village, to the store or somethin', and that he must get his own breakfast 'cause you won't be back till after he's gone to work over to Thankful's. That'll fix it. By crimus! That'll fix it fine. Look here, Hannah Parker; I've set out to do this and, by crimus, I'm goin' to do it. Come on now; let's."

Caleb was, as has been said, "sot" in his ways. He was "sot" now, and although Hannah continued to protest and declare she could not do such a thing, she yielded at last. Mr. Hammond left the Parker cottage in a triumphant mood. He had won his point and that had pleased him for a time; then, as he began to ponder upon that point and its consequences his triumph changed to misgiving and doubt. He had had no idea, until that forenoon, of marrying again. His proposal had been made on impulse, on the spur of the moment. He was not sure that he wished to marry Hannah Parker. But he had pleaded and persuaded her into accepting him that very night. Even if he wished to back out, how could he—now? He was conscious of an uneasy feeling that, perhaps, he had made a fool of himself.

He went to his room early in the evening and stayed there, looking at his watch and waiting for the rest of the family to retire. He heard Georgie's voice in the room at the end of the hall, where Mrs. Barnes was tucking the youngster in for the night. Later he heard Imogene come up the backstairs and, after her, Thankful herself. But it was nearly eleven before Heman Daniels' important and dignified step sounded on the front stairs and by that time the Hammond nerves were as taut as banjo strings.

It was nearly twelve before he dared creep downstairs and out of the back door, the key of which he left in the lock. Luckily the barn was a good distance from the house and Mrs. Barnes and Imogene were sound sleepers. But even with those advantages he did not dare attempt getting the buggy out of the barn, and decided to use the old discarded carryall, relic of "Cap'n Abner," which now stood under the open shed at the rear.

George Washington looked at him in sleepy wonder as he tiptoed into the barn and lit the lantern. To be led out of his stall at "midnight's solemn hour" and harnessed was more than George's equine reasoning could fathom. The harnessing was a weird and wonderful operation. Caleb's trembling fingers were all thumbs. After a while, however, the harnessing was accomplished somehow and in some way, although whether the breeching was where the bridle should have been or vice versa was more than the harnesser would have dared swear. After several centuries, as the prospective bridegroom was reckoning time, the horse was between the shafts of the carriage and driven very carefully along the road to the Parker homestead.

He hitched the sleepy animal to a pine tree just off the road and tiptoed toward the hollow, the appointed rendezvous. To reach this hollow he was obliged to pass through the Parker yard and, although he went on tiptoe, each footstep sounded, in his ears, like the crack of doom. He tried to think of some explanation to be made to Kenelm in case the latter should hear and hail him, but he could think of nothing more plausible than that he was taking a walk, and this was far from satisfactory.

And then he was hailed. From a window above, at the extreme end of the kitchen, came a trembling whisper.

"Caleb! Caleb Hammond, is that you?"

Mr. Hammond's heart, which had been thumping anything but a wedding march beneath the summer under-flannels, leaped up and stuck in his throat; but he choked it down and gasped a faint affirmative.

"Oh, my soul and body! Where HAVE you been? I've been waitin' and waitin'."

"What in time did you wait up there for? Why don't you come down?"

"I can't. Kenelm's locked the doors, and the keys are right next to his room door. I can't get down."

Here was an unexpected obstacle. Caleb was nonplused.

"Go home!" wailed the voice from above. "Don't stand there. Go HOME! Can't you SEE it ain't any use? Go HOME!"

Five minutes before he received this order Mr. Hammond would have been only too glad to go home. Now he was startled and angry and, being angry, his habitual stubbornness developed.

"I shan't go home neither," he whispered, fiercely. "If you can't come down I'll—I'll come up and get you."

"Shh—shh! He'll hear you. Kenelm'll hear you."

"I don't care much if he does. See here, Hannah, can't you get down nohow? How about that window? Can't you climb out of that window? Say, didn't I see a ladder layin' alongside the woodshed this mornin'?"

"Yes, there's a ladder there, but—where are you goin'? Mr. Hammond—Caleb—"

But Caleb was on his way to the woodshed. He found the ladder and laboriously dragged it beneath the window. Kenelm Parker had a local reputation for

sleeping like the dead. Otherwise Mr. Hammond would never have dared risk the
noise he was making.

Even after the ladder had been placed in position, Miss Parker hesitated. At
first she flatly refused to descend, asserting that no mortal power could get her
down that thing alive. But Caleb begged and commanded in agonized whispers,
and finally she was prevailed upon to try. Mr. Hammond grasped the lower end of
the ladder with a grip that brought the perspiration out upon his forehead, and the
lady, with suppressed screams and ejaculations of "Oh, good Lord!" and "Heavens
and earth! What shall I do?" reached the ground safe and more or less sound. They
left the ladder where it was, and tiptoed fearfully out to the lane.

"Whew!" panted the exhausted swain, mopping his brow. "I'm clean tuckered
out. I ain't done so much work for ten years."

"Don't say a word, Caleb Hammond. If I ain't got my death of—of ammonia
or somethin', I miss my guess. I'm all wheezed up from settin' at that open winder
waitin' for you to come; and I thought you never WOULD come."

As Caleb was helping the lady of his choice into the carryall he noticed that she
carried a small hand-bag.

"What you got that thing for?" he demanded.

"It's my reticule; there's a clean handkerchief and a few other things in it.
Mercy on us! You didn't suppose I'd go off to get married without even a decent
handkerchief, did you? I feel enough like a sneakin' ragamuffin and housebreaker as
'tis. Why I ever was crazy enough to—where have you put the horse?"

Mr. Hammond led her to where George Washington was tethered. The father
of his country was tired of standing alone in the damp, and he trotted off briskly.
The first mile of their journey was accomplished safely, although the night was
pitch-dark, and when they turned into the Bayport Road, which for two-thirds of
its length leads through thick soft pine and scrub-oak woods, it was hard to distin-
guish even the horse's ears. Miss Parker insisted that every curtain of the carryall—
at the back and both sides—should be closely buttoned down, as she was fearful of
the effects of the night air.

"Fresh air never hurts nobody," said Caleb. "There ain't nothin' so good for a
body as fresh air. I sleep with my window open wide winter and summer."

"You DO? Well, I tell you right now, I don't. I should say not! I shut every winder tight and I make Kenelm do the same thing. I don't run any risks from drafts."

Mr. Hammond grunted, and was silent for some little time, only brightening up when the lady, now in a measure recovered from her fright and the anxiety of waiting, began to talk of the blessings that were to come from their independent wedded life in a home of their own.

"We'll keep chickens," she said, "because I do like fresh eggs for breakfast. Let's see; this is the way 'twill be; you'll get up about five o'clock and kindle the fire, and—"

"Hey?"

"I say you'll get up at five o'clock and kindle the fire."

"ME get up and kindle it?"

"Sartin; you don't expect I'm goin' to, do you?"

"No-o, I suppose not. It come kind of sudden, that's all. You see, I've been used to turnin' out about seven. Seldom get up afore that."

"Seven! My soul! I always have my breakfast et by seven. Well, as I say, you get up at five and kindle the fire, and then you'll go out to the henyard and get what eggs there is. Then—"

"Then I'll come in and call you, and you'll come down and get breakfast. What breakfasts we will have! Eggs for you, if you want 'em, and ham and fried potatoes for me, and pie—"

"Pie? For breakfast?"

"Sartin. Laviny Marthy, my first wife, always had a piece of pie warmed for me, and I've missed it since. I don't really care two cents for breakfast without pie."

"Well now, Caleb, if you think I'm goin' to get up and warm up pie every mornin', let alone fryin' potatoes, and—"

"See here, Hannah! Seems to me if I'm willin' to turn out at that ungodly hour and then go scratchin' around the henhouse to please you, you might be willin' to have a piece of pie het up for me."

"Well, maybe you're right. But I must say—well, I'll try and do it. It'll seem kind of hard, though, after the simple breakfasts Kenelm and I have when we're alone. But—what are you stoppin' for?"

"There seems to be a kind of crossroads here," said Caleb, bending forward and peering out of the carryall. "It's so everlastin' dark a feller can't see nothin'. Yes, there is crossroads, three of 'em. Now, which one do we take? I ain't drove to Bayport direct for years. When we went to the Cattle Show we went up through the Centre. Do you know which is the right road, Hannah?"

Hannah peered forth from the blackness of the back seat. "Now, let me think," she said. "Last time I went to Bayport by this road was four year ago come next February. Sarah Snow's daughter Becky was married to a feller named Higgins— Solon Higgins' son 'twas. No, 'twa'n't his son, because—"

"Aw, crimus! Who cares if 'twas his aunt's gran'mother? What I want to know is which road to take."

"Well, seems to me, nigh as I can recollect, that we took the left-hand road. No, I ain't sure but 'twas the right-hand. There's a bare chance that it might have been the middle one, 'cause there was trees along both sides. I know we was goin' to Becky Snow's weddin'—"

"Trees 'long it! There ain't nothin' BUT trees for two square miles around these diggin's. Git dap, you! I'll take the right-hand road. I think that's the way."

"Well, so do I; but, as I say, I ain't sure. You needn't be so cross and unlikely, whether 'tis or 'tain't."

If the main road had been dark, the branch road was darker, and the branches of the trees slapped and scratched the sides of the carryall. Caleb's whole attention was given to his driving, and he said nothing. Miss Parker at length broke the dismal silence.

"Caleb," she said, "what time had we ought to get to Bayport?"

"About four o'clock, I should think. We'll drive 'round till about seven o'clock, and then we'll go and get married. I used to know the Methodist minister there, and—"

"METHODIST minister! You ain't goin' to a Methodist minister to be married?"

"I sartin shouldn't go to no one else. I've been goin' to the Methodist church for over thirty year. You know that well's I do."

"I snum I never thought of it, or you wouldn't have got me this far without settlin' that question. I was confirmed into the Baptist faith when I was twelve year old. And you must have known that just as well as I knew you was a Methodist."

"Well, if you knew I was one you ought to know I'd want a Methodist to marry me. 'Twas a Methodist married me afore."

"Humph! What do you suppose I care who married you before? I'm the one that's goin' with you to be married now; and if I was married by anybody but a Baptist minister I wouldn't feel as if I was married at all."

"Well, I shan't be married by no Baptist."

"No Methodist shall marry ME."

"Now, look here, Hannah—"

"I don't care, Caleb. You ain't done nothin' but contradict me since we started. I've been settin' up all night, and I'm tired out, and there's a draft comin' in 'round these plaguy curtains right on the back of my neck. I'll get cold and die and you'll have a funeral on your hands instead of a weddin'. And I don't know's I'd care much," desperately.

Caleb choked down his own irritation.

"There, there, Hannah," he said, "don't talk about dyin' when you're just gettin' ready to live. We won't fret about the minister business. If worst comes to worst I'll give in to a Baptist, I suppose. One reason I did figger on goin' to a Methodist was that, I bein' of that faith, I thought maybe he'd do the job a little cheaper for us."

"Cheaper? What do you mean? Was you cal'latin' to make a BARGAIN with him?"

"No, no, course not. But there ain't any sense in heavin' money away on a parson more'n on anybody else."

"Caleb Hammond, how much do you intend givin' that minister?"

Mr. Hammond stirred uneasily on the seat of the carryall.

"Oh, I don't know," he answered evasively.

"Yes, you do know, too. How much?"

"I don't know. Two or three dollars, maybe."

"TWO or three dollars! My soul and body! Is two dollars all you're willin' to give up to get MARRIED? Is THAT all the ceremony's worth to you? Two dollars! My soul!"

"Oh, let up! I don't care. I'll—I'll—" after a desperate wrestle with his sense of economy. "I'll give him whatever you say—in reason. Eh! . . . What's that foolhead horse stoppin' for now? What in the tunket's the matter with him?"

The matter was simply that in his hasty harnessing Mr. Hammond had but partially buckled one of the girths, and the horse was now half-way out of the shafts, with the larger part of the harness well up towards his ears. Caleb groaningly climbed down from the seat, rummaged out and lit the lantern, which he had been thoughtful enough to put under the seat before starting, and proceeded to repair damages. This took a long time, and in getting back to the carryall he tore a triangular rent in the back of his Sunday coat. He had donned his best clothes to be married in, and, to add to his troubles, had left his watch in the fob-pocket of his everyday trousers, so they had no means of knowing the time.

"That's a nice mess," he grumbled, taking off his coat to examine the tear by the light of the lantern. "Nice-lookin' rag-bag I'll be to get married."

"Maybe I can mend it when we get to Bayport," said Miss Parker.

"What'll you mend it with—pins?"

"No, there's a needle and thread in my reticule. Wait till we get to Bayport and then—"

"Can't mend it in broad daylight ridin up and down the main street, can you? And I'd look pretty shuckin' my coat in the minister's parlor for you to patch up the holes in it. Couldn't you mend it now?"

Hannah announced her willingness to try, and the reticule being produced, the needle was threaded after numerous trials, and the mending began. Caleb, holding the lantern, watched the operation anxiously, his face falling at every stitch.

"I'm afraid I haven't made a good job of it," sighed Hannah, gazing sorrowfully at the puckered and wrinkled star in the back of the garment. "If you'd only held that lantern steady, instead of jigglin' it round and round so, I might have done better."

Mr. Hammond said nothing, but struggled into his coat, and picked up the reins. He sighed, heavily, and his sigh was echoed from the back seat of the carryall.

The road was now very rough, and the ruts were deep and full of holes. George Washington seemed to be stumbling through tall grass and bushes, and the carryall jolted and rocked from side to side. Miss Parker grew more and more nervous. After a particularly severe jolt she could not hold in any longer.

"Land of love, Caleb!" she gasped. "Where ARE you goin'! It doesn't seem as if this could be the right road!"

"I don't know whether 'tis or not; but it's too narrow and too dark to turn 'round, so we've got to go ahead, that's all."

"Oh, heavens! What a jounce that was! Seems to me you're awful reckless. I wish Kenelm was drivin'; he's always so careful."

This was too much. Mr. Hammond suppressed his feelings no longer.

"I wish to thunder he was!" he roared. "I wish Kenelm or some other dam' fool was here instead of me."

"Caleb HAMMOND!"

"I don't care, Hannah. You're enough to drive a deacon to swearin'. It's been nothin' but nag, nag, nag, fight, fight, fight ever since this cruise started. If—if we row like this afore we're married what'll it be afterwards? Talk about bein' independent! Git dap there!" this a savage roar at George Washington, who had stopped again. "I do believe the idiot's struck with a palsy."

Hannah leaned forward and touched her fellow-sufferer on the arm. "Sshh, shh, Caleb!" she said. "Don't holler so. I don't blame you for hollerin' and—and I declare I don't know as I much blame you for swearin', though I never thought I'D live to say a thing like that. But it ain't the horse deserves to be sworn at. He ain't the idiot; the idiots are you and me. We was both of us out of sorts this mornin', I guess—I know I was—and then you come along and we talked and—and, well, we both went into this foolish, ridiculous, awful piece of silliness without stoppin' to figger out whether we really wanted to, or whether we was liable to get along together, or anything else. Caleb, I've been wantin' to say this for the last hour or more—now I'm goin' to say it: You turn that horse's head around and start right home again."

Mr. Hammond shook his head.

"No," he said.

"I say yes. I don't want to marry you and I don't believe you want to marry me. Now do you—honest?"

Caleb was silent for a full minute. Then he drew a deep breath.

"It don't make no difference whether I do or not, fur's I can see," he said, gloomily. "It's too late to start home now. I don't know what time 'tis, but we must have been ridin' three or four hours—seems eight or ten year to me—and we ought to be pretty near to Bayport. If we should turn back now we wouldn't get home till

long after daylight, and everybody would be up and wantin' to know the whys and
wherefores. If we told 'em we'd been ridin' around together all night, and didn't
give any reasons for it, there'd be talk enough to last till Judgment. No, we've just
got to get married now. That's all there is to it."

Hannah groaned as the truth of this statement dawned upon her. Caleb gathered the reins in his hands preparatory to driving on, when a new thought came to
him.

"Say, Hannah," he observed, "I suppose you left that note for Kenelm, didn't
you?"

Miss Parker uttered a faint shriek.

"Oh, my soul!" she cried. "I didn't! I didn't! I wrote it, but I was so upset when
I found I couldn't get the doorkey and get out that way that I left the note in my
bureau drawer."

"Tut, tut! Huh! Well, he may find it there; let's hope he does."

"But he won't! He WON'T! He never finds anything, even if it's in plain sight.
He won't know what's become of me—"

"And he'll most likely have the whole town out lookin' for you. I guess now
you see there's nothin' to do but for us to get married—don't you?"

"Oh! Oh! Oh!" wailed Miss Parker, and burst into tears.

Caleb groaned. "Git dap!" he shouted to the horse. "No use cryin', Hannah.
Might's well grin and bear it. The joyful bridal party'll now proceed."

But the horse refused to proceed, and his driver, peering forward, dimly saw a
black barrier in front of him. He lit the lantern once more and, getting out of the
carryall, discovered that the road apparently ended at a rail fence that barred further progress.

"Queer," he said. "We must be pretty nigh civilization. Got to Bayport, most
likely, Hannah; there seems to be a buildin' ahead of us there. I'm goin' to take the
lantern and explore. You set still till I come back."

But this Miss Parker refused to do. She declared that she would not wait alone
in those woods for anybody or anything. If her companion was going to explore so
was she. So Mr. Hammond assisted her to alight, and after he had taken down the
bars, the pair went on through a grove to where a large building loomed against the
sky.

"A church," said Caleb. "One of the Bayport churches, I cal'late. Wonder which 'tis?"

"There's always a sign on the front of a church," said Hannah. "Let's go around front and see."

There were no trees in front of the church, and when they came out by the front platform, Miss Parker exclaimed, "Well, I never! I wouldn't believe I'd remember so clear. This church seems just as familiar as if I was here yesterday. Why, what's the matter?"

Mr. Hammond was standing on the platform, holding his lantern up before a gilt-lettered placard by the church door.

"Hannah," he gurgled, "this night's been too much for me. My foolishness has struck out of my brains into my eyes. I can't read straight. Look here."

Hannah clambered up beside her agitated companion, and read from the placard these words:

FIRST BAPTIST CHURCH

REV. JONATHAN LANGWORTHY, PASTOR

"Good land!" she exclaimed. "Mr. Langworthy! Why, Mr. Langworthy is the minister at Wellmouth Centre, ain't he? I thought he was."

"He is, but perhaps there's another one."

"No, there ain't—not another Baptist. And—and this church, what little I can see of it, LOOKS like the Wellmouth Centre Baptist Church, too; I declare it does! . . . Where are you goin'?"

Caleb did not reply, neither did he turn back. Hannah, who did not propose to be left alone there in the dark, was hurrying after him, but he stopped and when she reached his side she found him holding the lantern and peering at an iron gate in a white fence. His face, seen by the lantern light, was a picture of bewildered amazement.

"What is it?" she demanded. "What IS it?"

He did not answer, but merely pointed to the gate.

"Eh? What—why—why, Caleb, that's—ain't that the Nickerson memorial gate? . . . It can't be! But—but it IS! Why—"

Mr. Hammond was muttering to himself.

"We took the wrong road at the crossin'," he said. "Then we must have switched again, probably when we was arguin' about kindlin' the fire; then we must have turned again when the harness broke; and that must have fetched us into Lemuel Ellis' wood-lot road that comes out—"

"Eh? Lemuel Ellis' wood-lot? Why, Lemuel's wood-lot is at—"

"It's at Wellmouth Centre, that's where 'tis. No wonder that church looked familiar. Hannah, we ain't been nigh Bayport. We've been ridin' round and round in circles through them woods all night."

"Caleb HAMMOND!"

Before Caleb could add anything to his astonishing statement the silence of the night was broken by the clang of the bell in the tower of the church. It clanged four times.

"WHAT!" exclaimed Caleb. "Only four o'clock! It can't be!"

"My soul!" cried Miss Parker, "only four! Why—why, I thought we'd been ridin' ten hours at least. . . . Caleb Hammond, you and me don't want to find a minister; what we need to look up is a pair of guardians to take care of us."

But Mr. Hammond seized her arm.

"Hannah," he cried, excitedly, "do you understand what that means—that clock strikin'? It means that, bein' as we're only five miles from home, we can GET home, if we want to, afore anybody's out of bed. You can sneak up that ladder again; I can get that horse and team back in Thankful's stable; we can both be in our own beds by gettin'-up time and not one soul need ever know a word about this foolishness. If we—"

But Miss Parker had not waited for him to finish; she was already on her way to the carryall.

At a quarter after seven that morning Thankful knocked at the door of her boarder's room.

"Mr. Hammond!" she called. "Mr. Hammond!"

Caleb awoke with a start.

"Eh?" he said.

"Are you up? It's most breakfast time."

Caleb, now more thoroughly awake, looked about his room. It was real; he was actually in it—and safe—and still single.

"Yes—yes; all right," he said. "I'll get right up. Must have overslept myself, I guess. What—what made you call me? Nothin'—er—nothin's happened, has it?"

"No, nothin's happened. But you're usually up by seven and, as I hadn't heard a sound from you, I was afraid you might be sick."

"No, no; I ain't sick. I'm feelin' fine. Has—has Kenelm Parker got here yet?"

"Yes, he's here."

"Ain't—ain't said nothin', has he?"

"Said anything? No. What do you mean? What did you expect him to say?"

"Nothin', nothin', I—I wondered what sort of a drive he and Imogene had yesterday, that's all. I thought it would be fine to hear him tell about it. You run along, Mrs. Barnes; I'll hurry and get dressed."

He jumped out of bed. He was tired and lame and his head ached—but, Oh, he was happy! He had stabled George Washington and reached his room without disturbing anyone. And, as Kenelm had, according to Mrs. Barnes, spoken and appeared as usual, it was evident that Hannah Parker, too, had gotten safely and undetected to her own apartment.

Thankful knocked at his door again.

"I'm sorry," she said, "but Melindy Pease hasn't sent home your mendin' yet. I'm afraid you'll have to do without your—er—your winter things for one more day."

"Hey? My winter—Oh, yes, yes. Well, I don't care. It's warmer today than 'twas yesterday."

"Oh no, it isn't; it's a good deal colder. I hope you won't catch cold."

"No, no, I shan't. I'm feelin' fine."

"Well, thank goodness for that."

"Thank goodness for a good many things," said Mr. Hammond, devoutly.

CHAPTER XIII

IF Kenelm noticed that George Washington seemed unusually tired that morning, or that the old carryall behind the barn had some new scratches on its sides and wheels, and leaves and pine needles on its cushions and floor, he did not mention what he saw. For a day or two both Mr. Hammond and Miss Parker were anxious and fearful, but as nothing was said and no questions were asked, they began to feel certain that no one save themselves knew of the elopement which had turned out to be no elopement at all. For a week Hannah's manner toward her brother was sweetness itself. She cooked the dishes he liked and permitted him to do as he pleased without once protesting or "nagging." She had done comparatively little of the latter since the announcement of the "engagement," but now she was more considerate and self-sacrificing than ever. If Kenelm was aware of the change he made no comment upon it, perhaps thinking it good policy to let well enough alone. Gradually the eloping couple began to feel that their secret was secure and to cease worrying about it. But Caleb called no more at the Parker cottage and when he and Hannah met they bowed, but did not stop to converse.

Miss Timpson's sudden departure from the High Cliff House caused less talk than Thankful had feared. It happened that the "cousin Sarah" to whose home Miss Abigail had fled, was seized with an attack of grippe and this illness was accepted as the cause of the schoolmistress's move. And Miss Timpson herself kept her word; she told no one of the "warning" she had received. So Thankful was spared the gossip and questioning concerning the snoring ghost in the back bedroom. For so much she was grateful, but she missed the weekly room rent and the weekly board money. The financial situation was becoming more and more serious for her, and as yet

Solomon Cobb had not made known his decision in the matter of the mortgage.

During the week following Miss Timpson's departure Thankful spent several nights in the rooms the former had vacated, lying awake and listening for sounds from the back bedroom. She heard none. No ghost snored for her benefit. Then other happenings, happenings of this world, claimed her attention and she dropped psychical research for the time.

The first of these happenings was the most surprising. One forenoon Kenelm returned from an errand to the village bringing the morning's mail with him. There were two letters for Mrs. Barnes. One was from Emily and, as this happened to be on top, Thankful opened it first.

There was good news in the letter, good news for Georgie and also for Mrs. Barnes herself. Georgie had been enjoying himself hugely during his stay in East Wellmouth. He spent every moment of pleasant weather out of doors and his energetic exuberance kept the livestock as well as the humans on the "Cap'n Abner place" awake and lively. He fed the hens, he collected the eggs, he pumped and carried water for George Washington; and the feeding of Patrick Henry was his especial care. That pig, now a plump and somnolent porker, was Georgie's especial favorite. It was past "hog-killing time" in East Wellmouth, but Thankful had given up the idea of turning Patrick Henry into spare ribs and lard, at least until her lively young relative's visit was at an end. That end was what Georgie feared. He did not want to go home. Certainly Thankful did not want him to go, and she and Captain Obed—the latter's fondness for his "second mate" stronger than ever— wrote to Miss Howes, begging her to use her influence with the family to the end that Georgie's visit might be prolonged until after Christmas, at any rate.

And in Emily's reply, the letter which Kenelm brought from the postoffice that morning, the permission was granted. Georgie might stay until New Year's Day.

Then [wrote Emily], he must come back with me. Yes, with me; for, you see, I am going to keep my word. I am coming to spend my Christmas vacation with you, just as I said I should if it were possible. There! aren't you glad? I know you are, for you must be so lonely, although one not knowing you as well as I do would never guess it from your letters. You always write that all is well, but I know. By the way, are there any developments in the matter of the loan from Mr. Cobb? I am very glad the renewal of the mortgage is to be all right, but I think he should do more than that. And have you been troubled in the other affair, that of your neighbor? You have not mentioned it—but have you?

Thankful had not been troubled in the "other affair." That is to say, she had not been troubled by E. Holliday Kendrick or his attorney. No move had been made, at least so far as anyone could learn, in the project of forcing her to sell out, and Heman Daniels declared that none would be made. "It is one thing to boast," said Mr. Daniels, "and another to make good. My—ahem—er—professional rival is beginning to realize, I think, that he has in this case bitten off more than he can—er—so to speak, chew. That young man has succeeded in ruining himself in this community and that is all he has succeeded in."

John said nothing. At his new boarding-place, Darius Holt's, he answered no questions concerning his plans, and was silent and non-communicative. He kept to himself and made no effort to regain his lost popularity or to excuse his action. Thankful saw him but seldom and even Captain Obed no longer mentioned John's name unless it was mentioned to him. Then he discussed the subject with a scornful sniff and the stubborn declaration that there was a mistake somewhere which would some day be explained. But his confidence was shaken, that was plain, and his optimism assumed. He and Mrs. Barnes avoided discussion of John Kendrick and his affairs.

Thankful read and reread the letter from Emily Howes. The news it contained was so good that she forgot entirely the fact that there was another envelope in the mail. Only when, as she sprang to her feet to rush out into the yard and tell Georgie that his plea for an extension of his visit was granted, was her attention called to this second letter. It fell from her lap to the floor and she stooped and picked it up.

The first thing she noticed was that the envelope was in a remarkably crumpled and dirty condition. It looked as if it had been carried in a pocket—and a not too clean pocket—for many days. Then she noticed the postmark—"Omaha." The address was the last item to claim her attention and, as she stared at the crumpled and crooked hand-writing, she gasped and turned pale.

Slowly she sank back into her chair and tore open the envelope. The inclosure was a dingy sheet of cheap notepaper covered with a penciled scrawl. With trembling fingers she unfolded the paper and read what was written there. Then she leaned back in the chair and put her hand to her forehead.

She was sitting thus when the door of the dining-room opened and a voice hailed: "Ahoy there! Anybody on deck?"

She turned to see Captain Obed Bangs' cheery face peering in at her.

"Hello!" cried the captain, entering the room and tossing his cap on the table. "You're here, are you? I was lookin' for you and Imogene said she cal'lated you was aboard ship somewheres, but she wa'n't sartin where. I've come to get that second mate of mine. I'm goin' off with a gang to take up the last of my fish weirs and I thought maybe the little shaver'd like to go along. I need help in bossin' the fo'mast hands, you see, and he's some consider'ble of a driver, that second mate is. Yes sir-ee! You ought to hear him order 'em to get up anchor. Ho! ho! I—Hey? Why—why, what's the matter?"

Thankful's face was still pale and she was trembling.

"Nothin', nothin', Cap'n Bangs," she said. "I've had a—a surprise, that's all."

"A surprise! Yes, you look as if you had." Then, noticing the letter in her lap, he added. "You ain't had bad news, have you?"

"No. No, not exactly. It's good news. Yes, in a way it's good news, but—but I didn't expect it and—and it has shook me up a good deal. . . . And—and I don't know what to do. Oh, I don't know WHAT I'd ought to do!"

The distress in her tone was so real that the captain was greatly disturbed. He made a move as if to come to her side and then, hesitating, remained where he was.

"I—I'd like to help you, Thank—er—Mrs. Barnes," he faltered, earnestly. "I like to fust-rate, if—if I could. Ain't there—is there anything I could do to help? Course you understand I ain't nosin' in on your affairs, but, if you feel like tellin' me, maybe I—Look here, 'tain't nothin' to do with that cussed Holliday Kendrick or his meanness, is it?"

Thankful shook her head. "No," she said, "it isn't that. I've been expectin' that and I'd have been ready for anything he might do—or try to do. But I wasn't expectin' THIS. How COULD anybody expect it? I thought he was dead. I thought sure he must be dead. Why, it's six year since he—and now he's alive, and he wants—What SHALL I do?"

Captain Obed took a step forward.

"Now, Mrs. Barnes," he begged, "I wish you would—that is, you know if you feel like it I—well, here I am. Can't I do SOMETHIN'?"

Thankful turned and looked at him. She was torn between an intense desire to make a confidant of someone and her habitual tendency to keep her personal affairs to herself. The desire overcame the habit.

"Cap'n Bangs," she said, suddenly, "I will tell you I've just got to tell somebody. If he was just writin' to say he was all right and alive, I shouldn't. I'd just be grateful and glad and say nothin'. But the poor thing is poverty-struck and friendless, or he says he is, and he wants money. And—and I haven't got any money just now."

"I have," promptly. "Or, if I ain't got enough with me I can get more. How much? Just you say how much you think he'll need and I'll have it for you inside of a couple of hours. If money's all you want—why, that's nothin'."

Thankful heard little, apparently, of this prodigal offer. She took up the letter.

"Cap'n Bangs," said she, "you remember I told you, one time when we were talkin' together, that I had a brother—Jedediah, his name was—who used to live with me after my husband was drowned?"

"Yes. I remember. You said he'd run off to go gold-diggin' in the Klondike or somewheres. You said he was dead."

"I thought he must be. I gave him up long ago, because I was sartin sure if he wasn't dead he'd have written me, askin' me to let him come back. I knew he'd never be able to get along all by himself. But he isn't dead. He's alive and he's written me now. Here's his letter. Read it, please."

The captain took the letter and slowly read it through. It was a rambling, incoherent epistle, full of smudges where words had been scratched out and rewritten, but a pitiful appeal nevertheless. Jedediah Cahoon had evidently had a hard time since the day when, after declaring his intention never to return until "loaded down with money," he had closed the door of his sister's house at South Middleboro and gone out into the snowstorm and the world. His letter contained few particulars. He had wandered far, even as far as his professed destination, the Klondike, but, wherever he had been, ill luck was there to meet him. He had earned a little money and lost it, earned a little more and lost that; had been in Nome and Vancouver and Portland and Seattle; had driven a street car in Tacoma.

I wrote you from Tacoma, Thankful [the letter said], after I lost that job, but you never answered. Now I am in 'Frisco and I am down and out. I ain't got any good job and I don't know where I will get one. I want to come home. Can't I come? I am sorry I cleared out and left you the way I done, and if you will let me come back home again I will try to be a good brother to you. I will; honest. I won't complain no more and I will split the kindling and everything. Please say I can come. Do PLEASE.

Then came the appeal for money, money for the fare east. It was to be sent to an address in San Francisco, in care of a person named Michael Kelly.

I am staying with this Kelly man [concluded Jedediah]. He keeps a kind of hotel like and I am doing chores for him. If you send the money right off I will get it I guess before he fires me. Send it QUICK for the Lord sakes.

Captain Obed finished the letter.

"Whew!" he whistled. "He's in hard luck, ain't he?"

Thankful wrung her hands. "Yes," she answered, "and I must help him somehow. But how I'm goin' to do it just now I don't see. But I must, of course. He's my brother and I MUST."

"Sartin you must. We—er—that is, that can be fixed all right. Humph! He sent this to you at South Middleboro, didn't he, and 'twas forwarded. Let's see when he wrote it. . . . Eh? Why, 'twas written two months ago! Where in the world has it been all this time?"

"I don't know. I can't think. And he says he is in San Francisco, and the postmark on that envelope is Omaha, Nebraska."

"Land of love, so 'tis. And the postmark date is only four days back. Why did he hang on to the thing for two months afore he mailed it? And how did it get to Omaha?"

"I don't know. All I can think of is that he gave the letter to somebody else to mail and that somebody forgot it. That's all I can think of. I can't really think of anything after a shock like this. Oh, dear! Oh, dear! The poor, helpless, incompetent thing! He's probably starved to death by this time and it's all my fault. I NEVER should have let him go. What SHALL I do? Wasn't there enough without this?"

For the first time Thankful's troubles overcame her courage and self-restraint. She put her handkerchief to her eyes.

The captain was greatly upset. He jammed his hands into his pockets, took them out again, reached for his own handkerchief, blew his nose violently, and began pacing up and down the room. Suddenly he seemed to have made up his mind.

"Mrs. Barnes," he said, "I—I—"

Thankful's face was still buried in her handkerchief.

"I—I—" continued Captain Obed. "Now, now, don't do that. Don't DO it!"

Mrs. Barnes wiped her eyes.

"I won't," she said, stoutly. "I won't. I know I'm silly and childish."

"You ain't neither. You're the pluckiest and best woman ever was. You're the finest—er—er—Oh, consarn it, Thankful, don't cry any more. Can't you," desperately, "can't you see I can't stand it to have you?"

"All right, Cap'n Bangs, I won't. Don't you bother about me or my worries. I guess likely you've got enough of your own; most people have."

"I ain't. I ain't got enough. Do me good if I had more. Thankful, see here; what's the use of your fightin' all these things alone? I've watched you ever since you made port here in South Wellmouth and it's been nothin' but fight and worry all the time. What's the use of it? You're too good a woman to waste your life this way. Give it up."

"Give it up?"

"Yes, give it up. Give up this wearin' yourself out keepin' boarders and runnin' this big house. Why don't you stop takin' care of other folks and take care of yourself for a spell?"

"But I can't. I can't take care of myself. All I have is invested in this place and if I give it up I lose everything."

"Yes, yes, I know what you mean. But what I mean is—is—"

"What do you mean?"

"I mean—I mean why don't you let somebody take care of you? That's what I mean."

Thankful turned to stare at him.

"Somebody—else—take care of me?" she repeated.

"Yes—yes. Don't look at me like that. If you do I can't say it. I'm—I'm havin' a—a hard enough time sayin' it as 'tis. Thankful Barnes, why—don't LOOK at me, I tell you!"

But she still looked at him, and, if a look ever conveyed a meaning, hers did just then.

"I ain't crazy," declared Captain Obed. "I can see you think I am, but I ain't. Thankful, I—Oh, thunderation! What is the matter with me? Thankful, let ME take care of you, will you?"

Thankful rose to her feet. "Obed Bangs!" she exclaimed.

"I mean it. I've been meanin' it more and more ever since I first met you, but I ain't had the spunk to say it. Now I'm goin' to say it if I keel over on the last word. Thankful, why don't you marry me?"

Thankful was speechless. The captain plunged desperately on.

"Will you, Thankful?" he begged. "I know I'm an old codger, but I ain't in my second childhood, not yet. I—I'd try mighty hard to make you happy. I haven't got anybody of my own in the world. Neither have you—except this brother of yours, and, judgin' from his letter and what you say, HE won't take any care; he'll BE a care, that's all. I ain't rich, but I've got money enough to help you—and him—and me afloat and comf'table. Thankful, will you?"

Thankful was still looking at him. He would have spoken again, but she raised her hand and motioned him to silence.

"Obed," she asked, after a moment, "what made you say this to me?"

"What made me say it? What kept me still so long, you ought to ask. Haven't I come to think more and more of you ever since I knew you? Haven't I been more and more sorry for you? And pitied you? I—"

She raised her hand again. "I see," she said, slowly. "I see. Thank you, Obed. You're so kind and self-sacrificin' you'd do anything or say anything to help a-friend, wouldn't you? But of course you can't do this."

"Can't? Why can't I? Self-sacrifice be hanged! Thankful, can't you see—"

"Yes. Oh yes. I can see. . . . Now let's talk about Jedediah. Do you think—"

"Jedediah be keelhauled! Will you marry me, Thankful Barnes?"

"Why no, Obed; of course I won't."

"You won't? Why not?"

"Because—well, because I—I can't. There, there, Obed! Please don't ask me again. Please don't!"

Captain Obed did not ask. He did not speak again for what, to Mrs. Barnes, seemed a long, long time. At length she could bear it no longer.

"PLEASE, Obed," she begged.

The captain slowly shook his head. Then he laughed a short, mirthless laugh.

"What an old fool I am!" he muttered. "What an old fool!"

"Obed, don't talk so! Don't! Do you want to make this—everything—harder for me?"

He straightened and squared his shoulders.

"Thank you, Thankful," he said, earnestly. "Thank you for sayin' that. That's the way to talk to me. I know I'm an old fool, but I won't be any more, if I can help it. Make it harder for you? I guess not!"

"Obed, I'm so sorry."

"Sho! sho! You needn't be. . . . I'm all right. I've been dreamin' foolish dreams, like a young feller after a church picnic dinner, but I'm awake now. Yes'm, I'm awake. Now just you forget that I talked in my sleep. Forget the whole of it and let's get back to—to that brother of yours. We've got to locate him, that's the first thing to be done. I'll send a telegram right off to that Kelly man out in 'Frisco askin' if what's-his-name—Jedediah—is there yet."

"Obed, you won't—you won't feel hard towards me? You won't let—this—interfere with our friendship?"

"Sho! Hush, hush, Thankful! You make me more ashamed of myself than ever, and that ain't necessary. Now the first thing is to send that telegram. If we locate your brother then we'll send him a ticket to Boston and some money. Don't you worry, Thankful; we'll get him here. And don't you fret about the money neither. I'll 'tend to that and you can pay me afterwards."

"No, no; of course I shan't let—"

"Yes, you will. There's some things you can't stop and that's one of 'em. You talked about our friendship, didn't you? Well, unless you want me to believe I ain't your friend, you'll let me run my own course this time. So long, Thankful; I'm off to Chris Badger's to send that telegram."

He snatched up his cap and was on his way to the door. She followed him.

"Obed," she faltered, "I—I—What CAN I say to you? You are SO good!"

"Tut! tut! Me good? Don't let Heman Daniels hear you say that. He's a church deacon and knows what goodness is. So long, Thankful. Soon's I hear from Kelly, I'll report."

He hurried from the house. Thankful watched him striding down the path. Not once did he hesitate or look back. She turned from the door and, returning to her chair by the center table, sat down. For a moment she sat there and then, leaning her head upon her arms on the table, wept tears of absolute loneliness and despair.

The telegram to Michael Kelly of San Francisco brought an answer, but a most unsatisfactory one. Jedediah Cahoon had not been in the Kelly employ for more than six weeks. Kelly did not know where he had gone and, apparently, did not care. Captain Obed then wired and wrote the San Francisco police officials, urging them to trace the lost one. This they promised to do, but nothing came of it. The weeks passed and no word from them or from Jedediah himself was received. His letter had come to prove that, at the time it was written, he was alive; whether or not he was still alive, or where he might be if living, was as great a mystery as ever. Day after day Thankful watched and waited and hoped, but her waiting was unrewarded, and, though she still hoped, her hope grew steadily fainter; and the self-reproach and the worry greater in proportion.

She and Georgie and Imogene spent Thanksgiving Day alone. Heman Daniels and Mr. Hammond were invited out and Captain Obed, who had meant to eat his Thanksgiving dinner at the High Cliff House, was called to Boston on business connected with his fish selling, and could not return in time.

Early in December Thankful once more drove to Trumet to call upon Solomon Cobb. The question of the renewal of the mortgage she felt must remain a question no longer. But she obtained little satisfaction from her talk with the money-lender. Mr. Cobb's first remark concerned the Holliday Kendrick offer to buy the "Cap'n Abner place."

"Did he mean it, do you think?" he demanded. "Is he really so sot on buyin' as folks say he is?"

"I'm afraid so."

"Huh! And he's hired his lawyer—that young cousin of his—Bailey Kendrick's son—to make you sell out to him?"

"Yes."

"What's the young feller done about it; anything?"

"No; nothin' that I know of."

"Humph! Sure of that, be ye? I hear he's been spendin' consider'ble time over to

Ostable lately, hangin' round the courthouse, and the probate clerk's office. Know what he's doin' that for?"

"No, I didn't know he had. How did you know it?"

"I knew. Ain't much goin' on that I don't know; I make it my business to know. Why don't you sell out to old Holliday?"

"I don't want to sell. My boardin'-house has just got a good start and why should I give it up? I won't sell."

"Oh, you won't! Pretty independent for anybody with a mortgage hangin' over 'em, ain't ye?"

"Solomon, are you goin' to renew that mortgage when it comes due?"

Mr. Cobb pulled his whiskers. "I don't know's I am and I don't know's I ain't," he said. "This Kendrick business kind of mixes things up. Might be a good idea for me to foreclose that mortgage and sell the place to him at my own price. Eh? What do you think of that?"

"You wouldn't do it! You couldn't be so—"

"So what? Business is business and if he's goin' to put you out anyhow, I don't see why I shouldn't get my share of the pickin's."

"But he ain't goin' to put me out."

"He says he is. Now—now—clear out and don't bother me. When that mortgage falls due I'll let you know what I intend doin' with it. If you pester me now I won't renew anyhow. Go along home and quit your frettin'. Long's you're there, you BE there. What more do you want?"

There was a good deal more of this sort of thing, but it was all quite as unsatisfactory. Thankful gave it up at last.

"I shan't come here again," she declared desperately. "If you want to see me you can come to my place."

"Humph!"

"Well, you will, or not see me. Why haven't you been there? Time and time again you have promised to come, but you never have. I shall begin to believe there is some reason why you don't want to go into that house."

She was on her way to the door, but Solomon called after her.

"Here!" he shouted. "Hold on! What do you mean by that? Why shouldn't I go into that house if I want to? Why shouldn't I?"

"I don't know; all I know is that you don't seem to want to. I can't say why you don't want to, but—"

"But what?"

"But, maybe, if someone that's dead and gone was here—he could."

"He—he—who? What? Hi! Where you goin'?"

"I'm goin' home."

"No, you ain't—not until you tell me what you mean by—by somebody that's dead and gone. What kind of talk is that? What do you mean?"

"Maybe I don't know what I mean, Solomon; but I think you do. If you don't then your looks belie you, that's all."

She went out of the "henhouse." As she drove away she saw Mr. Cobb peering at her through the window. He was "weeding" with both hands and he looked agitated and—yes, frightened. Thankful was more than ever certain that his mysterious behavior was in some way connected with his past dealings with her Uncle Abner, but, not knowing what those dealings might have been, the certainty was not likely to help her. And he had not said that he would renew the mortgage.

Georgie was the first to meet her when she drove into the yard. He had been spending the day with Captain Obed and had coaxed the latter into telling him stories of Santa Claus. Georgie's mind was now filled with anticipations of Christmas and Christmas presents, and his faith in Santa, which had been somewhat shaken during his year at kindergarten in South Middleboro, was reviving again. The captain and Imogene and Mrs. Barnes all helped in the revival. "Christmas loses three-quarters of its fun when old Santa's took out of it," declared Captain Obed. "I know, 'count of havin' been a young one myself a thousand year ago or such matter. This'll probably be the second mate's last Santa Claus Christmas, so let's keep this one the real thing for the boy."

So he and Imogene and Thankful—yes, even Kenelm—discussed Santa for Georgie's benefit and Georgie believed, although his belief was not as absolute and unquestioning as it had once been. He asked a great many questions, some of which his elders found hard to answer. His dearest wish was for an air-gun, but somehow Mrs. Barnes did not seem to think the wish would be gratified. She had a strong presentiment that the combination of Georgie and an air-gun and the chickens might not be a desirable one, especially for the chickens.

"But why won't he bring it, Auntie?" demanded Georgie. "You say he brings good boys what they want. I've been a good boy, ain't I?"

"'Deed you have. I wouldn't ask for a better one."

"Then why won't Santa bring me the gun?"

"Perhaps he'll think a gun isn't nice for such a little boy to have."

"But it is nice. It's nicer'n anything. If I'm good and I want it I don't see why I can't have it. I think Santa's mean if he don't bring it."

"Oh no, he isn't mean. Just think how good he is! He comes to every boy and girl—"

"No, he don't."

"Why yes, he does. To every good little boy and girl."

"He never came to Patsy Leary that lived up on the lots in Middleboro. Patsy said he didn't; he said there wasn't any Santa Claus, Patsy did."

"Hum! Perhaps Patsy wasn't good."

"Gee! Yes, he was. He can play baseball better'n any boy I know. And he can lick any kid his size; he told me he could."

This crushing proof of young Leary's goodness was a staggerer for Thankful. Before she could think of a reply Georgie asked another question.

"You say he'll come down the chimney?" he queried.

"Yes."

"The livin'-room chimney?"

"Yes, probably."

"No, he won't."

"Georgie!"

"How can he? He's so fat; he's ever so fat in the pictures. How can he get through the stovepipe?"

Mrs. Barnes' answer was evasive and Georgie noticed the evasion. However, his trust in his Aunt Thankful was absolute and if she said a fat man could get through a stovepipe he probably could. But the performance promised to be an interesting one. Georgie wished he might see it. He thought a great deal about it and, little by little, a plan began forming in his mind.

Three days before Christmas Emily Howes arrived at the High Cliff House. She was received with rejoicings. The young lady looked thinner than when she went away and seemed more grave and careworn. But when Thankful commented upon her appearance Emily only laughed and declared herself quite well and perfectly happy. She and her cousin discussed all topics of common interest except one, that one was John Kendrick. Once or twice Thankful mentioned the young man's name, but invariably Emily changed the subject. It was evident that she did not wish to speak of John; also it was, to Mrs. Barnes, just as evident that she thought of him. Thankful believed that those thoughts were responsible for the change in her relative's look and manner.

Christmas was to be, as Thanksgiving had been, a day free from boarders at the High Cliff House. Caleb was again "asked out," and Mr. Daniels, so he said, "called away." He had spent little time in East Wellmouth of late, though no one seemed to know exactly where he had been or why.

The day before Christmas was cold and threatening. Late in the afternoon it began to rain and the wind to blow. By supper time a fairly able storm had developed and promised to develop still more. Captain Obed, his arms filled with packages, all carefully wrapped and all mysterious and not to be opened till the next day, came in just after supper.

"Where's that second mate of mine?" whispered the captain, anxiously. When told that Georgie was in the kitchen with Imogene he sighed in relief.

"Good!" he said. "Hide those things as quick as ever you can, afore he lays eyes on 'em. He's sharper'n a sail needle, that young one is, and if he can't see through brown paper he can GUESS through it, I bet you. Take em away and put 'em out of sight—quick."

Emily hurried upstairs with the packages. Captain Obed turned to Thankful.

"How is she these days?" he asked, with a jerk of the head in the direction taken by Miss Howes.

"She's pretty well, or she says she is. I ain't so sure myself. I'm afraid she thinks about—about HIM more than she makes believe. I'm afraid matters between them two had gone farther'n we guessed."

Captain Obed nodded. "Shouldn't wonder," he said. "John looks pretty peaked, too. I saw him just now."

"You did? John Kendrick? He's been out of town for a week or two, so I heard. Where did you see him?"

"At the Centre depot. I was up to the Centre—er—buyin' a few things and he got off the noon train."

"Did you speak to him?"

"Yes, or he spoke to me. He and I ain't said much to each other—what little we've seen of each other lately—but that's been his fault more'n 'twas mine. He sung out to me this time, though, and I went over to the platform. Say," after a moment's hesitation, "there's another thing I want to ask you. How's Heman Daniels actin' since Emily come? Seems more'n extry happy, does he?"

"Why—why, no. He's been away, too, a good deal; on business, he said."

"Humph! He and—er—Emily haven't been extra thick, then?"

"No. Come to think of it they've hardly seen each other. Emily has acted sort of—sort of queer about him, too. She didn't seem to want to talk about him more'n she has about John."

"Humph! That's funny. I can't make it out. You see Heman got on that same train John got off. He was comin' along the depot platform just as I got to it. And the depot-master sung out to him."

"The depot-master? Eben Foster, you mean?"

"Yup. He sung out, 'Congratulations, Heman,' says he."

"'What you congratulatin' him for?' says I."

"'Ain't you heard?' says he. 'He's engaged to be married'."

Thankful uttered an exclamation.

"Engaged!" she repeated. "Mr. Daniels engaged—to be married?"

"So Eben said. I wanted to ask a million questions, of course, but John Kendrick was right alongside me and I couldn't. John must have heard it, too, and it did seem to me that he looked pretty well shook up, but he wa'n't any more shook than I was. I thought—Well, you see, I thought—"

Thankful knew what he had thought. She also was "shaken up."

"I don't believe it," she cried. "If—if—it can't he HER. Why, she would have told me, I'm sure. Obed, you don't think—"

"I don't know what to think. Heman's been writin' her pretty reg'lar, I know that, 'cause Chris Badger told me so a week after she'd gone. I don't know, Thankful; one thing's sartin, Heman's kept his engagement mighty quiet. How Eben learned of it I don't know, but nobody in East Wellmouth knows, for I've been soundin' ever since I struck here."

Thankful was greatly troubled. "I HOPE it ain't true," she cried. "I suppose he's all right, but—but I didn't want Emily to marry him."

"Neither did I. Perhaps she ain't goin' to. Perhaps it's just a round-the-stove lie, like a shipload of others that's set afloat every day. But, from somethin' John Kendrick said to me on that platform I knew he heard what Eben said."

"How do you know?"

"'Cause he as much as told me so. 'Is it true?' says he.

"'I don't know,' says I. 'First I'd heard of it, if 'tis.'

"He just nodded his head and seemed to be thinkin'. When he did speak 'twas more to himself than to me. 'Well,' says he, 'then that settles it. I can do it now with a clear conscience.'

"'Do what?' I asked him.

"'Oh, nothin',' he says. 'Cap'n Obed, are you goin' to be busy all day tomorrow? I know it's Christmas, of course; but are you?'

"'Not so busy it'll wreck my nerves keepin' up with my dates,' says I. 'Why?'

"'Can you spare a half-hour or so to come 'round to my office at—well, say two tomorrow afternoon? I've got a little business of my own and I'd like to have you there. Will you come?'

"'Sartin,' I told him.

"'Of course, if you're afraid of the moral leprosy—'

"'I ain't.'

"'Then I'll look for you,' says he, and off he went. I ain't seen him since. He come down along of Winnie S. and I had one of Chris Badger's teams. Now WHAT do you cal'late it all means?"

"I don't know. I don't know. But I can't think Emily—Hush! she's comin'."

Emily entered the room and Captain Obed began philosophically concerning the storm, which he declared was "liable to be a hooter."

He went away soon after. At the door, when he and Mrs. Barnes were alone, he whispered, "Ain't changed your mind, have you, Thankful? About—about what I said to you that day?"

"Obed, please! You said you wouldn't."

"All right, all right. Well, good night. I'll be around tomorrow to wish you and

Emily and the second mate a merry Christmas. Good night, Thankful."

After he had gone Thankful and Emily assisted Georgie in hanging up his stocking and preparing for bed. The boy seemed willing to retire, a most unusual willingness for him. His only worry appeared to be concerning Santa Claus, whom he feared might be delayed in his rounds by the storm.

"He'll be soaked, soppin' wet, won't he?" he asked anxiously.

"Oh, he won't mind. Santa Claus don't mind this kind of weather. He lives up at the North Pole, so folks say."

"Yes. Won't the chimney soot all stick to him when he's wet? He'll be a sight, won't he?"

"Perhaps so, but he won't mind that, either. Now, you go to bed, Georgie, like a good boy."

"I'm a-goin'. Say, Aunt Thankful, will the soot come all off on my presents?"

They got him into bed at last and descended to the living-room. The storm was worse than ever. The wind howled and the rain beat. Emily shivered.

"Mercy! What a night!" she exclaimed. "It reminds me of our first night in this house, Auntie."

"Does; that's a fact. Well, I hope there's nobody prowlin' around lookin' for a place to put their head in, the way we were then. I—what's that?"

"What? What, Auntie? I didn't hear anything."

"I thought I did. Sounded as if somebody was—and they are! Listen!"

Emily listened. From without, above the noise of the wind and rain and surf, came a shout.

"Hi!" screamed a high-pitched voice. "Hi! Let me in. I—I'm drownin'."

Thankful rushed to the door and, exerting all her strength, pushed it open against the raging storm.

"There's nobody here," she faltered.

"But—but there is, Auntie. I heard someone. I—"

She stopped, for, out of the drenched darkness staggered a figure, the figure of a man. He plunged across the threshold, tripped over the mat and fell in a heap upon the floor.

Emily shrieked. Mrs. Barnes pulled the door shut and ran to the prostrate figure.

"Who is it?" she asked. "Who IS it? Are you hurt?"

The figure raised its head.

"Hurt!" it panted. "It's a wonder I ain't dead. What's the matter with ye? Didn't you hear me yellin' for you to open that door?"

Thankful drew a long breath.

"For mercy sakes!" she cried. "Solomon Cobb! WHAT are you doin' over here a night like this?"

CHAPTER XIV

MR. COBB slowly raised his head. He looked about him in a bewildered way, and then his gaze fixed itself upon Mrs. Barnes.

"What—why—YOU!" he gasped.

"Eh?" stammered Thankful, whose surprise and bewilderment were almost as great as his. "Eh? What?"

"You?" repeated Solomon. "What—what are you doin' here?"

"What am I doin' here? What am I doin'?"

"Yes." Then, after another stare about the room, he added: "This ain't Kenelm Parker's house? Whose house is it?"

"It's my house, of course. Emily, go and fetch some—some water or somethin'. He's out of his head."

Emily hurried to the kitchen, Thankful hastened to help the unexpected visitor to his feet. But the visitor declined to be helped.

"Let me alone," he roared. "Let me be. I—I want to know whose house this is?"

"It's my house, I tell you. You ought to know whose house it is. Land sakes! You and I have had talk enough about it lately. Don't you know where you are? What are you sittin' there on the floor for? Are you hurt?"

Slowly Mr. Cobb rose to his feet.

"Do you mean to tell me," he demanded, "that this is—is Abner's place? How'd I get here?"

"I don't know. I ain't hardly had time to make sure you are here yet. And I'm sartin YOU ain't sure. That was an awful tumble you got. Seems as if you must have hurt yourself. And you're soppin' wet through! What in the WORLD?"

She moved toward him again, but he waved her away.

"Let me alone!" he ordered. "I was headin' for Kenelm Parker's. How'd I get here?"

"I tell you I don't know. I suppose you lost your way. No wonder, such a night's this. Set down. Let me get you somethin' hot to drink. Come out in the kitchen by the cookstove. Don't—"

"Hush up! Let me think. I never see such a woman to talk. I—I don't see how I done it. I left Chris Badger's and came across the fields and—"

"And you took the wrong path, I guess, likely. Did you WALK from Chris Badger's? Where's your horse and team? You didn't walk from the Centre, did you?"

"'Course I didn't. Think I'm a dum fool? My horse fell down and hurt his knee and I left him in Badger's barn. I cal'lated to go to Kenelm's and put up over night. I—"

He was interrupted by Emily, who entered with a glass in her hand.

"Here's the water, Auntie," she said. "Is he better now?"

"Better?" snorted Solomon. "What's the matter with you? I ain't sick. What you got in that tumbler? Water! What in time do I want of any more water? Don't I look as if I'd had water enough to last me one spell? I'm—consarn it all, I'm a reg'lar sponge! How far off is Kenelm's from here? How long will it take me to get there?"

Thankful answered, and her answer was decisive.

"I don't know," she said, "but I do know you ain't goin' to try to get anywhere 'till mornin'. You and I ain't been any too lovin', Solomon Cobb, but I shan't take the responsibility of your dyin' of pneumonia. You'll stay right here, and the first thing I'll do is head off that chill you've got this very minute."

There was no doubt about the chill. Solomon's face and hands were blue and he was shaking from head to foot. But his determination was unshaken. He strode to the door.

"How do I get to Parker's?" he demanded.

"I tell you you mustn't go to Parker's or anywhere else. You're riskin' your life."

Mr. Cobb did not answer. He lifted the latch and pulled the door open. A howling gust of wind-driven rain beat in upon him, drenching the carpet and causing the lamp to flicker and smoke. For a moment Solomon gazed out into the storm; then he relinquished his hold and staggered back.

"I—I can't do it!" he groaned. "I've GOT to stay here! I've GOT to!"

Thankful, exerting all her strength, closed the door and locked it. "Indeed you've got to," she declared. "Now go out into the kitchen and set by the stove while I heat a kettle and make you some ginger tea or somethin'."

Solomon hesitated.

"He must, Aunt Thankful," urged Emily; "he really must."

The visitor turned to stare at her.

"Who are you?" he demanded, ungraciously. Then, as another chill racked him from head to foot, he added: "I don't care. Take me somewheres and give me some-thin'—ginger tea or—or kerosene or anything else, so it's hot. I—I'm—sho—oo—ook all to—pi—ic—ces."

They led him to the kitchen, where Thankful prepared the ginger tea. During its preparation she managed to inform Emily concerning the identity of their unex-pected lodger. Solomon, introduced to Miss Howes, merely grunted and admitted that he had "heard tell" of her. His manner might have led a disinterested person to infer that what he had heard was not flattering. He drank his tea, and as he grew warmer inside and out his behavior became more natural, which does not mean that it was either gracious or grateful.

At length he asked what time it was. Thankful told him.

"I think you'd better be gettin' to bed, Solomon," she suggested. "I'll hunt up one of Mr. Caleb Hammond's nightshirts, and while you're sleepin' your wet clothes can be dryin' here by the cookstove."

Solomon grunted, but he was, apparently, willing to retire. Then came the question as to where he should sleep. Emily offered a suggestion.

"Why don't you put him in the back room, Auntie," she said. "The one Miss Timpson used to have. That isn't occupied now and the bed is ready."

Thankful hesitated. "I don't know's he'd better have that room, Emily," she said.

"Why not? I'm sure it's a very nice room."

"Yes, I know it is, but—"

"But what?"

Mr. Cobb had a remark to make.

"Well, come on, come on," he said, testily. "Put me somewheres and do it quick. Long's I've GOT to sleep in this house I might's well be doin' it. Where is this room you're talkin' about? Let's see it."

Emily took the lamp and led the way up the back stairs. Solomon followed her and Thankful brought up the rear. She felt a curious hesitancy in putting even her disagreeable relative in that room on this night. Around the gables and upon the roof the storm whined and roared as it had the night when she first explored that upper floor. And she remembered, now, that it had stormed, though not as hard, the night when Miss Timpson received her "warning." If there were such things as ghosts, and if the little back bedroom WAS haunted, a night like this was the time for spectral visitations. She had half a mind to give Mr. Cobb another room.

But, before she could decide what to do, before the struggle between her common-sense and what she knew were silly forebodings was at an end, the question was decided for her. Solomon had entered the large room and expressed his approval of it.

"This'll do first rate," he said. "Why didn't you want to put me in here? Suppose you thought 'twas too good for me, eh? Well, it might be for some folks, but not for me. What's that, a closet?"

He was pointing to the closed door of the little room, the one which Miss Timpson had intended using as a study. Thankful had, after her last night of fruitless spook hunting, closed the door and locked it.

"What's this door locked for?" asked Mr. Cobb, who had walked over and was trying the knob.

"Oh, nothing; it's just another empty room, that's all. There's nothin' in it."

"Humph! Is that so? What do you lock up a room with nothin' in it for?" He turned the key and flung the door open. "Ugh!" he grunted, in evident disappointment. "'Tis empty, ain't it? Well, good night."

Emily, whose face expressed a decided opinion concerning the visitor, walked out into the hall. Thankful remained.

"Solomon," she said, in a whisper, "tell me. Have you made up your mind about that mortgage?"

"Um? No, I ain't. Part of what I came over here today for was to find out a little more about this property and about Holliday Kendrick's offer for it. I may have a talk with him afore I decide about renewin' that mortgage. It looks to me as if 'twould be pretty good business to dicker with him. He's got money, and if I can get some of it, so much the better for me."

"Solomon, you don't mean—"

"I don't know what I mean yet, I tell ye. But I do tell you this: I'm a business man and I know the value of money. I worked hard for what I got; 'twa'n't left me by nobody, like some folks's I hear of. Don't ask me no more questions. I'll see old Kendrick tomorrow, maybe; he's expected down."

"He is? Mr. Holliday Kendrick? How do you know?"

"I know 'cause I found out, same as I usually find out things. Chris Badger got a telegram through his office from Holliday to John Kendrick sayin' he'd come on the noon train."

"But why should he come? And on Christmas day?"

"I don't know. Probably he ain't so silly about Christmas as the average run of idiots. He's a business man, too. There! Good night, good night. Leave me alone so's I can say my prayers and turn in. I'm pretty nigh beat out."

"And you won't tell me about that mortgage?"

"No. I'll tell you when my mind's made up; that ain't yet."

Thankful turned to go. At the threshold she spoke once more.

"I wonder what you say in those prayers of yours, Solomon," she observed. "I should imagine the Lord might find 'em interestin'."

"I'm glad I said it, Emily," she told her cousin, who was awaiting her in her bedroom. "I presume likely it'll do more harm than good, but it did ME good while I was sayin' it. The mean, stingy old hypocrite! Now let's go downstairs and fill Georgie's stockin'."

But that ceremony, it appeared, must be deferred. Georgie was still wide-awake. He called to Emily to ask if the man who had come was Santa Claus.

"The little rascal," chuckled Thankful. "Well," with a sigh, "he'll never make a worse guess if he lives to be as old as Methuselah's grandmarm. Emily, you sneak down and fetch the stockin' and the presents up here to my room. We'll do the fill-in' here and hang up the stockin' in the mornin' afore he gets up."

While they were filling the stocking and tying the packages containing gifts too bulky to be put in it Miss Howes cross-questioned her cousin. Emily had been most unfavorably impressed with Mr. Cobb during this, her first, meeting with him, and her suspicions concerning Thankful's financial affairs, already aroused by the lady's reticence, were now active. She questioned and, after a time, Thankful told her, first a little and then all the truth.

"I didn't mean to tell you, Emily," she said, tearfully. "I didn't mean to tell a soul, but I—I just couldn't keep it to myself any longer. If he doesn't renew that mortgage—and goodness knows what he'll do after he talks with Mr. Holliday Kendrick—I—I don't see how I can help losin' everything. It's either that or sell out, and I don't want to sell—Oh, I don't! I know I can make a go of this place of mine if I have another year of it. I KNOW I can."

Emily was very much excited and fiercely indignant.

"The beast!" she cried, referring to the pious occupant of the back bedroom; "the mean, wicked, miserable old miser! To think of his being a relative of yours, Aunt Thankful, and treating you so! And accepting your hospitality at the very time when he is considering taking your home away from you!"

Thankful smiled ruefully. "As to that, Emily," she said, "I ain't greatly surprised. Judgin' by what I've seen of Sol Cobb, I should say 'twas a part of his gospel to accept anything he can get for nothin'. But how he can have the face to pray while he's doin' it I don't see. What kind of a God does he think he's prayin' to? I should think he'd be scared to get down on his knees for fear he'd never be let up again. Well, if there IS a ghost in that room I should say this was its chance."

"A ghost? What are you talking about, Auntie?"

"Eh? Oh, nothin', nothin'. Did I say 'ghost'? I didn't realize what I said, I guess."

"Then why did you say it?"

"Oh, I don't know. . . . There, there, don't let's get any more foolish than we can help. Let's go to bed. We'll have to turn out awful early in the mornin' to get Georgie's stockin' hung up and his presents ready. Now trot off to bed, Emily."

"Aunt Thankful, you're hiding something from me. I know you are."

"Now, Emily, you know I wouldn't—"

"Yes, you would. At least, you have. All this time you have been deceiving me about that mortgage. And now I think there is something else. What did you mean by a ghost in that room?"

"I didn't mean anything. There ain't any ghost in that room—the one Solomon's in."

"In THAT room? Is there one in another room?"

"Now, Emily—"

"Aunt Thankful, there is something strange in some room; don't deny it. You aren't accustomed to deceiving people, and you can't deceive me now. Tell me the truth."

"Well, Emily, it's all such perfect foolishness. You don't believe in ghosts, do you?"

"Of course I don't."

"Neither do I. Whatever it is that snores and groans in that little back room ain't—"

"AUNTIE! What DO you mean?"

Thankful was cornered. Her attempts at evasion were useless and, little by little, Emily drew from her the story of the little back bedroom, of her own experience there the night of their first visit, of what Winnie S. had said concerning the haunting of the "Cap'n Abner place," and of Miss Timpson's "warning." She told it in a low tone, so as not to awaken Georgie, and, as she spoke, the wind shrieked and wailed and groaned, the blinds creaked, the water dripped and gurgled in the gutters, and the shadows outside the circle of light from the little hand lamp were black and threatening. Emily, as she listened, felt the cold shivers running up and down her spine. It is one thing to scoff at superstition in the bright sunlight; it is quite another to listen to a tale like this on a night like this in a house a hundred years old. Miss Howes scoffed, it is true, but the scoffing was not convincing.

"Nonsense!" she said, stoutly. "A ghost that snores? Who ever heard of such a thing?"

"Nobody ever did, I guess," Thankful admitted. "It's all too silly for anything, of course. I KNOW it's silly; but, Emily, there's SOMETHIN' queer about that room. I told you what I heard; somethin' or somebody said, 'Oh, Lord!' as plain as ever I heard it said. And somethin' or somebody snored when Miss Timpson was there. And, of course, when they tell me how old Mr. Eldredge snored in that very room when he was dyin', and how Miss Timpson's sister snored when SHE was sick, it—it—"

"Oh, stop, Auntie! You will have ME believing in—in things, if you keep on. It's nonsense and you and I will prove it so before I go back to Middleboro. Now you must go to bed."

"Yes, I'm goin'. Well, if there is a ghost in that room it'll have its hands full with Sol Cobb. He's a tough old critter, if ever there was one. Good night, Emily."

"Good night, Aunt Thankful. Don't worry about the—ha! ha!—ghost, will you?"

"No, I've got enough to worry about this side of the grave. . . . Mercy! what's the matter?"

"Nothing! I—I thought I heard a noise in—in the hall. I didn't though."

"No, course you didn't. Shall I go to your room with you?"

"No indeed! I—I should be ashamed to have you. Where is Imogene?"

"She's up in her room. She went to bed early. Goodness! Hear that wind. It cries like—like somethin' human."

"It's dreadful. It is enough to make anyone think. . . . There! If you and I talk any longer we shall both be behaving like children. Good night."

"Good night, Emily. Is Georgie asleep at last?"

"I think so. I haven't heard a sound from him. Call me early, Auntie."

Thankful lit her own lamp; Emily took the one already lighted and hastened down the hall. Thankful shut the door and prepared for bed. The din of the storm was terrific. The old house shook as if it were trembling with fright and screaming in the agony of approaching dissolution. It was a long time before Thankful fell asleep, but at last she did.

She was awakened by a hand upon her arm and a voice whispering in her ear.

"Auntie!" whispered Emily. "Auntie, wake up! Oh, DO wake up!"

Thankful was broad awake in a moment. She sat up in bed. The room was in black darkness, and she felt rather than saw Miss Howes standing beside her.

"What is it, Emily?" she cried. "What is the matter?"

"Hush, hush! Don't speak so loud. Get up! Get up and light the lamp."

Thankful sprang out of bed and hunted for the matchbox. She found it after a time and the lamp was lighted. Emily, wearing a wrapper over her night clothes, was standing by the door, apparently listening. Her face was white and she was trembling.

"What IS it?" whispered Thankful.

"Hush! I don't know what it is. Listen!"

Thankful listened. All she heard were the noises of the storm.

"I don't hear anything," she said.

"No—no, you can't hear it from here. Come out into the hall."

Cautiously and on tiptoe she led the way to the hall and toward the head of the front stairs. There she seized her cousin's arm and whispered in her ear.

"Listen—!" she breathed.

Thankful listened.

"Why—why," she whispered, "there's somebody down in the livin'-room! Who is it?"

"I don't know. There are more than one, for I heard them talking. Who CAN it be?"

Thankful listened again.

"Where's Georgie?" she whispered, after a moment.

"In his room, I suppose. . . . What? You don't think—"

Thankful had tiptoed back to her own room and was returning with the lamp. Together they entered Georgie's bed chamber. But bed and room were empty. Georgie was not there.

CHAPTER XV

GEORGIE had gone to bed that Christmas Eve with a well-defined plan in his small head. He knew what he intended doing and how he meant to do it. The execution of this plan depended, first of all, upon his not falling asleep, and, as he was much too excited to be in the least sleepy, he found no great difficulty in carrying out this part of his scheme.

He had heard the conversation accompanying Mr. Cobb's unexpected entrance and had waited anxiously to ask concerning the visitor's identity. When assured by his sister that Santa had not arrived ahead of time he settled down again to wait, as patiently as he could, for the "grown-ups" to retire.

So he waited and waited. The clock struck ten and then eleven. Georgie rose, tiptoed to his door and listened. There were no sounds except those of the storm. Then, still on tiptoe, the boy crept along the hall to the front stairs, down these stairs and into the living-room. The fire in the "airtight" stove showed red behind the isinglass panes, and the room was warm and comfortable.

Georgie did not hesitate; his plan was complete to the minutest details. By the light from the stove he found his way to the sofa which stood against the wall on the side of the room opposite the windows. There was a heavy fringe on the sofa which hung almost to the floor. The youngster lay flat upon the floor and crept under the fringe and beneath the sofa. There he lay still. Aunt Thankful and Captain Obed and Imogene had said there was a Santa Claus; the boy in South Middleboro had said there was none; Georgie meant to settle the question for himself this very night. This was his plan: to hide in that living-room and wait until Santa came—if he came at all.

It was lonely and dark and stuffy under the sofa and the beat of the rain and the howling gale outside were scary sounds for a youngster no older than he. But Georgie was plucky and determined beyond his years. He was tempted to give up and scamper upstairs again, but he fought down the temptation. If no Santa Claus came then he should know the Leary boy was right. If he did come then—well then, his only care must be not to be caught watching.

Twelve o'clock struck; Georgie's eyes were closing. He blinked owl-like under the fringe at the red glow behind the isinglass. His head, pillowed upon his outstretched arms, felt heavy and drowsy. He must keep awake, he MUST. So, in order to achieve this result, he began to count the ticks of the big clock in the corner. One—two—three—and so on up to twenty-two. He lost count then; his eyes closed, opened, and closed again. His thoughts drifted away from the clock, drifted to—to . . .

His eyes opened again. There was a sound in the room, a strange, new sound. No, it was not in the room, it was in the dining-room. He heard it again. Someone in that dining-room was moving cautiously. The door between the rooms was open and he could hear the sound of careful footsteps.

Georgie was frightened, very much frightened. He was seized with a panic desire to scream and rush up-stairs. He did not scream, but he thrust one bare foot from beneath the sofa. Then he hastily drew it in again, for the person in the dining-room, whoever he or she might be, was coming toward the door.

A moment later there was a scratching sound and the living-room was dimly illumined by the flare of a match. The small and trembling watcher beneath the sofa shut his eyes in fright. When he opened them the lamp upon the center table was lighted and Santa Claus himself was standing by the table peering anxiously about.

It was Santa—Georgie made up his mind to that immediately. There was the pack, the pack which the pictured Santa Claus always carried, to prove it, although in this instance the pack was but a small and rather dirty bundle. There were other points of difference between the real Santa and the pictures; for instance, instead of being clothed entirely in furs, this one's apparel seemed to be, for the most part, rags, and soaked and dripping rags at that. But he did wear a fur cap, a mangy one which looked like a drowned cat, and his beard, though ragged like his garments, was all that might be desired. Yes, it was Santa Claus who had come, just as they said he would, although—and Georgie's doubts were so far justified—he had NOT come down the living-room chimney.

Santa was cold, it seemed, for his first move was to go to the stove and stand by it, shivering and warming his hands. During this operation he kept looking fearfully about him and, apparently, listening. Then, to Georgie's chagrin and disappointment, he took up the lamp and tiptoed into the dining-room again. However, he had not gone for good, for his pack was still upon the floor where he had dropped it. And a few minutes later he reappeared, his pockets bulging and in his free hand the remains of half a ham, which Georgie himself had seen Aunt Thankful put away in the pantry.

He replaced the lamp on the table and from his pockets extracted the end of a loaf of bread, several doughnuts and a half-dozen molasses cookies. Then he seated himself in a chair by the stove and proceeded to eat, hungrily, voraciously, first the ham and bread and then the doughnuts and cookies. And as he ate he looked and listened, occasionally starting as if in alarm.

At last, when he had eaten everything but the ham bone, he rose to his feet and turned his attention to the pack upon the floor. This was what Georgie had been waiting for, and as Santa fumbled with the pack, his back to the sofa, the boy parted the fringe and peered at him with eager expectation.

The pack, according to every story Georgie had been told, should have been bulging with presents; but if the latter were there they were under more old clothes, even worse than those the Christmas saint was wearing. Santa Claus hurriedly pawed over the upper layer and then took out a little package wrapped in tissue paper. Untying the string, he exposed a small pasteboard box and from this box he lifted some cotton and then—a ring.

It was a magnificent ring, so Georgie thought. It had a big green stone in the center and the rest was gold, or what looked like gold. Santa seemed to think well of it, too, for he held it to the lamplight and moved it back and forth, watching the shine of the green stone. Then he put the ring down, tore a corner from the piece of tissue paper, rummaged the stump of a pencil out of his rags, and, humping himself over the table, seemed to be writing.

It took him a long time and was plainly hard work, for he groaned occasionally and kept putting the point of the pencil into his mouth. Georgie's curiosity grew stronger each second. Unconscious of what he was doing, he parted the fringe still more and thrust out his head for a better view. The top of his head struck the edge of the sofa with a dull thump.

Santa Claus jumped as if someone had stuck a pin into him and turned. That portion of his face not covered by the scraggly beard was as white as mud and dirt would permit.

"Who—who be YOU?" he demanded in a frightened whisper.

Georgie was white and frightened also, but he manfully crept out from beneath the sofa.

"Who be you?" repeated Santa.

"I—I'm Georgie," stammered the boy.

"Georgie! Georgie who?"

"Georgie Hobbs. The—the boy that lives here."

"Lives—lives HERE?"

"Yes." It seemed strange that the person reputed to know all the children in the world did not recognize him at sight.

Apparently he did not, however, for after an instant of silent and shaky inspection he said:

"You mean to say you live here—in this house? Who do you live with?"

"Mrs. Barnes, her that owns the house."

Santa gasped audibly. "You—you live with HER?" he demanded. "Good Lord! She—she ain't married again, is she?"

"Married! No—no, sir, she ain't married."

"Then—then—See here, boy; what's your name—your whole name?"

"George Ellis Hobbs. I'm Mr. Hobbs's boy, up to South Middleboro, you know. I'm down here stayin' with Aunt Thankful. She—"

"Sshh! sshh! Don't talk so loud. So you're Mr. Hobbs's boy, eh? What—eh? Oh, yes, yes. You're ma was—was Sarah Cahoon, wa'n't she?"

"Yes, sir. I—I hope you won't be cross because I hid under the sofa. They said you were coming, but I wasn't sure, and I—I thought I'd hide and see if you did. Please—" the tears rushed to Georgie's eyes at the dreadful thought—"please don't be cross and go away without leaving me anything. I'll never do so again; honest, I won't."

Santa seemed to have heard only the first part of this plea for forgiveness. He put a hand to his forehead.

"They said I was comin'!" he repeated. "They said—WHO said so?"

"Why, everybody. Aunt Thankful and Emily and Imogene and Cap'n Bangs and Mr. Parker and—all of 'em. They knew you was comin' tonight, but I—"

"They knew it! Boy, are you crazy?"

Georgie shook his head.

"No, sir." Then, as Santa Claus sat staring blankly with open mouth and fingers plucking nervously at what seemed to be the only button on his coat, he added, "Please, sir, did you bring the air-gun?"

"Hey?"

"Did you bring the air-gun I wanted? They said you probably wouldn't, but I do want it like everything. I won't shoot the hens, honest I won't."

Santa Claus picked at the button.

"Say, boy," he asked, slowly. "Who am I?"

Georgie was surprised.

"Why, Santa Claus," he replied. "You are Santa Claus, ain't you?"

"Eh? San . . . Oh, yes, yes! I'm Santa Claus, that's who I be." He seemed relieved, but still anxious. After fidgeting a moment he added, "Well, I cal'late I'll have to be goin' now."

Georgie turned pale.

"But—but where are the presents?" he wailed. "I—I thought you wasn't goin' to be cross with me. I'm awfully sorry I stayed up to watch for you. I won't ever do it again. PLEASE don't go away and not leave me any presents. Please, Mr. Santa Claus!"

Santa started. "Sshh!" he commanded in an agonized whisper. "Hush up! Somebody'll hear. . . . Eh? What's that?"

The front stairs creaked ominously. Georgie did not answer; he made a headlong dive for his hiding-place beneath the sofa. Santa seemed to be even more alarmed than the youngster. He glanced wildly about the room and, as another creak came from the stairs, darted into the dining-room.

For a minute or more nothing happened. Then the door leading to the front hall, the door which had been standing ajar, opened cautiously and Mrs. Barnes' head protruded beyond its edge. She looked about the room; then she entered. Emily Howes followed. Both ladies wore wrappers now, and Thankful's hand clutched an umbrella, the only weapon available, which she had snatched from the hall rack as she passed it. She advanced to the center table.

"Who's here?" she demanded firmly. "Who lit this lamp? Georgie! Georgie Hobbs, we know you're here somewhere, for we heard you. Show yourself this instant."

Silence—then Emily seized her cousin's arm and pointed. A small bare foot protruded from beneath the sofa fringe. Thankful marched to the sofa and, stooping, grasped the ankle above the foot.

"Georgie Hobbs," she ordered, "come out from under this sofa."

Georgie came, partly of his own volition, partly because of the persuasive tug at his ankle.

"Now, then," ordered Thankful; "what are you doin' down here? Answer me."

Georgie did not answer. He marked a circle on the floor with his toe.

"What are you doin' down here?" repeated Mrs. Barnes. "Did you light that lamp?"

"No'm," replied Georgie.

"Of course he didn't, Auntie," whispered Emily. "There was someone here with him. I heard them talking."

"Who did light it?"

Georgie marked another circle. "Santa Claus," he muttered faintly.

Thankful stared, first at the boy and then at her cousin.

"Mercy on us!" she exclaimed. "The child's gone crazy. Christmas has struck to his head!"

But Emily's fears were not concerning her small brother's sanity. "Hush, Auntie," she whispered. "Hush! He was talking to someone. We both heard another voice. WHO did you say it was, Georgie?"

"Santa Claus. Oh, Emmie, please don't be mad. I—I wanted to see him so—and—and when he came I—I—"

"There, there, Georgie; don't cry, dear. We're not cross. You were talking to someone you thought was Santa. Where is he?"

"He WAS Santa Claus. He SAID he was. He went away when you came—into the dinin'-room."

"The dining-room? . . . Auntie, WHAT are you doing? Don't!"

But Thankful had seized the lamp and was already at the threshold of the dining-room. Holding the light aloft she peered into that apartment.

"If there's anybody here," she ordered, "they'd better come out because. . . . Here! I see you under that table. I—"

She stopped, gasped, and staggered back. Emily, running to her side, was just in time to prevent the lamp falling to the floor.

"Oh, Auntie," cried the young lady. "Auntie, what IS it?"

Thankful did not answer. Her face was white and she moved her hands helplessly. And there in the doorway of the dining-room appeared Santa Claus; and if ever Santa Claus looked scared and apprehensive he did at that moment.

Emily stared at him. Mrs. Barnes uttered a groan. Santa Claus smiled feebly.

"Hello, Thankful," he said. "I—I cal'late you're surprised to see me, ain't you?"

Thankful's lips moved.

"Are—are you livin' or—or dead?" she gasped.

"Me—Oh, I'm alive, but that's about all. Hey? It's Emily, ain't it? Why—why, Emily, don't you know me?"

Miss Howes put the lamp down upon the table. Then she leaned heavily upon a chair back.

"Cousin Jedediah!" she exclaimed. "It can't be—it—Auntie—"

But Thankful interrupted. She turned to Georgie.

"Is—is THIS your Santa Claus?" she faltered.

"Yes'm," answered Georgie.

"Jedediah Cahoon!" cried Thankful. "Jedediah Cahoon!"

For Georgie's "Santa Claus" was her brother, the brother who had run away from her home so long ago to seek his fortune in the Klondike; whose letter, written in San Francisco and posted in Omaha, had reached her the month before; whom the police of several cities were looking for at her behest.

"Auntie!" cried Emily again.

Thankful shook her head. "Help me to a chair, Emily," she begged weakly. "This—this is—my soul and body! Jedediah come alive again!"

The returned gold-hunter swallowed several times.

"Thankful," he faltered, "I know you must feel pretty hard agin me, but—but, you see—"

"Hush! hush! Don't speak to me for a minute. Let me get my bearin's, for mercy sakes, if I can. . . . Jedediah—HERE!"

"Yes—yes, I'm here. I am, honest. I—"

"Sshh! You're here now, but—but where have you been all this time? For a man that is, I presume likely, loaded down with money—I presume you must be loaded down with it; you remember you'd said you'd never come back until you was—for that kind of a man I must say you look pretty down at the heel."

"Thankful—"

"Have you worn out your clothes luggin' the money around?"

"Auntie, don't. Look at him. Think!"

"Hush, Emily! I am lookin' at him and I'm thinkin', too. I'm thinkin' of how much I put up with afore he run off and left me, and how I've worried and laid awake nights thinkin' he was dead. Where have you been all this time? Why haven't you written?"

"I did write."

"You wrote when you was without a cent and wanted to get money from me. You didn't write before. Let me be, Emily; you don't know what I've gone through on account of him and now he comes sneakin' into my house in the middle of the night, without a word that he was comin', sneakin' in like a thief and frightenin' us half to death and—"

Jedediah interrupted. "Sneakin' in!" he repeated, with a desperate move of his hands. "I had to sneak in. I was scairt to come in when you was up and awake. I knew you'd be down on me like a thousand of brick. I—I—Oh, you don't know what I've been through, Thankful, or you'd pity me, 'stead of pitchin' into me like this. I've been a reg'lar tramp—that's what I've been, a tramp. Freezin' and starvin' and workin' in bar-rooms! Why, I beat my way on a freight train all the way here from New Bedford, and I've been hidin' out back of the house waitin' for you to go to bed, so's I'd dare come in."

"So's you'd dare come in! What did you want to come in for if I wa'n't here?"

"I wanted to leave a note for you, that's why. I wanted to leave a note and—and that."

He pointed to the ring and the bit of tissue paper on the table. Thankful took up the paper first and read aloud what was written upon it.

"For Thankful, with a larst merry Christmas from brother Jed. I am going away and if you want me I will be at New Bedford for two weeks, care the bark Finback."

"'I am goin' away'," repeated Thankful. "Goin' away? Are you goin' away AGAIN?"

"I—I was cal'latin' to. I'm goin' cook on a whaler."

"Cook! You a cook! And," she took up the ring and stared at it, "for the land sakes, what's this?"

"It's a present I bought for you. Took my last two dollar bill, it did. I wanted you to have somethin' to remember me by."

Thankful held the gaudy ring at arm's length and stared at it helplessly. There was a curious expression on her face, half-way between laughing and crying.

"You bought this—this thing for me," she repeated. "And did you think I'd wear it."

"I hoped you would. Oh, Thankful, if you only knew what I've been through. Why, I was next door to starvin' when I got in here tonight. If I hadn't eat somethin' I found in the buttry I would have starved, I guess. And I'm soaked, soppin' through and—"

"There, there. Hush! hush! Jedediah, you're gold-diggin' ain't changed you much, I guess. You're just as helpless as ever you was. Well, you're here and I'm grateful for so much. Now you come with me out into the kitchen and we'll see what can be done about gettin' you dry. Emily, if you'll just put that child to bed."

But Georgie had something to say. He had listened to this long dialogue with astonishment and growing dismay. Now the dismay and conviction of a great disappointment overcame him.

"I don't want to go to bed," he wailed. "Ain't he Santa Claus? He SAID he was Santa Claus. Where are my presents? Where's my air-gun? I want my presents. Oh—Oh—Oh!"

He went out crying. Emily ran to him.

"Hush, hush, Georgie, dear," she begged. "Come upstairs with sister—come. If you don't you may be here when the real Santa comes and you will frighten him away. Come with me; that's a good boy. Auntie, I will be down by and by."

She led the disappointed and still sobbing boy from the room. Thankful turned to her brother.

"Now you march out into that kitchen," she commanded. "I'll get you warm first and then I'll see about a bed for you. You'll have to sleep up on the third floor tonight. After that I'll see about a better room to put you in."

Jedediah stared at her.

"What—what," he faltered. "Do you mean—Thankful, do you mean you're goin' to let me stay here for—for good?"

"Yes, of course I do. You don't think I'll let you get out of my sight again, do you? That is, unless you're real set on goin' gold-huntin'. I'm sure you shan't go cook on any whaler; I've got too much regard for sailors' digestions to let you do that."

"Thankful, I—I'll work my hands off for you. I'll—"

"All right, all right. Now trot along and warm those hands or you won't have any left to work off; they'll be SHOOK off with the shivers. Come, Jed, I forgive you; after all, you're my brother, though you did run away and leave me."

"Then—then you're glad I came back?"

"Glad!" Thankful shook her head with a tearful smile. "Glad!" she repeated. "I've been workin' heavens and earth to get you back ever since I got that pitiful letter of yours. You poor thing! You MUST have had a hard time of it. Well, you can tell me all about it by and by. Now you march into that kitchen."

Another hour had passed before Mrs. Barnes reentered the living-room. There, to her astonishment, she found Emily awaiting her.

"Why, for goodness sakes!" cried Thankful. "What are you doin' here? I thought you'd gone to bed long ago."

Emily's reply was given in an odd tone. She did not look at her cousin when she spoke.

"No, no," she said, quickly. "I—I haven't gone to bed."

"I see you haven't, but why?"

"I didn't want to. I—I'm not sleepy."

"Not sleepy! At two o'clock in the mornin'? Well," with a sigh, "I suppose 'tain't to be wondered at. What's happened this night is enough to keep anybody awake.

I can't believe it even yet. To think of his comin' back after I've given him up for dead twice over. It's like a story-book."

"Where is he?"

"Up in bed, in one of the attic rooms. If he hasn't got his death of cold it'll be a wonder. And SUCH yarns as he's been spinnin' to me. I—Emily, what's the matter with you? What makes you act so queer?"

Emily did not answer. Mrs. Barnes walked across the room and, stooping, peered into her face.

"You're white as a sheet!" she cried, in alarm. "And you're tremblin' all over. What in the world IS the matter?"

Emily tried to smile, but it was a poor attempt.

"Nothing, nothing, Auntie," she said. "That is, I—I'm sure it can't be anything to be afraid of."

"But you are afraid, just the same. What is it? Tell me this minute."

For the first time Emily looked her cousin in the face.

"Auntie," she whispered, "I am—I have been frightened. Something I heard upstairs frightened me."

"Somethin' you heard upstairs? Where? Has Georgie—"

"No, Georgie is asleep in his room. I locked the door. It wasn't Georgie; it was something else."

"Somethin'—Emily Howes, do you want to scare me to DEATH? What IS it?"

"I don't know what it is. I heard it first when I came out of Georgie's room a few minutes ago. Then I went down the hall to his door and listened. Aunt Thankful, he—he is in there talking—talking to someone."

"He? Talkin'? Who?"

"Mr. Cobb. It was dreadful. He was talking to—to—I don't know WHAT he was talking to, but it was awful to hear."

"Talkin'? Solomon Cobb was talkin'? In his sleep, do you mean?"

"No, he wasn't asleep. He was talking to someone, or some THING, in that room. And that wasn't all. I heard—I heard—Oh, I DID hear it! I know I did! And yet it couldn't be! It couldn't!"

"Emily Howes, if you keep on I'll—WHAT did you hear?"

"I don't know. . . . Aunt Thankful, where are you going?"

Thankful did not answer. She was on her way to the front hall and the stairs. Emily rushed after her and would have detained her if she could, but Thankful would not be detained. Up the stairs they went together and along the narrow dark hall. At the end of the hall was the door of the back bedroom, or the larger room adjoining it. The door was closed, but from beneath it shone lamplight in sharp, yellow streaks. And from behind it came faintly the sound of a deep groan, the groan of a soul in agony.

"He's sick," whispered Thankful. "The man's sick. I'm goin' to him."

"He isn't sick. It—it's something else. I tell you I heard—"

Thankful did not wait to learn what her cousin had heard. She tiptoed down the hall and Emily followed. The two women crouched beside the closed door of Mr. Cobb's room. And within that room they heard Solomon's voice, now rising almost to a shriek, now sinking to a groan, as its owner raved on and on, talking, pleading, praying.

"Oh, don't—don't, Abner!" cried Mr. Cobb. "Don't, no more! PLEASE don't! I know what you mean. I know it all. I'm sorry. I know I ain't done right. But I'll MAKE it right; I swear to the Almighty I will! I know I've broke my word to you and acted wicked and mean, but I give you my solemn word I'll make everything right. Only just quit and go away, that's all I ask. Just quit that—Oh, there you GO again! QUIT! PLEASE quit!"

It was dreadful to hear, but this was not the most dreadful. Between the agonized sentences and whenever the wind lulled, the listeners at the door heard another sound, a long-drawn gasp and groan, a series of gasps and groans, as of something fighting for breath, the unmistakable sound of snoring.

Emily grasped her cousin's arm. "Come, come away!" she whispered. "I—I believe I'm going to faint."

Mrs. Barnes did not wait to be urged. She put her arm about the young lady's waist and together they tiptoed back to Thankful's bedroom. There, Mrs. Barnes's first move was to light the lamp, the second to close and lock the door. Then the pair sat down, one upon the bed and the other on a chair, and gazed into each other's pale faces.

Emily was the first to speak.

"I—I don't believe it!" she declared, shakily. "I KNOW it isn't real!"

"So—so do I."

"But—but we heard it. We both heard it."

"Well—well, I give in I—I heard somethin', somethin' that. . . . My soul! Am I goin' CRAZY to finish off this night with?"

"I don't know. If you are, then I must be going with you. What can it be, Auntie?"

"I don't know."

"There is no other door to that room, is there?"

"No."

"Then what CAN it be?"

"I don't know. Imogene's in her own room; I looked in and saw her when I took Jedediah up attic. And Georgie's in his with the door locked. And you and I are here. There can't be a livin' soul in that room with Solomon, not a livin' soul."

"But we heard—we both heard—"

"I know; I know. And I heard somethin' there before. And so did Miss Timpson. Emily, did—did you hear him call—call it 'Abner'?"

"Yes," with a shudder. "I heard. Who could help hearing!"

"And Cap'n Abner was my uncle; and he used to live here. . . . There!" with sudden determination. "That's enough of this. We'll both be stark, ravin' distracted if we keep on this way. My soul! Hear that wind! I said once that all the big things in my life had happened durin' a storm and so they have. Jedediah went away in a storm and he's come back in a storm. And now if UNCLE ABNER'S comin' back. . . . There I go again! Emily, do you feel like goin' to bed?"

"To BED! After THAT? Auntie, how can you!"

"All right, then we'll set up till mornin'. Turn that lamp as high as you can and we'll set by it and wait for daylight. By that time we may have some of our sense back again and not behave like two feeble-minded fools. Turn that wick up—WAY up, Emily Howes! And talk—talk just as hard as you can—about somethin' or somebody that's ALIVE."

CHAPTER XVI

EMILY obeyed orders as far as turning up the wick was concerned, and she did her best to talk. It was hard work; both she and her cousin found themselves breaking off a sentence in the middle to listen and draw closer together as the wild gusts whistled about the windows and the water poured from the sashes and gurgled upon the sills. Occasionally Thankful went to the door to look down the dark hall in the direction of Mr. Cobb's room, or to unlock Georgie's door and peer in to make sure that the boy was safe and sleeping.

From the third of these excursions Mrs. Barnes returned with a bit of reassuring news.

"I went almost there this time," she whispered. "My conscience has been tormenting me to think of—of Solomon's bein' alone in there with—with THAT, and I almost made up my mind to sing out and ask if he was all right. But I didn't have to, thank goodness. His light's still lit and I heard him movin' around, so he ain't been scared clean to death, at any rate. For the rest of it I don't care so much; a good hard scarin' may do him good. He needs one. If ever a stingy old reprobate needed to have a warnin' from the hereafter that man does."

"Did you hear anything—anything else?" whispered Emily, fearfully.

"No, I didn't, and I didn't wait for fear I MIGHT hear it. Did I lock the door when I came in? Emily, I guess you think I'm the silliest old coward that ever was. I am—and I know it. Tomorrow we'll both be brave enough, and we'll both KNOW there ain't any spirits here, or anywhere else this side of the grave; but tonight—well, tonight's different. . . . Ouch! what was that? There, there! don't mind my jumpin'. I feel as if I'd been stuffed with springs, like a sofa. Did you ever know a night as long as this? Won't mornin' EVER come?"

At five o'clock, while it was still pitch dark, Thankful announced her intention of going downstairs. "Might as well be in the kitchen as up here," she said, "and I can keep busy till Imogene comes down. And, besides, we'd better be puttin' Georgie's stockin' and his presents in the livin'-room. The poor little shaver's got to have his Christmas, even though his Santa Claus did turn out to be a walkin' rag-bag."

Emily started. "Why, it is Christmas, isn't it!" she exclaimed. "Between returned brothers and," with a little shiver, "ghosts, I forgot entirely."

She kissed her cousin's cheek.

"A merry Christmas, Aunt Thankful," she said.

Thankful returned the kiss. "Same to you, dearie, and many of 'em," she replied. "Well, here's another Christmas day come to me. A year ago I didn't think I'd be here. I wonder where I'll be next Christmas. Will I have a home of my own or will what I've thought was my home belong to Sol Cobb or Holliday Kendrick?"

"Hush, Auntie, hush! Your home won't be taken from you. It would be too mean, too dreadful! God won't permit such a thing."

"I sartin' hope he won't, but it seems sometimes as if he permitted some mighty mean things, 'cordin' to our way of lookin' at 'em. That light's still burnin'," she added, peering out into the hall. "Well, I suppose I ought to pity Solomon, but I don't when I think how he's treated me. If the ghost—or whatever 'tis in there—weeded out the rest of his whiskers for him I don't know's I'd care. 'Twould serve him right, I guess."

They rehung Georgie's stocking—bulging and knobby it was now—and arranged his more bulky presents beneath it on the floor. Then Thankful went into the kitchen and Emily accompanied her. The morning broke, pale and gray. The wind had subsided and it no longer rained. With the returning daylight Emily's courage began to revive.

"I can't understand," she said, "how you and I could have been so childish last night. We should have insisted on calling to Mr. Cobb and then we should have found out what it was that frightened him and us. I mean to go over every inch of those two rooms before dinner time."

Thankful nodded. "I'll do it with you," she said. "But I've been over 'em so many times that I'm pretty skeptical. The time to go over 'em is in the night when that—that snorin' is goin' on. A ghost that snores ought, by rights, to be one that's asleep, and a sound-asleep ghost ought to be easy to locate. Oh, yes! I can make fun NOW. I told you I was as brave as a lion—in the daytime."

It was easy to talk now, and they drifted into a discussion of many things. Thankful retold the story of her struggle to keep the High Cliff House afloat, told it all, her hopes, her fears and her discouragements. They spoke of Captain Bangs, of his advice and help and friendship. Emily brought the captain into the conversation and kept him there. Thankful said little concerning him, and of the one surprising, intimate interview between Captain Obed and herself she said not a word. She it was who first mentioned John Kendrick's name. Emily was at first disinclined to speak of the young lawyer, but, little by little, as her cousin hinted and questioned, she said more and more. Thankful learned what she wished to learn, and it was what she had suspected. She learned something else, too, something which concerned another citizen of East Wellmouth.

"I knew it!" she cried. "I didn't believe 'twas so, and I as much as told Cap'n Obed 'twasn't this very day—no, yesterday, I mean. When a body don't go to bed at all the days kind of run into one another."

"What did you know?" asked Emily. "What were you and Captain Obed talking of that concerned me?"

"Nothin', nothin', dear. It didn't concern you one bit, and 'twasn't important. . . . Hi hum!" rising and looking out of the window. "It's gettin' brighter fast now. Looks as if we might have a pleasant Christmas, after all. Wonder how poor Jedediah'll feel when he wakes up. I hope he slept warm anyhow. I piled on comforters and quilts enough to smother him."

Her attempt at changing the subject was successful. Emily's next question concerned Jedediah.

"What are you goin' to do with him, Auntie?" she asked. "He must stay here, mustn't he?"

"Course he must. I'll never trust him out of my sight again. He ain't competent to take care of himself and so I'll have to take care of him. Well," with a sigh, "it'll only be natural, that's all. I've been used to takin' care of somebody all my days. I wonder how 'twould seem to have somebody take care of me for a change? Not that there's liable to be anybody doin' it," she added hastily.

"Jedediah might be useful to work about the place here," said Emily. "You will always need a hired man, you know."

"Yes, but I don't need two, and I couldn't discharge Kenelm on Imogene's account. What that girl ever got engaged to that old image for is more'n I can make out or ever shall."

Emily smiled. "I shouldn't worry about Imogene," she said. "I think she knows perfectly well what she is about."

"Maybe so, but if she does, then her kind of knowledge is different from mine. If I was goin' to marry anybody in that family 'twould be Hannah; she's the most man of the two."

Imogene herself came down a few minutes later. She was much surprised to find her mistress and Miss Howes dressed and in the kitchen. Also she was very curious.

"Who's that man," she asked; "the one in the next room to mine, up attic? Is he a new boarder? He must have come awful late. I heard you and him talkin' in the middle of the night. Who is he?"

When told the story of Jedediah's return she was greatly excited.

"Why, it's just like somethin' in a story!" she cried. "Long-lost folks are always comin' back in stories. And comin' Christmas Eve makes it all the better. Lordy— There, I ain't said that for weeks and weeks! Excuse me, Mrs. Thankful. I WON'T say it again. But—but what are we goin' to do with him? Is he goin' to stay here for good?"

Thankful answered that she supposed he was, he had no other place to stay.

"Is he rich? He ought to be. Folks in stories always come home rich after they've run off."

"Well, this one didn't. He missed connections, somehow. Rich! No," drily, "he ain't rich."

"Well, what will he do? Will we have to take care of him—free, I mean? Excuse me for buttin' in, ma'am, but it does seem as if we had enough on our hands without takin' another free boarder."

Thankful went into the dining-room. Emily, when the question was repeated to her, suggested that, possibly, Jedediah might work about the place, take care of the live-stock and of the garden, when there was one.

Imogene reflected. "Hum!" she mused. "We don't need two hired hands, that's a sure thing. You mean he'll take Kenelm's job?"

"That isn't settled, so you mustn't speak of it. I know my cousin will be very sorry to let Kenelm go, largely on your account, Imogene."

"On my account?"

"Why, yes. You and he are engaged to be married and of course you like to have him here."

Imogene burst out laughing. "Don't you worry about that, Miss Emily," she said. "I shan't, and I don't think Kenelm will, either."

Breakfast was ready at last and they were just sitting down to the table—it had been decided not to call Jedediah or Mr. Cobb—when Georgie appeared. The boy had crept downstairs, his small head filled with forebodings; but the sight of the knobby stocking and the heap of presents sent his fears flying and he burst into the room with a shriek of joy. One by one the packages were unwrapped and, with each unwrapping, the youngster's excitement rose.

"Gee!" he cried, as he sat in the middle of the heap of toys and brown paper and looked about him. "Gee! They're all here; everything I wanted—but that air-gun. I don't care, though. Maybe I'll get that next Christmas. Or maybe Cap'n Bangs'll give it to me, anyhow. He gives me most anything, if I tease for it."

Thankful shook her head. "You see, Georgie," she said, "it pays to be a good boy. If Santa had caught you hidin' under that sofa and watchin' for him last night you might not have got any of these nice things."

Georgie did not answer immediately. When he did it was in a rather doubtful tone.

"There ain't any soot on 'em, anyhow," he observed. "And they ain't wet, either."

Imogene clapped her hand to her mouth and hurried from the room. "You can't fool that kid much," she whispered to Emily afterward. "He's the smartest kid ever I saw. I'll keep out of his way for a while; I don't want to have to answer his questions."

There were other presents besides those given to Georgie; presents for Emily from Thankful, and for Thankful from Emily, and for Imogene from both. There was nothing costly, of course, but no one cared for that.

As they were beginning breakfast Jedediah appeared. His garments, which had been drying by the kitchen stove all night and which Imogene had deposited in a heap at his bedroom door, were wrinkled, but his face shone from the vigorous application of soap and water and, as his sister said afterward, "You could see his complexion without diggin' for it, and that was somethin'."

His manner was subdued and he was very, very polite and anxious to please, but his appetite was in good order. Introduced to Imogene he expressed himself as pleased to meet her. Georgie he greeted with some hesitation; evidently the memory of his midnight encounter with the boy embarrassed him. But Georgie, when he learned that the shabby person whom he was told to call "Uncle Jed" was, although only an imitation Santa Claus, a genuine gold-hunter and traveler who had seen real Esquimaux and polar bears, warmed to his new relative immediately.

When the meal was over Jedediah made what was, for him, an amazing suggestion.

"Now," he said, "I cal'late I'd better be gettin' to work, hadn't I? What'll I do first, Thankful?"

Mrs. Barnes stared at him. "Work?" she repeated. "What do you mean?"

"I mean I want to be doin' somethin'—somethin' to help, you know. I don't cal'late to stay around here and loaf. No, SIR!"

Thankful drew a long breath. "All right, Jed," she said. "You can go out in the barn and feed the horse if you want to. Kenelm—Mr. Parker—generally does it, but he probably won't be here for quite a spell yet. Go ahead. Imogene'll show you what to do. . . . But, say, hold on," she added, with emphasis. "Don't you go off the premises, and if you see anybody comin', keep out of sight. I don't want anybody to see a brother of mine in THOSE clothes. Soon's ever I can I'll go up to the village and buy you somethin' to wear, if it's only an 'ilskin jacket and a pair of overalls. They'll cover up the rags, anyhow. As you are now, you look like one of Georgie's picture-puzzles partly put together."

When the eager applicant for employment had gone, under Imogene's guidance, Emily spoke her mind.

"Auntie," she said, "are you going to make him work—now; after what he's been through, and on Christmas day, too?"

Thankful was still staring after her brother.

"Sshh! sshh!" she commanded. "Don't speak to me for a minute; you may wake me up. Jedediah Cahoon ASKIN' to go to work! All the miracles in Scriptur' are nothin' to this."

"But, Auntie, he did ask. And do you think he is strong enough?"

"Hush, Emily, hush! You don't know Jedediah. Strong enough! I'm the one that needs strength, if I'm goin' to have shocks like this one sprung on me."

Emily said no more, but she noticed that her cousin was wearing the two-dollar ring, the wanderer's "farewell" gift, so she judged that brother Jed would not be worked beyond the bounds of moderation.

Left alone in the dining-room—Georgie had returned to the living-room and his presents—the two women looked at each other. Neither had eaten a breakfast worth mentioning and the same thought was in the mind of each.

"Auntie," whispered Emily, voicing that thought, "don't you think we ought to go up and—and see if he is—all right."

Thankful nodded. "Yes," she said, "I suppose we had. He's alive, I know that much, for I had Imogene knock on his door just now and he answered. But I guess maybe we'd better—"

She did not finish the sentence for at that moment the subject of the conversation entered the room. It was Solomon Cobb who entered, but, except for his clothes, he was a changed man. His truculent arrogance was gone, he came in slowly and almost as if he were walking in his sleep. His collar was unbuttoned, his hair had not been combed, and the face between the thin bunches of whiskers was white and drawn. He did not speak to either Emily or Thankful, but, dragging one foot after the other, crossed the room and sat down in a chair by the window.

Thankful spoke to him.

"Are you sick, Solomon?" she asked.

Mr. Cobb shook his head.

"Eh?" he grunted. "No, no, I ain't sick. I guess I ain't; I don't know."

"Breakfast is all ready, Mr. Cobb," suggested Emily.

Solomon turned a weary eye in her direction. He looked old, very old.

"Breakfast!" he repeated feebly. "Don't talk about breakfast to me! I'll never eat again in this world."

Thankful pitied him; she could not help it.

"Oh, yes, you will," she said, heartily. "Just try one of those clam fritters of Imogene's and you'll eat a whole lot. If you don't you'll be the first one."

He shook his head. "Thankful," he said, slowly, "I—I want to talk to you. I've got to talk to you—alone."

"Alone! Why, Emily's just the same as one of the family. There's no secrets between us, Solomon."

"I don't care. I wan't to talk to you. It's you I've got to talk to."

Thankful would have protested once more, but Emily put a hand on her arm.

"I'll go into the living-room with Georgie, Auntie," she whispered. "Yes, I shall."

She went and closed the door behind her. Thankful sat down in a chair, wondering what was coming next. Solomon did not look at her, but, after a moment, he spoke.

"Thankful Cahoon," he said, calling her by her maiden name. "I—I've been a bad man. I'm goin' to hell."

Thankful jumped. "Mercy on us!" she cried. "What kind of talk—"

"I'm goin' to hell," repeated Solomon. "When a man does the way I've done that's where he goes. I'm goin there and I'm goin' pretty soon. I've had my notice."

Thankful stood up. She was convinced that her visitor had been driven crazy by his experience in the back bedroom.

"Now, now, now," she faltered. "Don't talk so wicked, Solomon Cobb. You've been a church man for years, and a professor of religion. You told me so, yourself. How can you set there and say—"

Mr. Cobb waved his hand.

"Don't make no difference," he moaned. "Or, if it does, it only makes it worse. I know where I'm goin', but—but I'll go with a clean manifest, anyhow. I'll tell you the whole thing. I promised the dead I would and I will. Thankful Cahoon, I've been a bad man to you. I swore my solemn oath as a Christian to one that was my best friend, and I broke it.

"Years ago I swore by all that was good and great I'd look out for you and see that you was comf'table and happy long's you lived. And instead of that, when I come here last night—LED here, I know now that I was—my mind was about made up to take your home away from you, if I could. Yes, sir, I was cal'latin' to foreclose on you and sell this place to Kendrick. I thought I was mighty smart and was doin' a good stroke of business. No mortal man could have made me think diff'rent; BUT AN IMMORTAL ONE DID!"

He groaned and wiped his forehead. Thankful did not speak; her surprise and curiosity were too great for speech.

"'Twas your Uncle Abner Barnes," went on Solomon, "that was the makin' of me. I sailed fust mate for him fourteen year. And he always treated me fine, raised my wages right along, and the like of that. 'Twas him that put me in the way of investin' my money in them sugar stocks and the rest. He made me rich, or headed me that way. And when he lost all he had except this place here and was dyin' aboard the old schooner, he calls me to him and he says:

"'Sol,' he says, 'Sol, I've done consider'ble for you, and you've said you was grateful. Well, I'm goin' to ask a favor of you. I ain't got a cent of my own left, and my niece by marriage, Thankful Cahoon that was, that I love same as if she was my own child, may, sometime or other, be pretty hard put to it to get along. I want you to look after her. If ever the time comes that she needs money or help I want you to do for her what I'd do if I was here. If you don't,' he says, risin' on one elbow in the bunk, 'I'll come back and ha'nt you. Promise on your solemn oath.' And I promised. And you know how I've kept that promise. And last night he come back. Yes, sir, he come back!"

Still Thankful said nothing. He groaned again and went on:

"Last night," he said, "up in that bedroom, I woke up and, as sure as I'm settin' here this minute, I heard Cap'n Abner Barnes snorin' just as he snored afore his death aboard the schooner, T. I. Smalley, in the stateroom next to mine. I knew it in a minute, but I got up and went all round my room and the empty one alongside. There was nothin' there, of course. Nothin' but the snorin'. And I got down on my knees and swore to set things right this very day. Give me a pen and ink and some paper."

"Eh? What?"

"Give me a pen and some ink and paper. Don't sit there starin'! Hurry up! Can't you see I want to get this thing off my chest afore I die! And—and I—I wouldn't be surprised if I died any minute. Hurry UP!"

Thankful went into the living-room in search of the writing materials.

Emily, who was sitting on the floor with Georgie and the presents, turned to ask a question.

"What is it, Auntie?" she whispered, eagerly. "Is it anything important?"

Her cousin made an excited gesture.

"I—I don't know," she whispered in reply. "Either he's been driven looney by what happened last night, or else—or else somethin's goin' to happen that I don't dast to believe. Emily, you stand right here by the door. I may want you."

"Where's that pen and things?" queried Solomon from the next room. "Ain't you ever comin'?"

When the writing materials were brought and placed upon the dining-room table he drew his chair to that table and scrawled a few lines.

"Somebody ought to witness this," he cried, nervously. "Some disinterested person ought to witness this. Then 'twill hold in law. Where's that—that Howes girl? Oh, here you be! Here! you sign that as a witness."

Emily, who had entered at the mention of her name, took the paper from his trembling fingers. She read what was written upon it.

"Why—why, Auntie!" she cried, excitedly. "Aunt Thankful, have you seen this? He—"

"Stop your talk!" shouted Solomon. "Can't you women do nothin' BUT talk? Sign your name alongside of mine as a witness."

Emily took the pen and signed as directed. Mr. Cobb snatched the paper from her, glanced at it and then handed it to Thankful.

"There!" he cried. "That's done, anyhow. I've done so much. Now—now don't say a word to me for a spell. I—I'm all in; that's what I am, all in."

Thankful did not say a word; she couldn't have said it at that moment. Upon the paper which she held in her hand was written a cancellation of the fifteen-hundred-dollar mortgage and a receipt in full for the loan itself, signed by Solomon Cobb.

Dimly and uncomprehendingly she heard Emily trying to thank their visitor. But thanks he would not listen to.

"No, no, no!" he shouted. "Go away and let me alone. I'm a wicked, condemned critter. Nobody's ever cared a durn for me, nobody but one, and I broke my word to him. Friendless I've lived since Abner went and friendless I'll die. Serve me right. I ain't got a livin' soul of my own blood in the world."

But Thankful was in a measure herself again.

"Don't talk so, Solomon," she cried. "You have got somebody of your own blood. I'm a relation of yours, even if 'tis a far-off relation. I—I don't know how to thank you for this. I—"

He interrupted again.

"Yes," he wailed, "you're my relation. I know it. Think that makes it any better? Look how I've treated you. No, no; I'm goin' to die and go—"

"You're goin' to have breakfast, that's what you're goin' to have. And it shan't be warmed up fried clams either. Emily, you stay with him. I'm goin' to the kitchen."

She fled to the kitchen, where, between fits of crying and laughing, which would have alarmed Imogene had she been there, she tried to prepare a breakfast which might tempt the repentant money-lender. Emily joined her after a short interval.

"He won't listen to anything," said the young lady. "He has been frightened almost to death, that's certain. He is praying now. I came away and left him praying. Oh, Auntie, isn't it wonderful! Isn't it splendid!"

Thankful sighed. "It's so wonderful I can scarcely believe it," she said. "To think of his givin' up money—givin' it away of his own accord! I said last night that Jedediah's comin' home was a miracle. This one beats that all to pieces. I don't know what to do about takin' that thousand from him," she added. "I declare I don't. 'Course I shan't take it in the long run; I'll pay it back soon as ever I can. But should I pretend to take it now? That's what troubles me."

"Of course you should. He is rich and he doesn't need it. What have you done with that receipt? Put it away somewhere and in a safe place. He is frightened; that—that something, whatever it was, last night—frightened him so that he will give away anything now. But, by and by, when his fright is over he may change his mind. Lock up that paper, Aunt Thankful. If you don't, I will."

"But what was it that frightened him, Emily? I declare I'm gettin' afraid to stay in this house myself. What was it he heard—and we heard?"

"I don't know, but I mean to find out. I'm a sensible person this morning, not an idiot, and I intend to lay that ghost."

When they went back into the dining-room they were surprised at what they saw. Solomon was still sitting by the window, but Georgie was sitting in a chair beside him, exhibiting the pictures in one of his Christmas books and apparently on the best of terms with his new acquaintance.

"I'm showin' him my 'Swiss Family Robinson,'" said the boy. "Here's where they built a house in a tree, Mr. Cobb. Emmie told me about their doin' it."

Solomon groaned.

"You better take this child away from me," he said. "He came to me of his own accord, but he hadn't ought to stay. A man like me ain't fit to have children around him."

Thankful had an inspiration.

"It's a sign," she cried, clapping her hands. "It's a sign sent to you, Solomon. It means you're forgiven. That's what it means. Now you eat your breakfast."

He was eating, or trying to eat, when someone knocked at the door. Winnie S. Holt was standing on the step.

"Merry Christmas, Mrs. Barnes," he hailed. "Ain't drowned out after the gale, be you? Judas priest! Our place is afloat. Dad says he cal'lates we'll have to build a raft to get to the henhouse on. Here; here's somethin' Mr. Kendrick sent to you. Wanted me to give it to you, yourself, and nobody else."

The something was a long envelope with "Mrs. Barnes, Personal," written upon it. Thankful read the inscription.

"From Mr. Kendrick?" she repeated. "Which Mr. Kendrick?"

"Mr. John, the young one. Mr. Holliday's comin', though. He telephoned from Bayport this mornin'. Came down on the cars far's there last night, but he didn't dast to come no further 'count of bein' afraid to drive from the Centre in the storm. He's hired an automobile and is comin' right over, he says. The message was for John Kendrick, but Dad took it. What's in the envelope, Mrs. Barnes?"

Thankful slowly tore the end from the envelope. Emily stood at her elbow.

"What can it be, Auntie?" she asked, fearfully.

"I don't know. I'm afraid to look. Oh, dear! It's somethin' bad, I know. Somethin' to do with that Holliday Kendrick; it must be or he wouldn't have come to East Wellmouth today. I—I—well, I must look, of course. Oh, Emily, and we thought this was goin' to be a merry Christmas, after all."

The enclosure was a long, legal-looking document. Thankful unfolded it, read a few lines and then stopped reading.

"Why—why—" she stammered.

"What is it, Auntie?" pleaded Emily.

"It—I can't make out. I MUST be crazy, or—or somebody is. It looks like—
Read it, Emily; read it out loud."

CHAPTER XVII

CAPTAIN Obed Bangs rose at his usual hour that Christmas morning, and the hour was an early one. When he looked from his bedroom window the clouds were breaking and a glance at his barometer, hung on the wall just beside that window, showed the glass to be rising and confirmed the promise of a fair day. He dressed and came downstairs. Hannah Parker came down soon afterward. The captain wished her a merry Christmas.

Miss Parker shook her head; she seemed to be in a pessimistic mood.

"I'm much obliged to you, Cap'n Bangs," she said, "and I'm sure I wish you the same. But I don't know; don't seem as if I was liable to have many more merry Christmases in this life. No, merry Christmases ain't for me. I'm a second fiddle nowadays and I cal'late that's what I'm foreordinated to be from now on."

The captain didn't understand.

"Second fiddle," he repeated. "What have you got to do with fiddlin', for goodness' sakes?"

"Nothin', of course. I don't mean a real fiddle. I mean I shan't never be my own mistress any more. I've been layin' awake thinkin' about it and shiverin', 'twas so damp and chilly up in my room. There's a loose shingle right over a knot hole that's abreast a crack in my bedroom wall, and it lets in the dampness like a sieve. I've asked Kenelm to fix it MORE times; but no, all he cares to do is look out for himself and that inmate. If SHE had a loose shingle he'd fix it quick enough. All I could do this mornin' was lay to bed there and shiver and pull up the quilt and think and think. It kept comin' over me more and more."

"The quilt, you mean? That's what you wanted it to do, wasn't it?"

"Not the quilt. The thought of the lonesome old age that's comin' to me when Kenelm's married. I've had him to look after for so long. I've been my own boss, as they say."

She might have added, "And Kenelm's, too," but Captain Obed added it for her, in his mind. He laughed.

"That's all right, Hannah," he observed, by way of consolation. "Kenelm ain't married yet. When he is you can help his wife look out for him. Either that or get married. Why don't you get married, Hannah?"

"Humph! Don't be silly, Obed Bangs."

"That ain't silliness, that's sense. All you need to do is just h'ist the signal, 'Consort wanted,' and you'd have one alongside in no time. There's Caleb Hammond, for instance; he's a widower and—eh! look out!"

Miss Parker had dropped the plate she was just putting down upon the table. Fortunately it fell only a few inches and did not break.

"What do you mean by that?" she demanded sharply.

"I meant the plate. Little more and you'd have sent it to glory."

"Never you mind the plate. I can look out for my own crockery. 'Twas cracked anyhow. And I guess you're cracked, too," she added. "Talkin' about my—my marryin' Caleb Hammond. What put that in your head?"

"I don't know. I just—"

"Well, don't be silly. When I marry Caleb Hammond," she added with emphasis, "'twill be after THIS."

"So I cal'lated. I didn't think you'd married him afore this. There now, you missed a chance, Hannah. You and he ought to have got married that time when you went away together."

Miss Parker turned pale. "When we went—away—TOGETHER!" she faltered. "WHAT are you talkin' about?"

"When you went over to the Cattle Show that time."

"Is that what you meant?"

"Sartin. What are you glarin' at me that way for? You ain't been away together any other time, have you? No, Hannah, that was your chance. You and Caleb might have been married in the balloon, like the couples we read about in the papers. Ho! ho! Think of the advertisin' you'd have had! 'A high church weddin'.' 'Bride and groom up in the air.' Can't you see those headlines?"

Hannah appeared more relieved than annoyed.

"Humph!" she sniffed. "Well, I should say YOU was up in the air, Obed Bangs. What's the matter with you this mornin'? Has the rain soaked into your head? It seems to be softenin' up pretty fast. If you're so set on somebody gettin' married why don't you get married yourself? You've been what the minister calls 'unattack-ted' all your life."

The minister had said "unattached," but Captain Obed did not offer to correct the quotation. He joked no more and, during breakfast, was silent and absent-minded.

After breakfast he went out for a walk. The storm had gullied the hills and flooded the hollows. There were pools of water everywhere, shining cold and steely in the winter sunshine. The captain remembered the low ground in which the barn and outbuildings upon the "Cap'n Abner place" stood, and judged that he and Kenelm might have to do some rescue work among the poultry later on. He went back to the house to suggest that work to Mr. Parker himself.

Kenelm and his sister were evidently in the midst of a dispute. The former was seated at the breakfast table and Hannah was standing by the kitchen door looking at him.

"Goin' off to work Christmas Day!" she said, as the captain entered. "I should think you might stay home with me THAT day, if no other. 'Tain't the work you're so anxious to get to. It's that precious inmate of yours."

Kenelm's answer was as surprising as it was emphatic.

"Darn the inmate!" he shouted. "I wish to thunder I'd never seen her!"

Captain Obed whistled. Miss Parker staggered, but she recovered promptly.

"Oh," she said, "that's how you feel, is it? Well, if I felt that way toward anybody I don't think I'd be plannin' to marry 'em."

"Ugh! What's the use of talkin' rubbish? I've GOT to marry her, ain't I? She's got that paper I was fool enough to sign. Oh, let me alone, Hannah! I won't go over there till I have to. I'd ruther stay to home enough sight."

Hannah put her arms about his neck. "There, there, Kenelm, dearie," she said soothingly, "you eat your breakfast like a nice brother. I'LL be good to you, if nobody else ain't. And I didn't have to sign any paper afore I'd do it either."

Kenelm grunted ungraciously.

"'Twas your fault, anyhow," he muttered. "If you hadn't bossed me and driven me into workin' for Thankful Barnes 'twouldn't have happened. I wouldn't have thought of gettin' engaged to be married."

"Never mind, dearie. You ain't married yet. Perhaps you won't be. And, anyhow, you know I'LL never boss you any more."

Kenelm looked at her. There was an odd expression in his eyes.

"You bet you won't!" he said, slowly. "I'll see to that."

"Why, Kenelm, what do you mean?"

"I don't mean nothin'—maybe. Give me some more coffee."

Captain Obed decided that the present was not the time to suggest a trip to the High Cliff House. He went out again, to walk along the path and think over what he had just heard. It was interesting, as showing the attitude of one of the contracting parties toward the "engagement," the announcement of which had been such a staggering finish to the "big day" of the County Fair.

Winnie S. came whistling up the path from the village.

"Hi, Cap'n Bangs!" he shouted. "I was just goin' to stop at Hannah's to tell you somethin'."

"You was, eh?"

"Yup. Then I was goin' on to the High Cliff. I've got somethin' to take to Mrs. Thankful. What do you suppose 'tis?"

He exhibited the long envelope.

"John Kendrick sent it to her," he said. "I don't know what's in it. And he wants you to come to his office right off, Cap'n Obed. That's what I was goin' to tell you. He says not to wait till afternoon, same as he said, but to come now. It's important, he says."

John was seated at the desk in his office when the captain opened the door. He bowed gravely.

"Take off your hat and coat, Captain," he said. "Sit down. I'm glad you got my message and came early. I am expecting the other party at any moment."

Captain Obed was puzzled.

"The other party?" he repeated. "What other party?"

"My—er—well, we'll call him my client. He is on his way here and I may need you—as a witness."

"Witness? What to?"

"You will see. Now, Captain, if you'll excuse me, I have some papers to arrange. Make yourself as comfortable as you can. I'm sure you won't have to wait long."

Fifteen minutes later the rasping, arrogant "honk" of a motor horn came from the road outside. Heavy, important steps sounded upon the office platform. The door opened and in came Mr. E. Holliday Kendnick.

Captain Obed had known of the great man's expected arrival, but he had not expected it so early in the day. E. Holliday wore a luxurious fur-lined coat and looked as prosperous and important as ever, but also—so it seemed to the captain— he looked disturbed and puzzled and angry.

The captain rose to his feet and said, "Good morning," but except for a nod of recognition, his greeting was unanswered. Mr. Kendrick slammed the door behind him, stalked across the office, took a letter from his pocket and threw it down upon his attorney's desk.

"What's the meaning of that?" he demanded.

John was perfectly calm. "Sit down, Mr. Kendrick," he said.

"No, I won't sit down. What the devil do you mean by sending me that thing? You expected me, didn't you? You got my wire saying I was coming."

"Yes, I got it. Sit down. I have a good deal to say and it may take some time. Throw off your coat."

E. Holliday threw the fur coat open, but he did not remove it. He jerked a chair forward and seated himself upon it.

"Now what does that thing mean?" he demanded, pointing to the envelope he had tossed on the desk.

John picked up the envelope and opened it. A letter and a bank check fell out.

"I will explain," he said quietly. "Mr. Kendrick, you know Captain Obed Bangs, I think. Oh, it is all right. The captain is here at my request. I asked him to be here. I wanted a reliable witness and he is reliable. This," he went on, taking up the letter, "is a note I wrote you, Mr. Kendrick. It states that I am resigning my position as your attorney. And this," picking up the other paper, "is my check for five hundred dollars, the amount of your retainer, which I am returning to you. . . . You understand this so far, Captain?"

E. Holliday did not wait to hear whether the captain understood or not. His big face flamed red.

"But what the devil?" he demanded.

John held up his hand.

"One moment, please," he said. "Captain Bangs, I want to explain a few things. As you know, I have been acting as Mr. Kendrick's attorney in the matter of the property occupied by Mrs. Barnes. He wished me to find a means of forcing her to sell that property to him. Now, when a person owning property does not wish to sell, that person cannot be forced into giving up the property unless it is discovered that the property doesn't belong to that particular person. That's plain, isn't it?"

He was speaking to Captain Obed, and the captain answered.

"But it does belong to her," he declared. "Her Uncle Abner Barnes willed it to her. Course it belongs to her!"

"I know. But sometimes there are such things as flaws in a title. That is to say, somewhere and at some time there has been a transfer of that property that was illegal. In such a case the property belongs to the previous holder, no matter in how many instances it has changed hands since. In the present case it was perfectly plain that Mrs. Barnes thought she owned that land, having inherited it from her uncle. Therefore she could not be forced to sell unless it was discovered that there was a flaw in the title—that she did not own it legally at all. I told my client—Mr. Kendrick, here—that, and he ordered me to have the title searched or to search it myself. I have spent a good deal of time at the recorder's office in Ostable doing that very thing. And I discovered that there was such a flaw; that Mrs. Barnes did not legally own that land upon which her house stands. And, as the land was not hers, the house was not hers either."

Holliday Kendrick struck the desk a thump with his fist.

"Good!" he cried. "Good enough! I told 'em I generally got what I wanted! Now I'll get it this time. Kendrick—"

"Wait," said John. "Captain Obed, you understand me so far?"

The captain's outraged feelings burst forth.

"I understand it's durn mean business!" he shouted. "I'm ashamed of you, John Kendrick!"

"All right! all right! The shame can wait. And I want YOU to wait, too—until

I've finished. There was a flaw in that title, as I said. Captain Bangs, as you know, the house in which Mrs. Barnes is now living originally stood, not where it now stands, but upon land two or three hundred yards to the north, upon a portion of the property which afterward became the Colfax estate and which now belongs to Mr. Kendrick here. You know that?"

Captain Obed nodded. "Course I know it," he said. "Cap'n Abner could have bought the house and the land it stood on, but he didn't want to. He liked the view better from where it stands now. So he bought the strip nigher this way and moved the old house over. But he DID buy it and he paid cash for it. I know he did, because—"

"All right. I know he bought it and all the particulars of the purchase perhaps better than you do. A good deal of my time of late has been given to investigating the history of that second strip of land. Captain Abner Barnes, Mrs. Barnes' uncle, bought the land upon which he contemplated moving, and later, did move the house, of Isaiah Holt, Darius Holt's father, then living. Mr. Holt bought of a man named David Snow, who, in turn, bought of—"

Holliday Kendrick interrupted. "Snow bought of me," he growled. "Worse luck! I was a fool to sell, or so I think now; but it was years ago; I had no idea at that time of coming here to live; and shore land was of no value then, anyhow. The strip came to me as a part of my father's estate. I thought myself lucky to get anything for it. But what's all this ancient history got to do with it now? And what do you mean by sending me this letter and that check?"

"I'll explain. I am trying to explain. The peculiar point comes in just here. You, Mr. Kendrick, never owned that land."

E. Holliday bounced in his chair.

"Didn't own it!" he roared. "What nonsense are you talking? The land belonged to my father, Samuel Kendrick, and I inherited it from him."

"No, you didn't."

"I tell you I did. He left everything he had to me."

"Yes, so he did. But he didn't own that land. He owned it at one time, probably he owned it when he made his will, but he didn't own it at the time of his death. Your father, Mr. Kendrick, was in financial straits at various times during his residence here in Orham and he borrowed a good deal of money. The most of these were loans, pure and simple, but one at least wasn't. At one time—needing money badly, I presume—he sold this strip of land. The purchaser thought it was worth nothing, no doubt, and never mentioned owning it—at least, until just before he died. He simply had the deed recorded and forgot it. Everyone else forgot it, too. But the heirs, or the heir, of that purchaser, I discovered, was the legal owner of that land."

Captain Obed uttered an exclamation.

"Why, John Kendrick!" he shouted. "Do you mean—"

"Hush, Captain! Mr. Kendrick," addressing the red-faced and furious gentleman at his left, "have I made myself clear so far? Do you follow me?"

"Follow you? I don't believe it! I—I—don't believe it! Who was he? Who did my father sell that land to?"

"He sold it to his brother, Bailey Kendrick, and Bailey Kendrick was my father. Under my father's will what little property he had came to me. If anything is sure in this world, it is that that land occupied by Mrs. Barnes belonged, legally, to me."

Neither of his hearers spoke immediately. Then E. Holliday sprang to his feet.

"It belongs to you, does it!" he shouted. "It belongs to you? All right, so much the better. I can buy of you as well as anybody else. That's why you sent me back your retainer, was it? So you and I could trade man to man. All right! I don't believe it yet, but I'll listen to you. What's your proposition?"

John shook his head.

"No," he said. "You're wrong there. I sent you the retainer because I wished to be absolutely free to do as I pleased with what was mine. I couldn't remain in your employ and act contrary to your interests—or, according to my way of thinking, I couldn't. As I saw it I did not own that land—morally, at least. So, having resigned my employment with you I—well, I gave the land to the person who, by all that is right and—and HONEST, should own it. I had the deed made out in her name and I sent it to her an hour ago."

Captain Obed had guessed it. Now HE sprang from his chair.

"John Kendrick," he shouted, in huge delight, "you gave that land to Thankful Barnes. The deed was in that big envelope Winnie S. Holt was takin' to her this very mornin'!"

The happenings of the next few minutes were noisy and profane. E. Holliday

Kendrick was responsible for most of the noise and all of the profanity. He stormed up and down the office, calling his cousin every uncomplimentary name that occurred to him, vowing the whole story to be a lie, and that the land should be his anyway; threatening suit and personal vengeance. His last words, as he strode to the door, were:

"And—and you're the fellow, the poor relation, that I gave my business to just from kindness! All right! I haven't finished with you yet."

John's answer was calm, but emphatic.

"Very well," he said. "But this you must understand: I consider myself under no obligation whatever to you, Mr. Kendrick. In the very beginning of our business relationship you and I had a plain talk. I told you when I consented to act as your attorney that I did so purely as a matter of business and that philanthropy and kinship were to have no part in it. And when you first mentioned your intention of forcing Mrs. Barnes to give up her home I told you what I thought of that, too."

East Wellmouth's wealthiest summer resident expressed an opinion.

"You're a fool!" he snarled. "A d—d impractical fool!"

The door slammed behind him. John laughed quietly.

"As a judge of character, Captain Bangs," he observed, "my respected cousin should rank high."

Captain Obed's first act after E. Holliday's departure was to rush over, seize the young man's hand with one of his own, and thump him enthusiastically upon the back with the other.

"I said it!" he crowed. "I knew it! I knew you was all right and square as a brick all the time, John Kendrick! NOW let me meet some of those folks that have been talkin' against you! You never did a better day's work in your life. HE'S down on you, but every decent man in Ostable County'll be for you through thick and thin after this. Hooray for our side! John, shake hands with me again."

They shook, heartily. The captain was so excited and jubilant that he was incoherent. At last, however, he managed to recover sufficiently to ask a question.

"But how did you do it," he demanded. "How did you get on the track of it? You must have had some suspicions."

John smiled. His friend's joy evidently pleased him, but he, himself, was rather sober and not in the least triumphant.

"I did have a suspicion, Captain," he said. "In fact, I had been told that I had a claim to a piece of land somewhere along the shore here in East Wellmouth. My father told me years ago, when he was in his last sickness. He said that he owned a strip of land here, but that it was probably worth little or nothing. When I came here I intended looking into the matter, but I did not do so. Where the original deed may be, I don't know even now. It may be among some of my father's papers, which are stored in New York. But the record of the transfers I found in Ostable; and that is sufficient. My claim may not be quite as impregnable as I gave my late client to understand, but it will be hard to upset. I am the only possible claimant and I have transferred my claim to Mrs. Barnes. The land belongs to her now; she can't be dispossessed."

"But—but, John, why didn't you say so sooner? What made you let everyone think—what they did think?"

Before John could reply there came an interruption. The door opened and Thankful Barnes entered. She paid no attention to Captain Obed, but, walking straight to the desk, laid upon it the long envelope which Winnie S. had brought to her house that morning.

"Will you tell me," she asked, sharply, "what that means?"

John rose. "Yes," he said, "I will tell you, Mrs. Barnes. It is a rather long story. Sit down, please."

Thankful sank into the chair he indicated. He took up the envelope.

"I will tell you, Mrs. Barnes," he said, "why I sent you this deed. Don't go, Captain Bangs, you know already and I should like to have you stay. Here is the story, Mrs. Barnes."

He told it briefly, without superfluous words, but so clearly that there could be no possibility of a misunderstanding. When he began Thankful's attitude was cold and unbelieving. When he finished she was white and trembling.

"Mrs. Barnes," he said, in conclusion, "I'm a peculiar fellow, I'm afraid. I have rather—well, suppose we call them impractical ideas concerning the ethics of my profession, duty to a client, and that sort of thing. I have always been particular in taking a case, but when I have taken it I have tried to carry it through. I—as you know, I hesitated before accepting my cousin's retaining fee and the implied obligation. However, I did accept."

He might have given his reasons for accepting but he did not. He went on.

"When this matter of your property came up," he said, "I at first had no idea that the thing was serious. You owned the property, as I supposed, and that was sufficient. I had told my cousin that and meant to tell you. I meant to tell you a portion of what I have just told the captain here, but I—well, I didn't. Mr. Daniels' remarks irritated me and I—well, he put the case as a test of legal skill between himself and me, and—and I have my share of pride, I suppose. So I determined to beat him if I could. It was wrong, as I see it now, and I beg your pardon."

Thankful put a hand to her forehead.

"But you did—beat him, didn't you?" she stammered. "You found I didn't own the land."

"Yes. I found I owned it myself, legally. If I had found it belonged to anyone else, I—well, I scarcely know what I should have done. You see," with a half smile, "I'm trying to be perfectly frank. Finding that I was the owner made it easy."

She did not understand. "It made it easy," she repeated slowly. "But you gave it to ME!"

He leaned forward. "Please don't misunderstand me," he said earnestly. "As I see it, that land belonged to you by all that is right and fair. Legally, perhaps, it didn't, but legal honesty isn't always moral honesty. I've found that out even in my limited practice."

Captain Obed tried to put in a word. "Don't you see, Thankful?" he said. "John knew you thought you owned the land and so—"

"Hush! Please don't. I—I don't see. Mr. Kendrick, you—you have prided yourself on bein' honest with your clients, and Mr. Holliday Kendrick WAS your client."

John smiled. "I compromised there," he answered. "I returned his money and resigned as his attorney before I sent you the deed. It was a compromise, I admit, but I had to choose between him and—well, my honor, if you like; although that sounds theatrical. I chose to be honest with myself—that's all. The land is yours, Mrs. Barnes."

He handed her the envelope containing the deed. She took it and sat there turning it over and over in her fingers, not looking at it, but thinking, or trying to think.

"You give it to me," she said. "It was yours and you give it to me. Why should you? Do—do you think I can TAKE it from you?"

"Certainly, you must take it."

"But I can't! I can't!"

"Certainly you can. Why not?"

"Why NOT? After the things I've thought about you? And after the way I've treated you? And—and after Emily—"

"She didn't know either," broke in Captain Obed. "She didn't understand. She—"

"That's enough, Captain," interrupted John. "Mrs. Barnes, you mustn't misunderstand me again. Neither you nor—nor Miss Howes must misunderstand my motives. I give this to you because I honestly believe it belongs to you, not because I expect anything in return. I—I confess I did hesitate a little. I feared—I feared she—"

"He means Emily," broke in the irrepressible captain. "You mean Emily, don't you, John?"

"Yes," with some embarrassment. "Yes, I do mean Miss Howes. She and I had been—friends, and I feared she might misinterpret my reasons. It was not until yesterday afternoon, when I learned of the—of the engagement, that I felt certain neither you nor she could misunderstand. Then I felt perfectly free to send you the deed."

Captain Obed, who had grasped his meaning, would have spoken, but Thankful spoke first. She, evidently, was quite at sea.

"The engagement?" she repeated. "What engagement?"

"Miss Howes' engagement to Mr. Daniels. They were congratulating him on his engagement yesterday at the station. I overheard the congratulations. I had not known of it before."

At last Thankful understood. She looked at the speaker, then at Captain Obed, and the color rushed to her face.

"And even though Emily—Hush, Obed Bangs! you keep still—and even though you knew Emily was engaged to Heman Daniels, you could still give me and her—this?"

"Now, Mrs. Barnes, do you think—"

"Think! John Kendrick, I think I ought to get down on my knees and beg your pardon for what I've thought these last two months. But I'm thinkin' right now and you ain't. Heman Daniels ain't engaged to Emily Howes at all; he's engaged to that Bayport woman, the one he's been so attentive to for a year or more. Oh, it's true! Winnie S. told me so just now. The news had just come to town and he was full of it. Heman's over to Bayport spendin' Christmas with her this very minute."

Even Captain Obed had not a word to say. He was looking at John Kendrick and John's face was white.

"And I'll tell you somethin' else," went on Thankful, "somethin' that Emily herself told me last night. She might have been engaged to Heman Daniels; he asked her to be. But she wouldn't have him; she told him no."

John stepped from behind the desk. "She—she told him no," he repeated. "She . . . Why?"

Thankful laughed aloud. "That," she cried, "I SHAN'T tell you. If you don't know yourself then I ain't the one to tell you."

Obed was at her side. "That's enough," he ordered, taking her by the arm. "That's enough, Thankful Barnes. You come right along with me and fetch that deed with you. This young feller here has got some thinkin' to do, I cal'late. His mind needs overhaulin'. You come with me."

He led her out to the sidewalk and on until they reached the postoffice. Then, still grasping her arm, he led her into that building. The office was open for a few hours, even though the day was Christmas.

"Here!" he whispered, eagerly. "Stand here by the window where we can see whether he comes out or not."

"But, Obed, what are you doin'?"

"Doin'! I'm waitin' to see whether that boy is a permanent fool or just a temporary one. Wait now; wait and watch."

The wait was but momentary. The door of John Kendrick's office opened and John himself came out. He shut the door, but he did not wait to lock it. They saw him cross the road and stride off down the lane toward the shore.

Captain Obed laughed aloud.

"No," he cried, exultantly, "'twas only temporary. He's got his senses now. Thankful, let's you and me go for a walk. We shan't be needed at the High Cliff

House for a spell—and we won't be WANTED there, either."

CHAPTER XVIII

THE walk was a long one. It took them a good way from the more populous section of East Wellmouth, over the hills and, at last, along the beach at the foot of the bluff. It was an odd season of the year for a stroll by the seaside, but neither Thankful nor the captain cared for that. In fact it is doubtful if either could have told afterward just where they had been. There were so many and such wonderful things to tell, to speculate upon, and to discuss.

Thankful told of her brother's return, of Mr. Cobb's miraculous generosity, and, for the first time, of the ghostly haunting of the little back bedroom. In the latter story Captain Obed seemed to find much amusement. He was skeptical.

"I've heard of a good many ghosts in my time," he said, "but I never heard of one that could stand daylight or common-sense. The idea of your bein' troubled all this time by that snorin' business or whatever 'tis. Why didn't you tell me about it? I'd have had that spook out of that bedroom afore this, I bet you."

"It seemed so silly," confessed Thankful, "that I was ashamed to tell anybody. But there's SOMETHIN' there. I heard it the first night I came, and Rebecca Timpson heard it later on, and then Emily and I and Solomon heard it all together."

"Yes. Well, then, let's see WHEN you heard it. Every time 'twas when there was a storm; rain and wind and the like of that, eh?"

"Yes. I've slept in that room myself a good many times, but never when there was a gale of wind or rain. That's so; 'twas always in a storm that it came."

"Um-hum. And it always snored. Ho! ho! that IS funny! A ghost with a snore. Must have a cold in its head, I cal'late."

"You wouldn't laugh if you'd heard it last night. And it didn't snore the first time. It said 'Oh, Lord,' then."

"Humph! so you said. Well, that does complicate things, I will give in. The wind in a water-pipe might snore, but it couldn't say 'Oh, Lord!' not very plain. You heard that the first night, afore Kenelm and I got there."

"Yes. And there wasn't another person in that house except Emily and me; I know that."

"I wonder if you do know it. . . . Well, I'll have a whack at that room myself and if a spook starts snorin when I'm there I'll—I'll put a clothespin on its nose, after I've thanked it for scarin' old Sol into repentance and decency. It took a spirit to do that. No livin' human could have worked THAT miracle."

"I agree with you. Well, now I know why he acted the way he did whenever Uncle Abner's name was mentioned. I have a feelin'—at least I imagine there may have been somethin' else, somethin' we don't know and never will know, between Solomon and my uncle. There may be some paper, some agreement, hid around somewheres that is legally bindin' on the old sinner. I can't hardly believe just breakin' a promise would make him give anybody fifteen hundred dollars."

"Maybe, but I don't know; he's always been superstitious and a great feller for Spiritu'list camp-meetin's and so on. And he was always regular at prayer-meetin'. Sometimes that sort of a swab, knowin' how mean he actually is, tries to square his meanness with the Almighty by bein' prominent in the church. There may be the kind of paper you say, but I shouldn't wonder if 'twas just scare and a bad conscience."

"Well, I'm grateful to him, anyhow. And, as for John's kindness, I—I don't know what to say. Last night I thought this might be the blackest Christmas ever I had; but now it looks as if it might be one of the brightest. And it's all so strange, so strange it should have come on Christmas. It seems as if the Lord had planned it so."

"Maybe He did. But it ain't so strange when you come to think of it. Your brother came home on Christmas Eve because he thought—or I shouldn't wonder if he did—that you'd be more likely to forgive him and take him in then. Solomon came over when he did on account of his hearin' that Holliday Kendrick was comin'. All days, Christmas or any other, are alike to Sol when there's a dollar to be sighted with a spyglass. And as for John's givin' you the deed today, I presume likely that was a sort of Christmas present; probably he meant to give it to you for that. So the Christmas part ain't so wonderful, after all."

"Yes, it is. It's all wonderful. I ought to be a very, very happy woman. If John and Emily only come together again I shall be, sure and sartin'. Of course, though," she added, with emphasis, "I shan't let him give me that land. I'll make some arrangement to pay him for it, a little at a time, if no other way."

The captain opened his mouth to protest, but there was an air of finality in Thankful's tone which caused him to defer the protest until another time.

"Well—well, all right," he said. "That can be talked about later on. But how about yourself? I suppose you'll keep right on with the boardin'-house now?"

"Of course."

"It'll be pretty hard work for you alone, won't it? Especially if Emily and John should take a notion to get married."

"Oh, well! I'm used to bein' alone. I shan't mind—much. Why! here we are right at the foot of our path. I've been talkin' so fast I didn't realize we'd got here already. Do you suppose it's safe to go up to the house now, Obed?"

"I guess so. We can go in the kitchen way and I'll make noise enough to warn all hands that we're comin'. Who's that by the back door; John, ain't it? No, it ain't; it's Kenelm."

Kenelm and Imogene were standing at the kitchen door. When the captain and Mrs. Barnes drew near they saw that they were in danger of interrupting what seemed to be a serious conversation. Neither of the parties to that conversation noticed them until they were close at hand. Imogene had a slip of paper in her hand.

Captain Obed, whose mind was occupied with but one thought just then, asked a question.

"Imogene," he asked in a loud whisper, "where's Miss Emily?"

Imogene started and turned. Kenelm also started. He looked embarrassed.

"Eh!" cried Imogene. "Oh, it's you, Mrs. Thankful. I was wonderin' where you was. I've been havin' a little talk with Kenelm here. It's all right, Mrs. Thankful."

"What's all right?" asked Thankful.

"About your brother workin' here in Kenelm's place. He don't mind. You don't, do you, Kenelm?"

Mr. Parker, who had been standing upon one foot and pawing like a restless horse with the other, shifted his position.

"No-o," he drawled. "I—I don't know's I do."

Thankful was disturbed. "I'm sorry you said anything yet awhile, Imogene," she said. "My plans about Jedediah are hardly made yet. I do hate to make you lose your place, Kenelm. If I could see my way clear to keepin' two men I'd do it, but I declare I can't see it."

"That's all right, ma'am," said Kenelm. "I ain't partic'lar."

"He don't mind a bit, Mrs. Thankful," put in Imogene. "Honest, he don't. He don't have to work unless he's obliged to—not much anyhow. Kenelm's got money, you know."

"I know; at least I've heard he had some money. But 'tain't because he needs the money that I feel bad; it's because of his engagement to you, Imogene. I suppose you're plannin' to be married some time or other and—"

"Oh, that's all right, too," interrupted Imogene eagerly. "You needn't worry about our engagement. She needn't worry about that, need she, Kenelm?"

"No," said Kenelm shortly.

Captain Obed thought it time to repeat his first question.

"Where's Miss Emily?" he asked.

"She's in the livin'-room."

"Is—is anybody with her?"

Imogene nodded. "Um-hum," she said gleefully, "he's there, too."

"Who?" The captain and Thankful spoke in concert.

"Mr. John Kendrick. I let him in and I didn't tell her who it was at all. She didn't know till she went in herself and found him. Then I came right out and shut the door. Oh," with another nod, "I've got some sense, even if I did come from the Orphans' Home."

Captain Obed and Thankful looked at each other.

"Then he did come here," exclaimed Thankful.

"Course he did. I told you he wa'n't quite a fool. Been there some time, has he?"

"Yes. Shall I tell 'em you've come? I'll knock first."

"No, no." Thankful's reply was emphatic. "Where's the rest of the folks?" she asked.

"Georgie and Mr. Cahoon—your brother, I mean—have gone up to the village with the other one, the Cobb man."

"What have they gone to the village for?"

"To help Mr. Cobb get his horse and team at Chris Badger's. He's gone, you know."

"Who's gone?"

"Why, the Cobb one. He's gone home again. I tried to get him to stay for dinner; so did Miss Emily. We knew you'd want him to. But he wouldn't stay. Said he was goin' home. Seemed to me he wanted to get out of the house quick as ever he could. He gave Georgie a dollar for Christmas."

"WHAT!" Captain Obed leaned against the corner of the house. "A dollar!" he groaned. "Sol Cobb gave somebody a dollar for Christmas! Don't pinch me, anybody; I don't want to wake up. Let me enjoy my dream long as I can. Thankful, did you say Sol looked sick?"

"I said he looked pretty nearly sick when he came down this mornin'."

"I believe it. It must have been a mighty serious attack. Did Georgie take the dollar with him?"

"No. He left it with Miss Emily."

"That's a mercy. The outdoor air may make Sol feel more rational and soon's he came to his senses, he'd want that dollar back. Tut! tut! tut! Don't talk to ME! I shall believe in ghosts pretty soon."

Thankful looked troubled and annoyed.

"I'm awful sorry he went," she said. "The poor old thing! He was so miserable I did pity him. I must drive over and see him tomorrow, sure. But what makes me feel the worst," she added, "is to think of Jedediah's cruisin' up to the village dressed in the rags he was wearin'. He looked like—like somethin' the cat brought in. And everybody'll want to know who he is; and when they find he's my brother! And on Christmas Day, too!"

"Imogene!" it was Emily's voice. "Imogene, where are you?"

Captain Obed roared a greeting.

"Merry Christmas, all hands," he shouted. "Hey, you, John Kendrick; are you there?"

There was no answer. Thankful did not wait for one; she rushed into the house. John Kendrick was alone in the living-room when she reached it. Emily had fled. Thankful looked at Mr. Kendrick and the look gave her the information she wanted.

"Oh, Mr. Kendrick—John," she cried. "I shall call you John now; I can, can't I—where is she?"

John smiled. He looked ready to smile at all creation. "I think she is upstairs," he said. "At least she ran in that direction when she heard the captain call."

Thankful started for the hall and the stairs. At the door she turned.

"Don't you go away, John," she ordered. "Don't you dare go away from this house. You're goin' to have dinner here THIS day, if you never do again."

John, apparently, had no intention of going away. He smiled once more and walked toward the dining-room. Captain Obed met him at the threshold.

"Well?" shouted the captain. "Well? What have you got to say for yourself now, eh?"

John laughed. "Not much, Captain," he answered, "not much, except that I've been an idiot."

"Yup. All right. But that ain't what I want to know. I want to know—" he stopped and gazed keenly at his friend's face. "I don't know's I do want to know, either," he added. "I cal'late I know it already. When a young feller stands around looking as sheepish as if he'd been caught stealin' hens' eggs and grinnin' at the same time as if he was proud of it, then—then there's just one thing happened to him. I cal'late you've found out why she wouldn't marry Heman Daniels, eh? My, but I'm glad! You don't deserve it, but I'm glad just the same. Let's shake hands again."

They were still shaking and the captain was crowing like a triumphant rooster over his friend's good fortune and the humiliation in store for the "tattle-tales and character-naggers" among his fellow-townsmen when Imogene appeared.

"Is Mrs. Thankful here?" she asked. "Well, never mind. You'll do, Cap'n Bangs. Will you and Mr. Kendrick come out here to the back door a minute? I'd like to have you witness somethin'."

Captain Obed's forehead wrinkled in surprise.

"Witness somethin'?" he repeated. Then, with a glance at John, who was as puzzled as he, "Humph! I witnessed somethin' this mornin' and now I'm to witness somethin' else. I'll begin to be an expert pretty soon, won't I? Humph! What—well, heave ahead, Imogene. I'll come."

Imogene conducted them to the kitchen door where Mr. Parker still stood, looking remarkably foolish. Imogene's manner, however, was very business-like.

"Now then," she said, addressing the two "witnesses," "you see this piece of paper. Perhaps you'd better read it first."

She handed the paper to Captain Obed, who looked at it and passed it over to John. It was the statement, signed by Kenelm, in which he agreed to marry Imogene whenever she asked him to do so.

"You see what 'tis, don't you?" asked Imogene. "Yes. Well, now you watch and see what I do with it."

She tore the agreement into small pieces. Stepping into the kitchen she put the pieces in the stove.

"There!" she exclaimed, returning to the door. "That ends that. He and I," pointing to Kenelm, "ain't engaged any longer, and he don't have to work here any longer. Is it all plain to both of you?"

It was not altogether plain even yet. The expression on the faces of the witnesses proved that.

"Now, Kenelm," said Imogene cheerfully, "you can leave if you want to. And," with a mischievous chuckle, "when you get there you can give your sister my love, the inmate's love, you know. Lordy! Won't she enjoy gettin' it!"

When Kenelm had gone, which he did immediately and without a word, Imogene vouchsafed an explanation.

"I never did want to marry him," she said. "When I get ready to marry anybody it'll be somebody with more get-up-and-git than he's got, I hope. But I was ready to do anything to help Mrs. Thankful from frettin' and when he talked about quittin' his job right in the busy season I had to keep him here somehow, I just HAD to. He was kind of—of mushy and soft about me first along—I guess guys of his kind are likely to be about any woman that'll listen to 'em—and when his sister got jealous and put him up to leavin' I thought up my plan. I got him to ask me—he'd as much as asked me afore—and then I made him sign that paper. Ugh! the silliness I had to go through afore he would sign it! Don't ask me about it or I shan't eat any dinner. But he did sign it and I knew I had him under my thumb. He's scared of that sister of his, but he's more scared of losin' his money. And she's just as scared of that as he is. THEY didn't want any breachin' of promises—No sir-ee! Ho! ho!"

She stopped to laugh in gleeful triumph. John laughed too. Captain Obed scratched his head.

"But, hold on there; heave to, Imogene!" he ordered. "I don't seem to get the whole of this yet. You did agree to marry him. Suppose he'd said you'd got to marry him, what then?"

"He wouldn't. He didn't want to marry me—not after I'd took my time at bossin' him around a while. And if he had—well, if he had, and I'd had to do it, I would, I suppose. I'd do anything for Mrs. Thankful, after what's she's done for me. Miss Emily and me had a talk about self-sacrifice and I see my duty plain. I told Miss Emily why I did it that night when you all came home from the Fair. She understood the whole thing."

The captain burst into a roar of laughter.

"Ho! ho!" he shouted. "Well, Imogene, I said you beat all my goin' to sea, and you do—you sartin do. Now, I'd like to be on hand and see how Hannah takes it. If I know her, now that that engagement ain't hangin' over her, she'll even up with her brother for all she's had to put up with. Ho! ho! Poor old Kenelm's in for a warm Christmas."

And yet Kenelm's Christmas was not so "warm" after all. He told Hannah of his broken engagement, wasting no words—which, for him, was very remarkable—and expressing no regret whatever. Hannah listened, at first with joy, and then, when Imogene's "love" was conveyed to her, with growing anger.

"The idea!" she cried. "And you bring me over a message like that. From her—from an Orphans' Home inmate to your own sister! And you let her walk over you, chuck you out as if you was a wornout doormat she'd wiped her boots on, and never said a word. Well, I'll say it for you. I'll tell her what I think of her. And she was cal'latin' to sue YOU for breaches of promise, was she? Humph! Two can play at that game. I don't know's I shan't have you sue her."

"I don't want to. I told you this mornin' I didn't care nothin' about marryin' her. And you didn't want me to yourself. Now that it's all over you ought to be happy, I should think. I don't see what you're growlin' about."

"No, I suppose you don't. You—you," with withering contempt, "you haven't got the self-respect of—of a woodtick. I'm—I declare I'm perfectly prospected with shame at havin' such a brother in my family. And after cruisin' around with her and takin' her to the Cattle Show—"

"You went to the Cattle Show yourself."

"I don't care if I did. Now you march yourself upstairs and change your clothes."

"Aw, now, Hannah. These clothes are good enough."

"Good enough! For Christmas Day! I should think you'd be ashamed. Oh, you make me so provoked! If folks knew what I know about you—"

Kenelm interrupted, a most unusual thing for him.

"S'posin' they knew what I know about you," he observed.

"What? What do you mean by that? What have I done to be ashamed of?"

"I don't know. I don't know what you did. I don't even know where you went. But when a person crawls down a ladder in the middle of the night and goes off somewhere with—with somebody else and don't get home until 'most mornin', then—well, then I cal'late folks might be interested if they knew, that's all."

Hannah's face was a picture, a picture to be studied. For the first time in her life she was at a loss for words.

"I ain't askin' no questions," went on Kenelm calmly. "I ain't told nobody and I shan't unless—unless somebody keeps naggin' and makes me mad. But I shan't change my clothes this day; and I shan't do nothin' else unless I feel like it, either."

His sister stared at him blankly for a moment. Then she fled from the room. Kenelm took his pipe from his pocket, filled and lighted it, and smoked, smiling between puffs at the ceiling. The future looked serene and rosy—to Kenelm.

Christmas dinner at the High Cliff House was a joyful affair, notwithstanding that the promise of fair weather had come to naught and it was raining once more. John stayed for that dinner, so did Captain Obed. The former and Miss Emily said very little and their appetites were not robust, but they appeared to be very happy indeed. Georgie certainly was happy and Jedediah's appetite was all that might have been expected of an appetite fed upon the cheapest of cheap food for days and compelled to go without any food for others. Thankful was happy, too, or pretended to be, and Captain Obed laughed and joked with everyone. Yet he seemed to have something on his mind, and his happiness was not as complete as it might have been.

Everyone helped Imogene wash the dishes; then John and Emily left the kitchen bound upon some mysterious errand. Captain Obed and Georgie donned what the captain called "dirty weather rigs" and went out to give George Washington and Patrick Henry and the poultry their Christmas dinner.

The storm had flooded the low land behind the barn. The hen yard was in the center of a miniature island. The walls of the pigsty which Thankful had had built rose from a lake.

"It's a mercy Pat moved to drier quarters, eh, second mate!" chuckled the captain. "He'd have had to sleep with a life-preserver on if he stayed here."

They fed the hens and gave George Washington a liberal measure of oats and a big forkful of hay.

"Don't want him to go hungry Christmas Day," said Captain Obed. "Now let's cruise around and see if Patrick Henry is singin' out for liberty or death."

The pig was not, apparently, "singing out" for anything. When they reached the wall of the pen by the washshed he was not in sight. But they heard him, somewhere back in the darkness beneath the shed, breathing stertorously, apparently sound asleep.

Georgie laughed. "Hear him," he said. "He's so fat he always makes that noise when he's asleep. And he's awful smart. When it's warm and nice weather he sleeps out here in the sun. When it rains and is cold, same as now, he always goes way back in there. Hear him! Don't he make a funny noise."

Emily came hurrying around the corner of the house.

"Captain Bangs," she whispered. "Captain Bangs!"

The captain looked at her. He was about to ask why she whispered instead of speaking aloud, but the expression on her face caused him to change his question to "What's the matter?"

Emily looked at Georgie before replying.

"I—I want to see you," she answered. "I want you to come with me. Come quick. Georgie, you must stay in the kitchen with Imogene."

Georgie did not want to stay in the kitchen, but when he found Jedediah there he was more complacent. The ex-gold seeker and his tales of adventure had a tremendous fascination for Georgie.

Emily led the way toward the front stairs and Captain Obed followed.

"What's up?" he whispered. "What's all the mystery about?"

"We don't know—yet. But we want you to help us find out. John and I have been up to look at the haunted room and—and IT'S THERE."

"There! What?"

"The—the ghost, or whatever it is. We heard it. Come!"

At the door of the rooms which were the scene of Mr. Cobb's recent supernatural experience and of Miss Timpson's "warning" they found Thankful and John standing, listening. Thankful looked rather frightened. John was eager and interested.

"You found him, Emily," he whispered. "Good. Captain, you and I are commissioned to lay the ghost. And the ghost is in. Listen!"

They listened. Above the patter and rattle of the rain on the roof they heard a sound, the sound which two or three members had heard the previous night, the sound of snoring.

"I should have gone in before," whispered John, "but they wanted me to wait for you. Come on, Captain."

They opened the door of the larger room and entered on tiptoe. The snoring was plainly heard now and it seemed, as they expected, to come from the little room adjoining. Into that room the party proceeded, the men in the lead. There was no one there save themselves and nothing out of the ordinary to be seen. But the snoring kept on, plainer than ever.

John looked behind the furniture and under the bed.

"It's no use doin' that," whispered Thankful. "I've done that myself fifty times."

Captain Obed was walking about the room, his ear close to the wall, listening. At a point in the center of the rear wall, that at the back of the house, he stopped and listened more intently than ever.

"John," he whispered eagerly, "come here."

John came.

"Listen," whispered the captain. "It's plainer here than anywhere else, ain't it?"

"Yes. Yes, I think it is. But where does it come from?"

"Somewhere overhead, seems to me. Give me that chair."

Cautiously and silently he placed the chair close to the wall, stood upon it, and, with his ear against the wallpaper, moved his head backward and forward and up and down. Then he stopped moving and reaching up felt along the wall with his hands.

"I've got it," he whispered. "Here's the place."

His fingers described a circle on the wall. He tapped gently in the middle of the circle.

"Hark!" he said. "All solid out here, but here—hollow as a drum. It's—it's a stovepipe hole, that's what 'tis. There was a stove here one time or 'nother and the pipe hole was papered over."

"But—but what of it?" whispered Thankful. "I don't care about stovepipe holes. It's that dreadful noise I want to locate. I hear it now, just as plain as ever."

"Where could a stovepipe go to from here?" mused the captain. "Not into the kitchen; the kitchen chimney's way over t'other side. Maybe there was a chimney here afore the house was moved."

"But the snoring?" faltered Emily. "Don't you hear it?"

Captain Obed put his ear against the covered stovepipe hole. He listened and as he listened his face took on a new expression, an expression of sudden suspicion, then of growing certainty, and, a moment later, of huge amusement.

He stepped down from the chair.

"Stay right where you are," he ordered. "Don't move and don't make any noise. I'll be right back."

He hurried out. They waited. The snoring kept on and on. Suddenly it ceased. Then, in that very room, or so it seemed, sounded a grunt and a frightened squeal. And then a voice, a hollow voice which cried:

"Ahoy, all hands! I'm the ghost of Nebuchadnezzar's first wife and I want to know what you folks mean by wakin' me up."

The three in the back bedroom looked at each other.

"It's Captain Bangs!" cried Emily.

"It's Obed!" exclaimed Thankful.

"He's found it," shouted Kendrick. "Come on."

The captain was not in the kitchen when they got there. He had gone out of

doors, so Imogene said. Unmindful of the rain they rushed out and around the corner, behind and below the washshed. Patrick Henry was running about his pen,
apparently much disturbed, but Captain Obed was not in sight.

"Where is he?" demanded Thankful. "Where's he gone to?"

"Hello there, John!" cried a voice from the darkness at the rear of the pigsty
under the kitchen. "Come in here. Never mind your clothes. Come in."

John vaulted over the rail of the pen and disappeared. A few moments later he
came out again in company with the captain. Both were laughing heartily.

"We've got the answer," puffed Captain Obed, who was out of breath. "We've
laid the ghost. You remember I told you that day when we first explored this place
that old Laban Eldredge had this pigpen built. Afore that 'twas all potato cellar, and
at one time afore the house was made over there must have been a stove in that
back bedroom. There's no chimney, but there's cracks between the boards at the
back of that pigpen and any noise down here goes straight up between the walls and
out of that stovepipe hole like a speakin' tube. You heard me when I spoke to you
just now, didn't you?"

"Yes—yes," answered Emily. "We heard you, but—but what was it that snored?
What was the ghost?"

Captain Obed burst into a shout of laughter. "There he is," he said, pointing.

Thankful and Emily looked.

"What?" cried the latter.

"The PIG?" exclaimed Thankful.

"That's what. Georgie gave me a hint when he and I was out here just now.
Old Pat was asleep way in back there and snorin' like a steam engine. And Georgie
said he never slept there unless 'twas a storm, rainin' same as 'tis now. And every
time you heard the—ho! ho!—the ghost, 'twas on a stormy night. It stormed the
night you got here, and when Becky Timpson had her warnin', and last night when
Sol Cobb got his. Ho! ho! ho! Patrick Henry's the ghost. Well, he's a healthy old
spirit."

Emily laughed until the tears came into her eyes.

"The pig!" she cried. "Oh, Aunt Thankful! You and I were frightened almost to
death last night—and of that creature there. Oh, dear me!"

Thankful laughed, too, but she was not fully convinced.

"Maybe 'twas the pig that snored," she admitted. "And of course whatever we heard came up that pipe hole. But there was no pig there on that first night; I didn't buy the pig until long afterwards. And, besides, what I heard THAT night talked; it said, 'Oh, Lord!' Patrick Henry may be a smart pig, but he can't talk."

This was something of a staggerer, but the captain was still certain he was on the right track.

"Then somethin' else was there," he declared. "Somebody was down under the house here, that's sartin. Who could it have been? Never mind; I'll find out. We'll clear up the whole of this ghost business, now we've got started. Maybe we can find some hint in there now. John, go up and fetch a lantern, there's a good fellow, and we'll have a look."

John brought the lantern and by its light the two men explored the recesses of Patrick Henry's bed chamber. When they emerged, covered with dust and cobwebs, the captain held something in his hand.

"I don't know what 'tis," he said. "Maybe nothin' of any account, but 'twas trod down in the corner close to the wall. Humph? Eh? Why, it's a mitten, ain't it?"

It was a mitten, a much worn one, and on the inside of the wrist-hand were worked three letters.

"K. I. P." read Captain Obed. "What's 'K. I. P.' stand for?"

Imogene, who had joined the group, clapped her hands.

"I know," she cried. "Kenelm Issachar Parker."

Thankful nodded. "That's it," she agreed. "And—and—why, now I come to think of it, I remember hearin' Hannah pitchin' into Kenelm that first mornin' after our night at her house, for losin' his umbrella and a mitten."

"Right you are!" Captain Obed slapped his knee. "And Kenelm was out somewheres that night afore he and I came over here. He found his umbrella and he brought it home whole a week or so later. But it wa'n't whole all that time, because Seth Ellis told me Kenelm brought an umbrella in for him to fix. All turned inside out it was. Eh? Yes, sir! We're gettin' nigher port all the time. Kenelm came by this house that night, because 'twas him that saw your light in the window. I'll bet you he smashed his new umbrella on the way down from the club and crawled in here out of the wet to fix it. He couldn't fix it, so he left it here and came back after it the next day. And 'twas then he dropped this mitten."

Emily offered a suggestion.

"You said you saw someone hiding behind the henhouse that next morning, Captain," she said.

"So I did. And I thought 'twas one of Solon Taylor's boys. I'll bet 'twas Kenelm; he'd sneaked over to get the umbrella. It was him that said, 'Oh, Lord' that night; I'll bet high on it. When he thought of what Hannah'd say to his smashin' the umbrella she gave him it's a wonder he didn't say more than that. That's the answer—the whole answer—and I'll prove it next time I see Kenelm."

Which, by the way, he did.

Later in the afternoon John and Emily walked up to the village together. They asked Thankful and Captain Obed to accompany them, but the invitation was declined. However, as John had suddenly remembered that he had left his office door unlocked, he felt that he should go and Emily went with him.

"I presume likely," observed the captain, as he looked after them, "that I ought to feel conscience-struck for not sayin' yes when they asked me to come along, but somehow I don't. I have a sneakin' feelin' that they'll get on first-rate without our company, Thankful."

Thankful was silent. She was sitting by the window. The pair were alone together in the living-room now. Imogene and Jedediah and Georgie were in the kitchen making molasses candy.

"Well," observed Captain Obed, "that's so, ain't it? Don't you agree with me?"

Still there was no answer and, turning, the captain was surprised to see his companion wiping her eyes with her handkerchief.

"For thunder sakes!" he exclaimed, in dismay. "What's happened now? Are you cryin'?"

Thankful tried to smile. "No," she said. "I'm not cryin'. At least, I hadn't ought to cry. I ought to be awful happy and I am. Seein' those two go off together that way made me think that pretty soon they'd be goin' away for good. And I—I was a little lonesome, I guess."

"Sho! sho! You mustn't be lonesome. They won't get married yet awhile, I cal'late."

"No. I suppose not. But Emily will have to go next week back to her school, and she'll take Georgie with her. I'll miss 'em both terribly."

"Yes, so you will. But you've got your brother now. He'll be some company."

"Yes. But, unless he's changed more than I'm afraid he has, he'll be more responsibility than comfort. He means well enough, poor Jed, but he ain't what you'd call a capable person."

"Well, Imogene's capable enough, and she'll be here."

"Yes."

Silence for a time. Then Captain Obed spoke.

"Thankful," he said, earnestly, "I know what's worryin' you. It's just what you said, the responsibility of it all. It's too much for you, the responsibility of handlin' this big house and a houseful of boarders when they come. You hadn't ought to do it alone. You ought to have somebody to help."

"Perhaps I had, but I don't know who 'twill be. I can't afford to hire the kind of help I need."

"Why don't you take a partner?"

"A partner? Who, for goodness sakes?"

"Well—me. I've got some money of my own. I'll go in partners with you here. . . . Oh, now, now!" he added hastily. "Don't think there's any charity in this. There ain't at all. As I see it, this boardin' house is mighty good business and a safe investment. Suppose you and I go in partners on it, Thankful."

Thankful shook her head.

"You're awfully good," she said.

"No, I ain't."

"Yes, you are. But I couldn't do it, Obed."

"Why not?"

"You know why not. For the same reason I couldn't say yes to what you asked me a while ago. I can't let you help me out of pity."

"Pity!" He turned and stared at her. "Pity!" he repeated.

"Yes, pity. I know you're sorry for me. You said you were. And I know you'd do anything to help me, even—even—"

He interrupted.

"Thankful Barnes," he said, "did you think I asked you what I asked that time out of PITY?"

"Now, Obed—"

"Stop! Answer me. Did you think such a fool thing as THAT? You stay right where you are! I want you to look me in the face."

"Don't, Obed! Don't! Let me be. Don't!"

He paid not the slightest attention. He was bending over her, his hand beneath her chin, forcing her to look at him.

"Don't, Obed!" she begged.

"Thankful, you tell me. Did you think I asked you to marry me just because I pitied you. Just because I was sorry for you? Did you?"

"Obed, please!"

"Thankful, I've come to care for you more'n anything else in the world. I don't pity you. I've been pityin' myself for the last month because I couldn't have you—just you. I want you, Thankful Barnes, and if you'll marry me I'll be the happiest critter that walks."

"Oh, Obed, don't make it so hard for me. You said you wouldn't. And—and you can't care—really."

"I can't! Do you care for me? That's what I want to know."

"Obed, you and I ain't young folks. We're gettin' on towards old age. What would folks say if—"

He threw his arms about her and literally lifted her from the chair.

"I don't care a durn WHAT they say," he shouted, exultantly. "You've said what I was waitin' for. Or you've looked it, anyhow. Now then, WHEN shall we be married? That's the next thing for you to say, my girl."

They sat there in the gathering dusk and talked. The captain was uproariously gay. He could scarcely keep still, but whistled and drummed tunes upon the chair arm with his fingers. Thankful was more subdued and quiet, but she was happy, completely happy at last.

"This'll be some boardin'-house, this one of ours," declared the captain. "We'll build the addition you wanted and we'll make the city folks sit up and take notice. And," with a gleeful chuckle, "we won't have any ghost snorin' warnin's, either."

Thankful laughed. "No, we won't," she said. "And yet I'm awfully grateful to that—that—that pig ghost. If it hadn't been for him that mortgage would still be hangin' over us. And Solomon would never have been scared into doin' what he promised Uncle Abner he would do. Perhaps he'll be a better man, a more generous man to some of his other poor victims after this. I hope he will."

"So do I, but I have my doubts."

"Well, we'll never kill old Patrick Henry, will we? That would be TOO ungrateful."

Captain Obed slapped his knee.

"Kill him!" he repeated: "I should say not! Why, he's your Uncle Abner and Rebecca Timpson's sister Medora and old Laban Eldredge and I don't know how many more. Killin' him would be a double back-action massacre. No indeed, we won't kill him! Come on, let's go out and have a look at him now. I'd like to shake his hand, if he had one."

"But, Obed, it's rainin'."

"What of it? We don't care for rain. It's goin' to be all sunshine for you after this, my lady. I'm the weather prophet and I tell you so. God bless you, Thankful Barnes."

Thankful smiled.

"He has blessed me already, Obed," she said.

THE END

The Codes Of Hammurabi And Moses
W. W. Davies

QTY

The discovery of the Hammurabi Code is one of the greatest achievements of archaeology, and is of paramount interest, not only to the student of the Bible, but also to all those interested in ancient history...

Religion   **ISBN:** *1-59462-338-4*   **Pages:132**
MSRP $12.95

The Theory of Moral Sentiments
Adam Smith

QTY

This work from 1749. contains original theories of conscience amd moral judgment and it is the foundation for systemof morals.

Philosophy **ISBN:** *1-59462-777-0*   **Pages:536**
MSRP $19.95

Jessica's First Prayer
Hesba Stretton

QTY

In a screened and secluded corner of one of the many railway-bridges which span the streets of London there could be seen a few years ago, from five o'clock every morning until half past eight, a tidily set-out coffee-stall, consisting of a trestle and board, upon which stood two large tin cans, with a small fire of charcoal burning under each so as to keep the coffee boiling during the early hours of the morning when the work-people were thronging into the city on their way to their daily toil...

Childrens   **ISBN:** *1-59462-373-2*   **Pages:84**
MSRP $9.95

My Life and Work
Henry Ford

QTY

Henry Ford revolutionized the world with his implementation of mass production for the Model T automobile. Gain valuable business insight into his life and work with his own auto-biography... "We have only started on our development of our country we have not as yet, with all our talk of wonderful progress, done more than scratch the surface. The progress has been wonderful enough but..."

Biographies/   **ISBN:** *1-59462-198-5*   **Pages:300**
MSRP $21.95

The Art of Cross-Examination
Francis Wellman

QTY

I presume it is the experience of every author, after his first book is published upon an important subject, to be almost overwhelmed with a wealth of ideas and illustrations which could readily have been included in his book, and which to his own mind, at least, seem to make a second edition inevitable. Such certainly was the case with me; and when the first edition had reached its sixth impression in five months, I rejoiced to learn that it seemed to my publishers that the book had met with a sufficiently favorable reception to justify a second and considerably enlarged edition. ...

Pages:412

Reference   ISBN: *1-59462-647-2*   *MSRP $19.95*

On the Duty of Civil Disobedience
Henry David Thoreau

QTY

Thoreau wrote his famous essay, On the Duty of Civil Disobedience, as a protest against an unjust but popular war and the immoral but popular institution of slave-owning. He did more than write—he declined to pay his taxes, and was hauled off to gaol in consequence. Who can say how much this refusal of his hastened the end of the war and of slavery ?

Law   ISBN: *1-59462-747-9*   **Pages:48**
                                             MSRP $7.45

Dream Psychology Psychoanalysis for Beginners
Sigmund Freud

QTY

Sigmund Freud, born Sigismund Schlomo Freud (May 6, 1856 - September 23, 1939), was a Jewish-Austrian neurologist and psychiatrist who co-founded the psychoanalytic school of psychology. Freud is best known for his theories of the unconscious mind, especially involving the mechanism of repression; his redefinition of sexual desire as mobile and directed towards a wide variety of objects; and his therapeutic techniques, especially his understanding of transference in the therapeutic relationship and the presumed value of dreams as sources of insight into unconscious desires.

Pages:196

Psychology   ISBN: *1-59462-905-6*   *MSRP $15.45*

The Miracle of Right Thought
Orison Swett Marden

QTY

Believe with all of your heart that you will do what you were made to do. When the mind has once formed the habit of holding cheerful, happy, prosperous pictures, it will not be easy to form the opposite habit. It does not matter how improbable or how far away this realization may see, or how dark the prospects may be, if we visualize them as best we can, as vividly as possible, hold tenaciously to them and vigorously struggle to attain them, they will gradually become actualized, realized in the life. But a desire, a longing without endeavor, a yearning abandoned or held indifferently will vanish without realization.

Pages:360

Self Help   ISBN: *1-59462-644-8*   *MSRP $25.45*

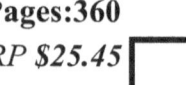

QTY

The Rosicrucian Cosmo-Conception Mystic Christianity *by Max Heindel*   ISBN: *1-59462-188-8*   **$38.95**
The Rosicrucian Cosmo-conception is not dogmatic, neither does it appeal to any other authority than the reason of the student. It is not controversial, but is: sent forth in the, hope that it may help to clear...   New Age/Religion Pages 646

Abandonment To Divine Providence *by Jean-Pierre de Caussade*   ISBN: *1-59462-228-0*   **$25.95**
"The Rev. Jean Pierre de Caussade was one of the most remarkable spiritual writers of the Society of Jesus in France in the 18th Century. His death took place at Toulouse in 1751. His works have gone through many editions and have been republished...   Inspirational/Religion Pages 400

Mental Chemistry *by Charles Haanel*   ISBN: *1-59462-192-6*   **$23.95**
Mental Chemistry allows the change of material conditions by combining and appropriately utilizing the power of the mind. Much like applied chemistry creates something new and unique out of careful combinations of chemicals the mastery of mental chemistry...   New Age Pages 354

The Letters of Robert Browning and Elizabeth Barret Barrett 1845-1846 vol II   ISBN: *1-59462-193-4*   **$35.95**
by Robert Browning and Elizabeth Barrett   Biographies Pages 596

Gleanings In Genesis (volume I) *by Arthur W. Pink*   ISBN: *1-59462-130-6*   **$27.45**
Appropriately has Genesis been termed "the seed plot of the Bible" for in it we have, in germ form, almost all of the great doctrines which are afterwards fully developed in the books of Scripture which follow...   Religion/Inspirational Pages 420

The Master Key *by L. W. de Laurence*   ISBN: *1-59462-001-6*   **$30.95**
In no branch of human knowledge has there been a more lively increase of the spirit of research during the past few years than in the study of Psychology, Concentration and Mental Discipline. The requests for authentic lessons in Thought Control, Mental Discipline and...   New Age/Business Pages 422

The Lesser Key Of Solomon Goetia *by L. W. de Laurence*   ISBN: *1-59462-092-X*   **$9.95**
This translation of the first book of the "Lernegton" which is now for the first time made accessible to students of Talismanic Magic was done, after careful collation and edition, from numerous Ancient Manuscripts in Hebrew, Latin, and French...   New Age/Occult Pages 92

Rubaiyat Of Omar Khayyam *by Edward Fitzgerald*   ISBN: *1-59462-332-5*   **$13.95**
Edward Fitzgerald, whom the world has already learned, in spite of his own efforts to remain within the shadow of anonymity, to look upon as one of the rarest poets of the century, was born at Bredfield, in Suffolk, on the 31st of March, 1809. He was the third son of John Purcell...   Music Pages 172

Ancient Law *by Henry Maine*   ISBN: *1-59462-128-4*   **$29.95**
The chief object of the following pages is to indicate some of the earliest ideas of mankind, as they are reflected in Ancient Law, and to point out the relation of those ideas to modern thought.   Religion/History Pages 452

Far-Away Stories *by William J. Locke*   ISBN: *1-59462-129-2*   **$19.45**
"Good wine needs no bush, but a collection of mixed vintages does. And this book is just such a collection. Some of the stories I do not want to remain buried for ever in the museum files of dead magazine-numbers an author's not unpardonable vanity..."   Fiction Pages 272

Life of David Crockett *by David Crockett*   ISBN: *1-59462-250-7*   **$27.45**
"Colonel David Crockett was one of the most remarkable men of the times in which he lived. Born in humble life, but gifted with a strong will, an indomitable courage, and unremitting perseverance...   Biographies/New Age Pages 424

Lip-Reading *by Edward Nitchie*   ISBN: *1-59462-206-X*   **$25.95**
Edward B. Nitchie, founder of the New York School for the Hard of Hearing, now the Nitchie School of Lip-Reading, Inc, wrote "LIP-READING Principles and Practice". The development and perfecting of this meritorious work on lip-reading was an undertaking...   How-to Pages 400

A Handbook of Suggestive Therapeutics, Applied Hypnotism, Psychic Science   ISBN: *1-59462-214-0*   **$24.95**
by Henry Munro   Health/New Age/Health/Self-help Pages 376

A Doll's House: and Two Other Plays *by Henrik Ibsen*   ISBN: *1-59462-112-8*   **$19.95**
Henrik Ibsen created this classic when in revolutionary 1848 Rome. Introducing some striking concepts in playwriting for the realist genre, this play has been studied the world over.   Fiction/Classics/Plays 308

The Light of Asia *by sir Edwin Arnold*   ISBN: *1-59462-204-3*   **$13.95**
In this poetic masterpiece, Edwin Arnold describes the life and teachings of Buddha. The man who was to become known as Buddha to the world was born as Prince Gautama of India but he rejected the worldly riches and abandoned the reigns of power when...   Religion/History/Biographies Pages 170

The Complete Works of Guy de Maupassant *by Guy de Maupassant*   ISBN: *1-59462-157-8*   **$16.95**
"For days and days, nights and nights, I had dreamed of that first kiss which was to consecrate our engagement, and I knew not on what spot I should put my lips..."   Fiction/Classics Pages 240

The Art of Cross-Examination *by Francis L. Wellman*   ISBN: *1-59462-309-0*   **$26.95**
Written by a renowned trial lawyer, Wellman imparts his experience and uses case studies to explain how to use psychology to extract desired information through questioning.   How-to/Science/Reference Pages 408

Answered or Unanswered? *by Louisa Vaughan*   ISBN: *1-59462-248-5*   **$10.95**
Miracles of Faith in China   Religion Pages 112

The Edinburgh Lectures on Mental Science (1909) *by Thomas*   ISBN: *1-59462-008-3*   **$11.95**
This book contains the substance of a course of lectures recently given by the writer in the Queen Street Hall, Edinburgh. Its purpose is to indicate the Natural Principles governing the relation between Mental Action and Material Conditions...   New Age/Psychology Pages 148

Ayesha *by H. Rider Haggard*   ISBN: *1-59462-301-5*   **$24.95**
Verily and indeed it is the unexpected that happens! Probably if there was one person upon the earth from whom the Editor of this, and of a certain previous history, did not expect to hear again...   Classics Pages 380

Ayala's Angel *by Anthony Trollope*   ISBN: *1-59462-352-X*   **$29.95**
The two girls were both pretty, but Lucy who was twenty-one who supposed to be simple and comparatively unattractive, whereas Ayala was credited, as her Bombwhat romantic name might show, with poetic charm and a taste for romance. Ayala when her father died was nineteen...   Fiction Pages 484

The American Commonwealth *by James Bryce*   ISBN: *1-59462-286-8*   **$34.45**
An interpretation of American democratic political theory. It examines political mechanics and society from the perspective of Scotsman James Bryce   Politics Pages 572

Stories of the Pilgrims *by Margaret P. Pumphrey*   ISBN: *1-59462-116-0*   **$17.95**
This book explores pilgrims religious oppression in England as well as their escape to Holland and eventual crossing to America on the Mayflower, and their early days in New England...   History Pages 268

QTY

The Fasting Cure *by Sinclair Upton*   ISBN: *1-59462-222-1* **$13.95**
In the Cosmopolitan Magazine for May, 1910, and in the Contemporary Review (London) for April, 1910, I published an article dealing with my experiences in fasting. I have written a great many magazine articles, but never one which attracted so much attention... New Age/Self Help/Health Pages 164

Hebrew Astrology *by Sepharial*   ISBN: *1-59462-308-2* **$13.45**
In these days of advanced thinking it is a matter of common observation that we have left many of the old landmarks behind and that we are now pressing forward to greater heights and to a wider horizon than that which represented the mind-content of our progenitors... Astrology Pages 144

Thought Vibration or The Law of Attraction in the Thought World   ISBN: *1-59462-127-6* **$12.95**
by William Walker Atkinson   Psychology/Religion Pages 144

Optimism *by Helen Keller*   ISBN: *1-59462-108-X* **$15.95**
Helen Keller was blind, deaf, and mute since 19 months old, yet famously learned how to overcome these handicaps, communicate with the world, and spread her lectures promoting optimism. An inspiring read for everyone... Biographies/Inspirational Pages 84

Sara Crewe *by Frances Burnett*   ISBN: *1-59462-360-0* **$9.45**
In the first place, Miss Minchin lived in London. Her home was a large, dull, tall one, in a large, dull square, where all the houses were alike, and all the sparrows were alike, and where all the door-knockers made the same heavy sound... Childrens/Classic Pages 88

The Autobiography of Benjamin Franklin *by Benjamin Franklin*   ISBN: *1-59462-135-7* **$24.95**
The Autobiography of Benjamin Franklin has probably been more extensively read than any other American historical work, and no other book of its kind has had such ups and downs of fortune. Franklin lived for many years in England, where he was agent... Biographies/History Pages 332

Name	
Email	
Telephone	
Address	
City, State ZIP	

☐ **Credit Card**   ☐ **Check / Money Order**

Credit Card Number	
Expiration Date	
Signature	

Please Mail to: Book Jungle
PO Box 2226
Champaign, IL 61825
or Fax to: 630-214-0564

ORDERING INFORMATION

web*: www.bookjungle.com*
email*: sales@bookjungle.com*
fax*: 630-214-0564*
mail*: Book Jungle PO Box 2226 Champaign, IL 61825*
or PayPal *to sales@bookjungle.com*

Please contact us for bulk discounts

DIRECT-ORDER TERMS

**20% Discount if You Order
Two or More Books**
Free Domestic Shipping!
Accepted: Master Card, Visa,
Discover, American Express

www.ingramcontent.com/pod-product-compliance
Lightning Source LLC
Chambersburg PA
CBHW080725020726
47503CB00010B/2790